Kitty Little

Freda Lightfoot

CORONET BOOKS

Hodder & Stoughton

ISBN 0 340 76899 1

Typeset by Palimpsest Book Production Limited,
Polmont, Stirlingshire

Printed and bound in Great Britain by
Mackays of Chatham plc, Chatham, Kent

Hodder & Stoughton Ltd
A division of Hodder Headline
338 Euston Road
London NW1 3BH

Freda Lightfoot

Freda Lightfoot was born and brought up in the mill towns of Lancashire. She has been a teacher, bookseller and smallholder but begun her writing career by publishing over forty short stories and articles and five historical romances under a different name. Having lived for many years in the Lake District and also in Cornwall, she now tries to divide her time between the two.

For Michael, brother-in-law, friend
and fellow thespian.
For my friends in the Troy Players, remembering all the
years of fun.
And for Sally, Antony and Lad, a promise not
forgotten, if somewhat delayed.

ACT ONE

London and the Lakes

1912

Chapter One

The girl standing in the theatre lobby seemed oblivious to the crowds milling and jostling about her. A young man inadvertently knocked her elbow and a stream of wine slopped over the rim of her glass to splash the extravagant silken folds of her new gown. But she didn't notice. Nor did she pay any heed to her attentive young escort who took the offender to task on her behalf. She was far too concerned with examining the photographs that lined the panelled walls. A lively scene from *Charley's Aunt*; the riotous comedy of *She Stoops to Conquer* recently performed at the Coronet Theatre; Vesta Tilley, Little Tich, Harry Lauder and other music-hall favourites, and the aristocratic figure of Henry Irving playing *Hamlet*. She stood before them all, enthralled.

In truth very few people noticed her either, or paid her the slightest attention if they did. Too tall and ungainly to be considered a classic beauty, only the dress might have excited interest, and had certainly been purchased by her socially aspiring mother with that purpose in mind. It was meant to take the wearer without shame to any social event a busy diary might throw up, hopefully attracting attention in the right quarters.

Undoubtedly exquisite, and of the purest silk, it was a wondrous example of the dressmaker's skill and artifice. Encrusted with bugle beads and rows of tiny, non-functional buttons, the boned bodice sported a daringly low-cut neckline and the multi-layers of the draped silk-voile skirt floated light as air against her legs. But shining forth above all this magnificence loomed the girl's face.

Quite bare of face powder or the current daring fashion for rouge, its healthy outdoor glow only added to its open, friendly aspect, which seemed quite at odds with the sophisticated image the dress presented. Some would consider the face to be that of a strong woman, one content with herself. A more shrewd observer might recognise that it revealed a flaw in an otherwise confident, practical nature; a young woman afraid to make the best of herself in case she should inadvertently reveal her vulnerability.

Though the hair was undoubtedly glossy and of a deep, dark brown, it was plainly styled in twin plaited coils which formed ear muffs nestling against her rounded pink cheeks. The eyes too might be a deep velvety brown and commendably alert and questioning, but the lashes were neither long nor curling, being rather short and functional. And beneath lay deep blue shadows and the faintest hint of fine lines, displaying evidence of many sleepless nights, which should hardly be present on a face that had barely attained maturity. It was, unquestionably, the face of someone who has known too early in life inordinate pain and the value of compromise.

When Katherine had first seen the dress in the dressmaker's private boudoir she'd refused, absolutely, to wear it.

'But it's a symphony of blues and lavender, girl,' her mother had insisted, quoting the fanciful language of the dressmaker in the carefully enunciated tones she adopted whenever she felt outclassed. 'You look a proper swank.'

Clara Terry, whose real name was Smith though changed in honour of the famous actress, Ellen Terry, smoothed a hand over the shimmering silk and, completely ignoring the scowl on her daughter's face, added, 'I picked this design out special, 'cause that's what yer wears for half mourning, ain't it?'

'I shall feel dreadfully overdressed.'

'Go on wiv yer. Draped skirts are all the rage this year.'

'An excellent reason for me not to wear one then. Anyway, I don't know that I even wish to go.'

Clara had registered utter shock and disbelief at this remark. 'Hark at 'er. What a bleedin' tale that is. Loves the theeaytre she does.' She made no mention of having invested a small fortune in goodwill and hot dinners waiting for Frank Cussins to come up trumps and buy an engagement ring for her darling girl. The theatre tickets had been another part of her strategy of inducement. Best seats in the stalls they were. Cost her a mint of money, not to mention all the rest.

Clara had liked young Frank from the start, for all he was a bit pasty-faced. She'd let him have the best room in her Ealing lodging house, second-floor front with a view over the common. And the minute she'd sized up the solid state of his insurance business she'd made sure Katherine was always the one to take up his tea or his hot shaving water. He'd taken quite a shine to the girl as a result. Took her up to town quite regular, though he was close with his money and would as soon settle for a walk by the river or a cream tea at the Lyons Corner House if left to his own devices. But men were like that. No imagination.

It had been Clara's idea to celebrate the engagement with an evening at the theatre, knowing how much Katherine would love it. Not that she'd any intention of revealing this fact, better Katherine thought it her fiancé's idea, and so Clara had adopted her most cajoling tones. 'Course you must go, cherub. Frank has got tickets 'specially, ain't he? And it's *Hullo Ragtime*, what that American chap wrote, Irving Brussels.'

'Berlin. Irving Berlin.'

'There y'are then. Yer knows all about it, so yer wouldn't want to miss it, would yer? Not when everyone says it's a hit. And you look a real duchess in that frock. Besides,' she'd persisted, 'you can't hide yourself away. Raymond wouldn't want you to. Life goes on.'

'To die so young is too cruel, Ma. So unfair.'

'Who said life was fair? And don't call me Ma, dearie. You know 'ow I detest it,' Clara hissed under her breath before smoothly lifting her voice and continuing. 'We can't bring him back, now can we? Nor be in mourning forever. Life must . . .'

'Don't say it must go on, not again! I can't bear it. How can we *go on*? I'm not in the mood for hi-jinks and parties. I can't flirt and jazz, drink cocktails and act as if everything is fine, because everything isn't fine.

Raymond is *dead*.' Katherine revealed in every sigh, every gesture, every irritable plucking of her fingertips upon the silk fabric, her desperate unhappiness.

"T'ain't a party, dearie, it's the theeayter. I thought you liked the theeayter?'

Katherine hadn't been near a theatre for over a year. Not since the motor accident which had robbed her of a loving brother. The last time they'd gone to see *Charley's Aunt* with Raymond's best friend, dear Archie. Her beautiful eyes filled with tears. 'I can't do it. It's *obscene!* Insensitive.'

Clara watched sadly as the protective shields went up, knowing that once her daughter had a bee in her bonnet, nothing would stop it buzzing. For all Clara regretted the death of her only son and had done her share of grieving these last months, she'd no intention of making it her life's work, as Katherine seemed set on doing. But then the poor girl couldn't help being soft as marshmallow inside, disguise it as she may, and the two had been especially close, them being twins and all.

Tears were rolling down Katherine's cheeks and she was sweeping them angrily away. 'I don't deserve to enjoy myself, or to see new American musicals. It would be like a betrayal. And how dare I even think of buying a new dress?'

As if coming to a decision, she'd begun to prise open loosely stitched buttons and scatter pins in every direction, sending the dressmaker scurrying about the room, picking them up as best she might. Clara, to her credit, simply shook her head in sorrow.

'I won't go and that's that.' But in the end she had allowed herself to be persuaded, and wasn't she glad?

It had been the most wonderful experience of her life. Now the show was over and people were streaming out on to a wet London street and she couldn't bear to drag herself away.

The performance had been stunning, the costumes dazzling, the music foot-tapping and heart-lifting, in particular 'Alexander's Ragtime Band' which she could hardly stop humming. Though she'd been keenly aware of herself, sitting up very straight and proper in the elegant gown in the orchestra stalls, she'd felt too as if she were up there with the actors on that stage, living each scene with them. The whole ambience of the theatre had filled her with an unexpected and thrilling excitement. Simply to experience row upon row of delighted, happy people laughing, applauding and singing, entirely caught up in the scenes enacted before them, had set her mind spinning. To Katherine, it felt as if for the first time ever, she was vividly and stupendously alive.

She even bestowed a dazzling smile upon the ever-patient Frank in his shiny suit and stiff collar, who'd somehow managed to irritate her beyond endurance all evening by attempting to anticipate her every need. She felt suffused with guilt suddenly since it was their engagement night after all. For a fleeting second the smile transformed her, making the fine lines vanish, winging the eyebrows upwards and seeming to lengthen the laughing eyes into a delightful almond shape, endowing the unremarkable face with a radiant and unusual beauty.

'Wasn't it all wonderful?'

'Of course, my dear. Don't I always know what is best for you?' Frank concluded in self-satisfied tones, and while he collected coats and capes and hailed a cab, Katherine experienced the slightest of chill winds across her shoulder blades.

When they arrived home, Frank lingered in the hall hoping for a goodnight kiss but Katherine hastily excused herself and made for the stairs, claiming she was tired. From the first landing she watched him disappear into the back kitchen, no doubt for a nightcap with Ma, then picked up her skirts and fled. But instead of going directly to her own room, tucked away in the front attic, she scrambled up the back stairs and slipped quietly into the top-floor back.

Archie Emerson was sitting up in bed, a muffler tucked in the neck of his striped pyjamas and an old cardigan draped loosely over his shoulders. His drawn face looked a sickly grey in the light of the gas mantle above his head and Katherine stifled the anxious enquiry concerning the state of his health which sprang instantly to her lips whenever she saw him.

Archie had survived the accident, physically at least, with barely a scratch. Outwardly he was unchanged, the same relatively fit young man, as raven-haired, blue-eyed and handsome as when he and Raymond had first met years ago at some motor rally or other. But this was merely the shell. Inside, Katherine could tell that, like herself, he was quite different. The accident had changed him.

It had been Archie who'd been driving the motor, probably far too fast, on a country road slick with rain and mud. It had run out of control, hit a tree

9

FREDA LIGHTFOOT

and Raymond had been killed outright. Guilt now ate away at Archie's soul. It was this awesome weight of responsibility, in addition to the normal grieving for a much-loved friend, which had led him into depression, personal neglect and near starvation till, in the end, he'd caught a ferocious attack of 'flu which had in turn resulted in pneumonia. For a while his life had hung in the balance and, with no family of his own, Katherine had brought him to Hope View to nurse him.

Surprisingly, Clara had not blamed Archie for her son's death, taking a philosophical view of the pranks of boys; she had gladly taken him in and ordered special egg custards and beef tea to be made for him. She didn't even charge him rent though she was not known for pampering her guests. At one time they'd feared they were about to lose him too but he'd been lucky and was now on the mend. Nevertheless, for all he enjoyed being the centre of attention, he couldn't bear to be fussed over.

Katherine flopped down on the bed beside him, lying flat out on the crumpled eiderdown.

'Hello, Kitty, old thing.' This was a pet name Raymond had given her from childhood, when he couldn't quite get his tongue round 'Katherine'. Now that he was dead, Archie continued to use it and she was glad. It reminded them both of happier days. She missed her twin sorely, as did Archie, so was content for him to act as Raymond's stand-in, a sort of surrogate brother. 'Good show, was it?'

'The best. You wouldn't believe how marvellous it was.'

'Did the actors declaim and rant and rave in suitably heroic fashion?' he teased.

She sat up, eyes bright, fixing her gaze earnestly upon his. 'No, they did not. They sang and danced and spoke with such *feeling*, you wouldn't believe. Not in the least Victorian but totally modern. A glorious riot of colour, wickedly clever scenery – and there was the most wonderful song performed by a woman with cropped hair, would you believe, topped with a huge ostrich feather.'

Unconvinced, as if determined to prove that he had missed nothing by being forced to remain in bed, Archie persisted. 'Surely the keynote of good drama is simplicity, in order to let the characters shine? The set should not in any way detract from the play.'

'Oh, I agree in principle. I mean, in the straight theatre, words, words, words are everything. The set doesn't need to be so important then as you can leave much more to the imagination of the audience. But this was a musical so those rules don't apply.' Katherine loved to air her views on the theatre, most of which she'd picked up from the constant stream of thespian tenants who had passed through the doors of Hope View over the years; years in which she'd grown up without a father, and with a mother whose sole aim was to carve out a vastly different future for her only daughter. Yet Katherine loved to soak up the many stories of theatrical life which buzzed all around her, longing for a taste of it herself. If she had a dream, it was that. To appear on stage. Sadly, she knew it was never likely to happen.

'But was it *art*, darling?' There was a mocking cynicism in Archie's tone, one she'd grown accustomed to of late. Katherine paid it no heed. Slapping playfully at him, she laughed.

'Don't be such an horrendous snob! Why should it not be? It was all so . . . so . . . oh, I don't know. Exciting, wonderful, marvellous! I simply adored it.'

He was laughing too, won over as always by her enthusiasm. 'You were glad you went then, after all?'

'Oh, yes.' She began at once to repeat her tale, frequently digressing into descriptions of a particular scene, the magnificence of the costumes and brilliance of the acting, gesticulating wildly with her slender hands and finishing with a detailed description of the pictures in the lobby. 'I was looking at a photo of some actor or other doing *Charley's Aunt*. Do you remember us all going to see it ages ago? Raymond doing a wonderful takeoff of Lord Fancourt Babberley. I laughed till I cried.'

'Light comedy,' Archie grumbled, snuffling into his handkerchief and reverting to his habitual air of gloom. 'Hardly Shakespeare, my dear.'

'But brilliant dialogue. Such wit. Don't patronise, Archie, it doesn't suit you. You know it's one of your favourites. Of course this show was entirely different.' And as she once again pressed home her point, he lay back on the pillows with a sigh and let his eyelids droop, making it clear that he was bone-weary, far too tired for further discussion. In truth she knew him to be miffed at having missed the show. It always amused her how he hated to lose an argument.

But then, recalling the lateness of the hour, she realised that he might indeed be tired. She stopped in mid-sentence and, leaning forward, kissed his lean cheek. 'Cocoa? You look all in.'

'Am rather, old thing.'

'Dearest Archie, I'm sorry for babbling on. I'll tell you all about it tomorrow, shall I?'

He knew that she would, so didn't trouble to reply.

As she crept out, pulling the door softly closed behind her, she heard him call after her. 'Don't drip cocoa on that new frock or Ma will kill you!' Giggling, she skipped along the landing, up the front stairs and into her own tiny room where she prudently stepped out of the dress before pulling on an old checked dressing-gown and heading for the kitchen.

After settling Archie for the night, Katherine returned to her room where she scowled at the pool of lavender-blue silk on the floor, only too aware of the reason why her mother had insisted on buying the dress, for all it must have cost a small fortune which she could ill afford. She'd wanted to make absolutely certain that Katherine looked her best for Frank so that their engagement went ahead. Yet there was never any doubt on that score. Frank would do exactly as Clara suggested. Nor did Katherine believe for one minute that the tickets for *Hullo Ragtime* had been his idea at all. Kind as he undoubtedly was, he'd never think of such a thing on his own account, not in a million years. He was far too unimaginative, bless his heart.

Oh, but it had been wonderful! Whatever sacrifices her mother had made in order to procure the seats, Katherine was truly grateful.

Even now she could feel her heart pounding with the excitement of it all and did a little tap dance all around

13

the floor before settling to sip her rapidly cooling cocoa. Swinging her long legs up over the arm of her chair, she arranged them in the most comfortable and unladylike position she could find and picked up her book, *Arms and the Man*, for a quiet read before bed.

But the book remained closed on her lap, the cocoa scarcely touched as it came to her that the thrill of the evening had been generated not by her engagement to Frank but by the show itself. Surely that was the wrong way round?

She sat as if dazed, eyes fixed upon the uncurtained attic window with its view of rooftops crowding in all around, their chimneys poking like fingers into the darkening sky. The sensation always made her feel slightly claustrophobic. Katherine hated London; sometimes wondered desperately if she was destined to live out her entire life in this smoky muddle of bricks and mortar.

She and Raymond had often talked of escaping to a new life, somewhere deep in the country. There seemed no such possibility now. They'd privately giggled about Frank Cussins as he pontificated on some worthy subject or other, saying he must have been born middle-aged with that receding hairline of his and the slightest hint of a double chin.

But in Clara's eyes at least Frank was an excellent catch, and Katherine had to admit that he was steadfast and earnest; she felt safe with him, for all he was very slightly on the dull side.

She lifted up her left hand to let a flicker of moonlight catch the tiny solitaire stone of her ring. Was it a real diamond? Had Frank chosen it himself, or had her mother had a hand in that too? Why didn't she feel excited? Why wasn't she happy? And if she wasn't, Katherine wondered why she'd allowed the engagement to take place at all.

Dear Lord, had she agreed to marry him out of pity? Or to please her mother?

'A girl must have a husband. Oh, dear me, yes. What would the world come to if gels refused to marry? Anarchy, no less,' Katherine recited, rather dramatically, to the empty room. She lifted her mug of cocoa as if in a toast, then drank it back in one like a shot of whisky before closing her eyes in pained resignation.

Or had she agreed simply because she'd been too filled with grief for her beloved Raymond to care?

A cold hand seemed to grip her heart, squeezing out all the excitement the evening had engendered. Now, too late, she faced reality. She was engaged to be married to a man she didn't even love. Tears seeped from beneath the sensible lashes and dripped on to her clasped hands.

She would have to tell him, of course, that it had all been a mistake; that she wasn't ready for marriage, not yet, while she still grieved. She slapped the tears firmly away with the flat of her hand. Over twelve months since Raymond had died, and still it felt like yesterday. Her mother said it was time to think of the future. But was marriage with Frank Cussins the right future for Katherine?

The next morning she hastily pulled on her favourite sweater, somewhat disreputable and with a hole in one elbow; dragged on a well-worn tweed skirt that finished just above the anklebone, revealing a darn in one stocking, and crept downstairs. She intended to avoid breakfast: kippers, judging by the smell that was wafting up from the dining room. Casting one anguished glance at the hall table, loaded yet again with social invitations her mother had no doubt procured for her, Katherine snatched up her coat and bolted for the front door, her one thought being to escape the anticipated grilling which always followed one of Clara's carefully planned outings.

Clara, though apparently fully occupied supervising Myrtle frying kippers while she herself scraped margarine on to wafer-thin slices of bread, kept the kitchen door half-open and one ear cocked since she was hell-bent on taking her errant daughter to task for snubbing Frank so pointedly during that long and *expensive* night at the theatre. So it was that she heard the front door slam and, instantly dropping the knife, ran to snatch it open again and stand dancing with frustration on the doorstep. Clara might well have yelled at Katherine to return this instant, were it not for the fact that such an action would make lace curtains twitch all along the street. Foiled by her recalcitrant daughter, Clara swore softly under her breath, snatched up a plate of bread, yelled at Myrtle to start on the washing up the minute she'd brewed the tea, and flounced off to the dining room in search of a more sympathetic ear.

Dear Frank was surely the best one to deal with Katherine when she was in one of her moods. He was also the ideal man to bring her grieving daughter back to life and offer her the future she deserved. Didn't Clara know from personal experience the other side

16

of the coin? What it was like to live alone, without the comforts a man could offer? The mere thought of the girl's ingratitude made her blood boil.

Clara kicked open the dining room door, smiling cursorily upon the guests waiting hopefully for their kippers as she slammed down plates of bread and marge. 'Mr Cussins, may I have a word?' she purred sweetly.

He glanced up from his seat at the window table and quietly removed the spectacles he had perched on the end of his nose so he could read the morning paper.

'Certainly, Mrs Terry.' It was a delightful little game they played, always being so punctiliously formal in front of the other guests. He carefully folded the paper and laid it neatly by his plate before getting up and weaving his way between the tables towards her.

Clara felt her heart give a little flutter of jealousy for he was indeed a fine figure of a man. Heaven help them, the girl didn't appreciate how fortunate she was. Twenty-one years old and still turning her nose up at every suitor who came along. Clara gave a simpering little giggle as Frank approached, while quietly sliding one or two slices of bread off a plate she considered too generously loaded and returning them to her tray. If that little madam didn't make an effort to treat this one with more respect she'd be left on the shelf, sure as eggs were eggs, and remain forever an old maid. The very idea made Clara shudder. She was determined that Katherine must be saved from herself no matter what the cost; dragged to the altar if necessary. Whatever had possessed her to run off this morning? She'd wring her bleeding neck, she would, when she got her hands on her.

These venomous thoughts, and any hope of a private conversation with Frank, were interrupted by Myrtle who burst through the kitchen door in a cloud of steam, cheeks scarlet with anger as much as from the heat of her surroundings.

'If that Mr Pickton don't keep his filthy 'ands to hissel, I'm 'anding in me notice this minute.'

'Dear Lord, what now?' Clara let out a heavy sigh. 'Right, I'll have a word with the old rogue. You get back to that washing up or you'll still be elbow-deep in suds come dinnertime.'

Ignoring the hungry diners, Clara excused herself to Frank with a beatific smile, pushed up her sleeves and prepared to do battle with the first-floor back. The fierce look in her eye seemed to indicate she'd be in possession of a vacant room come dinnertime. But the incident illustrated another good reason to have Katherine nicely settled. Clara had no intention of seeing her only child spend her life waiting hand, foot and finger on other folk's whims and peccadilloes.

Later, after her guests had finally been fed lukewarm kippers which they manfully swallowed, knowing how fruitless protest would be, she discovered the lavender dress exactly where it had fallen. Clicking her tongue with fresh annoyance, Clara hung it carefully in the cupboard, smoothing down the silken folds. It would come in very useful for the honeymoon at Clacton-on-Sea, as well as at cocktail parties in the garden suburbs.

Katherine, catching the first bus which happened along in her desperate effort to escape, was equally certain the gown was destined never to be worn again.

They were both wrong, for the life of this particular garment had barely begun.

Chapter Two

Sundays were Esme Bield's busiest day of the week. Even now as the second hymn boomed out under Miss Agnes's steadfast fingering and heavy footwork on the organ pedals, she was mustering the children ready to troop next door to Sunday School while her mind was busy calculating the slices of cold ham she might manage to cut from the woefully small bit of hock left in the larder at home. Following this cold and unappetising repast, there would be barely time to wash the dishes before Esme must return for the afternoon Sunday School which began promptly at two-thirty. After that there would be tea, plain bread and jam followed by the smallest slice of Madeira cake, and only then while her father, the Reverend Andrew Bield, snored in his wing-backed chair, would Esme be free to snatch a few minutes of complete bliss in the privacy of her room to devour the latest romance she had procured from the penny library. A Sunday, in fact, as predictable as any other.

The organ let out its customary squeak, rather like

a sigh of regret as it relinquished the final notes. As if primed by a starting pistol the children rose as one and crept down the aisle in a silent crocodile, too fearful of being struck down by the Almighty Himself to risk a whisper or even a backward glance as they shuffled out through the side door, thankful only to be free of the heavy formality of the church service. Esme too breathed a sigh of relief as she came out into the sunshine of the church yard.

The heavy scents of yew trees and damp grass tickled her nostrils enticingly as she hurried her little band along the overgrown paths. Here in this tiny hamlet of Repstone, one of many that clustered around the silvered surface of Carreckwater, primroses, violets and bluebells filled the verges with thick clots of colour; blossom hung in lacy white sprays from the hawthorn trees, brightened here and there by a blush of pink, heady scent intoxicating as it always was in spring.

But beyond this cosy, familiar world, lay quite another entirely, one that was stark and mysterious, where the lake gave way to an ocean of heather interspersed with steep slopes and fierce crags. And overseeing all, a magical panoply of blue-grey mountains that led from the heart of the Lakes to the shores of the Solway by way of Scafell, Esk Pike, Bowfell, Crinkle Crags and perhaps a brief detour to Great Gable; beguiling the would-be traveller into climbing their topmost peaks simply to see what lay beyond. Even the ribbon of dusty track linking the skeins of drystone walls on the closer hills, knitting them all together in great gleaming loops, seemed to lure one to venture onward and upward into the unknown. Yet those seemingly innocent sheep trods were not meant for the unwary. Esme had long believed the hills to possess personalities of their own. Sometimes they appeared sullen and brooding, sulkily reluctant to release the crisp new buds of bracken from the hard earth, while the crock-crock of the raven always brought a chill to her spine.

Today the scene held only a benign aspect, with the promise of spring in the air and the final melting of the snows on the tops bringing a fresh gush of sparkling water flowing down the becks into the shining lake below. The sweet sounds of young lambs calling to their mothers carried on a soft breeze and somewhere a skylark sang. It was as if the mountains had shaken out their skirts of green and lavender to bask in the golden May sunshine.

Esme smiled at the thought. The Lake District was surely meant for romantics and although she was happy to be counted among their number, without doubt loving this land in which she'd been raised, particularly on days such as this, there were times when its vast emptiness disturbed her, when its brooding dampness ate into her soul, robbing it of all light and hope.

Ushering her charges through the lych-gate into the schoolroom next door, she gazed upon those distant hills with longing. They represented freedom, an escape from the restrictions of a life bound by duty and dull routine; almost as if they were the gateway to an unknown world, for she'd rarely ventured further than neighbouring Carreckwater, except perhaps once in a while when she would go by train to the market town of Kendal, or in her father's dog cart to Windermere while the Lake Festival was on. There were regular charabanc outings to

Keswick or Ullswater with the Sunday School, of course, and once she had gone with her father to the city of Manchester, but only because he had a mission meeting to attend which he felt would be of benefit to her too. She'd been astonished by the bustle of people and traffic. Even the noise and the smoke had not dismayed her and the glories of the shop windows had been a revelation. She'd endlessly reiterated her gratitude to him, talking of little else for months afterwards.

Esme pulled open the heavy schoolroom door and ushered her charges inside. May was reputed to be a festive month. Some of the children from the more prosperous families sported new straw bonnets; others had decked out a hand-me-down with fresh ribbon. They'd enjoyed the traditional maypole dance on the first of the month, for all her father insisted it had pagan origins, and now sat in an obedient line on stout wooden benches, striving not to shuffle their small bottoms while she read them the story of Noah and his ark. It was a story that Esme loved for it signified a new beginning, an adventure for Noah, his three sons and all the animals fortunate enough to be chosen to accompany them on the expedition. How she longed to do likewise.

Later, over thin sliced brown bread and an even thinner coating of raspberry jam, her father reprimanded her on her choice.

'The New Testament would have been more appropriate, my dear. The Loaves and the Fishes perhaps, or the Prodigal Son.'

'Yes, Father. But the children do so love the Noah story. And they all drew wonderful animals. Little Amy

Rigg drew a whole delightful family of baby rabbits.'
Esme laughed but Andrew only grimaced.

'My point exactly, my dear. Encouraging the imagination is not wise. It only results in complete inaccuracy.'

She would like to have protested that imagination
was a gift that should be nurtured in any child and
did no harm at all to the value of the bible story, but
managed to bite back her words in time. She knew from
past experience how useless such arguments could be.

Satisfied that he'd made his point, Andrew patted her
arm as she began gathering up plates and cups. 'You're a
good worker, Mary.' He was calling her by her mother's
name as he often did when his mind was occupied with
church business. Esme was used to it so did not trouble
to correct him as he put his arms about her, holding her
close against him, one hand cupping her cheek, the other
resting lightly upon her buttocks while he dropped a kiss
upon her forehead and then her lips.

He was not an unkind man yet since the untimely
death of his beloved wife and helpmeet the Reverend
Bield had assumed Esme would take her place beside
him. He would have been utterly aghast had anyone
pointed out the unfairness of this; that perhaps playing
the role of parson's wife was not a task which his daughter
relished. It was, in his opinion, her bounden duty.

As she watched him turn and walk away to his study,
ostensibly to the pruning and tidying of his sermon while
in reality to a short nap, Esme wiped the kiss from her
lips without even realising she was doing it.

Much as she dreamed of escape one day, soaking
her pleasure-starved soul in an endless stream of cheap
romances, Esme too viewed her role in much the same

light. A labour of love that she was duty-bound to fulfil. Yet for some reason, perhaps the coming of yet another spring, she'd begun to question her fate more and more of late, hearing her life tick away minute by minute, hour by doleful hour, on the vicarage clock.

The moment her father had gone, she pulled the latest escapist delight from out of her knitting bag, opened it at the marker, and began to read. The door of the study opened again, causing her to drop the book hastily back into the beg as she turned to face him with a willing smile on a face flushed with guilt. Andrew Bield did not approve of any other reading matter than the Good Book on a Sunday, or on other days too, for that matter.

'Esme, don't forget to remind Mrs Phillips about the Sisterhood meeting on Tuesday evening. She is to lead the prayers.'

'Very good, Father. I expect she'll be at evensong, if not I'll call on my way home.'

'And you are to attend the Sewing Circle tomorrow afternoon, don't forget.'

Esme's heart sank. In addition to caring for her father, there were church meetings of one form or another on most evenings of the week, plus several afternoons. What with the Ladies' Guild, choir practice and various Sunday School teacher meetings, Monday had been her one free day. She clung to it now in frantic desperation. 'Oh, but I always go for a long walk on a Monday afternoon once I've finished with the washing. The fresh air does me a world of good, and you know I can't sew for toffee.'

'Then it's time you learned.' The door of the study closed upon her protests and the rosy cheeks of guilt now turned white with a pinched anger. He'd no right to take her for granted in this way. She couldn't go on like this, with no say in her own life, she really couldn't. She'd no time at all to herself. Esme was sure that she'd go mad if she didn't get away from parish duties soon.

Almost as swiftly as it had come, the flicker of rebellion died, superseded by the familiar gnawing guilt. Her mother was dead, after all, and her father desperately lonely. Surely the least she could do was to offer him her support?

In the following weeks as she went about her usual business, duly attending the Sewing Circle as instructed, Esme could feel the pitying eyes of the parish ladies upon her, their united gaze watching her every move, presumably because she was inept and rather plain. Esme would not for a moment have considered her plump, country rosiness pretty or imagine that her neighbours might see her as such. She kept her fair hair painstakingly tidy in one long plait; wound about her head it gave her a rather Scandinavian look. Rimless spectacles perched low upon her small nose, no matter how many times she adjusted them, and despite the radiance of her pale grey eyes, the rosebud mouth and silky bloom to her skin, she saw their gaze as censorious rather than kindly, their silence as a criticism rather than any sign of social ineptitude on their part, not for a moment thinking they might have some other reason to pity her.

If only she were twenty-one then she would be legally a woman and able to make her own decisions. Esme vowed to escape before her nineteenth birthday but that was only a few weeks away so quite how this was to be achieved was beyond her. She constantly reminded herself that of course her father had every right to dictate duties to her. He was burdened with a difficult and taxing occupation and it behoved her at least to do what she could to lighten his task.

Oh, but there were days when Esme wished someone would lighten hers!

She found Ida Phillips that evening in the ancient, flag-stoned kitchen of Repstone Manor, a square grey-stone building that had become a shadow of its former glory. The elderly woman was swathed in a huge wrap-around pinafore several sizes too large for her stick-like frame, chopping a stack of rhubarb preparatory to making jam, when Esme let herself in, unannounced, as was her wont.

'Esme dear, how kind of you to call. Slide the kettle on to the Aga this instant.' Ida's birdlike fingers flew as she found tea cups, saucers, the tin of home-made biscuits which she somehow always managed to produce, and in no time at all the pair were happily ensconced in their favourite pursuit: recalling happier times; those glorious golden days when Esme had been a young girl and the house had still possessed a family and a heart.

On this particular evening it soon became perfectly clear that Ida Phillips was bursting with excitement.

'You'll never believe what's happened?'

Esme laughed. 'I'm sure you're going to tell me.'

'He's written.'

'Who has?'

'The young master, of course, who else? Give me quite a turn it did to see his handwriting after all this time.'

'Oh!' Startled, Esme had a sudden vision of him, tall and lean in spanking new cricket whites, setting a topspin on an overarm as he sent the ball down the wicket towards her. A memory as sweet and fresh as dew. There were many such. She'd been fourteen, an impressionable adolescent, all freckles and coltish eagerness. Archie had been almost twenty-four and amazingly handsome. How she had loved him, even then. 'What did he say?' She edged anxiously forward in her seat, the tea and biscuits forgotten.

'That he's been proper poorly but he's on the mend now. See, ah'll show it thoo.' Ida got up from the table with cautious regard for her stiffening joints, to make frustratingly slow progress to the dresser. From a drawer she extracted a sheet of paper which she transferred into Esme's eager hand. 'Read it for yourself. The lad seems hale and hearty enough.'

'Is he coming home?' The question burst from Esme's lips even as she scanned the single sheet and discovered for herself that there was no mention of a visit.

Ida Phillips felt a surge of regret at having raised the poor child's hopes. Archie and Esme had grown up together, close friends and neighbours all of their young lives, for all there was nearly a decade between their ages. When he'd gone off on his travels the girl had cried as much as Ida, waiting eagerly for postcards and letters from Venice, Rome, Paris and other exotic locations. His last letter had stated simply that he was back in England, had had an accident but was all in one piece, save for a bit of a cold coming on. Since then, silence.

'At least the news is good, eh?' Ida did her best to let the girl down lightly. 'He never did care much for this place, though, not since his parents died. Tragic that were. Poor lad felt he'd no one left.'

'He had you.'

Ida's face softened. 'Aye, he allus had me. Never forgets his old Pips, he don't. But he's a man now, with a life of his own to lead. Happen he'll come home, happen he won't. We'll just have to wait and see, now won't we?'

'I suppose so.' Oh, but she did hope he would. Distracted by a sudden ache of longing, Esme reached for a second oat biscuit before finishing the first. Ida simply smiled.

Katherine had alighted from the bus when her fare had run out to find herself within walking distance of all the best theatres. It was then that the idea had come to her. What did she have to lose? Besides, once the crazy notion that she could become an actress herself had taken hold, there seemed no shifting it. Yet she didn't even get beyond the first porter who sat puffing a malodorous pipe, jealously guarding the back-stage entrance, warding off all-comers with a long arm and a short temper.

'No auditions today, girl,' he growled, wafting her away through a haze of smoke.

Katherine mustered every ounce of charm she possessed but it was clear from the start that he wasn't about to let her cross the threshold, not to see the producer, the stage manager, nor anyone. Not without a letter of introduction from her agent, which of course she didn't possess, or unless there were auditions on, which there certainly weren't as she could see by the fact there was no queue outside.

'Where would I find an agent, exactly?'

The porter peered at this tall, rather ordinary-looking girl from out of a pair of yellowed eyes half hidden behind dusty spectacles, then removing the pipe from his mouth, he knocked out the bowl and began to plug it with fresh tobacco, carefully tamping it down while he pondered on whether she was worthy of further consideration. 'You're new to this line of business then?'

'Is it so obvious?'

He lit the pipe, producing a small bonfire before it settled to a slow burn. Having got it drawing to his satisfaction, he grunted and turned his back on her. Then just as she prepared to go away, despair having finally demolished her resolve, he pushed a grubby sheet of paper across the narrow counter. 'There's a list of agents. Give them a try. Though I don't hold out much hope.'

She caught it with surprise and beamed at him with excited pleasure. 'Thanks ever so.'

His surprised gaze followed her as she strode away. By jove, what a difference that smile made. His jaw fell slack, the pipe forgotten, as he realised she was neither plain, dull nor in the least bit ordinary.

Katherine walked street after street till she decided she must have visited every address listed, and many she'd discovered on the way that were not, but had failed utterly to interest anyone into taking her on as a client.

Like the porter, some refused even to admit her beyond the outer office. Those who did lectured her on the fierce competition, pointing out that half the country seemed to imagine they could act, or make their fortune in the music hall. They fired questions at her to which she could give no suitable answers, the main one being that of experience. Some asked her to do a little step dance or sing a little ditty. The moment she confessed she could do neither, they lost interest. Others offered to do what they could if she agreed to pay them a large sum up front for their services, which sounded a shady deal even to Katherine's innocent ears. Such savings as she did possess were far too precious to be squandered without careful consideration. One even indicated he could most certainly find her work, in return for payment of a particular nature. Katherine had fled from that seedy office with all speed.

It took all of five hours' foot-slogging for her dream of being an actress, of treading the boards as these case-hardened agents called it, to be battered out of her. It had probably, she conceded, been foolish even to try.

The idea, so sparkling and brilliant when she'd first conceived it, promising a path to a marvellous new future, now lay tarnished and rusting in her mind. What had driven her even to think she could get a job on stage? Utter folly. A sort of madness, she supposed, born of a desperate need to escape. Was that how grief affected you in the end? There seemed no way out of the route into which Clara was resolutely funnelling her.

Feet aching, feeling dejected and low, not to mention cold and wet, with even the weather turning to a drizzly rain as if to echo her mood, Katherine caught the next bus home, preparing herself for the expected lecture.

On her daughter's return, Clara refused absolutely to speak to her. She would walk by her on the stairs and landing with her nose in the air and lips clamped tight shut, as if determined to make plain the injury caused by her lack of gratitude.

Frank, however, did his utmost during these early days of their engagement to please her. He took her to the zoo, to see the crown jewels in the Tower of London, for picnics and walks by the Serpentine. Best of all, he took her again to the theatre, this time to the music hall, where they marvelled at the magicians, wept at the melodrama, sang along with Marie Lloyd and cheerfully booed the pompous Master of Ceremonies. Seated high up in the gallery he ventured to kiss her but Katherine managed to turn her head just in time and the kiss landed on her cheek instead. Afterwards they ate jellied eels out of a paper bag. It was great fun, for all Archie mocked the outing as being fit only for the ignorant masses and not true theatre at all. Katherine responded by saying she greatly appreciated Frank's efforts to please her.

He was proving to be quite a gentleman in his bluff, self-deprecating way. Most evenings would find them in the parlour playing backgammon or chess quite companionably together. Almost like an old married couple, as Archie would caustically remark.

And as they played Frank talked, usually about the smart little house he was having built for them in the garden suburbs, while Katherine observed the guests seated morosely around the lounge, wondering if perhaps she should consider it a blessing not to have been taken up by a theatrical agent into this most insecure of professions. Amongst the motley collection of actors who occupied her mother's lodging house, few seemed to profit from it. Most appeared fairly down-at-heel in their luck. You only had to look at their clothes and footwear to know that. Nor did many put much effort into rectifying the situation as if, like her, they'd tried but soon lost heart. But then hope was something you'd largely abandoned if you chose to stay in this lodging house, despite its optimistic name.

Most actors managed to keep the wolf from the door by doing all manner of odd jobs such as being a waitress, shop assistant or barman which, generally speaking, they hated. Unfortunately, they never wanted to take on more regular work, in case a good part should turn up. They called this 'resting'. Others would lose their job through drowning their sorrows in too much drink, or 'a superfluity of alcoholic beverages' as Leonard, a one-time Shakespearean actor, preferred to call it.

Rents were paid weekly and, if unable to meet the cost, they were expected to visit Clara in her office with an explanation and proposed time-scale of when the debt might be settled. It was always a humiliating process for it was well known that Clara Terry was not a woman of sentiment. No rent – no room, was her policy. Poor payers were allowed two weeks' grace before they were evicted, their goods put out on the dusty pavement if necessary. In consequence nobody ever stayed very long at Hope View. Clients such as Frank Cussins, who paid on the nail each week, didn't take to drink and were clean in their habits, were a rarity indeed. But then he was far too predictable to be otherwise. No doubt once he had his house in the suburbs, he'd plant a neat little garden surrounded by a privet hedge which he would clip every Sunday. Katherine shuddered.

'I've just captured the last of your pieces, Katherine. Another game to me. I fear you're not concentrating.'

'Maybe I'm not up to your skill,' she said, not wishing him to query too closely what it was that so preoccupied her.

'I shall set the board out again and give you one or two pointers, shall I?'

Sighing deeply, Katherine paid scant attention as he punctiliously laid out the pieces once again, nor to the instructions he issued on her shortcomings as the game progressed.

'We must take another trip to the theatre one day,' he commented as he captured her bishop, 'so that you may wear your silk dress again.'

Katherine stretched her lips into a stiff smile, wishing she could feel more enthusiastic. 'That would be lovely.'

His eyes, set rather too close together, regarded her with a bright fondness and, encouraged by the smile, he leaned forward to whisper confidentially, 'Don't fret about Clara. She has a lot on her mind at present but she'll come round. I explained that a girl needs time to herself now and then, particularly when she's newly affianced.' Frank winked as he removed a knight, following it by two pawns. 'I also stressed how I observed many young women admiring your dress with some envy, which pleased her. And I pointed out that there's really no rush for us to wed. I perfectly understand that you need time to get over your grieving.' As if it were some sort of disease which would ultimately be cured.

Nevertheless Katherine appreciated his thoughtfulness. He was only being kind and he did understand about Clara. Her smile this time was more natural, filled

FREDA LIGHTFOOT

with relief. 'Thank you,' she whispered back. 'You're a brick.'

'Checkmate,' he said, gathering up her king, and they both laughed.

In between all of this 'social whirl', as Frank called it, Katherine continued to help her mother run the guest house. She laid the tables with limp, slightly off-white table cloths and tarnished silver, cleaned out the marble fireplace with its heavy brasses, dusted the collection of candlesticks on the overcrowded mantelpiece and polished the bulbous Victorian furniture. She also worked with resignation, if not contentment, alongside Myrtle in the kitchen.

In addition she tramped up the back stairs a dozen times a day with Scotch broth and any number of delicious milk puddings in an effort to tempt Archie's appetite back to normal and put some solid fat on his wasted muscles.

She would much rather have talked through these problems with him but whenever she took up his lunch or supper, he'd grunt and feign sleep, suffer from a fit of coughing or complain his head ached. Once or twice she'd been heartened to find him actually writing letters, which she gladly took to the post for him. But Katherine worried constantly about his state of health for he was still far from well and rarely in the mood for company. Even coercing him into the chilly bathroom to insist he shave or bathe was difficult enough, for she was quite sure he wouldn't bother to do either if she didn't insist. He seemed to have lost all interest and pride in himself.

Fending off beard growth or wearing a clean shirt didn't matter a jot, he told her, not in the general scheme of things, nor did it offer any protection against mortality; an argument she found difficult to repudiate.

For his part, Archie had no intention of recovering too quickly for wouldn't he then lose this delicious attention she gave so generously?

Sometimes, if he were feeling neglected, he would suffer one of his nightmares and Katherine would hear him and hurry to his bedside to cool his brow and soothe him. On better days he would allow her to coax him out of bed and they'd toast crumpets on long toasting forks held over the tiny bedroom fire and talk long into the night recalling old times, their memories of Raymond featuring strongly in these conversations. They would also discuss the future and what they might both like to do with their lives.

'I shall become a famous actress whom everyone flocks to see night after night,' Katherine would say. 'I shall keep half a dozen white Pekinese dogs, wear Turkish trousers and never go to bed before dawn.' An edge of passion crept into her voice and she could sense Archie watching her through amused, narrowed eyes. 'I won't have you mock me. You must write plays by the score for me to act in. Then you can travel around with me as my manager.'

'You'd best find some other companion to share that fantasy, dearest. I wouldn't have the energy. My chassis isn't what it was, and my crank shaft is on the blink.'

'Ever the defeatist.' Wiping a dab of butter from his chin and wrinkling her nose in a playful grimace. 'You're quite right, though, that is exactly what it is – a foolish fantasy. All the agents in London have turned me down so I've as much chance of becoming an actress as you have of turning into Leonardo da Vinci. It'll have to be Frank and the garden suburbs after all.'

And Archie would frown at her, and ponder this dilemma.

Chapter Three

Esme sat in the Sewing Circle making vicious little stabs into the towelling fabric. She had opted to make bibs for babies which, she reasoned, even she couldn't mess up since there were no armholes to worry over, no darts or pleats which always defeated her. But sewing on the bias binding was driving her mad with boredom. It had taken weeks to finish three pink and now she was on her second blue. Did the poor babies care if they were given the wrong one? she wondered.

Outside the window she could hear a skylark singing, the pure clarity of its song soaring heavenwards as the tiny brown bird hovered invisibly high above the church meadow.

'When you've finished your half dozen bibs, Esme, you can start on something more adventurous like smocking.'

'Thank you, Mrs Walsh.' She could hardly wait! Was that to be the summit of adventure and achievement in her life? To be allowed to put smocking on a child's frock?

Her father praised her warmly when she got home. 'I know needlework is not your forte, child, but think of those who will benefit from your efforts. Mrs Walsh distributes every scrap to those in the parish who do not have either the time or ability to sew, let alone the money to purchase clothes for their children. It is a generous act of mercy. Bless you.'

'I suspect they could get along much better without me. The cotton keeps getting tangled or breaking or slipping out of my needle, and it takes an age to re-thread every time.'

The Reverend Bield smiled. 'I'm sure your skills will improve. Practice makes perfect. Your mother was a splendid seamstress.'

'I am not my mother.'

'You're so like her, you must forgive me if at times I compare you with her. I miss her so very badly.'

'I know, Father. I'm sorry.'

He came to stand behind her where she sat at the table, cupping her cheeks between his hands as he tilted her head back so that he could kiss her brow. 'Well done, my child. No, not a child any longer. In fact you are growing up far too quickly.'

'Nineteen soon. My birthday, remember?' There was excitement in her voice and in her eyes as she looked up at him. Esme had asked for a book, one by Charles Dickens, on a sudden impulse to improve the quality of her reading matter.

'Of course,' he murmured, half to himself. 'Almost a woman. Just like my darling Mary.'

She was wondering if her request would be granted when she became aware of a small pressure upon her breast. Esme realised with a frisson of shock that his hands had slid down, one to her shoulder, the other entirely covering one breast, the fingertips flickering lightly over the nipple. She held her breath, waiting for him to realise and remove it. Instead of which, the pressure intensified, moving with a sensual purpose that made her feel trapped, unclean. She jerked upright, cheeks aflame.

'What is it, my dear? Don't be troubled. It's perfectly natural for me to wish to caress you. It was no more than genuine tenderness.'

Esme felt instantly guilty at her reaction, and slightly foolish. Was she turning into an hysterical spinster? Probably he'd grown confused again, thinking she was her mother.

He turned away, as calm and unruffled as if nothing untoward had taken place. 'I shall retire to my study until supper is ready. After we've eaten, I may read *Swiss Family Robinson* to you, by way of reward. How would that be, my child?'

Now she was his daughter again, one to be rewarded with the rare treat of a story. So everything must be all right, mustn't it?

The overwhelming responsibility of her father's love suddenly swamped her and she felt despair gnaw at her heart. Esme wanted to shout that she didn't need a reward for being a good girl, because there was no opportunity to be anything else. And she didn't want him touching her in that way. She was his daughter, not his wife. Would he please try to remember that? 'You said I was no longer a child,' was all she managed to utter, rather recklessly, to his retreating back.

She could hear the smile in his voice as he answered without even turning. 'You are *my* child, Esme, and I am immensely proud of you.'

Tears ran down her cheeks as she hurried to fetch the two tiny pieces of lamb's liver she intended to fry for supper from the larder. Esme felt as if she were drowning in his love. Suffocated by it. She rinsed the slivers of slippy offal beneath the cold tap, thinking of the long dull evening ahead. At least *Swiss Family Robinson* was an improvement upon their usual reading matter, though of course even they had spurned material possessions. He knew she loved books, and that was why he had offered to read to her. A reward for sewing babies' bibs.

Why wasn't she grateful for his care? As he frequently reminded her, he'd every right to caress her. He loved her, didn't he? Esme told herself stemly that her father would never hurt her, had never uttered a single unkind word, his one thought being to make people happy, and his beloved daughter content. Why couldn't she appreciate that fact? What was wrong with her? Was she incapable of love? And why did she lack his generosity of spirit? Guilt and rebellion warred within.

Banging the pans about on the old stove didn't help one bit. Nor did riddling the ash pan bring forth anything more than a belch of smoke and ash. He hadn't even thought to keep the fire stoked up with coke or wood while she was out, so how could she cook supper in a cold oven?

It took Esme the better part of an hour to heat the stove sufficiently to fry the liver, together with some onions and mashed potatoes. When she was done she was almost too worn out and choked with soot and smoke to eat.

Archie was in one of his more malleable moods and had agreed to sit at the small table in the window, obediently eating a good half of the fish pie Katherine had made especially for him. He much preferred the meals she prepared to the ones provided for the guests in the gloomy dining room. And while he ate, he watched the swing of her bare arms, the sway of her slender body as she busied herself changing his sweat-soaked sheets. Archie could sense she was about to bully him into some action or other and prepared himself to indulge her, though not perhaps without some protest.

'It's long past time you had a haircut,' she said. 'You're beginning to look quite Bohemian.'

'In that case I shall keep it this way, nice and long. I always did have Byronesque tendencies.'

Katherine stopped stripping the sheets long enough to glance up at him, slightly breathless. 'Don't think you can wriggle out of it with your flippancy. You need tidying up. Besides, some fresh air would be good for you. Frank will go with you, see you're all right.'

'Frank's the man for the job, is he?' And Katherine knew that he wasn't simply discussing a hair cut.

She tossed the soiled sheets to the floor, refusing to look at him directly or respond to his criticisms. 'Oh, do stop grumbling. Frank is perfectly harmless. He can even be good fun, if you give him half a chance.'

Archie stared at her, deliberately keeping his dark blue eyes unfathomable. He had his own opinions on

Frank Cussins which, so far, he had kept largely to himself. 'You aren't really going to marry the bounder, are you, Kitty-cat?'

Katherine was surprised by the tightness in his tone, holding his gaze for a long moment until it shifted and fixed itself on the rooftops instead. Inside she felt a small bud of rebellious anger start to unfurl. Everyone, even Archie, was far too concerned with telling her what to do with her life. 'We're engaged, aren't we? Anyway, Frank isn't a bounder. He's far too dull to . . . No, I didn't mean that.' She thumped the pillows, keenly aware of Archie's grin of triumph, for all he still kept his gaze firmly upon the rooftops.

'Yes, you did.'

Reaching for the clean sheets, Katherine began to unfold them in quick, jerky movements. 'Oh, for heaven's sake, just because he likes to enjoy life instead of going round with a long face like someone whose name I won't mention . . .'

'You mean he knows how to "give a girl a good time". Hurrah for Frank! Never thought you'd be influenced by such transitory delights.'

'It's called courting. We're walking out, as they say. He's a sweetie, and gloriously attentive.'

Archie glowered at her then coolly remarked, 'As any man would be when he goes fishing for a woman.'

'Don't be vulgar.'

'He isn't right for you, dear heart.'

Katherine pouted, largely because she suspected he might be right. She finished tucking in the blankets, smoothed out the pink cotton cover and turned it down in a neat fold. 'He is if I say he is. Anyway, I really don't see that it's anyone's business but mine.' She turned away. 'Are you staying there for a while, in the sun?'

'In the draught, more like.' His tone turned unexpectedly testy and irritable and she pulled a face at him.

'Dear me, we have got out of bed the wrong side this morning. It's long past time you rejoined the world, Archie Emerson, but don't take my advice. Lie here every day like a shrinking violet and lose the use of your legs if that's what you wish. See if I care.'

'I will.' Archie climbed stiffly between the sheets, leaning back upon the pillows with a dramatic sigh. As Katherine tucked the covers round him, mouth clamped tight shut with disapproval, the sight of the thin sticks of his wrists poking out from the sleeves of his old dressing gown filled her with a sudden rush of emotion that threatened to block her throat with tears. He looked so tired and so desperately ill, his once finely carved cheekbones now sunken and hollowed, that she was stricken with a rush of compassion. Leaning forward, she kissed him very gently upon his brow. The thought flew into her head that she might like to kiss him on the mouth, but she instantly quashed it. This was *Archie* after all. He smelt of camphor and the dreadful cigarettes he insisted on rolling for himself, and was the nearest thing she now had to a brother. 'Frank's very kind to me,' she said, firmly reasserting her point as she moved away from him.

'Of course. Darling Frank.' Archie smiled, having sensed her moment of indecision and revelled in it. Not for one moment did he look upon himself as a surrogate brother, though he recognised that was how she saw him. What he still hadn't worked out was whether this was to his advantage or not.

Long after the door had slammed behind her, his eyes remained riveted upon it.

Archie surprised everyone the following afternoon by setting out for a walk. He'd written another letter, he said, and wished to post it himself. Two in a month. He was becoming quite a scribe.

Feeling guilty for bullying him into taking exercise, Katherine ran after him, waving his red scarf like a flag. The sky was slate grey and she began wrapping the scarf about his scrawny neck, tucking the ends into the collar of his jacket as she would for a child, insisting that the wind might change and bring rain.

'Expert on the weather too, are you?'

'Don't be irritating!'

'And don't you nag. This is what you wanted, isn't it? For me to use the old legs again. Evidence that your splendid nursing skills have cured me.' A blustery spring breeze wrenched the scarf free and she struggled to tuck it back in place. 'Why don't you fasten the ends behind my back with a safety pin? And don't forget to tie on a label, in case I get lost.'

Katherine grinned suddenly, enjoying his black humour and, slipping her arm into his, fell into step beside him. 'Where shall we walk to then? Down to the Common? Or to the library to change your book? Oh, no, we haven't got it with us. I know, we could take a bus into town, go to Waterloo, Euston, Victoria or Paddington, and get on the first train that comes in.'

'What if it's going to the north of Scotland? That would be even wetter and colder.'

'But there'd be no London smog and grit, only clean, fresh air and the scent of heather. No nagging mother telling me what to do, what to think and even what to wear. Best of all, no miserable guests eating kippers for breakfast.' And no Frank, a small voice at the back of her mind quietly added.

'I thought they were rather fond of kippers in Scotland.'

'Herrings, isn't it?'

'Or mackerel?'

'Oh, shut up. We wouldn't know a soul,' she remarked on a note of surprise, warming to the dream. 'We could be anyone we wished. People of Mystery.'

'Absolutely, old thing.'

She laughed, hugging his arm closer as her mind enlarged upon the fantasy. 'We could be Bohemians together and live an outrageously free life, wandering the countryside and doing exactly as we pleased. You could take up painting, and I could act. How would that be?'

'Can't paint for toffee, darling, and you know how I dislike any sort of exertion.'

'You could be a descendant of Byron then, except that you shall write wonderful plays rather than poetry, and I could be the great-niece – or better still the long-lost child – of Ellen Terry, following in her famous footsteps. How about it?'

'You're engaged to be married to darling Frank.'

'Being engaged is one thing, getting married is quite another.' And then the buoyancy vanished from her tone and Katherine frowned. 'The truth is, I don't know anything about marriage, do you? Ma never set me any example of it.' She shuddered at the memory of sounds in the night from the room next to hers. 'How do people manage to stick together? Is it difficult, do you think, living with someone for an entire life time? Sounds fearfully risky to me.'

He considered the matter for barely a second before replying. 'Impossible, I should think.'

'Perhaps I won't marry anyone.'

'Steady the buffs. You must marry someone gloriously rich who'll devote his entire life to you and give you a brood of children to make you happy.'

Katherine began to giggle. Archie, with his wild mood swings, could one moment infuriate, the next captivate her. 'I'm not sure the two don't cancel each other out. Do children make one happy? I can't honestly see myself as a broody hen, can you?'

'Now who's being defeatist? Your dear mama expects you to marry, and marry well. It would signify her own escape from this godforsaken hellhole. All I'm saying is, for pity's sake don't let it be to that pubescent half-wit.'

'Perhaps I should marry you? No one would dare class you as such.'

'That's because few people possess half my wit.'

'Or I appreciate it more than most. We'd make a good team, you and me, without all that romantic stuff and nonsense to get in the way. Don't you think?'

'Would it?'

'What?'

'Get in the way?' His gaze held hers for so long that for the first time in his presence, Katherine felt her cheeks grow warm with embarrassment.

'You know what I mean. We're good chums, aren't we?'

He stuffed his hands in his pockets and quickened his pace so she had to run to catch up. 'I doubt marriage would suit my selfish nature, old thing, for all women fall at my feet in adoration. All that emotional angst and responsibility for another person's happiness. Where does it get you in the end?'

'That's a rather philistine, egotistical outlook.'

'Mayhap it is, dearie, but even so-called happy marriages can end in disaster.' His tone had grown oddly solemn and Katherine fell silent. The next instant he was grinning at her, as irreverent as ever. 'Though if this is a serious proposal instead of the indecent variety, which would be much more my style, I feel I should wear my new cravat, and perhaps my best smoking jacket.'

Katherine giggled. 'It might well become serious, if I should change my mind about Frank.'

A fleeting expression of panic crossed his features before he commented that he would be a poor bet as a husband since he might collapse at any moment from apoplexy, whatever that might be, and be nothing more than a dreadful burden. 'Wouldn't wish myself on any woman.'

'Ah, but I'm not any woman, you have no such dreadful disease, and you're on the mend.'

'Always so dreadfully finicky about detail. You should write the script of our conversations before we start, then I would know just what to say.'

'How could I hope to better your wit?'

'True, darling. I am rather remarkable.' Making them both double up with laughter so they had to grasp each other for support until Archie dissolved into a troubling cough that took some time to ease. It was a device, he'd found, which often served to end difficult conversations.

Rain had started to fall; fat, wet drops, so Katherine was naturally full of concern. 'Time to go home. We mustn't have you getting wet on your first outing.'

Archie jerked his head sideways to offer a further riposte and looked at her properly for the first time. His expression registered shock. 'Heavens, you haven't even brought your coat. What a nincompoop you are, rushing after me without a thought for yourself. You deserve a thorough scolding.' But he was smiling at her with such compassion, such a sweet, open tenderness, it made him look young and carefree again, banishing for a moment the horrors that haunted him. Katherine thought that despite his prickly nature and debilitating illness he was still beautiful. The perfect shape of his head, tilted with the arrogance of a Roman god, the raven curls that fell joyously about it and the deep blue eyes dancing with mischief, made him seem, outwardly at least, quite his old self. Perhaps it wasn't such a crazy idea to marry him. He was her very dear friend after all. 'Perhaps you'd better hang on to your best smoking jacket. I might really propose one day.'

'You're mad, Katherine Terry. D'you know that? Absolutely stark raving crackers.'

She grinned. 'I know. Isn't it wonderful?'

This was Clara's opinion too as they came into her kitchen, dripping pools of water all over the cracked linoleum. She continued to berate them as if they were recalcitrant school children while she rubbed Archie's head with a piece of old kitchen towel. Katherine watched with a kind of fascinated horror, thinking it probably still harboured fish scales left there by Myrtle's hands.

While they drank hot cocoa and nibbled ginger biscuits, dipping them into the frothing liquid, they carefully avoided each other's eyes so they could bear the brunt of Clara's stern lecture without collapsing into fresh giggles.

'It'll be a wonder if you don't go down with pneumonia again. Then how will you feel if he up and flippin' snuffs it, eh, girl?' Clara poked a long red finger nail into Katherine's shoulder and suddenly it didn't seem fun any more because it was true. Archie wasn't fit enough for an afternoon walk in the rain, let alone madcap adventures in Scotland.

'I'm sorry, Archie. I should never have bullied you into going out. It really was a stupid thing to do.' Was his face slightly flushed? Did he have a temperature? she worried.

'Nonsense, old thing. Never felt better. Did me a power of good.'

Clara folded her arms and glowered down at the pair of them, all scarlet lips and quivering bosom. Katherine thought she'd never looked more vivid, more alive, more beautiful, while she herself felt and looked like a drowned rat. Did other girls envy their own mother's beauty, even when it was slightly tarnished, as Clara's was?

'I hope you don't imagine you'll be able to boss Frank about in this way, madam, once you're married next month.'

'I beg your pardon?' Katherine stared at her mother, transfixed.

Archie scraped his chair back from the table. 'Think I'll go to my room, if you don't mind. I feel a sudden need for a lie down.'

She wanted to scream after him not to leave her but he'd gone, gently closing the door behind him, like a reproof. Clara was collecting mugs and dropping them in the sink for Myrtle to attend to later. When she returned to her place at the table, wiping her long white hands on the very same kitchen towel, she bestowed upon her daughter a huge wink. It gave her face an almost clownish look. 'He means to speak wiv you this evening, duchess, to fix it all up. See you don't go into one of yer moods. It's important you gives him the right answer. And you know what that must be, don't you?'

A wave of sickness hit her. 'It's too soon. I'm only twenty-one, Ma. There are months – years even before I need think about – about marriage and – and everything.'

'If you mean sex there's nothing to it. It's like riding a bike. Once you've got yer balance as it were, it gets easier. And yer not operating the handlebars after all.' Clara laughed, rather coarsely, as if she'd said something witty or meaningful.

The unspeakable reality of married life with Frank was not something which Katherine cared to consider too closely. So far they'd exchanged nothing more than a few clumsy kisses, always instigated by him and usually resulting in nothing more exciting than bumped noses. Then he would apologise for rushing her while in her heart Katherine knew he was showing admirable patience. She realised that this reaction didn't bode well for a happy marriage. Would she be any good at *It*? Was there something wrong with her that she hated even to think of sex? Perhaps she should put a stop to this terrible mistake before it was too late. 'I'm not sure that I even love him.'

'Leave it out. What's love got to do with anyfink, for God's sake?' Clara got up to reach into the top cupboard. Collecting a bottle of gin and rubbing a glass perfunctorily against her grubby skirt to clean it, she brought both to the table and proceeded to fill the latter to within an inch of the top. Katherine watched in silence, knowing that it said a good deal about where much of the money went in this household. Whatever rules she applied to her paying guests over the consumption of alcohol on the premises did not apply to Clara Terry. She took a long draught, closing her eyes in ecstasy. 'Wurf a fiver a glass that is. Nah, that sort of romantic rubbish don't last, even if you has it at the start. Better to let fings grow slowly. Get used to each other natural like.'

'I'm not sure I can.'

'I fought you and Frank got on well? Anyway,' she scanned her daughter critically, 'beggars can't be choosers. You're no oil painting, girl, great string bean that you are. And you'd be amazed how quickly the years roll by. Grasp the metal while it's hot, ain't that what they say? Frank Cussins is well placed financially for a young man still in his twenties, and not 'alf bad-looking. You have to give him that, girl. He don't come home drunk every night, do he? And there ain't so much as a sock out of place in his room. You might never get a better offer. Make no mistake about it, he's a catch.'

Katherine drew stubbornness about herself like a shell. 'If you insist on rushing me, I shall call the engagement off.'

Clara's affability fell away upon the instant. Her lips visibly tightened, pressing inward to leave specks of scarlet lipstick on her teeth. 'You'll do no such fing, madam. It's taken months of effort to bring him to this point. We need Frank Cussins, make no bones about it. He's wurf a bob or two, buying that luvverly house in the suburbs, and once the babies start popping out, I could sell up, or more likely close down, and come and help you wiv them.'

'You? Babies? You don't even like them. I'm not sure that I do.'

'I could learn. Same as you. All mothers love their own. So long as it don't start calling me Grandma, I can cope.' Clara feigned a shudder. 'I'd certainly be glad to be rid of this millstone round me bleedin' neck.'

If, in the argument which followed, Katherine had hoped to make her point, let alone to win it, she had reckoned without her mother's trump card.

'Refuse him and we'll both end up on Queer Street.' She leaned forward, squashing her full bosom against the table top so that it nearly met her plump chin. Her next words came in a sort of stage whisper, hissed out so fiercely into the silent kitchen that Katherine felt sure they must echo all over the house and she imagined ears pressed to keyholes, drinking in every one. 'Do you know how much money I owe on this place? More than I can pay off in one lifetime, that's how bleedin' much.'

Katherine stared at her mother in dawning horror.

'But *why*? I thought we were doing all right. We work hard enough, and the rooms are usually full.'

'It costs a flippin' fortune to run a house like this, and you don't fink what I charge this lot covers our lifestyle, do you? When they pays up, that is. Everyone knows I'm too soft fer me own good. Let 'em get away wi' murder, I do. Not to mention all them fancy frocks and folderols and such like you need for your socialising.'

'But I didn't ask for any of those things.'

'They were an investment, girl. I've told you that before. You're me best asset.' Clara refilled her glass to the brim, adding barely a dash of vermouth.

'I wish you wouldn't do that, Ma.'

Clara's patience snapped. 'Don't "Ma" me, and don't you look so po-faced. I've few enough pleasures, fer God's sake. Nor can I 'ang around waiting till it takes yer fancy to wed. Bills have to be settled, debts paid. Frank's eager to bring the wedding forward and so will you be, like it or not. In return he'll settle every bleedin' one. So don't you turn stubborn on me, girl. You'll wed within the month or we'll be coals and coke. Broke.'

Chapter Four

It was a Sunday, the last day of June and the evening before her birthday. Esme asked if they might postpone a further instalment of *Swiss Family Robinson* as she'd a letter to write.

Andrew Bield glanced up from his paper and frowned. 'To whom, might I ask? Not a sweetheart, I trust?' And she felt a spurt of resentment for having laid herself open to his interrogation.

'How could it be since I never go anywhere to meet a boy?'

Esme saw at once that some of her emotion had transmitted itself to her tone of voice for his expression turned from disapproval to one of sad disappointment, as if she had let him down in some way. 'Indeed I am only showing natural concern for you, my dear, a young girl of such tender years. Time enough for all of that nonsense later.' He waited, one brow raised in interested enquiry, thin lips curving into a conciliatory smile. 'Well?'

Guilt had dampened her moment of rebellion, as it always did. 'It's only to Archie. He's written to Mrs

Phillips, his housekeeper, from some boarding house he's staying in, in Ealing. I thought I'd like to write to him.'

Andrew Bield's smile broadened. 'Then for Archie's sake I am happy to postpone our reading for tonight. I'm sure it will do him no end of good to correspond with an old friend who remembers his dear parents.'

For a second Esme's defiance was rekindled. 'I'm writing as much for my sake as his. I'd like him to write back.'

'Of course you would. You're a dear child with a charitable heart.' He reached over to pat her cheek and she instinctively flinched away before she could prevent herself. Andrew halted, gazing down upon his daughter with a puzzled, slightly hurt expression in his pale eyes. 'I see you are tired. I shall take a late stroll by the lake into town. I may call upon poor Mrs Riley as she's been most unwell lately.'

'Netta Riley? At this time of night? But, Father, she lives in Tapworth Street, one of the worst streets in the Cobbles.'

'We live where we must. Judge not lest ye too be judged. She is entitled to succour in her sickness, the same as any other.'

'Of course.' Esme hung her head with shame. Her father was so utterly selfless, he'd risk catching some dread disease rather than fail to do his duty by one of his parishioners, while all she could think of was her own selfish right to an independence she probably didn't deserve.

He patted her head, tenderly tidying a few loose strands that had escaped the tightly wound plait. Esme did not move a muscle. 'You may leave my cocoa ready prepared but don't wait up for me. I may be some time. And don't spend too long on your letter, my dear. You need your rest.'

'Very well, Father.'

When he had gone, a peaceful silence folded in upon her and Esme closed her eyes in relief. Then on a burst of rebellion she unwound the neat plait and pulled it apart, shaking out the curling strands of fair hair and combing her fingers through in a moment of sheer ecstasy at being free to please herself, at last.

Father was a kind, sweet, darling man, she had to admit, even though grief over the early death of his beloved Mary had increased his tendency to vagueness over the years. Was it any wonder that his parishioners loved him, particularly the ladies? But then he always put the needs of others before his own.

True, it was beginning to worry her that his habit of confusing her name with her mother's had become more marked of late, but really the fault must be entirely her own. All she needed to do was to assert her own personality more forcibly though how this was to be achieved Esme hadn't quite worked out. Frowning, she reached for her writing pad. She wouldn't think any more about her own wretched problems, not tonight. Her father lived in a world of his own, one of rectitude and duty, as all parsons did. A fact she must simply accept.

Now what local gossip could she find to entertain Archie?

Esme awoke early the next morning, stretching her limbs deliciously in the warm cocoon of sheets. Today she had at last turned nineteen and drawn one small step closer to being her own woman. She smiled at the dust motes dancing in a ray of sunlight. What did it matter if dull routine continued as usual? Inside she could at least *feel* different.

She wondered if her father might buy her *Great Expectations*, or *The Old Curiosity Shop* perhaps. If he did not, she could only hope for something a little livelier than the copy of *Pilgrim's Progress* he'd bought for her last year which remained on her shelf, unread. And anything would be a change from *Swiss Family Robinson*.

From the crags surrounding the vicarage garden, she could hear the chack-chack of a merlin falcon. It sent her leaping from her bed to fling open her window and draw in lungsful of clear, crisp air.

'The first day of the month and I forgot to say "White rabbits",' she chided herself. 'Now I shall have bad luck.' But she was laughing as she pulled on her old grey pleated skirt and blouse for the day was already showing every promise of being hot. Perhaps, if she hurried over making her father's porridge and skimped on the dusting and cleaning today (since it was her birthday after all), she might have time to walk up through the woods and find some real rabbits.

Esme splashed water from the jug into the blue bowl and dipped her hands in it, enjoying the sting of its coolness on her warm cheeks.

Would anything ever change? This afternoon she must attend the Sewing Circle as usual, and no doubt be politely scolded for slipping out early last week. Tomorrow evening she must attend a special meeting of the Sunday School teachers where suitable infant hymns would be chosen and lessons planned. The only possible subject which might provoke interest or even a lively discussion would be over where to take the children for the summer picnic. The Superintendent would suggest a long walk in stout shoes. Mrs Walsh would opt for a steamer trip while Miss Agnes would offer dire warnings about children falling overboard. The children themselves might dream of a trip to the seaside, to Morecambe or Blackpool, but in the end they would do what they always did. They would take a charabanc to Arnside, then walk over to Fairy Steps and eat their picnic before trekking all the way back again.

On Wednesday there was to be tea and buns at the Mothers' Meeting, for which she'd promised to fill the urn with boiling water in good time. Someone recently returned from the Far East was to give a lantern-slide show. What relevance it would have to motherhood Esme couldn't imagine. Nevertheless it was an undoubted improvement upon the usual dull lecture on the problems of colic or nappy rash. And so the week would continue: dull, dutiful, all carefully set down in the parish diary.

But this morning, apart from the preparation of breakfast and lunch for her father, and because Esme was determined not to do a scrap of housework, she was free. Gloriously free. It was her birthday and she meant to enjoy what she could of it, meetings or no meetings.

She left the porridge simmering on the stove and ran all the way up the hill without even pausing for breath. In the woods she did indeed see several rabbits, moving through the dewy grass quite unafraid at this hour of the morning. A thin pearly light filtered down through the branches and here and there patches of blue sky glowed bright as a jewel, seeming to represent a glorious glimpse of freedom. One day, Esme vowed, she would journey to the very edge of its vastness. A magpie eyed her quizzically before flying off, perhaps in search of its mate. Esme watched it go. 'One for sorrow, two for joy,' she recited, anxiously looking for another.

She lingered for an hour or more, picking violets and garlic flowers, then heard the church clock strike ten before turning to run all the way home.

Reckless with joy on this glorious summer day, she didn't care that she was late. Father might not even notice. He would have eaten his breakfast by now and be in his study surreptitiously reading the morning paper while purporting to prepare his next sermon. He spent a good deal of time in his study, when he wasn't visiting his faithful flock. 'But not always working,' she said out loud, giggling to herself. 'Thinking I don't know what he's up to.'

Esme often talked to herself, largely because she liked to but also because there was rarely anyone else for her to converse with. The Reverend Bield did not approve of idle chatter.

He wasn't in his study when she arrived back, rather flustered and out of breath, feeling a nudge of guilt at having taken so long, despite her brave-hearted rebellion a moment ago. The porridge was where she'd left it, keeping warm on the hob, browning slightly at the edges where it had stuck to the pan. Her father's bed had been neatly made, Esme noticed, when she risked a peek around the bedroom door to check he hadn't overslept. Not that she ever remembered him doing so. Deciding he must have gone out early to see some sick parishioner, she ladled a portion of congealed porridge into a dish for herself, hungry after her morning's exercise and enjoying the healthy glow of her cheeks. Esme was on her second bowl when the knock came. She opened the door upon an agitated Mrs Phillips.

Afterwards she was to be grateful that it was her dear friend who brought her the news but for now she simply stared, knowing at once by the expression on the good lady's face that something was amiss.

'What is it?'

'I'll tell you inside, love, so half the street don't hear.' Ida Phillips quickly closed the door behind her as she drew the now trembling girl back into the suffocating warmth of the kitchen. 'Not that it won't be all round the village by dinner-time.' She sat Esme back at the table, moved the porridge dish out of the way, ran to the stove to slide the kettle back on and then looked desperately about for the tea pot.

'For pity's sake, Mrs Phillips, tell me. What's happened?'

Ida Phillips sat down rather suddenly, as if her legs could no longer support her. 'It's thee father. He's – well, there's nae easy way to say this, but he's . . .'

'He's dead, isn't he?' Esme heard the hollow echo of her own voice in the suddenly silent kitchen, and felt a huge surge of relief.

'It was so like the dear girl to save me the embarrassment of having to say it,' Ida would later confide to anyone prepared to listen. Esme Bield was, without doubt, a sensible lass but then she'd need every ounce of that good sense, to face what she had to face.

'I'm afraid so. But there's worse,' Ida continued.

Esme, ashamed of her initial reaction, felt strangely detached from reality, as if she were standing outside herself, calmly watching the conversation rather as an observer might. Part of her speculated on what could possibly be worse than death, while the rest worried over why she felt no grief. But then her father had often insisted that death was no more than the opening of a door. The older woman's cheeks, she noticed, had gone unusually pink, quite at odds with the paleness bad news was reputed to bring. 'Tell me. Whatever it is, I can bear it.'

'I reckon you'll have to.' Ida Phillips leaned forward and gripped Esme's hand with astonishing power. There were unshed tears in her faded eyes. 'It's the nature of his death which is going to make tongues wag, love.'

'Oh?' Esme suddenly didn't want to hear, but the words poured over her just the same, and Mrs Phillips's tiny frame seemed to shrivel like an empty string bag as she released them from her pinched mouth.

'He died in Netta Riley's bed. There now, that's the truth of it. If I didn't tell you someone else would have done so, and with more pleasure. No better than she should be, that woman, though it's happen wrong to speak ill of them wi' less sense than yerself, I dare say.'

Esme stared at her friend unblinking, her mind a blank. 'In her bed? Why? Was he ill? What on earth was he doing there?'

Ida looked at the girl and sighed. This conversation was clearly going to be even more difficult than she'd feared. 'You might well ask,' she said dryly.

* * *

The funeral was over in no time and the Church Commissioners wasted even less in informing Esme that her tenancy of the vicarage was now terminated. Her father's solicitor added to this stock of bad news by revealing that the Reverend Bield, not a material man in any sense of the word since he gave away most of the money he'd earned during his lifetime, had left what little worldly wealth remained, the sum of thirty guineas, to the Tapworth Street Mission. To his daughter, he left his best hunter watch and a single string of pearls which had belonged to her mother. The will stated that he knew she would not object to this decision since she possessed a charitable heart and the ability to earn her own living through service, as he had done.

Charity was not an emotion high in Esme's heart right at this moment, for she realised with a dreadful certainty that she had become, almost overnight, both penniless and homeless.

'What shall I do? Where am I to go?' she asked of anyone prepared to listen to her plight.

Miss Agnes clicked her tongue and sidled away, as if by engaging in conversation with the daughter of a parson who had died in a prostitute's bed would somehow rub some of the scandal on to her. And to think she had played the organ for him for twenty years! Mrs Walsh, less easily shocked by the weaknesses of men and being of a more practical nature, offered temporary accommodation in her attic, in return for various mundane chores on her farm. But it was Ida who put her finger precisely on the reality of the situation. Albeit she was in her way trying to help by suggesting, not unkindly, that Esme's best option as a single young woman with no visible means of support, was to become a paid companion or housekeeper to some kindly gentlewoman.

In that moment Esme had a clear vision of the life she faced. The Reverend Andrew Bield, her beloved parent, had been that worst of creatures, a hypocrite. No wonder they'd pitied her, those with the wit to guess. In the end even their pity would evaporate. She was to become one of the army of unmarriageable spinsters. Invisible, unloved, unnoticed, a leftover remnant of the Victorian age, dependent upon charity and service to survive. Through the death of her father she had simply escaped one life of service and duty for another, that would go on for as long as she lived and breathed, without even the redeeming factor of his love, suffocating and confusing as that had undoubtedly been.

Katherine turned on to her back and stared up at the grimy ceiling with hot dry eyes. The smell of stale cabbage along with the ubiquitous kippers Myrtle had cooked for breakfast lingered on, mingling with the suffocating fustinesss of too many people crowded into too small a space. But then these things always troubled her more when she was in 'one of her moods' as Clara called it.

Through the thin attic walls she could hear the gasps and small cries coming from her mother's bedroom next door, and the usual creaks and twangs of the bed springs. Being a voluptuous woman with, as she termed it, a lively appetite for life, she never seemed to go short of admirers. Leonard was apparently her latest conquest. Clara loved his white beard and the way he quoted poetry the whole time. Katherine pulled the pillow over her head and tried to shut out the too-familiar sounds.

Was this, she wondered, how she had come about? From one of her mother's more ardent lovers whose name she couldn't even remember? Clara herself firmly maintained she'd been properly and legally married and that her husband had deserted her the minute he saw he had two babies to support as well as a wife.

She would have dearly liked to learn more about her father for, as things stood, Katherine had no more faith in Smith being her true name than the more esoteric Terry. But Clara never enlarged upon the tale. It wasn't that she told lies exactly but simply preferred her life to seem dramatic. The role of deserted wife achieved that perfectly.

Breakfast was over but Katherine hadn't managed to avoid it completely. Now she stood at the kitchen sink, hands deep in suds as she went through the motions of washing up. Her eyes were fixed on the window as if seeking escape, for all there was nothing to see through it but the backyard wall. She was only vaguely aware of the activities going on around her: of Clara's voice yelling in the stairwell, Myrtle's sniffs and grumbles as she buttered wafer-thin slices of bread, the kettle starting to whistle. It stopped abruptly, though somehow Katherine knew that Myrtle hadn't made a move towards it.

If her choice was between slaving in the kitchen of Hope View for the rest of her life, tending to out-of-work actors and commercial travellers with her hopes and dreams of escape dead and buried with poor Raymond, then perhaps marriage with Frank in a new house in the garden suburbs didn't seem so bad after all.

Plans for the wedding seemed to escalate with alarming speed. When it came to organising anything which would result in a profit, Clara proved to be frighteningly efficient. A white lace gown had been purchased, wrapped in tissue paper and hung in her wardrobe with a lavender bag affixed to the hanger. The smell of it made Katherine feel slightly sick and she thought she would forever associate lavender with Frank. Mrs Capstick in middle back lent her some satin shoes and Leonard produced a blue garter for luck, though how he'd acquired it nobody dared ask.

Katherine couldn't quite take it all in. Despite his promises not to rush her, Frank hadn't even attempted to persuade her mother to postpone the wedding, had in fact cheerfully agreed on the third Saturday in July which was now perilously close. He'd arranged it all directly with Clara as if Katherine had no opinion whatsoever which, her mother tartly informed her, was the way the nobs went about things. It didn't seem at all the right way to Katherine, yet what could she do? She felt utterly powerless, couldn't even seem to get her brain to work the matter out properly. It seemed far easier to stand back and let the roller coaster hurtle on. The last thing she wanted was for her mother to lose Hope View to the bailiffs. Not only would they then have no income but no home either.

'You and me has to stick together, girl,' Clara kept repeating. 'We've no family now save each other, so must depend upon our own wit and ingenuity to get out of this 'ole.'

If Raymond were here, what would he have her do? Katherine repeatedly asked herself but came up with no answer. How could she? Raymond was dead.

Sometimes she felt as if she too didn't truly exist, as if she had neither past, present nor future, save the one Clara had invented for her. Only Archie supplied the one dissenting voice in the gathering excitement which was gripping Hope View with the kind of fervour usually reserved for a Royal event. Could he be right? He persistently begged her to think again, to wake up, to come to her senses; that she should learn to speak up for herself more. But how?

Yet perversely, throughout the hectic days of preparation, Katherine continued to defend Frank, pointing out his many strengths, even parroting her mother's words.

'He's good and kind.'

'Always ready for a laugh.'

'Generous to a fault he is.'

And even: 'He'll go far will Frank Cussins. I'm sure one day I'll be grateful for Ma's foresight.' Till Archie would shout 'piffle!' or something worse, and stamp off in high dudgeon.

Now, when his voice whispered against her ear, 'It's still not too late, you can stop this right here. Let your mother solve her own problems,' she stared at the engagement ring as it lay winking at her from the window sill where she'd set it while she washed the dishes, and shuddered.

'You have some other solution, do you?' Katherine tartly enquired, determined not to go over the whys and wherefores since she'd done so countless times before, then perversely found herself doing so anyway. 'Ma needs me. My father, whoever he was, let her down so badly by leaving her alone with two babies, she can't even bear to talk about it. How can I risk doing the same? I'm all she's got. I can't see her thrown out on the streets. I must help.'

'Not by playing the sacrificial lamb. There must be another solution.'

Katherine could feel the familiar swell of panic tighten in her breast. 'What can I do? I've already promised.'

'Frank Cussins won't make you happy. Don't trust the blighter, Kitty-Cat. He's as slippery as an eel.'

'You marry me then and pay off Ma's debts.'

'Told you, old thing. Marriage and me is like a sour cocktail. We don't mix. But I'd consider any other suggestions you might have. We could always run off together, as we once dreamed of doing.'

She felt angry with him for his continued flippancy. Why couldn't he see that she'd no alternative? 'This isn't the moment for jokes, Archie. This is real life, not fairyland.' She slapped a soapy cup down on the draining board with such force it was a wonder it didn't crack.

He picked up a tea towel and began to dry it with painstaking care. 'Don't do this to yourself, Kitty. Tell Clara to live her own life and let you live yours.'

Katherine couldn't even see the window now. Too much steam or moisture blotting her vision for some reason. Taking her hands from the water, she turned and ran from the kitchen and left Archie to finish the washing up by himself.

In only one respect did she win a small victory: Katherine refused, absolutely, to marry in church. She insisted her mother abandon plans for hiring a twenty-strong choir complete with organist that she couldn't, in any case, afford; adamant in her belief that it would be a sacrilege to say her vows in such a setting to a man she could never truly love.

But if Katherine had hoped to put Frank off by this obstinacy, she was mistaken. 'Just as well,' he said, firmly supporting her decision, 'or we might end up in Westminster Abbey being married by the Bishop of London.'

It was agreed that the marriage would take place, very quietly, at the nearest register office. Frank's brother would be best man and they wouldn't bother with a bridesmaid.

'But you'll be taken in a motor, duchess. Only the best for my girl,' Frank grandly informed her.

Katherine told him not to call her by that name. 'It sets me above everyone, and I don't care for it.'

'Right you are, darlin'.' She didn't think she liked that any better.

As if anxious to prove himself aware of his good fortune, Frank went out of his way to be agreeable in the days following: helping her buy clothes for a trousseau, taking her to see the new house and carefully explaining that there was no requirement for her to work, that all she would need do was to spend her days keeping it spick and span for the two of them. 'Like a pair of love birds we'll be. You can leave everything safely to me. Frank will look after you.'

And Katherine would thank him, while doing her best to suppress a shudder whenever he came near. Although his lingering glances revealed his increasing anticipation of the coming wedding night, she made absolutely certain that he had no opportunity for an untimely approach.

Should he lightly kiss her cheek, tuck back a stray curl or put a comforting arm about her waist to draw her close, she always managed to wriggle free and find something of great urgency to attend to elsewhere.

'Don't you worry, duchess,' he would say, smiling fondly. 'Frank can wait.' And she could almost sense his mouth watering. If the whole thing took on a dreamlike quality, leaving her suffering from a strong sense of unreality, Katherine put this down to the speed of events.

She did not for a moment doubt that he was sincere.

Nevertheless, deep in some secret part of her soul, there lurked the hope that something might happen to change the status quo; that she'd be released from this crazy promise to sacrifice herself in order to get her socially aspiring mother out of debt and keep a roof over their heads. If it wasn't so tragic, it would almost seem like the plot of a Victorian melodrama, or even a pantomine. Poor Beauty forced to marry the Beast. If only Frank Cussins could turn into a prince. Problem solved.

Was that what she was hoping for, a magic wish or a good fairy to save her? A knight on a white charger to ride to her rescue?

Nothing of the sort could happen, of course. Nothing and no one could possibly save her, not in real life. It was all her own fault for agreeing to the engagement in the first place. This princess would never find her Prince Charming and life, as Clara was so fond of reminding her, would go on.

The night before the wedding, Frank offered to take everyone out to the pub for a drink, except for Katherine of course who, as the bride, was expected to get an early night. In theory the outing was meant only for the men and even Archie was coerced into joining the party but she noticed that her mother considered herself included, without even being asked. In a way Katherine was thankful. Such residents as were left in the boarding house were female and content to remain in their own rooms. Katherine welcomed the prospect of time alone like a drowning man might gasp for air.

The moment they'd gone, with much loud finding of hats and scarves and ribald laughter, Katherine flew upstairs, two at a time, ran a deep hot bath and sank her cold, tense body into it. She lay back, telling herself that the moisture on her cheeks was caused by steam. Then, dressed in her comfortable old checked dressing gown, she sat on the edge of her bed, brushing her damp hair, gazing at the familiar chimney-pots.

'It's the garden suburbs for me now,' she told them. 'Cooking my husband's breakfast every morning, handing him his morning paper and his bowler hat; spending my days cleaning our lovely new house; tending the garden, going shopping and deciding what to cook for the evening meal. After which we'll play backgammon or chess. What a delightful life that will be. No more smog, smoke or grit. So do your worst, chimneys, it won't bother me.' At which point she burst into tears.

A long time later, worn out by worry and exhaustion, she slept.

It must have been well past midnight when Katherine woke, wondering what exactly had disturbed her. It was usually quiet here, in the top part of the house, where she was rarely bothered by the comings and goings of guests.

Then she heard the bed springs creak next door and the sound of muffled laughter. Of course, Clara, back home and up to her old tricks. Her animal grunts and groans increased in volume, as they so often did when she was the worse for drink.

Katherine considered slipping down to the kitchen to get herself a cup of cocoa until it was all over. She'd always hated the thinness of these walls. Before she was halfway out of bed, however, she heard her mother cry out in ecstasy the name of her lover. Katherine froze for in that moment she realised that her engagement was at an end.

Chapter Five

In the two years since she'd married, Charlotte had come to understand how very easy it was to make a mistake, and how difficult to right it.

She smiled at the enchantingly handsome young man so comfortably ensconced in her bed and permitted the satin dressing gown to slip one enticing inch further down her shoulder, revealing the pale orbs of her breasts, the flatness of her stomach and the promise of secrets that lay below. She could almost feel his eyes roving hungrily over her body; could see his tongue licking lips gone suddenly dry, as if desperate to slake his thirst.

'Have you cooled the wine?' Charlotte asked, her voice sweetly matter-of-fact.

'It's ready poured.' He was almost drooling, his breath coming short and ragged.

'And me 'usband sleeps like a babby.' She slid a fingertip into his mouth and felt him nip it gently, his tongue flicker urgently against the pad of it. Ever tantalising, she moved swiftly away. 'Perhaps it would be wise to check.'

'Lottie, don't leave me! Not like this.'

Charlotte was laughing as she slipped from the room, though the smile faded the instant she'd closed the door. Entering her husband's bedroom she found him, as expected, far from sleep for all the lateness of the hour. Seated at his desk by the wide bay window he scarcely troubled to glance up from the letter he was writing as she approached.

'His best stallion, remember. Rude Awakening. Rather an apt name, don't you think, since that's what young Tommy will get once the deed is done. I'm sure you can find some way to bring the subject into the conversation.' He cast her a sideways mocking glance. 'You do find time to talk, I suppose?'

'Of course.' Charlotte shivered and rubbed her arms, though the room was over-warm, even stuffy.

'Make sure he thinks the request comes entirely from you. Tell him I only ever give you dull grey mares with sway backs, and you're looking for something more spirited and challenging.'

'I came to see if you'd changed yer mind.'

He laughed, yet there was little mirth in the sound. 'It's young Lord Bickerstaff, now reposing in your boudoir, whose mind must be changed. He's refused to allow any of his stallions to service my mares but, as my own father taught me, there's more than one way of skinning a cat.'

Contrarily now Charlotte felt hot and light-headed, as if the closeness of the room were suffocating her. 'Why must you use *me* in your stupid schemes, as if I were simply another of yer damn' mares needing servicing?'

He got slowly to his feet and, grasping a lock of her

baby-soft golden hair, pulled her towards him, causing her to cry out. 'Why all the fuss, dearest? He's simply an eager young stud in need of a little pleasuring. And you're welcome to give it to him, so long as my price is met. Do I need to make my wishes plainer?'

Charlotte gazed into the handsome face mere inches from her own and knew a genuine hatred. She'd been fond enough of Magnus Radcliffe when she'd agreed to grace his home with her beauty and his bed with her passion, even if it were not quite the rapturous love match she'd once dreamed of. Charlotte had hoped all that would come later. Why should it not? In the meantime, she'd been more than content with her lot. He owned a large country estate, kept several horses and dubbed himself a gentleman farmer, having shaken off all connections with the origin of his wealth gained for him by his manufacturing father in the woollen trade.

Charlotte's lips curled with distaste as she wrenched herself from his grip and went to lean against the cold window frame, again rubbing her hands up and down her arms as if to rid herself of his touch upon the silky skin. 'It's plain enough, Magnus. Whether I'll succeed is another matter.'

'You *must*. You know I will not tolerate losing.'

She could see only her own face in the glass, made opaque by the fading evening light beyond, blanking out the scene of rolling parkland. Rain was streaming down, bouncing off the stone sill and rushing on down the façade of her prison walls. Charlotte had once thought this one of the finest country houses in Yorkshire, almost a palace. It had long since become otherwise to her.

The day she'd slipped in the snow and literally fallen

at his feet, exhausted after a hard day's work in the mill, had changed her entire life. Magnus Radcliffe, playing the role of perfect gentleman, had instantly come to her aid.

He'd looked upon her classic beauty with its neat straight nose, pert chin and porcelain skin and been mad to possess her. 'I always yearned to pick a girl out of the gutter,' he'd told her, dusting off the snow that clung to her coat with a lingering hand. And because he'd looked so handsome and his white teeth flashed so charmingly as he laughed, they'd married a mere three months later, causing quite a stir. 'My pretty waif,' he'd called her. 'My charming vagabond.'

Charlotte had let him call her whatever he wished, do with her as he willed, so long as she could live in a fine house on his Yorkshire moors, be waited upon by servants and have food in plenty to eat. Even now, in spite of all the strange demands he made of her, the comforts Magnus could offer counted for much.

Yet she'd never managed to feel the slightest degree of love for him. Would he have treated her differently if she had? No matter how hard she'd tried and however grateful Charlotte was to have escaped the rigours of the damp, overcrowded house where she'd been born, she never quite seemed able to satisfy Magnus Radcliffe. In one way or another she'd always fallen short of some desired perfection. Perhaps he didn't truly care for her either? Perhaps he'd picked her up that day simply to place her among his other business assets, like a possession. Maybe she didn't even deserve to be loved. Why should she? Nobody ever had before.

Jealous of her beauty, her own mother had largely ignored her. And a bully of a stepfather had spent time with her only to teach her how to steal from market stalls, which saved him the trouble of earning an honest crust. Charlotte had made strong objections to being schooled in thieving, when her mother was sober enough to listen, only to be accused of telling fibs.

'One of our Lottie's wild fancies,' she'd say, warning that if such wickedness were repeated, the child would be packed off to a wayward girls' home. Until that moment, Charlotte hadn't known what an untruth was but she soon learned to become an expert in both lying and stealing. Lies were what her mother expected, so that was what she was given.

'Eeh, our Lottie, where did you get this nice bit o' brisket?'

'Kaye's butchers let me 'ave it cheap.'

'Nay, see where yon pretty face'll get you. Tha'll go far, lass. Think on.'

As far as a prison cell if I'm not more careful, the young Charlotte worried, avoiding sight of her step-father's smirking face. She'd keep away from Kaye's for a while and try it on with another stall holder, but the fear of being caught was sharp in her. At least at first.

There were times when Charlotte would've liked to tell her stepfather to take the risks himself, but apart from the fact that he was a dangerous man to cross, he was fond of making lewd suggestions that he could find alternative ways for her to earn her keep. In the end, despite her better judgement, she'd got caught up in the excitement of it all and begun to steal on her own account. A scarf here, a pretty ribbon there, and always some tale to disguise the truth of what she was about. Charlotte became adept at making believe these items had been acquired legitimately, and that she was part of a normal, loving, happy family. In this way she created a protective shield about herself and, in a desperate attempt to disguise any lingering remnants of shame and guilt, came to live in a world of make believe.

Consequently she dealt with her feelings for Magnus Radcliffe in much the same manner, for the union hadn't worked out quite as either of them would have wished.

Their differences, surprisingly enough, were not caused by class. He, naturally, had taken it for granted she'd be eternally grateful, for what girl of her class would not? He could offer her the promised land: entry into a world far removed from her humble upbringing. It was a sign either of his arrogance, or of his security in Yorkshire society, that he was able to consider a match which a lesser man would balk at. And society had indeed accepted her, flocked to her door in fact, even if her vowels were rather too flat and her sense of humour at times bordering on the vulgar.

Yet much as the ladies of Halifax longed to ridicule her as nothing more than a novelty, and a cheap one at that, they forgave her because the new Mrs Radcliffe had that most precious commodity: style. Unconventional, eccentric, sometimes downright outrageous, but once seen never forgotten.

Charlotte's style seemed to demand she be tricked out with beads, earbobs, floating scarves, frills and furbelows which no one but a girl who completely lacked breeding would be seen dead in. And yet far from cheapening her, these tricks only added to her charms. They knew of no other young woman who would dream of wearing green gloves with a blue costume and making it seem the last word in chic, or a startlingly pink hat with a red coat and look simply ravishing in it. Nor anyone else of their acquaintance whose dresses were cut quite so low, or so prick-neat, nor whose skirts displayed such a vulgar show of ankle. There was no other word to describe this idiosyncratic attire except racy. From the top of her pale golden head to the toes of her dainty feet, every satin smooth curve of her petite body tantalised and bewitched. Her nose tilted to just the right degree, her eyes slanted, her lips . . . why, indeed, her lips never seemed anything other than blush pink and so fulsomely shaped they almost begged to be kissed. As for her figure, it was a miracle to these good Yorkshire ladies how it was she could keep it so neat without recourse to the iniquitous corset. Secretly they longed to emulate her and throw their own away but dared not.

In addition to heart-wrenching beauty, Charlotte Gilpin, as was, boasted a most engaging personality. She bubbled with energy and enthusiasm and had a wayward knack for mimicry which frequently left them in stitches. They were, quite simply, enraptured by her.

Was it any wonder if the ladies of the county set admitted, in the strictest confidence and only amongst themselves (should they ever feel the slightest twinge of resentment and jealousy), that they understood perfectly why their menfolk lusted after the girl.

But it was this ability to captivate men, Charlotte soon realised, which had first attracted Magnus to her and eventually proved the chief source of rancour between them. Even in the first year of her marriage, her life had become fraught with unexpected difficulties. He'd called her his prize, his golden chalice, and then proceeded to hand her round as if she were indeed a cup that others might drink from.

To Magnus Radcliffe, having men lust after his wife was all part of a game, one that bore a strong resemblance to the chances he took at the gaming table or at the races. He possessed something they wanted, therefore he could gamble with it. He might permit them a taste, a sip, so long as they returned the favour. Nothing gave him greater satisfaction than the sight of one of his friends or business rivals, young or old, jockeying to kiss her hand or anxious to lead her out on to the floor in a waltz. He did not mind who flirted with his wife, or how many *billets doux* she received, so long as he personally selected the *beaux* in question.

Today, for the first time and since necessity demanded it, he had decreed that a thirst be slaked completely, so long as the price was agreed beforehand.

He came to her now and pushed open her gown, allowing his gaze to wander over her nakedness. He smiled. 'Tell him you risk a good deal by allowing him into your bed. He will never know that the reverse is the case, so why should he argue the toss? Get his bond in writing, Charlotte, or your buttocks will do if you lack paper.'

She gazed at him, saying nothing. At one time she might have rebelled, even refused absolutely to comply, but she'd learned the value of obedience for there were precise rules to this game. She only had to flutter her lashes the very slightest degree in the wrong quarter, receive flowers from an admirer who hadn't first sought her husband's permission, for Magnus instantly to desire to reclaim what was rightfully his and inflict whatever punishment he considered appropriate. He would watch with brooding discontent in his dark eyes, fury building as she laughed and teased whichever poor soul she'd set out to enslave. Then Magnus would return the uninvited flowers with a curt note, or bar the sender from ever partaking of dinner at his table again.

Once, while attending an anniversary ball for an old friend, Magnus had discovered her dancing alone in the conservatory with a young captain.

'What is this?' The ominous quiet of his voice had so chilled her, she could only stare at him silently. Even her valiant partner had deemed it wise to hold his tongue.

Magnus had taken her arm in an iron grip and propelled her out into the garden in order to give full vent to his feelings on her questionable behaviour. Charlotte, desperately struggling to keep pace with his long strides, had been quite out of breath by the time she managed to wrench herself free from his grip. 'For pity's sake, what's up wi' thee? We were doing nowt wrong, only dancing.'

'Doing nothing wrong. You were doing *nothing* wrong.'

'Well then, why mek such a scene?'

He'd swallowed an outburst of rage. 'Do please watch your grammar, Charlotte. How many times have I told you? As for this latest charade, I do *not* recall giving you permission to disport yourself so openly with that fop.' Referring to Julian Webster, the son of one of his fiercest competitors at the race track.

'Julian is a poppet and wouldn't hurt a fly,' Charlotte had retorted, carefully rounding her vowels. 'And it were that hot in the ballroom.'

'*Was* too hot.'

'Like I said, too hot by 'alf.'

'Damn you, woman, you'll do as I say, do you understand?' He'd flung her to the ground, ripping her gown in the process. 'You'll offer favours to no man unless I say you may. *Is that quite clear?* I'll tell you with whom and when. Don't ever forget that *I* am in control. If you play the slut with me, woman, you'll be back where you came from, in the gutter.'

'You're me bloody 'usband, not me keeper!' she'd unwisely responded, some imp of madness making her hit out at him, partly from the folly of youth and partly the confidence she held in her own charms. She was soon to regret such recklessness.

He'd taken her home, stripped the clothes from her back and whipped her, using the silken cord from his dressing gown. Afterwards, as she sat sobbing, terrified of moving in case she exacerbated the pain in her back, he carefully explained how the punishment was not administered from lack of love on his part but was meant only to cure her of disobedience, in particular her persistent waywardness.

'Not forgetting me bad grammar,' she'd obstinately yelled back at him, receiving another leathering for her cheek.

Later, as she tenderly bathed her raw skin, Charlotte had noted with a mixture of relief and fear that he'd been clever enough not to break it, which meant that if he could get away with it once, he could do so again. Nevertheless the bruising took weeks to heal, serving as a spur to greater obedience, and causing her to work all the harder at being the wife Magnus demanded.

In this way, the peculiar nature of their relationship

continued to flourish. He as the master and she the slave. She must simper and smile and ply her charms to his will. And whenever Magnus judged that his wife had not quite put her heart into a prescribed task, thereby failing to procure whatever prize he'd set his heart on, he would say to her, 'Now what would you consider to be a suitable chastisement?' Charlotte would shake her head in mute distress for some of these punishments proved to be alarmingly imaginative.

He might lock her in a spider-infested closet for hours till she was ready to agree to anything just to be released from the crawling darkness, or twist her arm until she wanted to scream from the pain but dare not because he would beat her all the harder if the servants heard anything untoward. He might slap her till her head spun, pinch her till she was covered in purple bruises, or place tiny fierce bites all over her naked body. On one occasion he even made her crawl upon her knees, licking up crumbs from around his feet, begging his mercy for some supposed indiscretion, before he kicked her senseless as if she were a dog.

So now when he asked her to perform an intimate act with a man of his choosing, Charlotte was only too aware of the futility of argument. She had learned long since that it was far easier, and infinitely less painful to take the easy option of obedience. For the moment.

Until her plans for escape were all carefully in place.

Besides, she consoled herself, young Tommy Bickerstaff possessed a lean fit body hardened by long hours spent in the saddle. It could be worse. He might have chosen fat old Hugo Johnson to test her charms instead.

Turning from the window, she bestowed upon Magnus

what passed for a smile before quietly withdrawing from his presence to return to her ardent lover and carry out her husband's wishes to the letter, as a good wife should.

The stallion was delivered the very next day, tied up with a scarlet bow and a note saying that although it was merely a loan and the horse couldn't be offered as a gift, she was welcome to ride him whenever she so wished.

'That'll do for a first effort. You clearly pleased our young lord,' Magnus informed her with some degree of satisfaction. 'Though an outright gift would've been better. You must try harder next time.'

'For God's sake, who'd be daft enough to give away a prime stallion for one good . . .'

'*Don't* say another word. A lady never refers to the subject directly.'

Charlotte never did get to ride the animal, of course, much to her relief since horses were far outside her scope of knowledge, but Magnus made ample use of the time the horse was in his possession, even to the extent of bribing the groom who brought him each day.

Charlotte accurately guessed this would be the first of many such favours she'd be called upon to bestow. In no time, it seemed, she was proved entirely correct. Ownership of Rude Awakening was indeed soon transferred to her name, for all it was her grasping husband who always rode him. After this triumphant success, Magnus carefully considered every male of his acquaintance, weighing up the extent of their wealth and possessions and what they might possibly be prepared to part with, in return for a little dalliance with his enchanting wife.

His behaviour only deepened her loathing to a dangerously new level, yet there seemed to be nothing she could do about it at present. She had no money and no home besides this one, and Charlotte certainly had no intention of returning to the 'gutter', as he so charmingly termed it.

So the 'game' continued, exactly as Magnus wished it to, and Charlotte very nearly lost heart, unable to find the solution she sought; forced to comply obediently with his every whim. One day, though, she knew her time would come. She would bank upon it. In the meantime she made a private vow that although she would play the whore, if that was what he wished, she'd never permit her husband to hit her again.

It was unfortunate for Magnus Radcliffe that the moment he chose to repeat his bullying, he was seated astride Rude Awakening, cantering through the woods with his wife beside him on her more docile mare.

Despite all her best efforts Charlotte was a poor rider, struggling to learn only to pacify him. As they broke out of the woods and set the horses' heads to a track which threaded its way through dew-spangled meadows, Charlotte's cheeks glowed from the exercise, highlighting her loveliness to a breathtaking beauty. It was one of those magical mornings when an early sun promised quickly to disperse the skeins of mist that still clung to the hill tops and for a moment the sheer glory of it, and the excitement of the ride, filled her with a rare happiness.

She could never afterwards remember how it all came out. They'd reined in their horses to a quiet amble while they squabbled over something ridiculous such as who was to sit where at the dinner party that evening perhaps. She'd suggested Julian Webster be seated next to her while Magnus reiterated that it should be James Wisheart, a new neighbour who'd taken possession of the land adjoining their own. Or it might simply have been over which dress she should wear, Charlotte, as ever, favouring bright colours while Magnus preferred a more tasteful shade.

'I wish you to be nice to him, Lottie,' he'd informed her, his voice jerking slightly with the rhythm of the stallion's easy movement. 'It could prove highly beneficial to secure the friendship of such a wealthy man.'

'To hell with that! I'm done with playing the whore for you.' And then she'd told him she was pregnant. The words flew from her mouth without thought or planning. Instead of expressing pleasure and pride in the fact she was to produce an heir to his fortune, Magnus roared, *'Whose bastard is it?'*

Charlotte met his furious gaze with a red hot temper of her own. 'If it's impossible to tell, then you've only yourself to blame.' And she drummed her heels into the mare's flanks, making it spurt forward into a canter.

'Whore!' he shouted after her, his voice catching on the wind. 'I timed your performances so as to avoid any such confusion. If you've fallen, it must be because you've taken a lover on your own account.'

His arrogant assurance that he could control even the natural order of her own body, of life itself, suddenly seemed highly amusing and she threw back her head and laughed; hysterical, reckless laughter, which in turn excited the horse to increase its pace still further. She could hear the thundering hooves of Rude Awakening rapidly overtaking her. 'P'raps the poor little bugger's a bleedin' lord. That'd be summat, eh?' she yelled back at him.

'*You damned slut!* You'll get rid of it, d'you hear? I'll not have another man's by-blow. *I'll* decide when I'm ready for you to breed.'

Tears streamed down her cheeks though whether caused by the reckless ride or her own laughter, she couldn't rightly have said. 'What d'you reckon I am then? One of your brood mares?'

His instant response was to lash out with his riding crop, almost as a reflex action. The whip caught her full across her back and Charlotte jerked violently with the sting of it, ever sensitive on that part of her body which had already suffered ill treatment at his hands. He was screaming at her, demented with rage, lifting his arm to strike her again. Perhaps because she was such a poor rider, unsure of her seat, or because the horses, spooked by his violent outburst, had shifted their pace from a steady canter to a madcap gallop, instead of taking the punishment as he expected Charlotte reached out with one gloved hand and, more by good luck than judgement, grasped the thong of the whip. Whatever the reason, terrified of falling beneath the hooves of Rude Awakening, she held on, heaved on it as hard as she could without even considering the consequences. Or so she afterwards claimed.

The action caught Magnus off guard and, unable to hold his balance at the speed he was then moving, he

FREDA LIGHTFOOT

lurched sideways in his seat. Ahead of them reared a
fence and beyond that a ditch. Rude Awakening, feeling
the loss of control, missed his footing and panicked.
Snorting and pawing with fright he stopped short and
shied. Magnus was tossed like a cork right over the fence.

Charlotte too fell to the ground, still shaking with
hysterical laughter, at least until the pains started and
knifed her in two. Even so, one glance at the crumpled
body of her husband told her that losing this child was
the least of her worries.

The room stank of stale sweat, camphorated oil, and other
less edifying scents. Charlotte gazed bleakly upon the still
form of the man lying in the bed and knew a loathing that
increased with each passing day. There were no 'games'
now, no card parties, no dinner parties, nor any hope of
dalliance let alone dances with handsome young captains
in sweet-scented conservatories. Now there was only the
stench of sickness and hatred.

She'd lost the baby of course, had been told there
would be no further pregnancies. Sitting by her husband's bed, Charlotte knew there was little danger of
such a thing happening in any case. She shed no tears
for him, nor felt any sense of guilt. Why should she? It
had been he who had instigated the accident, by his own
hand, with a reckless violence she'd only responded to.
Being paralysed hadn't altered his nature one scrap. He
was still a brute. Always had been, always would be.

'I wish you'd been killed outright, you bully,' she
murmured.

Only when he slept did she find any peace, for the

house was still ruled by his iron will. He could still belittle her with his words; still order his affairs in that loud, demanding voice; still play the bully. And he blamed her entirely for the state he was in. Only the two of them were aware of her part in the 'accident' and he held this knowledge over her like a threat, using it to make her toe the line. So long as she did exactly as he ordered, no one else would learn the truth. Otherwise, as he constantly warned her, she could be charged with attempted murder. Charlotte had desperately wanted him to die that day and Magnus knew it.

Her face twisted with hatred at his power over her, even now, when that strong handsome body had been broken. She turned away and, without a backward glance at the prone figure in the high brass bed, strode from the room. Out on the landing Charlotte stood for a moment with her back to the bedroom door, breathing hard until the hammering of her heart, which a visit to the sick room so often brought on, gradually subsided and she had herself under control again.

She heard the housekeeper's step upon the stairs, bringing his supper no doubt. Charlotte straightened her slumped body and managed a smile. 'Good evening, Mrs Pursey.'

'Madam.' The woman scanned the mistress's slender figure with the kind of insolent glance which plainly stated what she thought of this common upstart who had married her master and was no better than she should be. Holding the laden tray high, Magnus's appetite having increased rather than abated as a result of his handicap, she waited to be allowed entry into the sick room. Charlotte remained where she was.

'He's asleep. I doubt it would be wise to wake him. You know how he hates to be disturbed.' She was always the one to suffer the full force of his anger, and although Charlotte understood, since only in sleep was he free from the knowledge of what he had lost, a business and fortune so cleverly garnered and now gradually crumbling away, she dreaded his temper.

There was also the most painful loss of all – his manhood. Even his friends were drifting from him for none knew how to deal with his increasing irascibility.

'He likes his tea prompt at six,' Mrs Pursey stoutly informed her.

Charlotte met the housekeeper's icy glare and considered holding it till she'd forced her to back down, but where was the use in aggravating the woman? For all there was no love lost between them, she needed Mrs Pursey. Without her, Charlotte would be even more of a prisoner of Magnus's whims and demands. Shrugging her shoulders, she stepped aside. 'Of course,' she said. 'I was forgetting.'

Far from releasing her from Magnus's tyranny the accident had made her an even greater prisoner of it. Instead of being married to a successful land owner with rising status and fortune, she was now encumbered with a cripple.

Entering her own bedroom, she locked the door carefully behind her, gazing about her with the desperation of a mouse caught in a trap.

Chapter Six

Trains were shunting and puffing by in every direction, whistles blowing, steam belching, people jostling and rushing to find a seat while Katherine stood bewildered on the platform, frozen with indecision. Finally gathering her courage, she stepped on to the train and it was here, hunched in a corner of a carriage, that Archie found her. She was astonished and filled with a rush of gratitude as he flung his bag on to the overhead rack and dropped into the seat beside her, breathing heavily.

'How did you know where to find me?'

It took several minutes before he could gather enough breath to speak, by which time the train was steaming steadily out of the station. 'You told me yourself once, remember? That you'd take a train to Scotland and see where you ended up. This is the Glasgow special. Ergo, here you would be. In any case, I slipped your taxi driver a guinea and he supplied me with your destination while you were extricating yourself from Clara's tantrum.'

She stared at him for a moment, then even as she began to laugh her eyes filled with tears. He handed her a large spotted handkerchief.

'No waterworks. This is what you wanted, isn't it? An adventure.' And Archie wanted Katherine, if not in holy matrimony then certainly in his bed. He'd told Clara that he would find her and bring her back, but nothing, certainly not Clara Terry, would prevent him from having her. He was quite delighted that Cussins had finally blotted his copybook.

'I didn't imagine it quite like this, though. All that shouting and the accusations, as if I were the guilty one.' She shuddered. 'It was all so – so *awful*! Is Frank furious? Did Ma really collapse or was it all show?' She didn't ask why her own mother had chosen to betray her in such a terrible fashion. Any discussion of that subject would be far too painful. 'And why are *you* here? I thought you hated scenes and didn't have the energy for adventures.'

'To answer your questions in order: absolute pandemonium. Frank swears his innocence and is threatening to follow you to the ends of the earth to bring you back, or else sue you for breach of something or other. Clara is blaming it all on the drink she'd consumed at the party, as well as indulging in hysteria, largely because the guests are fleeing from the house like rats leaving a sinking ship. And you're right about my abhorrence of scenes though it all proved rather entertaining in a macabre sort of way. As for an "adventure", well, here's your chance, Kitty old thing. But if I'm to join you, you'll just have to make allowances for my greater age and do it slowly. Can't let you disappear over the blue horizon by yourself, now can I? Chocolate?' offering her a Nestlés bar with a huge grin.

Faced with such stalwart friendship, Katherine found the rush of tears was now for quite a different reason and even felt a smile tugging at the corners of her mouth. 'Thank you,' was all she could manage as she took the proffered piece.

They sat nibbling the chocolate as the train picked up speed till it seemed to thunder along, pounding in time to the questions in her head, questions she couldn't answer. *I'm running away! I'm running away! Where shall I go? Where shall I go?*

'Had you any particular spot in mind?' Archie asked, as if he'd heard.

She gazed at the photographs lining the walls of the carriage: *The Forth Bridge. Blackpool Tower. Margate Sands*. There was a taste of ash and soot in her mouth, an aching pain in her chest and a great empty void in her head, as if thinking were something she didn't dare risk in case it resulted in other pictures, the kind she had no wish to see. 'I don't know. I thought I'd get off when I saw somewhere I fancied.'

'Good idea.'

'I'm not sure how much money I have with me.' She was rather worried about money.

Archie gave a little snort. 'Don't think about such boring practicalities now, old bean. Time for some shuteye.'

'It was the right thing to do, wasn't it?'

'Absolutely.'

How could she stay after that fiasco? She would make a new beginning, a new life for herself. Who knew where they might end up? So long as Frank or, worse, Clara didn't come after her, she'd be all right.

'I do know of a place we could try,' Archie sleepily commented, stretching his long legs out and folding his arms, preparatory to a doze.

She looked at him with fresh hope. 'Where?'

'Quiet little spot in the Lake District. No one would dream of looking for you there, certainly not Frank Cussins.' But even before she could ask for more details, he'd resolutely closed his eyes and settled to sleep. Taking the hint, Katherine tucked her cardigan beneath her cheek and for once did exactly as she'd been instructed without a word of argument.

The journey was long and hot and tiring. She felt close to exhaustion but Archie's fragile state of health always filled her with such fear that she daren't for a moment complain. They'd been travelling for what seemed like hours before alighting at the small station of Oxenholme, where they caught a connection to Windermere. There they found overnight accommodation in a terraced house. The rooms were small and cramped, with only one shared bathroom for the five guest bedrooms and no sign of hot water from the rickety cistern, the house's major appeal being that it was close to the station.

'At least it doesn't smell of kippers,' Archie whispered as they were shown to their separate rooms. 'And you know where I am should you need a shoulder to cry on, old thing. Just tap on my door.'

She felt grateful for his thoughtfulness. Since they didn't want to encourage any awkward questions they'd pretended to be brother and sister, Archie and Katherine Emerson. It seemed like a good idea at the time, though it was one she would later come to regret.

An appetising supper of mutton stew followed, and a welcome cup of tea, if not the hoped for excellent night's sleep. Katherine listened as each and every lodger climbed the stairs, there was much opening and closing of many unknown doors, and finally she heard Mrs Stokes, their landlady, call to the cat and draw the bolts. Even as silence finally settled upon the little house she tossed and turned in the strange bed, one moment hot, the next cold, her over-tired body becoming tangled in the coarse sheets while her mind replayed recent events with a painful clarity.

Why had Frank slept with Clara, her own *mother*? Had she repelled him with her own shy reserve? Or was she so lacking in charms he'd felt unable to love her in quite that way? Katherine felt diminished by Frank's betrayal, as if she were a non-person, someone who wasn't woman enough for him to desire.

She heard the clock in the hall strike midnight and still she lay, wide-eyed and frustrated, as misery engulfed her. What was wrong with her? Was she so dull and stupid that even her own mother had to invent a father for her, and satisfy her daughter's fiancé's physical needs? Katherine remembered Archie's exhortations to tap on his door should she be in need of a friend; an offer which he'd generously repeated as they'd climbed the stairs to their separate beds after supper. Moments later she was doing just that and, without waiting for a response, slipped inside his room.

*   *   *

'Are you asleep, Archie?'

'If I was, I'm certainly not now.' She heard the rustle of an eiderdown as he started to sit up.

'Don't put on the light. I feel so awful. Will you hold me?'

'Kitty . . .'

'Please, just for a little. You're my big brother after all.' She slid beneath the sheets, pushing her shivering body close against the warmth of his. Wrapping her arms about his waist so that she didn't roll out of the hard narrow bed, she laid her cheek against his chest and realised with a small shock that he was naked. He wore no pyjamas. But then, wasn't it just like Archie not to remember to pack any?

He, thinking of the silk spotted pyjamas which remained unpacked in his valise, smiled in the darkness. He had known she would come.

'Am I so dreadfully unattractive?' Katherine whispered.

It was some seconds before he found his voice. 'Are you referring to Frank, old thing?' He sounded rather odd and Katherine guessed she must have woken him from a deep sleep after all.

'Of course I'm referring to Frank. He clearly finds Ma far more attractive than me. What does that say about my supposed charms?'

'That the fellow needs his head examining.' His arms came gently about her, rocking her as if she were a child. But she wasn't a child, she was a woman, a living breathing, healthy young woman who'd barely set out on the journey of passion which seemed to so fascinate men.

Why then was she less fascinating than her own mother, who was well past forty?

'Do *you* like me?' she softly asked. 'I mean, if we weren't just good friends and you a sort of adopted brother, would you find me . . . attractive?' Katherine tried to see his face, catching only the glitter of his eyes in a stray shaft of moonlight. They seemed to be studying her with an equal intensity.

'A chap would be mad not to.' Yet despite his words, he shifted slightly away from her. Had she annoyed him by barging into his bed in this bold manner? Or was he finding the scent of the Pear's soap that she'd used to wash herself with far less intoxicating than Clara's Ashes of Violets? Frank had obviously liked that. She felt awkward suddenly, naive and rather foolish.

'I'll take you back to your room, dear heart, you shouldn't be here – like this.' Archie made as if to get out of bed, knowing she would resist. He was right.

'No. I don't want to go. I need to know what's wrong with me.'

'There's nothing wrong with you. Frank is the one to blame.'

'I don't believe you.'

'My dear love, I would do anything to prove how absolutely delightful you are. Anything in the world.'

'Would you?'

'Of course. But what could I possibly do to convince you?' His voice had grown soft against her ear, beating like a pulse in her veins.

Katherine stroked his cheek, placed a kiss on the naked chest, then on to his chin and the roughness of his cheek. She found the acrid scent of his maleness oddly pleasing and somehow disturbing. 'Show me, Archie. I never let Frank even kiss me properly. Is it any wonder if he . . . Teach me how to make love. I want to learn how to be a woman.'

She felt his body growing tense and stiff beside her. Was that because she repelled him, because he thought her gauche? He hardly seemed to be breathing. 'I think you should go, Kitty. This isn't right. What if the old dragon downstairs should . . .'

She stopped his protests with a kiss. A real kiss this time, clumsy and over-exuberant but full on the lips, like a child imitating grown-up passion. Katherine felt a quiver run the length of his body, a shudder that could only be excitement, and it both surprised and pleased her. Even so, an inner voice warned her that this was wrong, that she shouldn't be here in Archie's bed. Stubbornly she turned a deaf ear to it, made reckless by her pain. What did convention matter when she'd been so betrayed, by her own mother not just her fiancé? Archie's arms tightened about her, his mouth warm and demanding against her own, bringing with it a pulsing excitement she hadn't expected. To Katherine the moment was spellbinding, a startling revelation, so very different was it from Frank's fumbling efforts. Perhaps she wasn't frigid after all. Perhaps she just needed a little practice, with the right man.

She captured his face between her hands and spoke to him with breathless urgency. 'I trust you, Archie, never to hurt me. I trust you absolutely. Clara made *It* – no, I shall say the word – *sex*, sound so crude. It quite put me off. And Frank – Frank never inspired me. All my fault I expect.'

'No, Kitty. Don't ever think that,' he groaned, his voice a hoarse whisper now, and even as he spoke he was peeling her night-gown from her shoulders.

She sat up suddenly and pulled it off in order to help him, smiling as his gaze fastened hungrily upon the nakedness of her breasts; smooth-skinned and rather small in her own estimation, though pertly uptilted. She felt only gratitude for his admiring gaze. To her surprise Katherine recognised in his choked, 'Oh, God,' that perhaps he might find her attractive after all. His eyes upon her were blessedly uncritical, uncondemning, not mocking her gangling limbs or flat chest as Clara had so often done. His reaction gave her renewed courage. 'Show me,' she whispered. 'I want to *know!*'

'Kitty, for pity's sake . . . I'm not the man for you. I'd ruin your life.' His protests were weak and she, suddenly the all-knowing, all-powerful woman, recognised them as such.

'I don't believe that for a minute,' she laughed as she straddled him and, arching her back, placed his hand upon one breast, rubbing it gently back and forth over the rosebud nipple. 'Is this what I'm supposed to do? Tell me. Teach me how to be a woman. You always said life was for living, Archie, that only friendship mattered. Well, you're my very best friend, so who better to teach me how to make love?'

'I hope you're sure, Kitty-Cat. This could all be a terrible mistake.' But even as he half mumbled the words, his mouth moved to suckle her breast, making her cry out with surprise and pleasure. She lost all control from that moment on. His hands and mouth seemed to develop a life of their own, moving and caressing every secret part of her, stroking, teasing, tantalising, awakening sensations in her she hadn't known possible. Just to experience the demanding pressure of his lips against hers, the roughness of his skin bruising her breasts, and the weight of his body upon hers, squeezing the breath from her lungs as he entered her, stirred a desire in her so deeply profound, so sweetly insistent, that Katherine could hardly believe she'd never previously discovered its existence. It was as if this great and overpowering need had been present inside her all along, just waiting to be fanned into life by his touch.

Katherine was the first to wake. She stirred with reluctance, so comfortable and safe was she, wallowing in a sense of warmth and well-being. She drew her feet up beneath the blankets and the thought came to her through a haze of sleep that she could lie here all day, so cosy, so safe, so . . .

And then she remembered.

Her eyes flew open and went straight to Archie's supine figure, fast asleep beside her. *What had she done?* What had she been thinking of? A wave of embarrassment washed over, filling her with an overwhelming instinct to flee.

Very quietly, so as not to disturb him, she slid from the bed, snatched up her night-gown and crept swiftly from the room, praying she would not bump into their landlady as she fled naked along the landing. Collecting her wash bag she locked herself in the bathroom, since thankfully no one else in the house seemed to be up at this early hour. She ran a deep bath, guessing Mrs Stokes would be furious with her for taking all the hot water, but they'd be leaving straight after breakfast so what did it matter?

What did anything matter? Last night she'd lost her virginity. No, not lost it – given it away with gladness and joy. She could feel her cheeks burn with shame at the memory.

Had she completely lost her reason? She'd slept with Archie Emerson, her dearest friend, who up until last night she'd thought of as a surrogate brother. She'd even passed him off as such.

What would he think of her now? How could she ever face him again? Katherine felt utterly appalled by her own wantonness. Why had she done it? For revenge on Frank? Surely not. Why would she risk spoiling a perfect friendship for such a shallow reason? Katherine lay back in the hot, softly lapping water, going over their lovemaking, step by blissful step, remembering the mounting tension, the breathless excitement, the touch of lips and fingers and the glorious intensity of fulfilment. Surely all of that emotion must have a deeper purpose than simply physical. Whatever Katherine might lack in practice, she was certainly fully conversant with the theory of sex, thanks to Clara's open approach to the subject. She understood that men could enjoy it without love. Besides, hadn't she been given ample proof of that fact already, from her own fiancé?

But could a woman? 'A woman's needs are different,' her mother had told her so a dozen times or more. 'Except for harlots.'

So what did last night make her?

Why, a woman in love of course. What else could those marvellous feelings mean?

The water had gone cold by the time she stepped out to rub herself down briskly with the towel. She did not examine her vulnerability or naivety now. Katherine gave no credence to the insecurities she'd felt so sharply in the uneasy hours of the night. In the time it took her to climb back into her clothes and tidy her hair ready for breakfast, she became perfectly convinced that not only was she head over heels in love with Archie Emerson but that, having given herself to him, she must marry him. In her innocence, she could think of no other reason to explain such behaviour.

The only question that remained was – did Archie feel the same way about her?

He had seemed to find pleasure in her too thin, too tall body, Katherine reasoned as she buttoned up her boots. But if men truly were different, then how could one ever know for certain what they felt? It was most perplexing. Yet surely Archie was not like other men? He was her special friend and would never take advantage.

Having boosted her waning self-confidence, Katherine smoothed down her skirt and viewed herself in the spotted mirror over the bathroom sink. The scrubbed, shining face that looked back at her still wore the mantle of youth but in the eyes she detected a new excitement, a knowledge which hadn't been there before. She was quite certain that when she walked into the dining room for breakfast, everyone would know what had taken place the previous night. They would witness the love emanating from them both.

Archie could hardly bring himself to get out of bed. He'd been aware of her slipping out and been thankful for it. The hiatus before he must face her would give him time to think, to work out a way to handle this tricky situation, for he was feeling the slightest prompting of guilt.

He would have liked to blame her for what had happened, blame anyone but himself for that matter, yet how could he? He was the mature adult. He should have shown more control instead of his usual display of selfish need.

She was a young girl, doubtless a virgin, for God's sake, wounded and hurt, who had turned to him for comfort. And what had he done? Had he picked her up and taken her back to her own bed? Indeed not. Had he reassured her that she was perfectly lovely and would one day meet the kind of young man she deserved, that she should be grateful to Clara for saving her from the odious Frank Cussins? No, he had not. Instead, he'd shamelessly taken advantage of her naivety.

What excuse could he possibly offer? He made no bones of the fact that he'd lusted after her for months; had relished the care and attention she gave so unstintingly, impatiently waiting for her grieving to pass. But not for a moment had he considered taking the relationship any further.

It wasn't that he even loved her. No, he corrected himself. That wasn't strictly true. Of course he loved her. Any man with eyes in his head would adore Katherine Terry, but that didn't necessarily make him the right man for her. He loved her as he would a younger sister. No, that couldn't be true either or he wouldn't have been capable of what he'd done last night. Oh, God, was he completely debauched?

He cut himself shaving, had to stick a piece of tissue paper on the wound to stop it from bleeding. The breakfast gong sounded and Archie braced himself for a painful confrontation. He could only hope that she'd be grown up about it so they could pretend it had never happened and go on being friends. That would by far be the best way.

The two of them sat at the check-clothed table in the tiny dining room, each stiffly seated on a straight-backed chair, silently chewing their way through a substantial breakfast, the likes of which had never been seen at Hope View throughout its entire existence. He spoke not a word to her, hadn't even ventured a good morning. Nor, for that matter, had she to him. Katherine could tell by the way he was avoiding her eye that he was embarrassed.

A wall of silence rose solidly between them, thickening and growing while inside she felt a sickening realisation unfurl. *He wasn't even going to mention it!* Disappointment bit deep, souring the taste of food in her mouth, making it seem like sawdust. She set her breakfast aside, half eaten.

'Don't you want it?' Katherine shook her head and Archie said something about it being a shame to waste good food as he helped himself to a slice of her bacon and two of her sausages.

How could he eat so heartily while her own stomach churned with nerves, quite robbing her of appetite?

Finally he laid down his knife and fork with a sigh, drained a second cup of tea and addressed her in his usual bright and cheery voice. 'I say, old thing, you're a bit quiet this morning. Sleep all right?' Just as if she'd spent the night down the landing in her own room, and not curled up beside him.

She flashed him a wavering smile but, anxious not to let him see how his careless tone hurt her, responded equally brightly, 'Like a log.'

Another silence during which Archie finished off three slices of toast and marmalade. She felt the absence of emotion like a slap in the face. He gave no sign of the tender love which had been so prevalent during the night. Could Clara have been right after all? Sex, to the male of the species, as Frank and now Archie had so clearly demonstrated, was of no consequence. Well, then, it was certainly of no consequence to her either. 'And you? Did you sleep well?' she politely enquired, with a calculated brightness.

'Like a top.'

'Excellent.'

He set down his cup. 'We'd best be on our way then.'

'Yes, why not?' And thrusting back her chair, almost knocking it over, she went in search of the landlady to settle their bill.

The silence deepened between them as the bus trundled along but then they left the small town behind and Katherine forgot their discord as she caught her first glimpse of the breathtaking beauty of the mountains. Their brooding splendour, backlit by a brilliant haze of light, the silver sheet of water that was Lake Windermere rippling at their feet, could well have been stage managed by Mother Nature entirely for her benefit. The glorious view acted like a balm to her sore heart, solace to her injured pride. Katherine resolved not to worry about what had taken place between them but to behave in a more mature fashion. She was a woman after all, not a child.

She didn't enquire where it was they were going as the bus branched left by the steamer pier although Archie informed her that the remains of a Roman camp known as Galava lay beneath the green meadow; that they were heading towards Clappersgate, Skelwith Bridge and ultimately Carreckwater, that the hills she could see now were the Langdales. Katherine could barely take it all in, but gazed about her in wonder as they continued down a maze of winding lanes, up hill and down dale, so entranced was she by the beauty of it all. It all felt quite extraordinary, just as if she were coming home.

And then, in what seemed like the middle of nowhere, he asked the driver to stop and they both stood in the empty lane watching as the bus drove away, leaving a swirl of dust in its wake. Archie finally set off without a word along a wide dirt track with Katherine trudging alongside, dragging her battered old suitcase and not caring where this path, or her life, might be leading.

The moment she saw the house Katherine knew that the adventure had begun. It stood four-square in the centre of a small gravelled courtyard, rather like an oversized doll's house. The paintwork was faded and cracked. It possessed no Ionic columns, no porticoes or Gothic additions of any sort, not even a porch; simply a solid oak door and eight sash windows all shuttered against the sun. Clumps of grass and thistles grew up here and there through the gravel, a gate swung off its hinges, creaking eerily in the wind, and the fallen branch of a tree had smashed down part of what might have been a stable.

Nevertheless the house possessed undoubted charm. At right angles to it stood a cluster of barns and outbuildings, the whole surrounded by a drystone wall. Beyond these lay satin green meadows, tall beech and oak trees, a flagstoned packhorse bridge over a babbling beck which led in turn down to the edge of the lake, glittering and still in the morning sun. And towering over the entire scene as if keeping guard reared the mountains, now no longer blue-grey and distant but close at hand, revealing every scar of rock, every patch of bracken, as if she could reach out and touch them. Yet their awesome grandeur took her breath away as they soared endlessly upward, their topmost peaks veiled by wreaths of mist, like a shy bride. After Ealing, it seemed like a little piece of heaven had fallen from the sky at her feet.

'This is yours?' She was utterly incredulous.

Archie merely signified his assent by a casual raising of his eyebrows.

Katherine wanted to ask why, if he owned even a fraction of this glorious beauty, he'd chosen to live at wretched Hope View. Instead, leaving her suitcase on the gravel path since she hadn't the strength to drag it another inch, she obediently followed him along an overgrown path which led around the side of the house, fighting her way through stinging nettles and clinging ivy.

'Sorry about this, but we never use the front door these days.'

Excitement was sharp in her. What would they find

inside this intriguing mansion? Katherine couldn't wait to explore.

Pushing open the door, Archie marched straight into a bright sunny kitchen, throwing its two surprised occupants into first stunned disbelief and then a whirl of excitement. There were squeals of delight and hugs of welcome. He was lifting and swinging each of the women around in turn, head thrown back, laughing like a delighted young boy.

Only when it was over, tears wiped away, laughter and joy subsiding, did he manage to extricate himself and turn to her.

Katherine had remained standing by the kitchen door throughout, startled by the very presence, let alone the effusively warm greeting, of these two strangers. It made her feel like an outsider, though she'd no right to complain for that was indeed what she was. He was introducing her now as 'Little Kitty, my very best friend and adopted sister', a glint of wicked mischief shining in his navy blue eyes, for who but he had ever dubbed her 'little'?

Even so, she felt a pained disappointment that he should class their friendship as akin to siblings. This careless introduction seemed to eradicate those precious intimate moments of the previous night, as if they'd never taken place.

Feeling bemused and raw with wounded pride, she found herself shaking hands with a tiny, birdlike elderly woman and then a pretty, young, plump one with the most enormous pale grey eyes that peered at her with frank curiosity from behind a pair of spectacles which seemed largely redundant on the end of her small nose.

'Hello.' She felt awkward and unwanted, deeply resentful of the way the girl was hanging on Archie's arm and laughing up into his face. In that moment Katherine realised that she'd always thought of him as her very own and, either because of the change in their relationship, or in spite of the damage her recklessness had evidently done to their friendship, she'd really no wish to share him.

Chapter Seven

It was a wonderful healing summer, a period which brought colour to Archie's sallow cheeks. Katherine decided to adopt the name Kitty, and added to it a new surname of Little. Why not? It was about as accurate as Terry, chosen by her mother, and far more fun. Kitty Little. A new persona for a new beginning. Perhaps, she thought, it would bring her better luck.

Esme too was enjoying a new start. Nurtured and cosseted by Mrs Phillips, or Mrs Pips as Archie called her, she positively blossomed. He declared that the three of them would become firm friends, a triumvirate united against the world. Esme and Kitty viewed the notion more cautiously but went along with it as best they could, for Archie's sake.

Shortly after their arrival, Esme had commenced employment with a Mrs Randle who lived in a tall Edwardian villa that stood on the shore of the lake in the nearby village of Carreckwater. The exercise was not a success. Mrs Randle had a list of rules as long as her arm which, unhappily for Esme, she frequently and unwittingly transgressed. She was expected to cook, clean and care for her employer from six in the morning till nine at night, with one half day off per fortnight. She was not allowed to have friends in, nor was she permitted to set foot outside the house or venture on any errands without Mrs Randle's express permission. This was carried out to the letter, even to the extent of every door being kept locked both inside and out at all times, which created in her new maid a not unnatural claustrophobia.

'Anyone would think I was being held prisoner,' Esme declared as, after a mere two weeks of this, she packed her bags on her first afternoon off and, leaving a note of explanation, returned to Repstone. 'I'd rather starve.'

'Starve you won't, my lamb,' Mrs Pips assured her, sliding a large piece of apple pie on to her plate, though acknowledging her employer's part in providing this fare by adding, 'I'm sure the master would never hear of such a thing.'

'Absolutely not, sweetie,' Archie agreed. In truth he hadn't the faintest idea how much money resided in the various bank accounts and shares left to him by his people, but so long as he had any cash at all, he was more than willing to share it with his friends, he told them. What better purpose could there be for it?

'Thank you, Archie. I do appreciate your hospitality, really I do.'

'Heavens, don't call it that. What are friends for?' Esme's smile was trusting as she gazed up at him, causing Archie to pat her on the head as if she were still fourteen and had asked if she might borrow his tennis ball. 'Don't you fret, old thing. Won't see you on your uppers.'

Kitty, feeling annoyed and oddly neglected, remarked,

'Perhaps Esme would prefer to be independent. She could always try for employment in a bigger house where there are more servants and less for her to do, or in a larger town perhaps. Just because one employer is bad, doesn't mean they all are, and she needs to earn her keep.' Even as she uttered these dreadful words she was aware of everyone looking at her, as well they might for who was she to speak of independence? Wasn't she in the same boat? But the jealousy, once having been born, seemed set on growing.

Archie had never once referred to that night of intimacy and, following his lead, neither had she. Yet despite the strict rules she set herself, Kitty couldn't help feeling that he belonged exclusively to her. She found herself watching the way he moved, walked, smiled and laughed, and not simply because she was concerned for his health. She sought evidence in his words, and in his frequent glances across to her when they were sharing some joke, that their relationship had changed in some subtle way, had become special; that they shared a bond and it was Esme who was the outsider.

Yet she found none.

Not that it mattered, the new Kitty told herself stoutly, and if she ached with love for him, at least he wasn't aware of the fact. She should be glad that their friendship at least seemed to have survived her immature advances. Once since their arrival at Repstone Manor she'd considered going to his room then decided that perhaps it wasn't such a good idea, not with Esme around. After all, it was surely up to him to come to her. Since he made no effort to do so, she felt rebuffed but also gauche and rather foolish for even wanting him to. The same sort of embarrassment that washed over now. 'I – I'm sorry, I only meant she might like – that we all should try to contribute something.'

Archie shrugged his shoulders. 'Let's enjoy what little is left of this cracking summer first, eh? Plenty of time for earning a crust later.'

And so they did. Each day they would work in the garden, reclaiming it from the wilderness of weeds that had overtaken it, perhaps discovering a hidden statue or shrub flowering beneath a tangle of bindweed. Better still a row of raspberry canes luscious with fruit. Later, lying on their backs in the sun, they ate them all one by one.

They paddled in the beck, cooling their feet in the flow of tingling water, splashing each other and screeching with delight. When they grew tired of that, they took their costumes and towels down to the lake and, gasping against the cold, plunged or dived in, or pottered about in an old clinker-built boat Archie had found in one of the boat houses. On lazier afternoons they might light a fire on the shingle and fry sausages in a battered old pan Mrs Pips found for them, Archie reciting poetry with his Panama hat tilted over one eye. Wherever they went, whatever they did, it was always a threesome and if there was the slightest competitive edge as to which of the two girls would bring tea, or fetch Archie's cushion or book, neither remarked upon it. Certainly he didn't, accepting their attentions as if they were his by right, yet showing nothing more than casual gratitude to either.

At other times their attempts to outdo each other would become less subtle. When Kitty stated that she approved of the tighter hobble skirts, Esme dismissed them as cheap and tawdry. If she expressed an interest in the fashionable new game of tennis and regretted that it wasn't included in the Olympic Games in Stockholm, Esme said it wasn't quite proper to leap and run about in a silly game showing your ankles.

'Heavens, you're a prude!'

'I certainly am not.'

'Yes, you are.'

'Am not.' Esme went quite red in the face with embarrassment; the memory of her father's touch, and of his ignominious death, suddenly looming close.

Archie quietly intervened. 'She's a parson's daughter, old thing,' as if that explained everything and they would stop squabbling, call a temporary truce in order to please him and enjoy what was left of the summer.

Charlotte had discovered a delightful way to bring joy into her life. Not from the bottle of gin that she remembered gracing her mother's bedside table, nor particularly from the fit, lithe bodies of the young men who so often occupied her bed these days. There they were given a delectable taste of what they most desired but only because it served her purpose to do so.

Her purpose. No one else's.

This was her one triumph over Magnus. That she could now choose her own lovers and not have to perform at his direction. Even more satisfying was the pleasure she derived from cheating on him now, when in the past, he himself had taken such care to teach her the tricks of the trade.

This afternoon she let her silken robe fall upon the

floor and climbed into bed beside today's chosen candidate. She'd already decided that this must be the last time with Alderman Miles Pickering. He'd been an exciting lover once, imaginative and considerate, but he'd grown a touch too demanding of late, making assumptions, taking liberties. Today, for instance, it had been reckless of him to arrive so early, before Magnus had eaten supper. She didn't greatly care whether her husband was aware of her activities or not, for all it was a dangerous game she played, but she'd certainly no wish to be gossiped about by the servants. That could cause irreparable damage to her comfortable way of life.

As she leaned enticingly over her lover, his hands instantly fastened upon her breasts. Gently but firmly Charlotte disengaged them, casting her eyes down with every appearance of innocence. 'No teeny proof of your love today, my sweet?' she pouted. 'No little solace to compensate me for the risks I take for you?'

Charlotte never named a price, but she managed to make it clear nonetheless to whomever her current lover was, that she required continual proof of their devotion; that there were dangers in their coupling for which she deserved due recompense. It irked her that this subterfuge was even necessary but ever since the accident, Magnus had neglected to provide her usual regular allowance. An oversight no doubt, but worryingly inconvenient.

'I'd never forget you, dear Lottie.' Alderman Pickering slid a necklace about her throat, fastening it with fingers that shook with desire. The stones, surely diamonds, winked brilliantly in the light from the bedside lamp.

'What a darling man you are.' Older men, she'd

discovered, had more class, and usually more brass to go with it. 'But you must call me Charlotte, not Lottie. Always Charlotte. Like the lady I am. Don't forget, love.'

Greedy hands gripped her waist to pull her roughly down in a tangle of silken sheets. 'How could I forget?' panting hotly as he devoured the creamy smoothness of her neck, his impatience getting the better of him. 'You're the most beautiful, the most enchanting wom – lady in my life. In all the world.'

She put back her head and laughed with delight at his exuberance. How delicious it was, how *exciting!*

When he entered her, plunging and gasping to reach his climax, her laughter turned to cries of carefully orchestrated pleasure. Charlotte writhed and moaned, whimpered and groaned with sufficient artifice to convince her lover that he pleased her, while keeping her mind engaged elsewhere. Nothing she did was ever quite what it seemed. Despite the apparent satisfaction she found in the coupling, her pleasure, and therefore her security, came from the money that was piling up in a secret store at the back of the mahogany wardrobe, and in the delightful trinkets and gifts from her many admirers that filled the dressing-table drawers. These represented the tangible means by which she would eventually escape this living hell.

The ravishingly beautiful Mrs Radcliffe might be a thoroughly good sport and enormous fun, but above all else, she was a manipulative woman with a hard-headed desire to have her own way in everything.

*　　*　　*

The warmth of the summer lingered on into September, the days shortening, the lone cry of the curlew sounding piercingly sad as it soared in the thermals over coppiced oaks, glorious in a blaze of reds and golds. They would go for long healthy walks over Loughrigg or Scaife Heights, and once to Skelwith Force where they nearly did themselves a mischief by plunging over the rocks into the rushing icy water.

Even today with the rain bucketing down they'd walked for miles, entirely circling the lake and had run home soaking wet and giggling, chased by huge flashes of light which split the sky. When they'd finally stood dripping on Mrs Pip's clean floor it had been Esme who'd run for the towels and, taking them from her, Kitty who'd dried Archie's hair, fearful he might come down with 'flu again. He'd tried to fend off both of them, complaining loudly about their fussing.

They toasted crumpets for tea and Kitty said it reminded her of evenings spent at Hope View by the fire in Archie's room. Esme swiftly responded by reminding him how he'd taught her to play cricket. This desire of hers to prove an earlier claim always discomfited Kitty. For a long time, Archie had been Raymond's friend, not hers. Only since her twin's death, during Archie's illness and slow convalescence had he become more than a distant, older figure to her.

'I recall you were as ham-fisted as any other little girl,' he lazily responded to Esme. 'Once broke the greenhouse windows, don't you know. Not with the ball but by letting go of the damned bat. Went like a bullet straight into the peach house.' Kitty, at least, ached with laughter at the picture this presented.

'It's fortunate the cricket season is over, I dare say,' he chortled. 'Though how we shall endeavour to amuse ourselves when the weather turns sour, I cannot think. I'm no lover of the Lakes in winter.' He eyed Kitty speculatively, for there were other winter pastimes he wouldn't mind pursuing, and wondered whether this competitive edge he'd noticed between them could possibly work in his favour. He was already regretting his remarkably chaste summer. Where was the fun in that?

'Which only goes to show what a dull townie you've turned into,' Esme retorted, though her tone was teasing.

They did at least agree that empires were crumbling, both in Europe and at home; that the unrest in the Balkans was disturbing. 'England can expect great change in the years ahead,' Kitty vehemently stated, always outspoken in debate. 'Why should women have no say, no vote, despite all the efforts of the suffragists? We should be in Parliament as well as men. There should be women judges, women solicitors, women doctors. Why should we always be expected to marry and devote our lives to waiting on a man?'

'Or become someone's servant if we don't,' Esme agreed with feeling. 'Men seem to be the only ones with any power.'

'I think I'd better stay out of this conversation,' Archie dryly remarked then got to his feet and stretched lazily. 'I reckon I've heard enough of your theories for one night. Never was hot on the ambition front myself. So far as I'm concerned, life is for living. If there's enough in the coffers to get by, I'm content.' He grinned at them, winged eyebrows lending a roguish, devil-may-care quality to the lean, high-cheekboned face. 'Cheerio, sprites, I'm off to hit the sack.'

When he'd gone the two girls exchanged wry smiles. They both fondly believed they understood him perfectly. He was not an ideas man, nor did he hold strong opinions about anything. Archie was a follower not a leader, bone idle much of the time and entirely selfish, but a dear, sweet man for all that.

'He's nowhere near as fragile as he used to be,' Esme concluded. 'I can see an enormous improvement in him.'

Kitty frowned, not fully understanding the comment but unwilling to admit as much. 'We thought we'd lost him when he developed pneumonia. I can't tell you what a relief it is to see him so well and happy.' She explained about the dark depression that had settled upon him following the accident which had killed Raymond.

Grey eyes gazed into brown. 'I can see that his health matters to you very much.'

Kitty looked away. 'And to you.'

This was the nearest either had come to an acknowledgement of their feelings. It left both of them silent for a whole half minute, after which Esme admitted to having suffered the slightest tinge of jealousy and Kitty voiced similar sentiments. This seemed to square things a little between them and they poured themselves more wine in thoughtful silence.

Then Kitty took the opportunity to ask Esme if she'd ever had a boy friend, which she seemed to find amusing, saying what few opportunities there'd been in her previous life for fraternising with boys.

'So you've never . . . you know?'

'Lord, no. Why? Don't say that you . . . ?'

Kitty quickly denied it, her fingers crossed against the lie. 'You're supposed to ensure that a man's intentions are honourable first, aren't you?'

'Absolutely.' And they both chuckled.

'Besides, you could easily get pregnant that way, couldn't you?'

'Not the first time,' Esme spoke with assurance, as if she were an expert on the subject. 'Not if you were a virgin.' Her mind was still on Archie. 'He hasn't been home in years nor seemed so happy since – well, since his parents . . . you know. It was so terribly tragic.'

Kitty rolled over on to her stomach and set her glass down carefully on the shabby Persian rug. 'No, I don't know. What happened?'

'They died, at least his mother did, in a hotel fire while they were touring the continent. Archie had just left school. He'd have been seventeen or eighteen. I remember there was talk of him going on to university but first the whole family was to enjoy a year of travelling together. They got on so well, you see. It all ended abruptly and horrifically. Archie and his father were out at the casino at the time. Fay, that's Mrs Emerson, died instantly it was believed, from all the smoke.'

'Dear Lord, how awful. What happened to his father?'

'He tried desperately to save her, searching the burning ruins for hours until someone managed to stop him. He couldn't forgive himself for leaving her alone that night, poor man. Drove him mad in the end. Finished his days in some sort of institution, not knowing who or where he was. Archie thought it rather a blessing when he finally died.'

'I suppose so.' Katherine felt awe-struck by this tragic tale. In all the time Archie and her brother had been friends, he'd given no hint of anything like this. She said as much now.

'He can't bear to talk about it. Won't even let himself think of it, I should imagine. Certainly he never spoke of the fire once in the years following, seemed to block it right out of his mind.'

'It does explain his somewhat cavalier approach to life,' Katherine conceded, as well as his attitude towards marriage and his reluctance to be responsible for another person's happiness. Poor Archie. For a fleeting second she considered revealing to Esme the true state of their relationship, perhaps in a rash attempt to prove her supremacy. But tears were glistening in the other girl's eyes, spilling over to run unchecked down her rosy cheeks as she agreed that the loss of his parents in such tragic circumstances had indeed damaged him. The words died on Kitty's lips unspoken. How could she wound Esme further when they both cared about him so deeply? She reached out to wrap her arms about the other girl, and it was in that moment that they finally acknowledged not only the love each felt for the same man, but the birth of a new friendship. The next instant they were mopping tears from each other's eyes, and laughing at their own foolishness.

'Let's drink to friendship. You, me, and Archie. The two of us to look after him forever, our very dear friend.'

'Absolutely.'

Their friendship thus established, dissension was banished for good in several more glasses of Archie's excellent wine and, all inhibitions gone, each was finally able to admit that he wasn't actually in love with either of them so where was the use in squabbling? He saw Esme as a young girl and Kitty as his adopted sister.

'But what if things were to change? I mean, what if Archie were to – choose – one of us. What then?' Kitty asked eventually.

Silence lay heavy for some moments. It was Esme who broke it. 'Were that to happen, the other would simply have to accept it, wouldn't she? Take a step back, as it were. But our friendship must remain.'

Kitty considered her over the rim of her wine glass. 'That could prove difficult.'

'But surely not impossible?'

'Let's hope not.'

'We must keep a pact, Kitty, to remain friends, no matter what. I've never had such a good friend as you. And I'd hate – well – anything to stand in the way of that.'

'So would I. It's been a wonderful summer. The best ever.' And Kitty realised suddenly that it was true. But what next? Where did they go from here? 'Right then. A pact. Whichever he chooses, the other will gracefully accept defeat, but the two of us will remain friends forever.'

'Forever.' And they both drank to this.

The next day Mrs Phillips placed one of her excellent breakfasts before each of them. The aroma from the laden plate of bacon and eggs had no sooner reached Kitty's nostrils than she flew from the room to be sick in the cloakroom toilet.

'Too much red wine last night,' she admitted rather shamefacedly on her return. Archie offered his commiserations and Esme, with a wry smile, a slice of dry toast.

Kitty continued to feel nauseous over the next few days, making a private vow that in future she would be more abstemious. Esme insisted on coddling her by bringing her breakfast in bed till the sickness passed. It was while she lay about bored in bed that the idea came to her. 'I know what we can do now that summer is over. We'll put on a play.'

The other two laughed. 'A *play*? Where? We don't have a theatre.'

'By the lake. We'll invite people to come and watch. Something light and funny,' she said, warming to her idea. 'Shakespeare perhaps. There must be a copy of his plays somewhere in the house.'

'I'm sure there is, dear heart, but won't we be rather short of bodies? I mean,' Archie pointed out in all reasonableness, 'there are only three of us.'

To Kitty this was a trifling matter which presented no problems at all for, as she sensibly pointed out, they need only do selected scenes and they could each perform several parts. Even Esme agreed that it might be fun.

They chose *As You Like it* since the copse by the lake, with a little imagination, would lend itself to represent the Forest of Arden. They couldn't guarantee the weather, of course, but they'd just have to hope for a typically golden autumn day for which the Lake District was, after all, famous.

Esme was to play Celia, as well as Oliver, one or two servants and a shepherdess. Archie was to be Duke Frederick and Orlando, who is loved by Rosalind. This latter part Kitty bestowed upon herself along with various other minor roles.

'What happens if Celia has a scene with Oliver? I can't talk to myself,' Esme objected.

'We'll cut that bit out. Shakespeare won't mind, I'm sure.' Which sounded rather like sacrilege but in the circumstances they all agreed it couldn't be avoided.

They wrote out tickets and programmes. Posters were drawn up to advertise the production and stuck up in village Post Offices, on walls and even trees, and since it was a scattered farming community with little in the way of entertainment, word spread quickly.

The attics of Repstone Manor were raided, Mrs Pips offering to alter anything which looked vaguely suitable for costumes. Several dreadfully old-fashioned ball gowns were discovered, although Esme begged to wear the lavender silk. For some unknown reason, Kitty had thrown the gown in with her other belongings when she'd hastily packed.

'It certainly looks better on you than it did on me, if slightly long,' she conceded. Mrs Pips tacked it up and Esme strutted back and forth, transformed by the dress and the way her pale blonde hair was flowing loose over her shoulders. Again the prick of jealousy stabbed, making Kitty almost regret her offer, and she set about searching with greater diligence for a suitably bewitching gown for herself.

The best she could find was a rather dull green which did nothing for her complexion. It boasted a high neck, long sleeves and hung loosely at her waist. Even when she'd found a belt to use as a girdle around her hips, she knew it wouldn't make anyone's heart beat faster, certainly not Archie's. However, Kitty did discover an excellent outfit for when Rosalind was pretending to be a boy, a genuine doublet and hose which some previous Emerson must have had made for a fancy dress party.

'How tall and elegant it makes you look,' Esme commented admiringly.

'I am tall. Despite my name.' And the new Kitty Little did indeed feel elegant, and not in the least ungainly. It was a good feeling.

When the day arrived, as sweet and golden as they could have wished, with falling leaves scattering like jewels upon the azure and white reflections of sky and cloud in the flat calm lake, they marked the front of the acting area with a row of candles set in tins. These would serve as footlights. Others they hung from the branches of trees to give a truly romantic glow. The scene seemed utterly magical, entirely appropriate for the play, and certainly delighted the fifty or so people who turned up for the performance, including Miss Agnes and Mrs Walsh who made a point of sitting on the front row so they could see what the daughter of their late notorious vicar was up to these days.

Esme noticed them as soon as she went on stage but valiantly pressed on, concentrating on remembering her words. It was all for charity in any case, so perfectly respectable. It had been her idea that instead of charging admission, donations should be collected for fruit, flowers and gifts in aid of the sick and old. Mrs Pips, dressed as an Elizabethan houswife, collected the offerings and provided refreshments in the shape of tea and orange juice, not forgetting a substantial supply of her excellent biscuits.

Kitty was in her element. This was what she'd always longed to do: to act, to perform, to make people laugh. How she loved it! Esme too proved skilful, finding it easy to learn lines and moving with a natural grace. Archie was simply himself, handsome and debonair, merrily strumming a ukulele disguised as a beribboned lute as he sang one or two songs they'd improvised. And when the Rosalind he loved masqueraded as a boy and suggested that he practise his lovemaking techniques upon him (or rather her), he had the whole audience roaring with laughter at the expressions of shock and horror upon his face. For all it was acting, those kisses nonetheless left Kitty weak at the knees, reminding her of a previous, more serious encounter.

Without doubt the play was a riotous success, the audience demanding several 'curtain calls'. 'I didn't realise you were such a fine actor,' she whispered to Archie as they took yet another bow, grinning from ear to ear with the excitement of it all.

'You were the star, dear heart. You make a better chap than a girl, old thing, with all that manly hey-hoing and those dashing tights. Perhaps I should call you my adopted brother instead of my sister.' Then he strolled away to change, his laughter echoing back to her from across the garden.

Kitty stood watching him go, stricken to the core.

She told herself sternly that he hadn't meant to be unkind. It was simply another example of that acerbic wit of his. He'd be devastated to think he'd hurt her by implying she wasn't in the least bit feminine. He probably hadn't meant that at all. He'd just been teasing. Having fun. Being typically Archie.

Unfortunately it no longer seemed any fun at all to be his dear adopted sister, let alone his *brother!* But then it was surely all her own fault for feeling foolishly jealous and mooning over him like some love-sick schoolgirl. Plus the fact that she hadn't been feeling quite herself lately. Clearly she was in imminent danger of making far too much of this typically male thoughtlessness. Even so, as she ran to her room, Kitty was appalled to find her cheeks wet with tears.

Chapter Eight

Now that the excitement of the play was over, they all suffered from a terrible sense of anticlimax. A warm September changed into a damp October and the days were shortening. Day after day they were confined to the house and their restlessness increased. 'Even I'm bored now.' Archie's voice emerged after a fit of coughing as he lay swathed in woollen scarves and jumpers. 'Pips has lit a fire in the library and is serving tea. That is the sum of our excitement for today.'

'If we're so gloomy now, how will we fare when winter really arrives?' Kitty asked, to which nobody had an answer.

The next morning the grey clouds retreated and after a lazy morning and a late lunch, Archie came across Esme where she lay flat on her back on a grassy slope by the lake.

'Enjoying the sun? Don't blame you, old thing.' He propped his back against the sun-warmed wall, rested his elbows on his knees and, gazing up into a pale blue sky puffed with soft cloud, remarked on what a wondrous glow the copper beech made. In fact, all the trees bordering the lake were basking in an unexpected blaze of glory: emerald, saffron, gold and deep olive greens. A family of moorhens paddled off into the shallows, clearly irritated at having been disturbed. Out in the centre of the lake, a couple of fishermen in a lone boat were plying their rods. 'Perhaps we should have a go at that,' Archie idly remarked. 'Catch some char or pike for tea.'

Esme, worrying over Kitty's remark about the coming winter and wondering what she should do with her life, said something to the effect that if she went fishing, she'd probably only catch eels and toads.

Archie attempted to jolly her out of her miserable mood. 'Don't run yourself down, old thing. You're more capable than you realise – not perhaps as organised as Kitty, but you have other strengths.'

'Do I?' Esme turned her gaze full upon him, surprised by the warmth in his.

'I remember when you were no more than a tiddler, always being there for a chap, ever the loyal friend and good sport.' He seemed pleased to see her relax and smile, commenting on how he understood about 'the glums' getting the better of a person at times. 'We had some fun once, you and I, eh? All those tennis parties and picnics on the lake in the old steamboat. You falling in and frightening Ma half to death.'

'Oh, she was always kind to me, was your lovely ma. And good to my own mother, a humble vicar's wife. And I remember helping Mrs Pips to make coconut ice and sticky bonfire toffee.'

'Burning it more like,'

'And getting it all in my hair.' They were both weak

with laughter, chortling with delight at happy memories, then almost simultaneously the laughter faded as if each had more serious concerns nowadays and levity wasn't quite appropriate.

'They're all dead. Pater, Mater, Kitty's beloved brother, your people too.'

'Yes.'

'A chap gets lonely with all his family gone. A gel too, I dare say. Dashed bad luck for both of us. But we have each other, eh? Remember that, old thing.'

'You know you'll always have me Archie. If you want me.'

'Of course I'll always want you, old thing.' There was a hint of surprise in his voice, almost as if he'd only just realised that this was true. 'You know a chap isn't always proud of what he does or how he behaves,' he remarked enigmatically. 'Grief and disappointment can do strange things to a person, don't you know. But as you say, I have you. My dear little solace. My best chum. So you understand absolutely why I need our special sort of friendship?' Then quite unexpectedly he kissed her, his mouth warm and clumsily demanding upon hers, tasting faintly of a cigarette he'd recently smoked.

Esme experienced a sudden and dizzying panic as a rush of memories clouded her mind; pictures of herself as a child in a bath, the face of her father smiling down at her, whispering something in her ear that she really didn't wish to hear. Fingers. Hands. Touching. And then, quite unexpectedly, came a sudden kindling of desire for these were Archie's lips upon hers, Archie's hand upon her breast, feeling as if it had every right to be there and not at all unpleasant.

'It's all right, isn't it?' he murmured, smoothing his hand along her leg as he pushed up her skirt. 'You don't mind, do you? A chap has needs, don't you know. I'll be careful and I won't hurt you, old thing.'

And nor did he. The weight of his lean body upon hers seemed easily bearable, the thrust of him moving inside her an astonishing delight. If Esme could have found words in that magical moment, she would have spoken of her great love for him, told him her true feelings. But her heart seemed too full, the sensations she was feeling too overwhelming, the excitement so tight in her chest each word died in her throat even as it formed.

'Mum's the word, old thing,' he murmured softly against her ear when he was done. And of course Esme was used to keeping secrets. She'd certainly keep this one, for hadn't she always been willing for Archie to choose whichever game he wanted to play? The only difference being that this was a more grown-up sort of game, one she was only too eager to share without thought or question.

Kitty felt quite herself again, full of energy, apart from one or two odd symptoms to which she'd resolved to pay no heed. If they were still in evidence by Christmas, she'd maybe go and have a chat with the doctor. For now she was far too concerned with working on a plan for their future. The success of the play had given her an idea. Filled with fresh enthusiasm, she'd decided that they couldn't idle their days away at Repstone Manor for much longer. They had to work, earn money, do something useful, and Kitty believed she had the perfect solution. One evening, over the customary bottle of wine and after much clearing of her throat, she put the plan to them.

'The play was a huge success. Agreed?'

'Absolutely, dear heart. The locals have talked of little else since.'

'Then why don't we do another? Why don't we, in fact, do any number of plays?'

Archie dryly pointed out that it was too damned cold to put one on by the lake now, and the drawing room would prove rather inadequate as a theatre.

Kitty said that wasn't her plan at all.

She slipped from the sofa to sit cross-legged on the rug in her favourite spot, warming her back against the fire. 'What I mean is that it might be fun to start our own theatre company. Not just here, by the lake, where we can perform each summer. The rest of the time we could be travelling players and take our plays round the village halls and schoolrooms of Lakeland, Yorkshire and Lancashire. Anywhere, in fact, where we can get bookings. Think how many people never get the chance to see live theatre, never see a play of any sort, let alone Shakespeare. You could recite your favourite ditties, Archie, and I could try writing some new plays. We might even put on a musical if we could find someone who can sing. We'd need one or two more actors to join us, obviously, but that shouldn't be too difficult.'

She was speaking rapidly now as the ideas bubbled out and Archie was smiling indulgently at her, as he so often did when she was having one of her 'enthusiasms' as he called them. 'And you'll play the lead, I suppose?'

'Sometimes. You too, of course, and Esme.'

'Me?' Esme had been listening entranced, more than ready to agree to this thrilling scheme. She'd looked upon playing Celia as a lark, a summer caper, but hadn't she always yearned for some excitement in her life? Now here was the chance. The solution to everything. 'Count me in. Anything is better than being someone's paid companion. What would we call ourselves?'

'The Lakeland Travelling Players, what else?'

Thus the LTPs, as they came to be known, were born. It felt almost as if the idea had been there all along, simply waiting to be discovered.

The sound of Mrs Pursey hammering on her bedroom door, insisting she come and calm her poor husband upon the instant, interrupted Charlotte's lovemaking.

'Miles, get up, get up! You must go. For God's sake, *go!*' Her relationship with Alderman Pickering had proceeded without a hiccup for some weeks now; so well in fact that she'd awarded him a reprieve. He'd proved to be far more grateful and generous in return for her attentions than she could ever have hoped. Now she dragged on her satin dressing gown, unlocked the bedroom door and managed to squeeze through without the housekeeper sneaking the smallest glance into the room, which was just as well or she might have seen the bare buttocks of the Town Mayor elect as he hopped on one leg in a tangle of trousers and braces.

'What is it? What's happened?'

'It's the maister. He's gone off his head. Demented he is.'

'I'll not have that *damned-Presbyterian-faced-nincompoop*

136

anywhere near me!' Magnus was sitting up in bed, face purple with rage, mouth wide and snarling. 'You serve my supper, woman. You owe me that much at least, lazy *harlot* that you are!'

At a loss to know how to deal with his black mood, Charlotte found she was trembling as always in response to one of his tantrums. Inwardly she prayed Alderman Pickering had made a safe if undignified escape out of her bedroom window and over the orangery roof. It was the reason she'd chosen that room, safely tucked away at the back of the house. 'I've told you before, I don't like you to call me that. I am what you and my stepfather made me, neither more nor less.' Aware too late of the interested presence of Mrs Pursey still lingering in the doorway, she instantly regretted these hasty words uttered in the heat of the moment. Charlotte took a step closer to her husband, offered soothing, well-practised phrases in an attempt to calm him. They had no effect at all as he continued to storm at her.

'Look at you, bloody mess that you are. Half-dressed at this time of day.'

'I was about to bathe and change for dinner.' How dare he upbraid her in front of the servants? This woman in particular who had never liked her. It was too much. Charlotte whirled about and ordered the housekeeper to leave, closing the door on her startled face. Perversely, Magnus now countermanded his earlier demands.

'Don't you tell *my* housekeeper what to do,' he yelled. 'I *need* Mrs Pursey. She at least takes proper care of me.'

'I thought you wanted me to feed you?' Charlotte managed a smile, picked up the fork and offered it to him. 'Come along now, open wide, there's a good boy. Eat up then you'll get better.'

But Magnus was not in the mood for her wheedling today. He snatched up the dinner plate and flung it at her. Charlotte ducked and it hit the wall instead. With one swipe he sent the milk jug, tea pot, and cup and saucer flying from the bedside table to smash into a dozen pieces. Shards of pottery lay scattered over the carpet and Charlotte gazed in disgust at the resulting mess. The supper, roast pork with buttered carrots and Cook's special creamed potatoes, hung in globules of congealed grease on the silk-patterned wallpaper. A posy of squashed raspberries clung to the gas mantle while Magnus was now giving vent to his rage by ripping his pillows to shreds, sending a snowstorm of feathers flying everywhere. Dear Lord, demented was certainly the word. She felt hysteria rise in her throat; the memory of the accident hanging over her like the Sword of Damocles. 'Magnus, give over! Stop this at once. What the 'ell are you doing to me? Is this some sort of revenge?'

Instantly he did stop, as if to consider the matter, an odd sort of frown on his flushed face. 'Revenge, you say? No, not yet, my lovely. I'll choose the time and place for that. But it'll come, Lottie, make no mistake. Play the devoted wife and whore all you wish, it will come. And you won't know from where or when.'

Fear flared within her. Surely he didn't guess about her regular stream of attentive lovers? She'd been so discreet not even the servants guessed. At least she hoped not. Charlotte strove to tease him into a better humour. 'What are you saying, ye daft 'a'porth? You can't blame me for Rude Awakening shying like that, now can you?

It's your own bleedin' temper that's at fault. You shout at poor Mrs Pursey, now you're shouting at me. What can we do to please you?'

He stared at her for a long moment while a slow smile spread across the once handsome but now somewhat bloated face. He leaned forward to speak in a hissing whisper, as if not wishing anyone to overhear for all they were quite alone in the room. 'We both of us know the truth, do we not, my love? Remember *I* am still in control; that I *know* you tried to kill me. Pity you didn't succeed. But perhaps one day I shall return the compliment. With or without the use of my bloody legs you are still my wife, and I can do with you exactly as I please.'

In the silence which followed this devastating statement, Charlotte could hear the loud ticking of the mantel-clock which seemed in fierce competition with the beating of her own heart. She felt suddenly desperately vulnerable for in those few seconds he'd wiped away the false sense of security she'd wrapped about herself. Now, each swing of the pendulum reverberated in her head, ticking her life away, and outside the four walls of this stifling bedroom she was only too aware that the house buzzed with servants' gossip like angry bees.

She realised, in that moment, that she had no choice but to escape, if only for a little while, before the reality of her situation drove her quite mad. To leave Magnus entirely, Charlotte decided, would be a mistake, since she had no wish to relinquish her rights to his vast fortune. When he did ultimately die, and she prayed each night that it would be soon, every last penny would be hers. And didn't she deserve it?

Nevertheless she had no wish to risk being carted off to a police cell in the interim, while she waited for his demise. The servants had never liked her, had always resented a woman of their own class setting herself above them. They would lose no opportunity to place the blame on her, if they got the slightest whiff of scandal. And if her presence so infuriated Magnus that he kept her short of funds and was now making veiled threats, what might he not utter in his next rage, or the one after that? Once the truth was out, that his fall had been a deliberate act on her part, who would save her? Mrs Pursey for one would be the first to call in the police.

It was Charlotte herself who called the doctor on the telephone Magnus had had installed for his business dealings. He came, young and earnest, eager to make headway in his chosen profession, to find poor Mrs Radcliffe utterly distraught. She sobbed out her concern for her demented husband, begging he be given some draught to cool his blood, to help him sleep and come to terms with his disability – before managing to faint at the doctor's feet, quite spectacularly on cue.

When she came round, it was to find herself ensconced in her own bed, the concerned young doctor holding *sal volatile* to her nose. She spluttered and choked, then smiled weakly at him, all her senses on alert.

'I really don't feel able to cope, Doctor,' she said in a voice trembling with fatigue. 'Magnus is so demanding. I fear I shall go mad if I don't get some rest soon.' She looked appealingly up at him from beneath silken lashes.

The doctor not only agreed with this self-diagnosis, he ordered the agitated young wife to take a complete rest, some sea air, for a month at least; expressing his fears that he could very well have two patients on his hands if a nurse were not engaged to relieve her.

And so it was arranged.

Unusually, Charlotte insisted on doing the packing herself, carefully folding several of her most valued gowns and shawls, not forgetting numerous pairs of her finest Italian leather shoes, for she meant to travel the continent, not for one month but two, three if she could possibly afford it, and had no wish to be poorly dressed. All of these prized possessions were placed between layers of tissue paper in two large leather valises, brought down from the attics.

Lastly, she emptied the trinket box, stowing these carefully preserved gifts into her vanity case. They could be sold if necessary, though she'd no intention of staying away too long. Magnus was a rich man and she needed to maintain access to that wealth. Her heart was hammering hard in her breast as she worked swiftly and quietly. She'd given careful instructions to the household not to tell him of her imminent departure, warning them of the risks of upsetting their master further.

Finally she collected the leather purse which hung on a nail at the back of her wardrobe. The mere weight of it in her hand made her feel better, for the money would ensure she had no need to return to this claustrophobic prison until it suited her to do so. Charlotte had funds, beauty, youth and an agile brain. All she needed now was her freedom.

It was Mortimer who drove her to the station and loaded her luggage on to the train already waiting in the station. Charlotte had no idea where it was bound, nor did she care: she wanted only to get away, to escape, to taste some unknown adventure. She thanked him with a generous tip and apologised for deserting the household at this difficult time.

The young chauffeur, who had always carried something of a torch for his attractive mistress and had no time at all for the master, was sympathetic, assuring her that he understood her plight. He'd risked his job by asking Cook to make up a small hamper for her. The request had been met with sulky protest that she'd 'do nowt for a young madam who deserted her husband', so he'd made it up himself. He stowed this on board beside her then returned to the platform, carefully closing the carriage door. 'Just to keep you going, ma'am, should you feel peckish like.'

Charlotte was so moved by this thoughtfulness that for a second she dropped her cool front. 'Bless you. That old goat wouldn't give me the time of day without charging me for it.'

Privately, young Mortimer hoped that the rumours circulating in the servants' hall weren't true. Not that there was any proof she'd deliberately made the maister fall from that horse. How could she? Little scrap of a thing like her. It was an accident, plain as plain. Anyroad, Maister Radcliffe was still alive and well, if not exactly hale and hearty. No wonder she needed a rest for he'd never been an easy man. 'If you want 'owt doin, I'm your man. Just give me a shout.'

'I will. Oh, I will. Thank you again, Jeffrey. You're a dear sweet boy.' And leaning down through the carriage window, she planted a kiss on his cheek.

Flushed and flattered by her use of his Christian name, not to mention the kiss, young Mortimer remained on the platform until her train was no more than a puff of steam in the distance.

When Charlotte opened the hamper an hour or so later, just as they were crossing the Pennines, she found he had also included that morning's paper. Glancing through it as she ate the cucumber sandwiches and tiny egg rolls, she discovered in the personal column an advertisement which quite caught her attention. It announced that a newly formed company of travelling players was seeking actors and actresses interested in joining such an enterprise for the coming winter season. An address followed, one which she realised could coincidentally be found along the very same line upon which this train was bound. It seemed that fate, at last, was smiling upon her.

The need for sea air and even the pleasures of the continent paled into insignificance beside a sudden, piquant desire for fame. Actresses were always adored, their admirers crowding the stage door for a mere glimpse of their idol. Charlotte decided there and then that it was long past time she had some fun. And where better to use her skills than as an actress? Hadn't she been one all her life?

The girl standing before them with her mid-calf hobble skirt, and huge astrakhan fur collar and cuffs trimming a high-waisted three-quarter-length coat, made them all feel dowdy in the extreme. Kitty and Archie were both festooned in cobwebs as a result of having spent the afternoon yet again delving through the many attics, searching for anything suitable to use for costumes or props. Esme had been helping Mrs Pips to cook and despite being enveloped in a large wrapover apron, had managed to get dough in her hair and flour all over her face.

Now here they were confronted by this wondrous creature, dressed to the nines, groomed to perfection, and very nearly interviewing them with her probing cornflower blue gaze. Even her hat was of the very latest fashion, tall-crowned and wide-brimmed, shading what was undoubtedly one of the loveliest faces they had yet seen amongst all of the would-be actors they'd interviewed thus far.

Kitty cleared her throat. 'Would you care to take off your coat and make yourself more comfortable?'

It unnerved her somewhat to note the stack of luggage which the cab driver had set in the hall, almost as if the newcomer assumed the job to be hers already and she was moving in, lock, stock and barrel. But when the young woman noticed her interest, she merely smiled and offered no explanation whatsoever.

Tea and crumpets were served in the sitting room beside a bright, roaring fire. Archie had been adamant that any auditions be conducted in a civilised fashion. They were, after all, choosing people who would be living with them day in and day out, so it was equally important that they be the sort one could get along with, and not simply be able to recite Shakespeare, for goodness' sake. Miss Gilpin, as she introduced herself, drank hers without any pretension of lifting her little finger but declined a hot buttered crumpet in favour of a thin slice of bread and butter. Esme concluded this to be wise, in view of the fineness of the blue wool costume the removal of her fur trimmed coat had revealed. Were such an outfit hers, she knew she'd be dripping butter and jam all over it in an instant.

'What is it exactly that you wish me to perform for you?' Miss Gilpin asked finally, from her perch on the edge of the sofa. 'I must confess right away that I've boundless enthusiasm, a love of poetry, but very little actual acting experience.'

Her vowels were most carefully enunciated with the trace of an accent Esme recognised instantly as Yorkshire but to Kitty, being a Londoner, meant nothing more than northern.

She heard Archie's almost inaudible sigh of disappointment and cast a quick glance across at him. It was clear, from the rapt expression upon his face that he was utterly enchanted by this woman and although she did not wonder at it, her own heart seemed to turn a slow somersault down into the pit of her stomach.

Her dreams had grown ever more disturbing of late, for whatever their relationship had once been it had changed irrevocably on that fateful night. All she wanted was for him to come to her, as she had once gone to him, except this time with love in his heart. Yet he offered nothing more than friendship, sometimes not even that for there were times when he seemed to go out of his way to ignore or avoid her completely. She dared not risk even a glance in Esme's direction, knowing she would be feeling as alarmed as Kitty herself at the prospect of providing Archie with the opportunity of seeing this exquisite creature each and every day. What a pair of heartsick fools they were!

For a moment Kitty's brain cleared and centred upon

that admission of total inexperience. Ignoring the fact that she herself, who certainly intended to tread the boards, was no better placed in this respect, Kitty decided that self-confessed lack of experience was surely an excellent reason to turn the girl down – though Archie was even now assuring Miss Gilpin that it was of no account at all besides the attributes of boundless enthusiasm and a love of poetry. Kitty half expected him to add 'and incredible beauty' – but noted he prudently restrained himself.

She drew in a deep breath, holding it far too long in order to steady her nerves, before bestowing a sympathetic smile upon the aspiring actress. 'Experience of some kind would naturally be beneficial. Perhaps, after tea, you could recite one of your favourite poems to us, so that we might judge.'

'Oh, indeed, you can easily do that, can you not, Miss Gilpin? I'm certain she'll perform excellently,' Archie agreed, nodding vigorously, as if she were his protégé and he her proud mentor. 'What a splendid notion.'

'We do have many other people to see,' Esme put in, speaking for the first time.

'I'm sure you must have.'

Ever since they'd placed the advertisement in *The Times*, of all newspapers, they'd been inundated with requests; largely from out-of-work actors, making the last two weeks an absolute frenzy of interviews. The best of the bunch had been Jacob Warburton who wore a pair of eyeglasses which rattled annoyingly against a silver fob watch as each dangled from a pocket of a yellow checked waistcoat, straining over a rotund stomach. He claimed still to get regular parts, though they suspected it was chiefly in pantomime. Nevertheless he clearly had both talent and experience and Kitty could see him as a wonderful villain, so he was duly engaged.

Then there came Suzannah – 'Call me Suzy' – Grant, who'd once possessed a superb singing voice, now sadly marred by the eternal cigarette which she held in a long tortoiseshell holder to her scarlet lips. She assured them that it would pass muster for the provinces, and gave them a rendition of 'Sweet and Low' to prove it.

They'd also engaged a young female pianist who wore droopy cardigans, was troubled with her adenoids and had scattered her music with haphazard untidiness all over the carpet. Once seated at Archie's grand piano, however, she'd captivated them with her Chopin, thrilled them with her Liszt, and best of all had them out of their seats and jazzing when she changed to 'Darktown Strutters' Ball.' She was instantly hired.

And then had come Felicity Fanshaw. Felicity described herself as a suffragette, dangerously close to forty and the onset of despair but ruthlessly good-humoured about it. She'd arrived on a bicycle wearing long corduroy shorts, a skinny jersey clinging to her flat chest and a battered felt hat rammed down over cropped black hair. She'd delighted them all with the way she could parody herself let alone others; an actress in every sense.

Apart from this oddly assorted crew, they'd been besieged by any number of arrogant young men seeking acquaintance with pretty girls, only two of whom were actually taken up; one with foppish curly hair worn rather long as a protest, he claimed, though against what exactly he didn't make clear, and another very serious and plain young man who had a wonderfully

deep voice which carried to the far end of the library
with ease.

Of pretty girls themselves there had been a paucity
of applicants, probably because their respective mamas
thought joining a theatre company one short step from
entering a brothel. And now here was Miss Charlotte
Gilpin, breathtakingly beautiful and engagingly frank.
Perhaps, Kitty thought, she did not have a mama.

'Tell us something of your family, Miss Gilpin?'

'All dead, I'm afraid. I was raised in an orphanage
since when I've had all manner of jobs, both in and out
of service.'

'How very sad, Miss Gilpin,' Archie put in, his face
mournful.

'Call me Charlotte, please. I hate to be formal.'

Kitty, determined to be businesslike, resolutely continued, 'Your last position, Miss Gilpin, must have been
with a fine house indeed, since you look quite unlike
any maid I have ever seen and clearly have already
left their employ,' making a pointed reference both to
her modish attire and the stack of luggage in the hall.
'Why was that exactly?' She was interested to note a
slight flush appear upon the velvety cheeks. The young
woman turned her eyes downward for a moment to fix
them upon her clasped hands before meeting Kitty's gaze
with her own, as clear and frank as you please and with
the faintest glimmer of tears in it.

'It was indeed the kindest family imaginable who
quite took me to their hearts. I began as companion
to Lady Ballacombe, and for a time was unofficially
engaged to her son. But then he was killed in a riding
accident. I stayed on for a while as we both grieved

for him but finally decided that, difficult as it would be to break away, it was time for me to set the past aside and move on.' As she related the story with a compelling sincerity and depth of feeling, the result of hours of practice in the train, tears coursed a sorrowful trail over her pale cheeks and Archie hurried to mop them away with a corner of his handkerchief. He was so clearly moved by this further evidence of the cruelty of life, his hand was visibly shaking as he did so.

Kitty and Esme exchanged horror-stricken glances. Not for the world did they wish to upset Archie. They could only hope that the audition would brand her a complete failure. If only they'd known, this was the finest proof they would ever receive that Charlotte Gilpin could indeed act.

After tea they all repaired to the library where the auditions proper took place. Charlotte recited 'The Lady of Shalott' and although Kitty, pressed against the far wall, longed to claim that she couldn't hear a word, or that it was done without any emotion whatsoever, she felt any such criticism would have been unfounded. Charlotte's performance was superb.

'I could sing a little ditty too, if you like.' Her voice was clear and pure, her pretty face a picture of impish delight. She sang 'A Little of What You Fancy', putting in actions and even dance steps, singing with such flirtatious innuendo that despite herself Kitty found herself laughing. Whatever doubts she might have had about engaging Charlotte Gilpin were now quite dispelled.

She was a natural. The applause from them all when the piece was over proved as much, and nothing either Kitty or Esme could say would avoid the inevitable. She was hired.

Chapter Nine

By the middle of October the actors arrived, one by one, as their previous engagements came to an end, and went straight into rehearsals. Kitty had devised an interesting programme. They were to open with *The Pedlar Woman*, a short play she'd written herself during those lazy summer weeks, followed in the second act by scenes from *The Tempest*. In between would be fitted a rousing folk song or two, an epic poem and a delightful number called 'Daisy Bell' which involved Sam, one of the juveniles, and Suzy singing a duet using Felicity's trusty old bicycle.

They managed to collect two trunks full of costumes which included various hats, canes, pairs of shoes and even a couple of wigs they'd found tucked away in the attic. In addition they gathered together acetylene lighting, a wind-up gramophone, a mirror, a window frame, and a fireplace which Jacob Warburton made out of cardboard.

It was agreed that Kitty was to be overall actor-manager, Archie would keep the accounts and Esme would act as secretary. It was her unenviable task to write scores of letters to schools, churches, the YMCA, various women's organisations and other likely venues throughout the north. Fortunately actors did not expect to be paid during rehearsals but in this situation so many miles from town they had to be given bed and board and, if they didn't start earning their keep soon, would be forced to find other employment. Time, therefore, was of the essence.

But everything was progressing smoothly and Kitty didn't mind the hard work. In fact she revelled in it. This was her dream and she resolved to make it come true. All personal problems must now be put to one side. The play must come first. She threw herself into finding curtains for the stage and, with Archie's permission, pestered Mrs Pips until that good lady agreed to take down the long red velvet drapes that hung in the library.

'You're stripping the house bare,' she complained.

'We're shutting it up, Pips old thing, so what does it signify?' Archie said, looking faintly sheepish.

The housekeeper had welcomed the return of her young master with joy, cherishing the hope that his stay would be permanent. To see him going off on what she termed 'theatrical gallivanting' was a bitter blow. On the tip of her tongue hovered the ever-present desire to ask what his parents might have had to say about such a shocking state of affairs, but wisely she managed not to.

Kitty, guessing how the older woman was feeling, sat her down amidst the chaos and asked her, point blank, to join them. Ida Phillips, for the first time in her life, was struck dumb. When she did find her voice it was only to repeat what Kitty had said.

'Come with you?'

Archie gave a whoop of joy. 'What a splendid idea! Why don't you, Pips? We'll need someone to keep us in order.'

'I dare say you will. Not to mention someone to sort out all the mess you seem to be mekking of these 'ere clothes. But who'd look after the house while I was off gallivanting wi' you lot?'

'I could ask old Joe who used to help out with the gardening to act as caretaker, keep an eye on the place.'

'Forgive me for asking,' Kitty gently put in, 'but is there a Mr Pips?' Or any little pippins, she'd have liked to add. It appeared there were not. The Phillipses had never been so blessed and Ida was a widow. 'There you are then. What is there to keep you here? Come with us and have an adventure.'

If Ida Phillips thought that at well past sixty she was perhaps a mite old for adventure, one glance at her beloved Archie's pleading expression and all doubts melted like a snowball in sunshine. After all, she'd known him since he was a wee lad in short breeches, and felt responsible for him now his people were gone. Only one doubt remained. 'Where would I be sleeping? I'm too old to do aught daft like sleep in a tent or suchlike.'

Kitty burst out laughing. 'Oh, no, we're expecting to be given hospitality in people's houses. It's part of the deal they must agree to before we come and perform.' The only problem was that, to date, they hadn't received a single reply to the scores of letters Esme had sent out, but Kitty refused to be downhearted. It was far too soon.

'And could you manage to give one or two of these old

dresses long trains, do you think?' Kitty pleaded. 'For the Shakespeare.'

'Eeh, heck, what have I let meself in for?' Mrs Pips moaned, but at once began picking through for likely candidates. The matter seemed to be settled.

On their way out of the kitchen Kitty casually remarked how they never seemed to have a minute alone these days and Archie laughingly agreed.

'Actually, there is something I'd like to discuss with you,' she began when, as if on cue, Charlotte appeared through the open conservatory door. Archie flew to her aid and Kitty noticed how she pressed her voluptuous body tantalisingly close to his as she heaped a pile of kindling into his outstretched arms. He was laughing down into her lovely face, instantly forgetting Kitty's request and utterly oblivious to the chaos of the other actors dashing hither and thither about their various chores.

'Archie, my saviour! I can't carry these dreadful logs another minute.'

Kitty bit down hard on her lower lip and went back upstairs.

Over the next few days she couldn't help noticing the lingering glances that passed between them, and that whatever task Charlotte was given, she always managed to secure Archie's assistance. Whether it was a pile of dresses or simply a single hat box she had to move, within seconds he'd be carrying the whole caboodle for her. Kitty even discovered them peeling potatoes together one morning when it was Charlotte's turn to do kitchen duties, and she was perfectly certain that Archie had never peeled a potato in his life before.

Esme too had evidently been keeping a close eye on events and shared her reservations. 'Did you see the little minx sidling off with him? Just as if there weren't a million and one jobs waiting to be done. They spent hours in the attics the other day and only brought down a wicker chair, would you believe?'

'And a lovely fur cape, which will come in very useful.'

Esme sniffed her disapproval. Acutely aware she was sounding very like an old maid, she dryly commented that she believed Charlotte Gilpin to be no better than she should be, exactly as Miss Agnes and Mrs Walsh, her late father's parishioners, might have said.

Kitty looked thoughtful but then, wanting to be fair, said, 'You may be right but everyone likes her and she's undoubtedly talented as well as beautiful and charming. And she can be quite sweet and funny.'

'But she isn't pulling her weight, Kitty. You should ask her to leave.'

'I can't do that.' And she watched with sadness as her friend strode away, chin high, aware how deeply it hurt Esme to see Archie so enraptured. What would her reaction be if she learned the truth about Kitty's own intimate moments with him?

Dear Lord, what should she do? She couldn't ignore the problem for much longer.

And so it went on, day after day, and the pain of watching them together grew worse. She watched them sharing secrets, teasing each other, feeding each other titbits. Unable to bear it, Kitty would squirrel herself away for hours in the small sitting room on pretext of checking costs or revising her play when in fact she would be gazing bleakly out of the window. She strove to beat back her uncharitable thoughts, yet still they remained. Was Charlotte paying so much attention to Archie simply because he owned this magnificent if faded old manor house?

And their increasing closeness meant it was even more difficult for Kitty herself to find a moment alone with him. In fact, the need to speak to Archie was becoming quite urgent, though if she ever did find the opportunity, she hadn't the first idea what she'd say.

She'd discovered the tenderness about her breasts some weeks ago and had at first ignored it. Filled with a mixture of fear and excitement, she'd smoothed her hand over her stomach. Though still flat, it felt somehow different, firmer, slightly swollen inside, and she spread her fingers as if cradling the child in her womb. A baby, a human life, forming within her, she was certain of it. A small person who surely deserved the best in life, even if she or he hadn't been planned. She felt an unexpected thrill at the prospect of becoming Archie's wife, for surely he would be only too delighted to marry her, the moment he knew? And then she realised that she couldn't tell him at all since he might feel trapped.

Hadn't he said he would hate to be responsible for another person's happiness? How marriage would not suit him in the least? Archie loved to tease and flirt, to enjoy life and have fun. But he disliked anything in the least unpleasant, and neither during their night of shared intimacy, nor since, had he once spoken of love.

Despite these reservations Kitty remained resolutely optimistic. Archie was kind and caring. They were good friends, and she felt certain he would stand by her. She just had to find the right moment to tell him, when he wasn't being swamped by Charlotte. And it could surely wait a little longer, till they had everything properly organised.

Their most difficult problem was transport. One evening after rehearsal they were all sitting gloomily in the drawing room, worrying over which of them was capable of repairing the old Jowett motor that was quietly rusting away in the barn, when fate took a hand. There came a terrified scream from the kitchen and, bursting in upon the assembled company, Mrs Pips declared that there was 'some devil lurking out t'back'.

All the men snatched up some tool or other, Jacob grabbing the fire irons while Mrs Pips herself wielded a wooden rolling pin. They all followed the trail of soap suds she'd left, back to the kitchen, and Archie flung open the door to find a sorry-looking creature standing on the doorstep. Stocky, not an inch over five foot five, with rain dripping from the flat cap pulled down over his ears, he grinned cheerily back at them from beneath a nose blue with cold.

'Strike me down with a feather if it isn't Reg Bright! I last saw you years ago when we were caught scrumping apples together,' Archie exclaimed. 'Well, we won't go into that now. Come in, man. You're soaking wet. Take off your coat. Fetch him a cup of tea, Pips. No, a double whisky would be better. I'll get it myself.'

It turned out that Reg's parents both used to work on the estate years ago and he and Archie had been pals when they were boys, though where he'd been these last several years he wasn't saying and nobody liked to ask.

Mrs Pips produced a plate brimming with shepherd's pie left over from their supper, having recovered from the shock of seeing his leering grin through the kitchen window. Esme brought him a mug of hot cocoa which she considered far more suitable than whisky. Reg looked into her sunny, smiling face and was instantly certain he'd landed on his feet good and proper, if not in heaven itself. As he ate, he listened with avid attention to Archie's account of the Lakeland Players, and how they were needing a handyman to help with scenery and transport.

'I'm your man,' he said through a forkful of Mrs Pip's excellent pie.

And he did indeed prove to be a valuable asset. Esme spent most of the next morning handing spanners and oil rags to Reg as he lay on his back under the Jowett, worriedly enquiring if he was quite safe under there.

'Aye, lass. It's gooin' gaily weel. We'll 'ave this motor running in no time, noo I've got meself a canny mechanic's mate to help me like.'

Esme laughed, never having thought of herself as such before, but it sounded rather modern and unfussy to be smeared with oil, and not at all how a parson's daughter would be expected to behave. 'It's time you had a brew. I'll go and put the kettle on.'

'Eeh,' said the invisible voice from beneath the car, 'tha'll mek a reet good wife for some lucky bloke. What a little treasure!'

She hurried away to fetch him a mug of tea and a steaming pasty she'd made earlier, wondering if she wanted to be anyone's little treasure except perhaps Archie's. Though any hope she'd once had in that direction seemed to be quickly fading.

Reg also built a large box called a rostrum, under Kitty's careful direction. It measured six foot by three and could, she said, be used as a boat, shop or railway carriage, indicate a separate room on stage, or even the balcony for Romeo and Juliet. Turned upside down and with two pairs of wheels attached, it became a trailer. This was somewhat precariously hooked on to the back of the repaired motor where it could be filled with many of the group's properties.

It seemed they were very nearly ready, for all Reg continued to fiddle with his spanners under the Jowett, while Archie hovered, offering advice and perfunctory assistance. Except that there were still no bookings, and rehearsals were fizzling out as enthusiasm waned.

Frantic for the company at least to make a start, as well as to justify her place in the group, Esme set about writing yet another score of letters. Felicity Fanshaw volunteered to ride around on her bicycle distributing leaflets. Tessa Crump, the pianist, said she couldn't cycle to save her life but she'd be happy to deliver them by hand, if they thought it would do any good. Not that she could walk *very* far, she warned them, due to her bad back. In the end she caught any number of buses into Keswick, Kendal, Penrith and several towns and villages in between and did in fact walk for miles posting leaflets through dozens of letter boxes. Rod and Sam went along to help and make sure she didn't get lost.

Suzy rashly volunteered to sing to the tourists waiting at the steamer pier in Ambleside, and Jacob Warburton organised an impromptu scene from *Twelfth Night* in the market place at Kendal.

Within days of this huge effort they received not just one booking but three.

Their first was two nights in a small village near Settle in Yorkshire, then on to the Forest of Bowland in Lancashire, followed by three nights back in the wilds of Westmorland and Cumberland. More were even now being confirmed in places as diverse as Skipton and Preston, Harrogate and Workington.

Over the next few days engagements poured in. Fitting them all into their diary proved quite a task, demanding several telephone calls to confirm or rearrange events. It also involved lengthy discussions about Post Office boxes and telegrams and the co-ordination of information with Mrs Waldron, their friendly postmistress, who agreed to pass bookings on to them while they were on tour.

'We're in business,' Kitty squealed, hugging Esme tight then rushing to do the same with Jacob and Suzy, Reg and Archie and all the other members of the company who were coming to feel like a family to her. Everyone else was equally excited. She particularly noted the embrace between Archie and Charlotte, which was surely lengthier than necessary.

'By heckmondwyke,' Charlotte said, 'but we deserve this! We've worked our socks off.' Which made them all fall about laughing, not simply because of the hammed up Yorkshire accent but because, so far as the speaker was concerned, it was largely untrue.

'You look worn out,' Kitty remarked as she saw Esme take off her spectacles and rub her eyes tiredly.

'You look a bit peaky yourself.'

'Thanks.'

'It'll all be worth it in the end, I dare say.' Esme smiled then pulled a wry face. 'No doubt it'll be worse once we're on the road.'

'Probably.' Kitty's own happy smile faded to be replaced by a quick frown of concern. How on earth was she going to cope with a baby on top of everything else? She almost blurted out her secret there and then, might well have done so had they not been interrupted.

'What a po-faced pair you are.' Charlotte flung her arms about both girls and hugged them tight. 'Come on, cheer up, for God's sake. We're on our way.'

Archie was beside them in a second, declaring they should celebrate properly, and dashed off to return with a couple of bottles of red wine.

Rehearsals were forgotten as the afternoon did indeed turn into a celebration. Kitty had taken to wearing her thick brown hair fastened into a chignon, nestling heavily in the nape of her neck, and she always carried a small silver hunter watch attached to the waistband of her skirt in order to time scenes more accurately. Today she left the watch off and let down her hair, in reality as well as metaphorically.

Charlotte danced a wild gypsy number then Tessa played 'villain' music for Rod and Sam's clowning. Reg and Esme became engaged in a noisy game of snap while Felicity Fanshaw and Suzy sat huddled in a corner chatting. Jacob recited various Shakespearean monologues before ending up snoring on the couch, well gone on the whisky.

Perhaps it was the wine which finally loosened Kitty's

inhibitions for she went boldly up to Archie and asked if he'd mind stepping outside as there were one or two things she wanted to say to him. Charlotte, observing the quick exchange and seeing Kitty saunter away down the path, hurried quickly over just as he was about to follow.

From the moment of her arrival when Charlotte had first introduced herself, reverting to her maiden name for the sake of prudence, she'd envied the trio's close-knit friendship and vowed to infiltrate it. No one, in Charlotte's opinion, had a right to be happier than herself. For all he was a whey-faced, rather sad creature, Archie was charming, pleasant, agreeable, even rather sexy in a gentle, well-bred sort of way. And if he were not her usual sort of man, then he certainly fitted the bill so far as the size of his pocketbook was concerned. 'Darling Archie,' she purred, slipping her arm through his and neatly blocking his exit, 'would you do me a *huge* favour?'

He glanced down as if surprised to find her there, and smiled. Her lovely hair was all tangled, her face flushed from the dancing. She looked like a naughty child at a party, a most delightful imp of a child. From the first moment he'd clapped eyes on Charlotte Gilpin, Archie had felt drawn to her. There was a magnetism about the girl. She possessed the kind of earthy, animal quality that no man could precisely put a name to but all recognised as utterly irresistible. 'Name it. Your wish is my command.'

Charlotte's optimism soared. This was indeed progress, which so far had been frustratingly slow. She could see by the way he was looking at her that he was interested. Often she would sense his eyes upon her, yet at other times he barely seemed to notice her presence. Too damned cautious perhaps. 'You turn a girl's head with your flattery,' she said, reaching up to kiss his cheek lightly, so that her breasts grazed his chest.

Archie laughed softly. 'Minx! And don't you lap it up?' He glanced over her head through the open door into the garden, his gaze narrowing as he watched Kitty walk uncertainly away along the garden path. He felt torn, wanting to be with both girls. 'We'll talk later. Kitty needs a word first.'

Charlotte clicked her tongue sympathetically but maintained her hold on his arm as she slid one hand over his chest, then stroked his cheek. 'I need your help, Archie dear, with the teeniest little problem. I really don't know how to tell Kitty but I need to go away for a few days, maybe a week. Just to check on things at home. My mother hasn't been well,' she fabricated, adopting a suitably sad tone. For all Charlotte welcomed the bookings, she was afraid to neglect Magnus for much longer in case he did something outrageous, such as disinherit her. A brief visit home might sweeten him. And once the tour got underway, who knew when she'd have the time?

Archie frowned, looking vaguely anxious. 'I didn't realise you had a mother.'

Charlotte put back her head and laughed, revealing perfect white teeth which she could tell he did not fail to observe. 'Everyone has a mother, darling.' She offered him assurances that she'd be back in good time for the start of the tour. 'If you could just explain to Kitty for me? Please?' She pressed her slender body against his once more so that he could breathe in the scent of her perfume. 'I shall miss you, of course,' she murmured. 'There's something so *exciting* about you.'

'And you,' Archie murmured, half to himself.

'I'm glad you noticed.' She was smiling tantalisingly up at him from beneath lowered lashes, lips pouting so that her meaning was all too clear. He wanted her. Didn't every man? And she wished him to know that she would not be unwilling. Charlotte felt giddy with power as she always did when out to enslave her latest victim. Emboldened, she placed her soft lips against his ear and reminded him that her room was conveniently close to the back stairs. She couldn't have made it plainer.

But his eyes were once more upon the door through which Kitty had so recently passed, searching the now empty path almost as if he could see her waiting for him in the shrubbery. 'Sorry, what did you say?' He wasn't even listening.

Charlotte felt herself flush with annoyance and her eyes narrowed, but she manufactured a giggle to disguise her fury. 'I said, you and I could perhaps enjoy a little drink together later,' But he was making excuses, actually setting her to one side, and the next moment was striding away leaving her quite alone.

A cold wind blew a flurry of leaves into the hall. 'Bugger!' Charlotte swore loudly and comprehensively, revealing her true background in several more blunt words, then slammed the door shut and stormed upstairs. Once in the privacy of her room, she strode back and forth, ranting and raving, steaming with fury as she hurled books from shelves, following these with a vase of flowers that Esme had placed there earlier in the day. Never, in all her life, had a man actually refused her. But she knew who to blame. Oh, indeed she did. And wouldn't she make her sorry!

Warmly dressed in their winter coats and galoshes, they walked at a leisurely pace down the pitted track that had once been the main carriage drive of Repstone Manor. A bright winter sun slanted probing fingers through the bare branches of the beech trees that lined the way. Even the mountains seemed to be drawing back as if to let in more light on this crisp, late October day. Had it been Charlotte walking beside him, Kitty thought, the sunlight would have turned her hair to a golden halo, her elfin neatness entirely suiting the woodland scene.

Kitty drew the edges of her own shabby, three-year-old raincoat close and linked Archie's arm in the kind of friendly way she'd once taken for granted. Yet now, because of the tension inside her, it felt awkward. How would he react to being told he was about to become a father? All her worries about him feeling trapped into marriage rushed to the fore. He might even insist they abandon the travelling theatre project, sack the actors and give up on her dream, which was the last thing she wanted.

Kitty was suddenly filled with indecision.

'Penny for them?'

'Oh, I was just thinking what excellent progress we're making now the bookings are starting to come in,' she prevaricated, then kicked at a stone, annoyed with herself for missing a golden opportunity. 'We'll be ready in good time, so long as everyone pulls their weight.'

'Are you suggesting someone isn't? Just because Charlotte has to rush home to spend a few days with a sick mother doesn't mean she's slacking.'

Kitty stared at him in astonishment. 'Rush home? When did she decide that? She hasn't asked for time off.'

'She asked me, and I said she could.'

'Isn't that just a perfect example of her selfishness? Our final week of rehearsals and with all the packing to be done at the start of the tour, she skives off. It's too much.'

'She'll be back in a few days, in ample time for our first engagement, Kitty old thing.'

'Oh, she won't risk offending you, that's for sure.' The evening was bitterly cold and Kitty pulled her scarf closer about her neck.

He frowned at her. 'And what's that supposed to mean?'

Without stopping to consider the effect of her words, Kitty said, 'She's only using you, that's all. Having you run errands and do tasks she's perfectly capable of carrying out herself. She treats you like a servant at times.'

Archie's frown had turned to a scowl. 'I like to help, don't you know. Hardly turns me into a skivvy, does it?'

His displeasure at her criticism chilled her like a draft of icy wind, yet Kitty felt quite unable to retract a single word. Her heart was pumping madly and although she knew everything was going wrong, that all her carefully rehearsed phrases were seeping from her mind, she felt powerless to prevent them. Instead, all the envy and jealousy she'd nursed for Charlotte over these last weeks simply poured out of her mouth. 'She certainly overplays the Little-Miss-Helpless act. It's utterly nauseating. I'm only suggesting that you should be careful.'

'Charlotte has had a difficult time,' he testily remarked, 'losing her fiancé and not having any people of her own to turn to. Would've thought you, at least, could understand how she feels, old sport.'

'Yes, I lost Raymond but I don't go round expecting preferential treatment because of it.' She could hear her own voice sounding uncharacteristically carping and high-pitched, as if the pain of her jealousy had destroyed all her sense of reason.

Archie had stopped walking and was standing staring at her, his face stiff with displeasure. 'What was it, exactly, that led you to this observation, Kitty? Her open, friendly nature, or because she's prepared to admit when she's taken on too much and ask a man for assistance now and then?'

The sick sensation in the pit of her stomach felt very like fear. Kitty was terrified about the changes taking place in her body, invaded as it seemed to be by this new little stranger who was going to spoil everything, turn her life upside down, perhaps even ruin her dream, and she hadn't the first idea how to cope. She longed for Archie to realise what was happening to her without her having to tell him. She wanted him to proclaim his undying love for her, to insist that *her* happiness was all he cared about, but she couldn't for the life of her work out how to make him say these things. And here she was embroiled in a quarrel she'd never intended. She became aware that Archie was still talking, still comparing her unfavourably with Charlotte.

'With that stubborn independence of yours, you never seem to need help of any kind, certainly not from a mere male, and particularly not from me.'

'Now you're being ridiculous.' A small voice at the back of her head was warning her to play the helpless female, to own up to her own vulnerability. Yet a contrary voice reminded Kitty that the last time she'd shown such weakness, she'd found her life taken over by a selfish mother and her engagement announced to a man she didn't even love. 'I don't go around making eyes at a man just because he has money in the bank. I'm my own woman, or at least I hope I am. Charlotte Gilpin, on the other hand, has already admitted to one engagement which could be considered above her station. I'm perfectly certain she'd have no objection to another. She's a grasping little gold digger, that much is obvious.'

The silence that followed this outburst was appalling. The stunned expression of shock and disbelief on Archie's face, the hard anger in his eyes, made Kitty instantly wish every reckless word unspoken. He looked bigger, broader, darker of brow, somehow far more masculine and aggressive than she'd ever seen him before. His tone, when he finally spoke, was chilling.

'That's what you think, is it?'

It was too late to back down, not without looking foolish. 'Yes, that's what I think.' And it was true. Kitty did believe that Charlotte Gilpin was after Archie's money. The girl had entranced him with her winsome charm, her tales of woe, her *fragility*, and because of the tragic loss of his own family and grief for Raymond, he couldn't resist her.

'That's the cruellest, most heartless thing I've ever heard you say.'

One glance at his tight-lipped expression told Kitty that further argument was futile. Having given him the perfect excuse to defend Charlotte, she'd unwittingly widened the gulf between them. Turning on her heel, she began to walk, almost run, from him, blinded by tears, her booted feet slipping over the ruts in the drive. But by the time he caught up with her, even more grimly silent than before, her eyes were quite dry and her chin tilted high for Kitty realised she'd just lost the perfect opportunity to tell him about the baby, and not for a moment would she allow him to see how much that hurt.

Chapter Ten

Magnus was in a temper. Where had Charlotte been all this time, he wanted to know? What kind of a wife was she to spend so long away, wandering the world on some endless holiday?

'For God's sake, is it any wonder with you like a bear with a sore head the minute I come home? And I haven't been on holiday, not the whole time anyroad. I've been staying with Mam for some of it,' Charlotte improvised, remembering her tale to Archie.

'Why? I thought the two of you didn't get on.'

'She's still me mother and she's been ill.' In no time at all Charlotte had invented a whole case history of troubles and tribulations for her poor mother, on whom she hadn't in fact clapped eyes since she married Magnus. 'I'm her only surviving child, and she doesn't have the advantage of a Mrs Pursey to wait upon her hand, foot and finger, so who else is there to see to her but me?'

Magnus, still sulking, was not so easily mollified. 'What about your stepfather? Isn't he still around?'

Charlotte was tempted to say that he'd run off with

some young floozy and left her mother in the cart, but common sense prevailed as too many lies were difficult to keep track of, so she reluctantly cut that dramatic story from her repertoire. Besides, if her mother had been left alone then there'd be no reason why the old woman couldn't have come to stay with them, thereby destroying a useful alibi. 'And what use would he be?' she scoffed. 'What use is any man?' She brushed a brief kiss upon Magnus's cheek. 'I'll go and instruct Mrs Pursey to cook your favourite hot pot and we'll enjoy the meal together, here in your room, to celebrate my return. All on us own, eh?'

'All on *our* own,' he reminded her, eyes glinting nonetheless.

'Whatever you say. Wensleydale cheese and fruit loaf for afterwards, eh?'

'Lovely.'

She did her best to placate him over the few days she was there, reading the papers to him each morning, instructing Mrs Pursey in the preparation of more of his favourite dishes, allowing him titbits and treats that the doctor had denied him, in view of his rapidly increasing girth. And she even let him kiss and fondle her now and then, although managed to avoid any further intimacy on the grounds that it was bad for his blood pressure. Charlotte's reward was the restoration of her allowance.

'Young Lord Bickerstaff is to be wed,' he informed her with relish one morning as he lay propped against his pillows reading the paper. 'What a disappointment for you.'

'Tommy Bickerstaff was your choice, not mine.'

Magnus chuckled. 'Even your latest beau, what was

his name? – Alderman Miles Something-or-other – has found himself a bride half his age, the old roué.'

'Pickering? How did . . .' No, Charlotte thought. Best not to investigate too closely how much Magnus knew about her affairs. But for some reason this news utterly devastated her. It felt like a betrayal. As if everyone could find romantic bliss but herself. It somehow hardened her resolve to have Archie, no matter if he was secretly lusting after Kitty. He'd find she wasn't so easily put off. Oh, dear no.

It took five days not three before she managed to extricate herself from Magnus's house, which was cutting it a bit fine. Even then she'd been driven to write herself a letter, purporting to come from her mother, begging her to return since the old woman had suffered a further relapse. Charlotte read the letter to Magnus with tears rolling down her cheeks, declaring her own sorrow at being forced to leave him when matters between them were on the mend.

He'd railed against it, of course, raging at her for leaving him so soon. Unfortunately, because of his condition, his control over her was slipping and he knew it. Magnus believed she should have no other life beyond these four walls, that Charlotte belonged to him absolutely and must stay by his side, morning, noon and night.

'If you don't come back soon, I'll get out of this damned bed and come looking for you myself!' he shouted as she'd left, gently closing his bedroom door after her with an audible sigh of relief.

She was on the afternoon train, complete with luncheon hamper, again especially prepared by Mortimer the ardent chauffeur, except that this time she knew where she was going and found herself welcomed back if not exactly with open arms, then with relief, by Archie at least.

'Thank goodness! There'd have been all hell to pay if you'd been late.'

Charlotte pouted sulkily. 'Thanks very much. I'm surprised you noticed I'd gone.'

'Of course I did.'

'Good. A girl likes to be missed.' She had a way of lifting her shoulders when she smiled that was so sensual Archie almost reached out for her there and then. But it was true, he had missed her. He'd found himself thinking more and more of Charlotte recently. She was beautiful and sensual, amusing and lively. Positively fizzed with vigour and fun.

As he smiled thoughtfully down upon her, Charlotte was embroidering the story of her mother's failing health, now so well rehearsed she almost believed it herself. It was a fiction which could well prove useful in the months ahead. 'I hated to leave her. I'll have to go back to her from time to time,' she wept, dabbing at a tear.

'Of course you will, old thing. Just say the word. I'm sure we can manage to give you the necessary time off. Don't cry. I can't bear to see a woman cry.' He put an arm about her, patting her awkwardly on the shoulder.

'Kitty mightn't agree.'

'I'll see to Kitty. Don't you fret.'

'Will you? Darling Archie.' And twisting her head a little so she could reach, she kissed him with an enticing sweetness, so very gently that he thought he might have imagined the flicker of her tongue brushing ever so lightly over his lips. He gazed wonderingly into those cornflower blue eyes, but when the lids drooped he allowed the kiss to deepen and did not draw away.

The next morning Charlotte caught up with Kitty on the stairs. She'd come up with a carefully devised plan which she fully intended to make work. It was vitally important that these new friends of hers behaved as she wished them to behave. She might not love Archie Emerson but she intended to have him all the same, along with everything he represented. He would be good insurance in case her expectations from Magnus went awry. 'I know you don't think much of me, Kitty, but I'd like to explain . . .'

'Charlotte, I . . .'

'No, it's all right, I understand. I can see it every time you look my way.' Charlotte sank down on the edge of a stair but Kitty remained where she was, tall and stiffly dignified beside her. 'I'd just like to say that it's easy for you, always having had loads of friends. I've had nowt, 'ceptin' what I grabbed wi' me own fair hands.' This was so close to the truth that Charlotte began to feel uncomfortable so hurried quickly on. 'I know you think I've been monopolising Archie but the truth is – I've only been putting in a word for Esme.'

The words came out in a rush. They were followed by a stunned silence and then Kitty sank down beside her on the stair. 'Esme? What do you mean, "putting in a word" for her?'

'Well, Esme's that shy, she'd say nowt on her own account, would she? She's pining after him, anyone wi' half an eye can see it.' A sideways glance at Kitty's face told Charlotte not only that she'd inadvertently stumbled upon the truth but a good deal more besides. Her mouth fell open. 'Lord above, you're potty about him an' all!'

'Don't be ridiculous.'

'It's all right, I'll not breathe a word. Eeh, you poor love.' And now Charlotte's mind was racing, noting the depth of pinched misery in Kitty's expressive face, the pallor of her skin, the bleakness in her eyes; calculating, observing, playing with possibilities.

Kitty, finding herself discovered and unable to deny the truth, almost sobbed out loud. 'You won't tell him?'

''Course not, what d'you take me for? So that's why Esme's hangin' back? Because she reckons you have first call on his affections, being t'boss like.'

Kitty hastily explained about their pact and Charlotte sadly shook her head.

'Ah, well, that explains a good deal,' she murmured sympathetically, almost wanting to laugh out loud at her own cleverness. 'I'm sorry to say you're the loser, love. Told me he's been like a brother to you since you lost your own. That's how he thinks of you. As his dear little sister.'

'Sister!' The tone was bleak for all Kitty recognised the truth of Charlotte's words.

'It's Esme Archie loves, lass. No doubt about that. Plain as the nose on your face. He virtually admitted as much to me the other night.' Charlotte felt perfectly safe devising this fiction, since she didn't believe Kitty had the courage to challenge Archie about it.

'He did?' Kitty's voice was barely above a whisper.

'Oh, aye. Worships the ground she walks on but reckons she'd think he were too old for her. How blind can a chap be? Men! If he knew how she truly felt, there'd be no holding him, eh?'

Neither of them spoke for long moments. Kitty sat with her arms wrapped tight about her knees, hardly able to breathe, the pain of disappointment was so overpowering. Charlotte wasn't telling her anything she hadn't already suspected. Though it hurt to have it confirmed, she must face the truth. She must be brave. Archie didn't love her, not like a man should. He never had. She should be pleased for Esme, that she at least had a real chance of happiness. Tears were rolling unchecked down her cheeks and Charlotte was putting her arms around her, drawing her close as if she truly cared and was not, in fact, the cause of them.

'Who needs men eh? More trouble than they're worth.'

'I'll not stand in her way,' Kitty sobbed. 'I promised her.'

'Here, have a good blow.' She handed Kitty a large silk handkerchief, far too fine actually to use. 'As for our other differences, well, I may not be as practical as you, or as capable, but I'll pull me weight in other ways when the tour starts, see if I don't. Till then, I'll try to do better on the work front, I promise.'

Kitty looked into those bewitching blue eyes glistening with moist sympathy and felt a sudden rush of warmth for this diminutive figure. Perhaps she'd entirely misjudged her. Perhaps Charlotte wasn't so selfish and greedy as she'd imagined. All the time she'd been thinking of Esme, not herself. Archie was right. The girl clearly knew what it was to suffer, and that's why she was so kind and understanding. Leaning forward, Kitty kissed her on the cheek. 'Friends?'

Charlotte blinked, looking faintly stunned as if no one

had ever offered such a thing to her before. 'Aye. Why not, eh? Friends.'

Only two days to go before the start of the tour and Esme's role of mechanic's mate had been superseded by that of assistant wardrobe mistress to Mrs Pips, who set her darning holes in stockings which would be needed by the men in the Shakespeare.

'Though I don't hold with chaps in women's clothing,' Mrs Pips muttered through a mouthful of pins, her thin face looking quite pink and not half so disapproving as she sounded. 'They don't have the legs for one thing.'

Giggling, Esme allowed herself to be pressed into service as a model for various dresses which needed pinning and tacking up. Kitty then sent her dashing to the Post Office with another bunch of letters, for which purpose Felicity Fanshaw kindly loaned her bike. On her return she painted scenery, fashioned spears and shields for the halberdiers and tackled any number of other jobs, of which she quite lost count.

Smiling fondly at her friend's obvious enthusiasm, Kitty drew back into the shadows of the barn as Esme hurried past bearing an armful of linen. It was there that Archie found her. 'We never did finish our talk.' His voice, soft in her ear, made Kitty jump and she scolded him for creeping up on her so quietly. 'Are we still friends? I recall a time when you were not so unwilling to have me near. Could you be avoiding me, my sweet, when all I desire is to recreate those magic moments we once enjoyed?'

His fingers were caressing her cheek, his breath soft against her skin, and Kitty felt bathed in a hot panic. Had she not known otherwise, she would have sworn this was genuine, but it was obviously an example of Archie's droll wit.

She managed to laugh up at him. 'Can't you see that I'm desperately trying to prepare every last detail in time for our first night? Which is less than two days off in case you hadn't noticed.'

'You might at least apologise.'

'For what?'

'Kitty, don't be obtuse. Are you telling me you believed all that nonsense you were saying about Charlotte?'

'Well, yes, I did think it true at the time, but perhaps I was a bit hard on her.'

'Excellent. A degree of sympathy at last. Now we've got that out of the way, what about us? Or are you too busy playing the famous director to find time for an old friend these days? I mean, a chap has needs, don't you know, and you've neglected me for far too long.'

She stared at him, dumbfounded. What was he saying? Charlotte said that it was Esme he loved and wanted so Kitty mustn't take his words too literally. He was simply teasing her and she must remember to keep to her pact with her friend. She pushed him away, her laughter now high-pitched, sounding unnatural even to her own ears. 'If you've so much redundant energy, go and help Esme with those curtains, for goodness sake, but keep out of my way.'

And as she marched off across the courtyard, Archie called after her, 'Why must you always be so damned bossy, Miss Kitty Little?'

Hearing his voice, Charlotte hurried out just in time to see Kitty slam the barn door behind her. Smiling to herself, she crossed the yard to comfort the now glowering Archie, for wasn't her little scheme working just beautifully?

As if to prove his words, Kitty crammed in several extra rehearsals, putting the company through its paces, insisting they go over and over a scene until it was polished to perfection, for there was no question but that they needed all the rehearsal time they could squeeze in. This was what she'd dreamed of for so long and now that the moment had arrived, she couldn't allow herself to relax for a second, for that way lay failure. Besides, wouldn't it also give her too much time to think? Even when Suzy suggested she might be overdoing it, Kitty merely increased the work schedule.

'Full dress rehearsal at two, and please make sure you know your lines this time.'

This was what was important. Nothing else mattered.

Kitty told herself firmly that she could manage perfectly well without a man. Which law stated that a woman had to be married before she could bring up a child? It might be considered morally shocking but all this conventional nonsense about marriage being an honourable estate meant very little in the face of her predicament. You had to cope with life as it was presented to you, not as some romantic ideal. She'd never been interested in domesticity and servitude before, so why start now?

Because she loved Archie, of course. Because her body

ached for him. Not for a moment could she get the image of him out of her head. Yet if Esme was his choice than she must not spoil things for them. What was to be gained by forcing a man into fatherhood and marriage? Nothing.

Charlotte paid particular attention to Kitty's almost frantic behaviour, observing her closely, noting the tired lines beneath her eyes, the way she sometimes put her hand to her aching back or stomach when she thought no one was looking. If Kitty carried another secret, the sooner Charlotte prised it out of her, the better. It could prove essential in her campaign.

She went to her and, gently remarking on how tired she was looking, suggested that since this was their last day, they should cancel the afternoon rehearsal as they all deserved some time off before the start of the tour. 'We could go shopping, have tea. Maybe try the flicks?'

'An excellent idea,' Esme agreed. 'I could do with a break.'

Kitty conceded that perhaps an afternoon off would do them all good.

Rod and Sam declared their intention of going for a long hike. Felicity and Suzy were to take turns on the bicycle and make their way to Hawkshead for an afternoon tea of gingerbread and rum butter. Jacob buried his head in the newspaper in case he should be required to do anything energetic and Tessa opted for a long hot bath to nurse a cold she was quite certain was coming on. Archie and Reg were happy to spend the afternoon polishing the Jowett, which had been tuned and tinkered into as near perfect a condition as it was capable of.

'While we can wallow in sentiment, weep at Mary Pickford or laugh at Fatty Arbuckle,' Esme said, round cheeks pink with the anticipated pleasure.

In the end they sat nibbling Fry's chocolate bars, listening to the warbling sounds of a tinny piano as they watched some third-rate fantasy about a poor girl who'd lost touch with civilisation. She was discovered by a jungle explorer who carried her off supposedly to have his wicked way with her, though this was barely hinted at. Then, instead of returning to New York where she could enjoy theatres and nice frocks, she opted instead to remain in the back of beyond with lover-boy.

It was so utterly ridiculous that the three girls came out clinging to each, weak with laughter.

'What must she have been thinking of?' Charlotte cried. 'It would be like a living death, all that heat and jungle and creepy-crawlies.' She shuddered. 'Can't these picture magnates come up with anything more realistic than that comic book nonsense?'

'But he clearly adored her,' Esme reminded them. 'And he was something of a matinée idol. Would that real life could be so tidily arranged!'

'"Came the dawn the two lovers walked off together into the sunset",' Charlotte quoted from the subtitles, clutching her breast in pseudo-anguish and then flinging her arms out in such a parody of the actor's movements they all doubled up with laughter again.

They climbed aboard the bus to take them back to Repstone, deeply involved in an argument about whether the cinema really would damage the theatre. Charlotte believed that it would, while Kitty resolutely argued that customers who went twice a week to a picture house would also be keen to see live theatre, if they were given the opportunity. 'Which is why we're starting a theatre company,' she announced as she flopped into a seat. 'Oh, fizz, where are the dratted return tickets?' And she began searching through her pockets and in her bag so she could show them to the conductor when he came round.

Esme, on quite a different tack, said, 'Perhaps being in love is more important than any of this new materialism. Perhaps that's what the picture was trying to tell us.'

'Give up everything for love, you mean?' Charlotte said scornfully, pursing her lips as she applied fresh lipstick. 'What utter rubbish! How would they live? I certainly couldn't. I'm a gel who likes her comforts.'

'We'd noticed,' Kitty dryly remarked, still rummaging.

'Tickets, please.'

The conductor was upon them and Kitty, on her feet by this time, was growing frantic, begging the others to check pockets and bags as she couldn't find them anywhere.

'Then you'll have to pay again, love,' said the conductor with a cheery grin.

'We've just spent all our money,' Esme moaned, insisting Kitty hand her the bag so she could look while Charlotte batted her eyelashes at the conductor. The contents of Kitty's bag were strewn all about the seat. No tickets. A thorough search of every pocket again produced the same result.

'I'll have to put you off,' the conductor sternly warned them.

'Oh, come on, be a sport,' Charlotte wheedled. 'It's late and we're a long way from home.'

'That's naught to do wi' me. I'm only doing me job.'

'Put a truncheon in yer hand, and you'd be the spitting image of those daft Keystone Cops that were on before the big picture.'

A ding-ding of his bell and within minutes the three girls found themselves standing on the side of the road, gazing at each other in horror as the bus trundled off into the night without them.

'Thanks for being so helpful, Charlotte dear,' Kitty dryly remarked.

'How far is it?'

'About three miles.'

The short autumn day was already growing dark with a fitful moon floating in and out of streaks of cloud. The lane seemed quite deserted. Somewhere an owl hooted, making Charlotte shiver.

'Oh, dear!'

'You shouldn't have annoyed him by comparing him with Buster Keaton's "daft cops".'

'My charms must be slipping.'

Esme said, 'Best foot forward, girls.' So arm in arm they did just that, striding out as best they might, soon giggling again, as much at their predicament as over the picture.

Perhaps it was the loneliness of the country road with its eerie rustlings and strange hoots and calls, the brooding mountains seeming to close in on them as they reared up like a black ridge against the pale moonlight, or because this was the first time they'd spent so long alone in each other's company. Or perhaps the fun they'd enjoyed together that day, a little shopping (mainly of the look and dream variety), tea and a sticky bun, followed by first house at the pictures, had drawn them closer. Whatever the reason, the three girls were soon exchanging confidences.

Charlotte was giving a riotous, if carefully edited, version of her love life which neglected to make any mention of a husband, and seemed to involve any number of encounters with ardent young men all desperate to deprive her of her virtue.

'You didn't succumb, did you?' Esme asked in shocked tones, and then blushed furiously as she realised the impertinence of her own question. 'Sorry. Don't answer if you don't want to.'

'I've no secrets from my friends,' Charlotte grandly and inaccurately assured them. 'This is the modern world, darling. A new dawn with Victorian England dead and buried.'

'Oh, Charlotte, you are a caution,' Esme chuckled.

'I never give owt to a man I can't easily part with,' she finished rather enigmatically, and winked. 'Right. It's someone else's turn now. What about you? Tell us your dark secrets, Esme. Or is the daughter of a parson above such earthly desires as sex and love?' she probed, giving a wicked little chuckle.

Embarrassment fired Esme's face as images of her father came to mind. 'It isn't funny. Being a parson's daughter doesn't cut you off from the real world, nor from sin.'

'True. Even parsons do IT, I suppose. Else how would you be here?'

If anything Esme's blush deepened, all too cruelly

highlighted by the moon which chose to sail out in full glory at precisely that moment, revealing the depth of her discomfiture.

Kitty put her arm about her friend's shoulders, throwing Charlotte a silent warning to leave the topic be. 'It's all right, Esme. We've all gone a bit silly over watching that daft picture and getting thrown off the bus. I'm sure Charlotte didn't mean to offend.'

'As if I would,' she said, sounding genuinely contrite and giving Esme's hand a reassuring squeeze. 'All mouth, that's me. Anyway, you can tell us anything you like. We're your very best friends.'

As Esme remained mute, walking along with shoulders hunched and chin sunk into her chest, the other two girls exchanged puzzled glances though neither had the heart to press her further. But it was plain to them both in that moment that Esme did indeed have a secret. One she clearly had no wish to share.

'Right then, it's Kitty's turn. Tell us your life story. Have you any dark secrets?' Charlotte half glanced at Kitty's all too eloquent features, at the way her hand crept protectively to her waist. This was the moment she'd been carefully leading up to and not for anything would she let this one go. 'Lord above, you've got one an' all. Go on, tell us. Spill the beans.'

Kitty studied herself in the mirror. Ignoring the huge brown eyes brimming with tears, she examined her profile. There was still no obvious sign beyond a slight thickening of her waistline; far too thin for a woman in a delicate condition. Perhaps she had indeed been working too hard and should take more care. That's what Esme and Charlotte had both said.

Letting her friends into her secret had been a good thing in a way, something of a relief, for she couldn't deny she was going to need their support in the months ahead. Yet it had been the hardest thing she'd ever done. Each had been astonished, even shocked, in their different ways and both had urged her to visit a doctor. Esme had generously volunteered to go with her and Kitty of course had sworn them both to secrecy, trusting them not to breathe a word to a soul.

It felt almost as if the baby were a ticking bomb, marking off the hours of her freedom, about to explode and destroy her.

Charlotte had been the one to ask the identity of the father but not for the world would Kitty reveal it. That fact remained her secret and always would. It was entirely against her nature to tell an untruth but how could she admit to that one crazy night she'd spent with Archie? Not so much for her own sake, for all she was ashamed of having practically thrown herself at him, but because of her promise to Esme.

Since it was generally known that Kitty had once been engaged, what harm would it do for them to believe Frank was the father? She was never likely to see him again. And there was little point now in Archie learning that the child was his and feeling obliged to marry her, when really it wasn't Kitty he loved at all but Esme.

Determined to make her sacrifice worthwhile and keep their friendship intact, Kitty dashed away the tears of self-pity and went to find Esme where she was scribbling more letters in the small sitting room, evidently anxious not to allow the LTPs to rest on their laurels. Without hesitation, so as to give herself no time for regrets, Kitty blurted out what Charlotte had informed her the other morning on the stairs: that it was Esme Archie loved, but that he was nervous of approaching her because of the difference in their ages.

She stared at Kitty unblinking through her round spectacles. 'I-I'm not sure I understand?'

'I want you to know that I won't stand in your way. I'll keep our pact. I value our friendship too much. Archie's too for that matter.'

'He hasn't said anything to me but I've always – hoped.'

Esme's complete lack of confidence in herself endeared her to Kitty all the more and she put her arms about her friend and hugged her. 'When has he had the chance to speak to you with all this work going on? I'm sure he will. Be patient.' And, biting her lip, she hurried away, quite unable to say anything further.

Chapter Eleven

It was agreed that Reg would drive the motor and trailer outfit, with Archie acting as navigator and back-up driver. 'Esme could ride with us,' Reg blurted out, his neck turning a dull red at expressing himself so forcibly in public. 'We'll squeeze what boxes we can into the boot and stack the rest beside her on the back seat. So long as she doesn't mind a bit of a crush.'

Kitty agreed that this seemed a good idea since Esme had been the one to take the bookings. Charlotte, however, had her own views on these arrangements for the last thing she wanted was for Esme to be in such close proximity to Archie. Her original plans hadn't taken into account the fact that the dutiful little mouse was actually potty about him, too, which could create further complications. Not that she considered Esme much of a threat. She knew she would soon have Archie safely in her own grasp.

'You'd have no objections if I came along too, would you? Train travel makes me horribly sick, and I could act as navigator to one driver while the other sleeps.'

'It didn't seem to prevent you from visiting your mother,' Kitty very reasonably pointed out, 'and Esme can map read perfectly well. I'm sorry, Charlotte, but I doubt there'll be room for two passengers in the car.'

Infuriated at having her plans blocked, she went at once to Archie, fluttering her eyelashes quite unashamedly. 'Kitty says that since train travel makes me sick, she's no objection to my travelling in the motor with Esme if there's room.' The lie slipped sweetly off her tongue, as always. 'You could squeeze me in, couldn't you, Archie?'

'Absolutely, old thing. If you don't mind travelling with your feet on one box and another on your lap,' he good-naturedly agreed. 'Being train-sick must be a terrible bore.'

Kitty, when she heard of this decision, was hard put to know whether to be amused by Charlotte's obvious connivance, or infuriated by it. But because there had been a distinct warming of relations between them and she'd no wish further to upset Archie, she resigned herself to going along with it. What did it matter anyway?

It was freezing in the old Jowett. Esme had made up hot water bottles but these soon lost their heat. She'd put on all her warmest clothes including two pairs of socks, several jumpers and a woolly hat, not to mention a couple of blankets, but even so within an hour of their setting out, she was shivering with cold. For this reason if for no other she was heartily glad of Charlotte's company since the two girls could snuggle up together on the back seat in a futile attempt to keep warm as the wind blasted around them, whistling through the cracks and flaps of the canvas hood of the old car.

'I feel like we're off to explore the Arctic,' Charlotte giggled.

With Hardknot and Scafell glowering down upon them, the latter with its head wreathed in thick swirling cloud, they rattled through Windermere and Kendal, then branched off towards Kirkby-Lonsdale. Visibility was poor with sweeping rain much of the time and progress pitiably slow. Worse still, every road they chose seemed to be filled with pot holes. They lost count of the number of times they took the wrong turn and had to back track or make a detour. The tarpaulin covering the trailer came loose and it took Reg and Archie an age to fix it as it flapped like a live thing in the wind.

'Has Archie declared himself yet?' Charlotte whispered, and Esme shook her head, blushing furiously. She found it dreadfully embarrassing to have her private affairs discussed in this public fashion.

'Perhaps he needs a bit of encouragement,' Charlotte commented. 'Shall I say something? Give him the nod like?'

Esme sent her a look of pure gratitude. Since she was so desperately shy, perhaps Charlotte's speaking up for her would be the perfect solution. 'Would you, Charlotte? I'd be so grateful.'

They were about eight miles west of Ingleton when the clouds lifted and Charlotte decided it was time to stop for lunch. They were all eager to escape the cramped confines of the overcrowded motor and Esme spread a couple of old raincoats on the grass verge where they could at least enjoy a brief spell of fickle sunshine.

While Charlotte sat next to Archie, Reg placed himself beside Esme. 'Can't remember the last time I had a picnic. I'm reet glad you came with us.'

'It seemed sensible since I made the booking.' Esme kept a good six-inch strip of raincoat between them while she concentrated on eating her egg sandwich. If it was true that it was she Archie loved, then what would he think of her sitting so close to Reg?

Leaning close, he whispered against her ear, 'D'you reckon she'll catch him?'

Esme felt her blood run cold. 'Who?' she asked, dreading his answer.

'Little Lottie here. See how she hangs so attentively upon his every word. If ever a lass set her cap more plainly at a chap, I've yet to see it. Archie looks like he can't believe his luck, eh?'

Esme could think of nothing to say to this. It was true the pair were sitting remarkably close together in deep and intimate conversation, but what of it? Hadn't Charlotte promised she'd get him to declare his love for Esme?

'Hey up, they're off.' And it seemed he was right. Charlotte was brushing crumbs from a becomingly crumpled linen dress, declaring her need to stretch her legs and inviting Archie to accompany her to make sure she didn't get lost or abducted. Without demur he did so and the pair of them strolled off arm in arm, leaving Esme so heartsore it felt as if a horse had kicked her in the chest and winded her.

Reg munched his way stolidly through a pile of

sandwiches. She managed to nibble only one, her appetite quite gone. Disappointment cut through her like a knife. Was it possible that what Reg had suggested was right? That Archie was indeed keen on Charlotte? Or was he just being himself, jolly and friendly as always? In that moment, it hardly seemed to matter. He didn't seem the least interested in her. Esme was beginning to feel that she had imagined those intimate moments by the lake, or perhaps he regretted them.

Then again, it might be because she was the sort of person no one would ever truly love. Her father clearly hadn't loved her and, much as she might prefer to push the painful memories into obscurity, he really hadn't treated her as a father should. In a way she'd been invisible to him. He hadn't seen her as a real person at all. Was she invisible to Archie too? Esme found little comfort in such a thought, only a sharpening of her misery.

Her arm tucked securely under Archie's, Charlotte began by divulging 'secrets' of her own, spinning a few yarns of her sad life in order to gain a few confidences in return. Except that she succeeded rather too well.

'I know how it feels to be disappointed in love,' he said, with very little prompting. 'I thought Kitty and I might get together at one time, but nothing came of it.'

Kitty, always Kitty. Ever between them with her soft brown eyes, unprepossessing looks and sound common sense. 'What about little old me? Won't I do instead? Or am I too plain and Yorkshire for a member of the landed gentry?' Charlotte slanted a gaze up at him, lifted her rosebud lips in the hope he might succumb and kiss her of his own accord this time.

Instead he playfully pinched her pert little nose. 'Ever the flirt, Charlotte. You're a very beautiful and exciting woman. One any normal, red-blooded male would be only too pleased to call his own. I swear, if it weren't for Kitty, I might well be tempted myself.'

In that moment she almost hated him – stupid, stubborn fool that he was. Charlotte certainly hated Kitty whose fault this must be. She allowed her eyes to fill with tears. 'Oh, Archie. Don't say such things. I didn't realise you were spoken for. I'd never hurt Kitty, not for the world.'

He laughed. ''Course I'm not "spoken for". Heaven forbid! Anyway, what an idea. Kitty is a sweet, dear girl but tough as old boots. She's her own woman. Bit of a suffragist at heart, don't you know. Fiercely independent and never one to admit she *needs* help from anybody, least of all a chap.'

'But does this chap want to be needed?' teased Charlotte, tapping his arm with one polished fingernail.

'I wouldn't say no to a little light dalliance.' Charlotte was appalled, inwardly raging that it was proving so damned difficult to capture Archie and all his lovely money. She pulled him to a halt, turned him to face her and traced her fingertips lightly over the fullness of his mouth, pouting her lips so delectably that surely any man would cut his own throat rather than risk losing her. 'But does it have to be with Kitty? Darling Archie, you always think the best of everyone, I'm sure, but you really shouldn't be so trusting.'

He frowned. 'I'm not sure I follow you?'

'The truth is, I doubt Kitty is quite so independent as you imagine. At least, I don't think she can afford to be for much longer. Oh, dear, what have I done.' She put a hand to her mouth and half turned away, as if she couldn't bear to witness his distress. 'I'm that sorry, really I am.'

'Sorry about what?'

'No, I've said too much already. I *would* tell you, if I could, really. Only I promised, hand on heart, I'd keep her secret.' And she gazed appealingly up at him, soft blue eyes brimming with tears.

His jaw set rigid, Archie took her by the arms and gave her a little shake. 'You can't plague me in this fashion, Charlotte. Tell me, is something wrong with Kitty? I need to know.'

'Nothing wrong exactly. Entirely natural I should say. I mean, she was *engaged* once, wasn't she?' And as light began to dawn in his blue eyes, Charlotte spilled forth Kitty's secret, which she'd promised so faithfully to keep.

It was almost pitiful to see Archie so sadly disillusioned. 'She must have lied to me,' was all he kept saying, over and over. 'She can't have been a virgin after all, can she?'

'Did she tell you that she was?'

'I assumed . . . er . . . it came up in conversation once.'

Had Charlotte been a woman who possessed a heart, she might well have been moved by the sight of such anguish. She could have sworn that he was very near to tears.

'Poor sweet darling, did you think she was pure as the driven snow? She really isn't worthy of your

195

consideration. There are other women,' she very reasonably pointed out, and for a long moment they looked deep into each other's eyes, reading far more into that single glance than they could ever speak with mere words. It revealed to them both that they had much in common: an innate obsession with self; a desperate need for excitement, for physical pleasure and fulfilment, even danger. They were kindred spirits in so many ways.

Charlotte found little difficulty in seducing him after that. He was angry, so no wonder he welcomed the comfort she offered.

He offered no resistance as she pulled him down into the sweet-scented grass, though they were both soaked through in seconds. The linen dress was swiftly peeled away, as was an array of apricot silk undergarments, revealing the tantalising softness of those voluptuous breasts entirely for his pleasure. Tongue probing, teeth nipping at his lower lip, her mouth met his with new urgency, while the persistence of her exploring hands served to heighten his need and kindle a dangerous excitement within him. And if, when he finally took her, pounding into her in the long damp grass of a country meadow, the name he cried out in his climax was not hers, Charlotte refused to allow this small fact to trouble her. It was, after all, her body he was pleasuring.

When the small party resumed their journey, refreshed and rested, Esme recognised in the tightness of Archie's expression that whatever had taken place between the two of them during that walk had not improved her own chances one little bit. Charlotte's little shrug of apology when Esme glanced enquiringly across at her confirmed this fear. No doubt any preference he'd had for her had all been a mistake, a figment of Charlotte's vivid imagination.

While Reg and Charlotte broke into a cheery chorus of 'Oh, Mr Porter', Archie barely glanced in Esme's direction and didn't speak a word to anyone. She did her best to join in but as the Jowett lurched into yet another pot hole and she heard the sickening hiss of a burst tyre, she closed her eyes in silent despair and knew she'd be heartily thankful when this nightmare journey was over.

The rest of the company arrived merrily enough at the village hall where the performance was to be held, full of excitement and eagerly looking forward to their first night, only to find the door locked and no sign of a key holder, let alone a key.

It was early-afternoon, a thin drizzle was starting and Kitty, feeling responsible for the whole enterprise, was anxious to get set up, find their digs and have time to rest and eat after their long journey before the show started prompt at eight. Yet there was no one here and a chill of concern sprang up in her. Everything had been going smoothly up until now. Even the train journey had been reasonably pleasant, and surprisingly useful. Kitty had marshalled her troupe into an impromptu rehearsal as the train rattled south, much to the fascinated amusement of the other passengers.

'Don't worry about them,' she'd said, smiling brightly at her team. 'I'll read in for Charlotte and it'll be good practice to have an audience at last.' Which proved to be entirely correct as the passengers soon became engrossed in the drama of whether Miranda would gain her true love in *The Tempest*, applauding with gratifying enthusiasm at the end of the extract. Kitty suspected one or two deliberately missed their stops in order to see the end.

Now here they were, stuck on the doorstep of a locked village hall in a rapidly worsening shower of rain.

'Shouldn't there be a welcoming committee with offers of accommodation waiting?' complained Suzy, hammering on the green-painted door. 'Really, I'm not used to such shabby treatment.'

More importantly in Kitty's eyes at least, there should have been evidence of the transport with Reg and Co. on board, not to mention all their equipment which had been expected to arrive first. Where were they? The pinch of concern had grown into a knot of cold fear. What if there had been an accident?

'Nor am I accustomed to being kept waiting, I do assure you,' Jacob Warburton was saying, examining his fob watch for the umpteenth time. 'If no one comes soon, I for one will not wait indefinitely.'

Kitty viewed this high-handed attitude with fortitude since these actors wouldn't have agreed to join a new group of travelling players if they'd been at the top of their profession with other, more lucrative, offers of work. Nevertheless she was concerned. To save costs and get everyone on their toes from the start, since it would more often than not be a one-night booking, Kitty had elected not to arrive a day early. Now she regretted that decision, based on optimism that the team would pull together, high on energy due to first-night nerves.

Taking their cue from the two grandees, grumbles

quickly spread amongst the rest of the cast. Only Felicity Fanshaw remained relaxed and silent, leaning against her bicycle which had fortunately survived its journey in the guard's van. 'Probably had a puncture. Motor cars, in my experience, are always breaking down. Bicycles are far more reliable.'

'Yes, of course.' Why hadn't she thought of that? Kitty breathed a sigh of relief. She must simply be patient. In the meantime she could do something about getting them all inside, out of the rain.

Having found the caretaker and gained entry it took less than five minutes to place a table and four chairs on the small, bare platform which stood at the end of the hall, ready for *The Pedlar Woman*, their first one-act play. But they could do little more until the Jowett arrived. Without the fitup, as the whole rig and stage equipment was termed, they couldn't even begin preparations. Not without the curtains and lighting, folding flats, cardboard fireplace, or the trees and bushes they'd so painstaking fashioned from strips of wood and hessian for the Shakespeare. Nor the numerous boxes of costumes.

One or two would-be landladies were already hovering at the door, peeping curiously inside, anxious to see what a real live actor looked like in the flesh. One glimpse told them they were disappointingly similar to everyone else. The next hour was fully taken up with assigning accommodation as several more village ladies drifted in to offer the loan of their spare room in a show of civic pride and duty.

The Players soon discovered that the decision on who was to sleep where was largely in the hands of these good women who insisted on making their own selection, a trait they were to find repeated time and again in the weeks to come. Some would only board females while others took quite the opposite view.

'Oh, no, I do like a man about the house. They're so much easier to please.'

Smothering her giggles, Kitty would watch Rod or Sam being borne away by some motherly matron and wonder whether she should feel pity or envy for the care he would undoubtedly be given.

She arranged digs for Archie and Reg with a whiskery lady who ran the local tea shop, thinking they'd at least be sure of being well fed. Mrs Pips was to stay at the Rectory. Suzy was stationed with the school mistress and Felicity Fanshaw with a dear old lady who promised her currant buns for tea. Kitty, Esme and Charlotte when they arrived, and Tessa Crump, their scatterbrained pianist, were to share a couple of rooms at the home of the church organist who also acted as clerk to the parish council. It had been she who'd made the booking and now informed them that tickets were still being sold at the Post Office, for no one wished to miss the show, not for the world.

'Well, that's a relief at least,' Kitty commented with a smile, half glancing at the door where she imagined she'd caught a flicker of movement that might have been Esme but unfortunately wasn't. 'A show does need an audience.'

By half-past five everyone had gone ahead to their digs save for Kitty herself and Tessa who was attempting to come to grips with an instrument that had clearly stood in that spot since Victoria was a girl. It boasted twin candelabras which, Kitty feared, might be the only lighting they would have for the entire performance if the Jowett didn't arrive soon. And how they would manage without Charlotte, Esme or the two men, she daren't even imagine. She tried to keep her mind off such worries.

'How is it? In tune?'

Tessa grimaced. 'It'll do,' playing a few notes of 'Green Grow the Rushes-O' to prove her point. Kitty pulled a face too, not quite convinced.

By six, even Tessa had drifted away to unpack, change and grab a bite to eat. She'd promised to return with a sandwich for Kitty who steadfastly remained, still sitting on her bag and chewing her nails, anxiously worrying over what she would do if they didn't turn up at all, when she heard the cough of an engine and realised the Jowett had finally arrived.

Tightening her resolve not to make a fuss, since that wouldn't solve anything, she ran out to greet them. All that really mattered, she told herself, was that they were here at last and, if everyone buckled to, might just get the fitup done in time. 'Did you have a terrible journey?' she began and skidded to a halt.

Apart from Esme, who was in floods of tears, the other three were all screaming with laughter and singing at the tops of their voices. 'Dear Lord,' Kitty said, shocked to the core. 'You're drunk.'

The curtains opened on that first night to a packed house with everyone struggling to remember their lines, be in the right place at the right time and become accustomed to unfamiliar surroundings. The set was somewhat has-tily hooked together, the curtains hung slightly wonky and the cardboard fireplace bore no sign of the artificial glow it should contain. The door which Reg had so carefully constructed stuck fast and refused to open, forcing Esme to make her exit by walking around it which brought gales of laughter from the audience. Suzy had to be prompted twice, Rod and Sam were each late for an entrance and Archie missed one altogether. But he was by this time suffering from a thumping headache which Kitty considered he fully deserved.

Reg had been at great pains to express his regret over the ill-fated journey, not once but over and over again, relating the tale at least a dozen times. Apparently they'd suffered not one puncture, but two. On the second occasion while he'd got down to mending the tyre, since they'd already used the spare wheel, the other three had been entertained with parsnip wine provided by a nearby householder. Poor Esme had assumed it to be innocuous enough, since it was home-made, but it had made her rather ill. By the time Reg was done, he too had been persuaded to partake of a glass or two, to 'wet his whistle after all that work', and between them they were soon far gone and completely forgot the time.

'It's a wonder,' he said, 'we didn't end up in a ditch.'

Any further post-mortem into the whys and where-fores had been postponed for it had taken several cups of stewed tea and a good deal of ducking in cold water before any of them were fit to go on stage. Now, as they stumbled through a diabolical performance, there were stifled giggles from other members of the cast, but from

Kitty only a stiff-lipped and ominous silence as she held to her resolve to be patient and forgiving. Though no one was in any doubt that this dammed-up reserve of fury would ultimately explode.

Charlotte, at least, appeared as composed and beautiful as ever and enchanted the audience with her recitations, not to mention a superb and lively performance as Miranda. Even Esme managed to pull herself together and deliver her lines with creditable aplomb, if with exceptional concentration. Despite everything, the show was a huge success. The residents declared they could never remember a more enjoyable evening in the entire history of the village, and the parish clerk instantly booked them for a second occasion later in the year.

Afterwards, several bottles of beer were downed to celebrate their success since everyone was too elated to go to bed, though Archie and the rest of the party from the Jowett opted to stick with lemonade. Rod went out and bought them each a hot meat pie from the cook shop and they all sat in a happy row on the edge of the platform, eating and drinking, laughing and talking all at once.

Despite what had very nearly proved to be a catastrophic start to their tour, to Kitty it suddenly felt like the most perfect night of her life. 'Wasn't it wonderful?' she kept saying, high on euphoria. All her dreams seemed to have come to fruition. The simple glory of hearing an audience roar with laughter in all the right places, be silent and sorrowful when the mood of the play dictated it, and then the heady joy of the tumultuous applause at the end of the performance was more gratifying than she could ever have bargained for. They'd even enjoyed her own play, loudly applauding *The Pedlar*

Woman. 'This is the life. What glorious fun we're going to have.'

She looked about for Archie, ready to share her happy mood and to apologise for being so grumpy with him earlier; though by rights the apologies should be coming from him.

He was standing some way off and although she was perfectly certain that he'd heard her call out his name, he slipped out through the door to vanish into the darkness. Seeing him go, Esme burst into a fresh paroxysm of tears and fled out of the back door in the opposite direction. Whatever was the matter with her? Had Archie hurt her in some way to cause her to react so badly? He was behaving like a child dodging a well-deserved scolding. His complete disregard for punctuality on this, their first night, coupled with no sign of the due apology, served to demolish the last of her patience and the dam of her anger finally burst.

'Where the hell is he off to now? Drat the man!' she yelled. 'I'll not have it.' And jumping down from the platform, Kitty snatched up her coat and marched after him. None of the rest of the company dared move a muscle. She'd reached the door, even had her hand on the iron sneck that held it closed, when the world seemed to shift and tilt and she fainted clean away.

It was Charlotte who insisted on calling in the local doctor and Esme who put her to bed, scolding her gently for allowing her anger to get the better of her. The doctor examined Kitty and coldly gave his opinion that, in view of her condition, she should be in a home for wayward girls; that if she were his daughter she certainly would be. When he had gone the three girls stared at each other in shocked dismay.

Charlotte said, 'Oh, dear. How very cross he sounded. Now we know what you are.'

'A wayward girl,' Kitty agreed. 'My reputation in ribbons. Scarlet ones, no doubt.'

'What would Father's parishioners have said?' Esme murmured on a rare note of dry humour and, despite their differences, they looked into each other's eyes and collapsed in a fit of nervous giggles, rolling about with hoots of laughter as if having a baby out of wedlock were a huge joke and not a moral calamity.

'I'd still prefer this to be our secret, if you don't mind,' Kitty managed, when the paroxysms of mirth had finally subsided.

'Of course, darling,' Charlotte sweetly agreed.

Kitty was up at seven the next day as usual, ignoring Esme's exhortations to take heed of the doctor's advice and rest. 'You can't go on working this hard.'

'But I can and I must,' she said. 'Doesn't the show always have to go on? Besides, I shall have another mouth to feed soon.'

As time went by, if Kitty ever doubted the wisdom of her decision to keep her secret from Archie, or if she became filled with an overwhelming desire to share the miracle of this new life with him, watching Esme sink into gradual despair always managed to curb that need. The girl hardly seemed to touch her food, drifting about half the day in soulful reverie, never hearing when anyone spoke to her, constantly jumping at shadows. As for her performances, she'd had more prompts over these last few nights than throughout the entire tour.

She wasn't the only one to be concerned. Reg confided his worries to Kitty one day, as if he expected her to have a solution at her fingertips.

Everyone saw her as a strong person and that was what she strived to be. But sometimes Kitty could take no more and would snatch an hour or two between rehearsals to walk on the Lakeland hills, hoping the lone cry of the curlew or the soft hues of the heather would bring a solution. In the solitude of the countryside her tears could fall unchecked, and when there were none left to shed she would walk back to their digs and lie awake at night, dry-eyed and sleepless in countless strange beds, only to find the next day that her vibrant energy was entirely lacking and her brain too tired and bemused for her to give a good performance.

With an increasing sense of helplessness, she berated herself for not having spoken to Archie; for not making it clear to him that if he truly loved Esme, she wouldn't stand in his way. Yet day after day she kept making excuses for why she'd failed to do so. Perhaps because she was too afraid of making a fool of herself, for why should she assume he even needed her permission? More likely she didn't speak to him because in her heart of hearts she prayed that Charlotte might be wrong. Deep within her burned a stubborn hope that it was she Archie truly loved, and that one day he would say as much. Until that glorious moment dawned, or perhaps until she summoned up the courage to reveal her condition, Kitty became utterly obsessed with concealing it. She took to wearing flowing skirts and loose tops, adopting a bohemian style of dress which attracted either a teasing jocularity or rare compliments, but thankfully little curiosity.

Esme was the one who helped most by bringing her tea in bed each morning, insisting she rest whenever she could do so without exciting notice from the others.

What was she thinking of, to allow herself to fall into such a state?

They were at the start of a wonderful adventure, the realisation of a dream, and she was putting the entire project in jeopardy simply because she couldn't come to terms with losing a man she'd never had any hope of possessing, nor could find the courage to cut out of her heart completely.

Chapter Twelve

The tour was a resounding success though costs were heavy, the actors alone being paid two guineas a week. On a good night the show might take as much as fifteen pounds, on a bad one little more than a pound.

They learned to perform in all manner of venues and to every size of audience. They played in a delightful little schoolroom in Kirkby Lonsdale where they had to change their costumes in the shop next door. In Keighley the hall was the exact opposite, vast if rather draughty, but the audience had travelled from as far afield as Ilkley to watch them. Sometimes the venue wouldn't have electricity and they'd have to use their acetylene lamps or perhaps resort to candles in tins, praying they didn't set fire to the place. Once they performed in a freezing barn right in the middle of a farmer's field with the sound of cows lowing noisily from adjoining stalls.

Whatever the difficulties, once the show was under way, the atmosphere became thick with excitement. Everybody loved to be entertained. It was always the audience who made it all worthwhile yet each one was different. Some would relish every joke, roaring with laughter from start to finish. Others would be quieter, more thoughtful. The audience in Barrow-in-Furness, for instance, had consisted chiefly of miners who sat polite and quiet throughout, yet their applause at the end proved their enthusiastic response.

Throughout the cold short days of November and early-December as the LTPs continued their progress through the towns and villages of Lakeland, Yorkshire and Lancashire, Charlotte observed with pleased satis-faction how Archie barely exchanged a word with Kitty beyond what was essential for the smooth running of the show. He seemed to go out of his way to avoid her and the tension between the two old friends grew day by day.

Even so she took no chances. Charlotte took care to add fuel to the disappointment he felt in Kitty. Should he ever cast lingering glances in the stupid girl's direc-tion, Charlotte would point out how she was racketing through some task or other without even consulting any-one else's opinion or stopping to think for five minutes. And, most important of all, she would remind him of Kitty's hypocrisy and lack of morals, so that his mouth would tighten with fresh disapproval.

Archie's doleful mood affected everyone. Esme too seemed to be on the brink of despair half the time, poor girl, her eyes following his every move with a pitiful misery, rather like a pathetic dog begging for a titbit from its master.

Indeed, matters were proceeding entirely to plan. All Charlotte need do now was to crush the last vestige of hope which might still be lingering in either of them. She must make it quite clear that the current state of affairs was permanent. Perhaps it was due to her particularly devious mind, or this special gift she had for divining the secrets people believed they'd kept well hidden, but manipulating them all into behaving as she wished was proving to be remarkably simple. And highly entertaining.

She began with Esme.

It was the last week of the tour and Kitty was scolding Charlotte, as usual, for coming down late for breakfast.

'Esme has hardly touched hers. I'll grab a slice of toast and a cuppa while she finishes it. We'll be over in ten minutes. Promise.' She knew that Kitty was most anxious for Esme to eat properly.

'See that you are.'

The others went off with Kitty to rehearse in the local schoolroom where their final performance was to be held that very night. When the landlady disappeared back into the kitchen, Charlotte grabbed the opportunity to enquire, in a sympathetic, woman to woman sort of way, if Archie had yet declared himself. She tutted sorrowfully when Esme shook her head and confessed that he hadn't, not in so many words. 'He seems to be ignoring me completely these days.'

'I did try,' Charlotte assured her, smiling sadly through the lie. 'I made it abundantly clear that you would not repel his advances. Give him time. It's never easy to bring men to the point and he's probably suffering terrible guilt after having let Kitty down by getting drunk on the first night.'

'I'm not at all concerned,' Esme said, the pallor of her face showing otherwise. She longed for Archie to utter those magic words, for him to speak of his love for her.

Instead he seemed hardly to notice that she was around. 'I'm being stupid, I know. I dare say if it were you, you'd give him the glad eye or whatever you call it. You'd know how to encourage him.'

'And you can't bring yourself to do that?' Charlotte gently enquired, and had to struggle to hide her elation when Esme pulled off her spectacles and began to rub them quite vigorously on a corner of her jumper. 'Too shy, eh? Even though you've known him all these years? Well, would you believe it? Never mind, mebbe that's why you can't. Because you know him a bit too well.'

Esme looked up at her and frowned. 'Do you think so? Do you think that might be why Archie never quite tells me how he feels?'

'By Heckmondwyke, it might well be. Now why didn't I think of that?' Ye Gods, Charlotte thought, this was all getting amazingly convoluted. And almost wished she'd never started down this road. But then she remembered her plan. All she had to do was follow her instincts.

'There wouldn't be any other reason he'd hang back, would there?' she casually enquired. 'I mean, that time we were on our way home from the flicks and we were sharing secrets, talking about parsons and – well – *you know, IT*, and you went all coy. Well, I did wonder if there was something . . .' And seeing Esme's cheeks turn crimson Charlotte dropped her piece of toast and put a hand to her mouth as if in shock, but actually to disguise the burst of satisfaction which shot through her. She'd hit the jackpot yet again. It must take her sort of twisted mind to work these things out. 'Oh, heck, me and my big mouth,' she said with mock concern. 'That's it, isn't it? You poor bugger.'

Esme stared at her, wide-eyed and appalled. 'You mustn't say anything. No one must know. He meant nothing by it.'

''Course he didn't. No man does. Nay, don't worry about me knowing. Had a few problems in that department myself over the years.' Charlotte put out a consoling hand to pat Esme's shoulder. 'My stepfather was a shocker too when he was drunk. I want you to know, love, that whatever that parson father of yours did, your secret's safe with me. I'd never tell a living soul, particularly Archie.' And there it was, just handed to her on a plate nice as ninepence, exactly what she needed to block Esme's path for good and all. 'Wouldn't be safe in the circumstances, now would it?'

Esme had replaced her spectacles and was staring at Charlotte, bewildered. 'Safe? I don't quite understand what . . .'

'Hell's teeth, nobody knows men better than me, chuck. And there's one thing they hate above all else.'

'What's that?' Esme was almost breathless with her need to understand even a half of what seemed so obvious to Charlotte. Archie and she had once been such good friends, more than friends you might say, yet despite everyone assuring her that he cared, he barely glanced her way any more. He seemed completely locked up in himself, and possibly Charlotte. It didn't occur to her that he might be behaving in this way with Kitty and Charlotte too, that the problem might lie elsewhere, perhaps even within his own flawed nature. To Esme, with her low self-esteem, if something went wrong, then it must be she who was to blame for it and not those who were brighter and cleverer than she. This fact had been made clear to her from a very early age. Obedience and duty were all, self-worth was nothing. The inconsistencies of men, of life itself, were a puzzle to her, filled as each was with strange emotions and conflicting signals, all seemingly at odds with each other.

Charlotte was looking at her with the kind of pity in her eyes that filled Esme with the sudden, cold realisation that she might not care for what she was about to hear. Nevertheless, if her more experienced friend could shed some light upon these mysteries, then it would surely be to her benefit to learn. 'Tell me, Charlotte. I need to know.'

'Men don't like tarnished goods, d'you see, love? They only like them what's untouched by human hand. Not that they'd be against taking advantage of any girl what gave them half a chance, you understand.' She winked broadly. 'But they'd never tek such a girl home to mother, as it were, let alone down the aisle. Not one that had been – spoiled – in any way. D'you see?'

And now Esme understood perfectly why Archie had not declared himself. She was one of those girls, cheap and worthless. Her father had known it, and so had Archie. It was really all her own fault.

Charlotte was noting with satisfaction the way Esme's skin had gone a muddy grey colour. Twisting a smile of satisfaction into one of complicity, she tapped the side of her nose. 'Not a word, eh? Let's hope he hasn't heard any rumours because what a chap don't know, won't hurt him. He'll hear nowt from me. I'll not queer your pitch.' And congratulating herself on a task well done, Charlotte retired to her room where she took an envelope, already stamped and addressed, from out of a secret pocket in her suitcase. Then, with a jaunty lilt to her step, she walked along to the village Post Office and dropped it into the post box.

And that should settle Madam Kitty.

On this, the last night of the tour, the show did not go well. Esme's performance was dire. Her depression was now so complete, her introspection so deep, that her level of concentration had fallen to an all-time low. She came on stage without an essential piece of property and had to go off again to fetch it. Then she started to say lines from the wrong play, ever a fear since they performed scenes from two or three at a time. In consequence she lost the drift entirely, panicked, and failing to hear Suzy madly prompting in the corner, completely dried. She stood frozen on stage, shaking with terror, while Kitty was obliged to précis all of her speeches in order to clarify the scene for the bemused audience.

Once off-stage, before Kitty had a chance to offer a consoling word, Esme fled to the dressing room in floods of tears where she locked herself away for hours. Kitty knocked on the door, Charlotte gave her a brisk talking to and Reg pleaded with her through the keyhole, all to no avail. All they could hear were great gulping sobs. Even Archie failed to shift her.

'Come on, old thing,' he calmly informed the closed door. 'Everyone else has gone home. If you don't come out soon, we'll have to call out the dratted fire brigade, don't you know. And what if they get it wrong and squirt us all with water, thinking we're on fire, eh? We'd be the soggiest actors in the history of the theatre.' But the door remained firmly closed, his wit failing to have any effect.

It was Suzy who finally persuaded Esme out, with her motherly warmth. She gathered her close in a swathe of silk wraps, cheap scent and sticky greasepaint, then bore her off for a nip of something warming. 'Which is sure to do the trick, darling girl. Then it's a good rest for us all.'

Christmas was upon them and, satisfied at a job well done, the company was looking forward to a couple of weeks' rest with their families before the start of rehearsals for the second tour. There would be new plays, new parts to learn, each member of the cast hoping there might be a good one for them. For now they went off happy and content, with a lively buzz about them born from a tired sort of excitement.

Charlotte too went home to her 'ailing mother' feeling quite certain that it was safe to leave Archie, Esme and Kitty alone since their close-knit relationship was now fractured beyond repair. And it seemed she was right.

The one-time triumvirate of friends ate a delicious turkey dinner with all the trimmings, but there was a distance between them, a stilted quality to their conversation, and most evenings found them all in their respective beds by nine. Mrs Pips, who'd cooked and served to the best of her ability, became increasingly disturbed by the odd behaviour of her dear charges. Something was going on that she couldn't quite put her finger on but she'd get to the bottom of it, oh, dear, yes, if the happiness of her boy was concerned. She attempted to jolly them into playing cards or backgammon, fondly describing it as a peaceful rather than a merry Yuletide. 'A time for resting and recuperating and going for long walks. That's what you all need. You've all worked far too hard.'

The weather was certainly perfect for walking. The air had become dry and utterly still, the days short while the nights were hard with frost. Even the sounds of the lake seemed muted as its waters flowed more sluggishly while ice formed around the edges, cracking and creaking like snapped twigs. A few powdery flakes of snow fell, crusting the tops of the fells like frosted icing on a cake, and they all realised that if temperatures dropped still further, there could well be a blizzard. Great swathes of snow would then blanket the land and lanes alike, which could well put paid to their next tour. This was due to begin in about three weeks' time and the possibility of not being able to travel and meet their commitments was a constant worry.

Kitty spent most evenings in her room, writing or blocking out moves on bits of paper, ready for when rehearsals started next week, which all proved to be good therapy. Even so, more personal concerns kept intruding upon her thoughts.

What should she do about Esme, whose depression was now deeply alarming? Kitty wondered if perhaps the problem lay with their pact, made for the best of reasons but beginning to create a barrier to their friendship. Perhaps Esme came to the same conclusion for the next day she approached Kitty and announced that her depression had been caused by her own foolish obsession with Archie. She'd come to realise now that it was all a mistake.

'If it were truly me he loved, he'd have said so by now. He's had ample opportunity after all. Perhaps I don't even love him. Perhaps it was all a silly schoolgirl crush, an illusion. Anyway, I want you to know that I release you from our pact. Let's put an end to it. I always did think you should be his choice, Kitty, so you're free to have him. Go and tell Archie what you feel.'

Kitty could hardly believe her ears. 'Oh, Esme. I don't know what to say.'

'Don't say anything to *me*. Say it to Archie. That was our agreement, remember, to give each other a chance. I've had mine, now it's every woman for herself.'

'But we'll stay friends?'

'Of course.'

Then Kitty was laughing and hugging her and crying, all at the same time.

It was the next evening after supper, when Kitty was helping Archie bring in more logs, that she decided to take her chance. Esme had gone to bed early and for once the two of them were alone. It was bitterly cold, with a sharp frost glistening upon drystone walls lit by the light of a full moon. The panoply of surrounding hills loomed eerily ghostlike above them, the silence so complete that Kitty felt it might snap like glass. Or like her frayed nerves.

Not that he was making it easy for her. He seemed ever more withdrawn of late, as if entirely preoccupied with his own thoughts, living in another world. What would he say? How would he react to the prospect of becoming a father? His attitude lately had switched constantly from adult petulance to boyish charm, so she didn't know what to expect. If only she could win from him a declaration of undying love *before* she told him. Then she would know that he wanted her for herself and not simply out of duty.

But he'd hurt her by his stubborn neglect these last weeks, hurt Esme too, and she couldn't quite let that go unchallenged. Her back was aching and she'd much rather be snuggled down in her own warm bed but then, if she gave up now, she might never find the courage to tell him at all. 'This miserable Christmas has all been your fault.' She tossed the words at him, rather as she did the logs into the basket, stamping her booted feet in an effort to keep warm as she waited for his response.

'Is this another lecture?' Archie mildly enquired, though his voice, she noted, was almost as cold and hard as the weather. 'I rather thought I'd escaped one, since you've been avoiding me for weeks.'

'*Me* avoiding *you*! Huh! Rather the other way around.'

He leaned on the door jamb and watched her struggle, as if at a loss to know what to believe or how to deal with the matter. He thought she looked pale, not at all her normal self, but nor for that matter was Esme which in her case he put down to the stress of the tour. Unless it was all due to moods. But then feminine matters were largely a mystery to him. Far too tedious and complicated. Quite beyond any mere male.

Charlotte was far easier to understand, a woman influenced by her sensual and physical needs rather than emotion. Nor did she have Kitty's obstinate determination to be a 'modern woman'. Charlotte wasn't feisty and difficult but vulnerable and fragile, passionate and exciting. He almost salivated with pleasure at the memory of their nights together. But she could be surprisingly sensitive too. She'd been desperately upset to shatter his illusions over Kitty, his dearest friend.

Women were utterly incomprehensible to him. Delicious. Adorable. To be enjoyed, of course, but never taken too seriously as they could so rarely be understood. He must take care, though, how he dealt with Kitty. Even now she was glaring at him with apparently murderous intent and, as always when overtired, becoming ever more quarrelsome. 'I'm still waiting for that apology.'

'Apology for what?'

'For being drunk in charge of a Jowett for a start, not to mention running the risk of killing yourself as well as ruining our first night.' Why on earth was she fussing about that now? she asked herself.

Archie asked much the same question, though he seemed entirely unconcerned at being reminded of his indiscretion. Raking long fingers through his thick dark curls, he simply sighed, 'Lord, didn't set out to be late, Kitty old thing. What of it? Relax. No harm done, eh?'

How she hated to be told to relax! Esme had been saying much the same for weeks now. Oh, if only she didn't feel so guilty about Esme. It was one thing to agree that the pact had been abandoned, quite another to banish it completely from her mind. 'No harm done? Except to my nerves.'

She tried to pick up the basket of logs but found it too heavy. Annoyed with herself, Kitty began to unload some into her already aching arms, acutely aware of Archie standing by, saying nothing, merely watching her with a half smile on his handsome face. It made her irritation with him flare all the more, despite her best intentions to remain calm. 'It could've been a disaster. You could all have ended up in a ditch. Not to mention almost ruining the show.'

'No one noticed anything wrong at all.'

'The audience certainly noticed you tottering on with that silly grin on your face, apologising for missing your cue and nearly falling over the footlights.'

He laughed out loud at the memory. 'That was rather a hoot. I felt certain I would end up in the lap of that very large lady in the front row.'

At one time she might have laughed with him. Tonight his phlegmatic approach to life, his flippancy in addition to her own delicate condition and the inner war she was fighting over grasping happiness for herself at Esme's expense, made Kitty stubbornly refuse to weaken. 'Don't you dare laugh. It isn't a game. There's a good deal of money involved.'

'I realise that, dear heart.' Archie judiciously changed his tone to coolly matter-of-fact, that of a business partner discussing the state of trade. Still he made no move to help with the logs. 'Much of it mine, I seem to recall.' He noticed that for some reason this infuriated Kitty all the more and, better still, found that he really didn't care. He certainly had no intention of being emotionally bullied.

'It wasn't *our* money I was thinking of, neither yours nor mine. I was thinking of the ticket money the audience pay to be entertained by a load of *half-cut amateurs*. And I'm not your dear heart!' Oh, but how she wished that she was. Tears starting into her eyes, Kitty snatched up an extra log, desperately struggling to balance it on top of the armful she already carried. She'd almost managed this impossible feat when her foot slid on the frozen ground and the whole pile toppled from her arms. Shock jarred through her, swiftly followed by a jolt of fear as she landed heavily. Lord, had she hurt the baby?

Archie was beside her in a second, lifting her up, asking if she was all right while scolding her in a surprisingly tetchy manner. 'You've been doing far too much lately and you really shouldn't. Not in your current state of health.'

Kitty had been about to shake herself free from his hold. Instead she stared up at him, mouth open in shock. 'My current . . .'

Now he was smiling at her, shaking his head as if at a naughty child. 'You should have told me yourself but it's all right, Kitty, I know about the baby.' His tone was soft, conciliatory.

'What?'

'I'll admit it knocked me for six at first when Charlotte told me. A nice girl like you – getting in such a fix. But I can understand how . . .'

'*Charlotte* told you?'

He knew that he must choose his words with care, and he did. 'Don't be cross with her for splitting on you. She's concerned, that's all. We both are. Esme too, I warrant, though we haven't discussed it and I swear no one else knows yet. These things happen in the best of circles. I'm sure everything will work out for you. Just requires a few adjustments, eh?'

She couldn't quite take in what he was saying, started

to brush his hands away as if anxious to stave off his pity, and then it dawned on her that he *knew*, perhaps had known for weeks, and yet had said *nothing*. *Why hadn't he?* Red hot fury rushed through her as Kitty struggled clumsily to her feet, absolutely refused to be carried and marched furiously into the house. Finding herself still holding a log, she tossed it on to the fire in a final declaration of independence, causing a shower of sparks to fly up the chimney. Wasn't it just like him to leave her to stew? Probably thought it all a grand joke. He really was far too careless for words. 'Why do you always have to make such an *ass* of yourself? Mooning over Charlotte half the time, *and* you've hurt Esme.'

Kitty was aware that he'd kicked shut the door but her heart was beating so fast she didn't dare turn around to check. He dropped the basket by the hearth. 'Esme? Was she sitting on the front row too?'

This was too much and Kitty turned upon him in a fury. 'Can't you *ever* take anything seriously?'

'Why should I? Life's too dashed short, don't you know.' He began to unbutton her coat, smoothed one hand over the curve of her stomach as he drew her close. How she excited him when she was in a tantrum. She became utterly irresistible. Even the glorious Charlotte paled into insignificance beside Kitty when she was in a rage. 'Don't be cross, old sport. I'd much rather we were friends again, like we used to be. What d'you say? Come to the fire. Let me warm you. There are far better things we could be doing while we still have the chance. Before real life closes in, eh?'

His fingers were sliding beneath her blouse now, seeking her ripe breasts, and Kitty thought he meant because of her pregnancy. His touch set her on fire and she gazed up at him, utterly enraptured, repeating to herself the astonishing fact that he knew, *and didn't seem to mind*.

'Drat you, Archie Emerson! You're utterly impossible.'

'Amoral is perhaps a better word, darling.'

'And selfish and stubborn and . . .' But her protest was weak, the tone softly caressing, for, oh, didn't she want him? Didn't she need him to love her?

He made love to her there and then on the faded Persian rug before the blazing fire, stripping off her clothes with eager hands, allowing her no time to think as he took her with a swift and dominating insistence. Kitty barely had time to cry out her delight before it was over. He gently scolded her, silencing her with more kisses, reminding her that Mrs Pips was in the housekeeper's room above, and Esme not too far away.

Afterwards he whispered that this should remain their secret. Again thinking of the baby and dazed with love for him, Kitty readily agreed. Besides, how could she bear the guilt of witnessing Esme's jealousy if she ever learned they'd become lovers? She still had to break it to Esme that the child she carried was Archie's. For all their pact was now at an end, some instinct warned her to tread softly on her friend's sensibilities.

It was the following morning and Kitty was returning from one of her long walks over Claife Heights when she saw two familiar figures walking towards her from the direction of the house. One of them was Archie and she waved to him. She'd been humming happily to herself as her boots crunched over iced puddles and crisp bracken, dreaming and making delicious little plans about weddings and celebrations. She gave a little skip of pleasure as she hurried to meet him, and then realised who the other man was. Kitty skidded to a halt, hardly able to believe her eyes.

'What on earth are you doing here?' Frank looked just the same: thinning hair slicked flat to his head, black shiny suit, tie too tightly knotted.

'You didn't imagine I'd ever forget you, duchess, did you?' She'd rather hoped he might. Kitty gritted her teeth even as she smilingly offered him her hand. Frank grasped her by the shoulders and gave her a resounding kiss. 'I think I'm worth more than that, don't you?'

While she surreptitiously wiped the kiss away, feeling suddenly bemused about why he was there and how in fact he'd found her, Archie's voice boomed out in its jovial way. 'Was going to leave it to you, old thing, to break the good tidings but dropped one too many hints, I'm afraid. No harm done, though. Frank's jolly pleased. Rather fancies the prospect of fatherhood, don't you, old chap?' And he slapped the grinning Frank on the back.

Kitty stared at Archie in stunned disbelief as the truth slowly dawned. He hadn't realised the baby was his at all. He'd thought it was Frank's.

1914

Chapter Thirteen

The people of Lakeland took the LTPs to their hearts. The Players travelled the length and breadth of the north, from the mill towns of Lancashire where the factory girls shrieked with laughter, to the dales of Westmorland and Cumberland, Yorkshire and beyond. Without question they were a success, for all they hadn't found it easy. During the year since that momentous first tour, any number of village halls, schoolrooms, repertory theatres, and even one or two seaside pavilions, had been granted the pleasure of a show from the LTPs. With all the unease over the situation in Ireland and trouble in the Balkans, 'going to a show' was a welcome and cheap diversion. The wind might blow, rain, hail or snow might cloud the Lakeland skies, but if the LTPs had a booking, no matter what the weather they would be there as promised and the show would go on.

On this winter's night early in 1914 they were in Kendal at the St George's Hall, in rehearsal with *Cinderella*. This was their own version, written and produced by Kitty herself. For much of the year even this famous theatre was now proud to be known as one of the finest picture houses in the north. But for a few weeks it was once again given over to live theatre. A professional company, currently in the middle of its annual run of Shakespeare, had agreed to take a week's break so the LTPs could present a pantomime for the townsfolk.

Draughts cut through the empty auditorium from every direction. Esme was wearing her coat as she worked on a new backcloth; even so her hands felt stiff with cold. She and Reg, now official stage manager, had spent hours slapping size on to the hessian cloth in order to stiffen it, followed by yet another missed night's sleep painting it so that it would be ready for first night tomorrow. Reg had chalked out the grid pattern into which Esme sketched the outline, gradually building up a picture of a ballroom. After that it had simply been a question of filling in the squares with the appropriate coloured paint. It was laborious and painstaking work since there were only the two of them. Reg was a bit slapdash but Esme had come to enjoy working with him. They made a good team.

Ever since her disastrous performance on the last night of that first tour, she'd confined herself to backstage work, for which she'd proved to have quite a talent. It certainly provided ample opportunities to be alone with her lover for many intimate moments in some shadowy corner.

The company had all tried to persuade her to continue with her acting. Jacob had related countless horror stories of his own, one of losing his wig when playing in *The Rivals*. Suzy told of the night her voice had vanished completely and Tessa Crump promised to play the piano very loudly if ever Esme should forget her lines in future.

All to no avail. Even Kitty's more practical suggestion that she have extra private rehearsals was not taken up. Esme had, in short, lost her nerve.

'Now all we have to do is slide the chain into the bottom hem to weight it.'

'Slave driver,' Reg said, wiping his brow. 'Pity we don't have a giant darning needle.'

Esme playfully punched him and got down on her knees, chain in hand. 'We'll pull it through with wire and a long stick. Idiot!'

'I wish I'd got a big darning needle to stitch us two together. That'd be grand. I'd be a happy man to go through life with the pair of us all sewn up.'

'Reg, I've warned you before about those fantasies of yours,' Esme scolded, but she was smiling. He was a predictable if unexciting man, kind and caring, never taking liberties but patiently hoping for her to give him the word to take their relationship further. Esme tolerated these constant hints of his faithful devotion with warm good humour, for all she'd no intention of ever succumbing to his charms. For Reg was not her secret lover. Archie was.

There had been a time when she'd imagined she'd lost him but one glorious pink and green spring afternoon he had come to her and they'd made love, just as wondrously as that first time by the lake. Since then Esme had grown and blossomed. The youthful plumpness had fine-tuned to more slender lines, which Archie described as sweetly pretty. She was no longer a child but a woman.

Esme believed he could easily have chosen Charlotte for her greater beauty, or Kitty with her dignified loveliness and driving efficiency. Instead he preferred herself, a plain and dull little mouse. For this reason she was perfectly satisfied that he loved her, as much as Archie was capable of loving anyone, but didn't expect or ask anything of him. Not duty, commitment or marriage, any more than she craved either excitement or fame. Charlotte's warning, coupled with Archie's attitude in the early days of their relationship, had made a deep impression upon her. Esme saw herself as a ruined woman and was more than grateful for whatever he was prepared to offer.

Not that any hint of their affair must ever be revealed. Kitty, as her dearest friend, was of course aware that Esme still adored Archie but had no idea they were lovers. No one must know. It was their own delicious secret. He preferred to keep their private life just that. Entirely private. And for all that the foolish pact was over, Esme agreed with him. She was rather a private person too.

So, in the circumstances, she was more than content to leave the accolades for acting to Charlotte, Kitty and the other members of the group. Didn't they deserve it? Charlotte in particular gloried in the fame the LTPs had brought her, parading about in fashionably exotic costumes so that no one would be in any doubt she was a famous actress. While Esme, being a stage hand, took no trouble at all over her appearance, usually opting, as she had today, for a pair of Reg's old dungarees. Finding her splattered with paint or glue was so common an occurrence the company didn't expect to see her any other way. Certainly Archie didn't mind. That was a pet name he had for her. His 'little ragamuffin'.

'It's ready to fly,' she called now, tying the last tape that fastened the finished backcloth on to its baton. This moment always excited her: seeing the results of their handiwork *in situ*. It took both their combined strength on the pulley to hoist the painted ballroom scene up into place. 'To think we'll have to drop and haul that thing back up into the flies every night,' she gasped, rubbing her aching arms.

'I could manage it on my own. It's too heavy for you in any case.'

'And let you take all the credit. No fear!' And they grinned at each other, in perfect accord.

'It looks grand. You should be stage manager, Esme, not me. You're so talented. I'm just a pair of strong hands.'

'For goodness' sake, you're always putting yourself down. Don't!' And she beamed at him as if she would never dream of doing anything so foolish, trying not to notice the gratitude in his eyes. 'Come on, we've work to do.'

Their main difficulty, as always, lay in creating a set in the limited time in which they had access to the stage. Erecting the fitup, curtains and lights at speed had become second nature to them; pantomime, however, was technically more demanding, requiring trickery such as wires, special lighting effects, flashes and painted backcloths. Not to mention the harlequinade where magical scenes, transformations or gauzes were involved.

'It won't do.'

The familiar voice at her elbow made Esme swing about, annoyed by the unexpected interruption. 'I beg your pardon?'

Charlotte was looking as glamorous as ever, from the tip of her ridiculous flower pot hat with its spiky feather, through the extravagantly pleated, magenta silk dress with its hobble skirt so narrow at the hem she could hardly walk in her tiny pointed shoes. She looked as if she were dressed for a cocktail party rather than a rehearsal. 'There are too many shadows.'

'We haven't got all the lights in place yet.'

'And we need more depth. When I walk down the staircase in my ball gown – I assume it will be a *wide* staircase? – I have to make an impact. So, either you move the cloth back a couple of feet, or we'll need an apron at the front. Preferably both.'

'For God's sake, Charlotte, it's the Dress tonight. We haven't time to start rehanging backcloths, let alone construct an apron,' Reg protested. 'In any case, this is one of the biggest stages we've ever performed on, so where's the problem?'

'I insist,' she said, flicking a pair of gloves agitatedly into one hand over and over to emphasise her point, 'it simply *will – not – do*! The colours are too dark and splodged all over the place. Either repaint it, move it or take it down this instant.'

Tight-lipped, Esme retained her patience with difficulty. It was ever so in discussions with Charlotte. 'We'll let Kitty decide, shall we?'

'What must I decide?'

The next hour turned into one of those hellish arguments the company had grown used to over the months. In so many ways they'd come together almost like a family, Jacob and Tessa Crump taking the parental roles, respectively doling out advice or aspirins, whether asked for or not. Rod and Sam, along with other young people who joined the Players from time to time, as the mischievous, bright young things. Esme and Kitty two hardworking, independent young women. Archie standing slightly apart, the languid young hero, quiet and somewhat enigmatic. And Reg, Esme's loyal and most stalwart supporter.

'Which leaves Suzy Grant and Felicity Fanshaw as a pair of maidenly aunts who act like sisters but aren't quite,' Kitty had once declared when she and Esme had giggled over this notion one night after too many glasses of wine.

There was of course one other member of the Lakes Players, perhaps the most important so far as Kitty was concerned. This was Dixie, her darling baby daughter.

Dixie had caused quite a stir when she'd arrived on scene back in April 1913, not least because her mother was not married, never had been, nor seemed to have any intention of becoming an honest, respectable woman.

At the time of Dixie's birth one or two well-meaning people had hinted she should be adopted or put into an orphanage. Kitty had shown complete outrage at both suggestions. From the moment she set eyes on her, Kitty was entirely enslaved. Dixie belonged to her and always would.

But the decision had resulted in a certain notoriety, and from time to time scandalous comments would appear in some local newspaper or other, wherever the group happened to be performing. Her name, always *Miss* Kitty Little, would be prefixed by such adjectives as *infamous*, *outrageous* or even *disreputable*. She was considered something of a social pariah in the bohemian gypsy dresses and trailing scarves which had become her accepted mode of dress. Kitty ignored them all and usually the furore died down after a while. It didn't seem in any way to harm their takings at the door, rather the reverse. She was certain people came to see her as much as the play.

Admittedly takings had fallen off a bit lately but Kitty put that down to competition from the new rage for cinema. Available theatres were becoming an increasing rarity and posters needed to proclaim that their show was live to encourage people to come. It wouldn't last, everyone said so. Cinema was no more than a fad. Live theatre would always prevail.

At nearly nine months, Dixie was a contented baby who loved nothing better than to sit in her pram and watch proceedings with surprising alertness, when she wasn't crawling about the stage getting under everybody's feet. She possessed an impish grin, pale auburn hair and the most enchanting chocolate brown eyes, very like Kitty's own, fringed by dark lashes. She was hugely adored, properly if unconventionally cared for and thoroughly spoiled by all members of the company. Already she'd appeared in several plays as a babe in arms and would no doubt soon be treading the boards wherever a child actor was called for just the moment she'd found her feet, which wasn't far off. She was treated as a sort of mascot, always managing to lift spirits if someone had 'the glums', and so far as Kitty was concerned, the identity of her child's father was nobody's business but her own. Let them speculate as they wished.

It never ceased to amaze her that Frank was still here, hanging on to her like the proverbial limpet.

'Saw a piece about the LTPs in a local paper,' he'd glibly informed her when she'd asked how, exactly, he'd found her. 'It gave all the details of your latest tour. What an adventure! So I thought, why not pop up north and join you?'

'How's Ma?' she'd asked, accepting his explanation without question.

Clara, it seemed, was well, having found herself a new young man; the third, apparently, since that fateful night. Frank doubted this one would hang around any longer than the others. Kitty couldn't help but smile. Her mother Clara was a survivor, albeit one who would lurch from one man to another all her life, each of them far too young and entirely unsuitable. Why could she never simply be herself? Vowing not to make the same mistake, Kitty decided she was probably wise to remain single.

Frank had proved surprisingly sanguine about the generally held belief that Dixie was his child. Not once had he refuted the rumour, though he could easily have done so, choosing instead to use it as a means to make further attempts to persuade her into marriage. His efforts in that direction had so far proved fruitless, a state of affairs upon which Kitty held firm.

Even if she didn't have Clara to warn her of the unreliability of love, since that terrible Christmas when Archie had been only too ready to wear blinkers and shift the blame on to Frank, despite having been prepared to enjoy the favours she offered, Kitty was even more determined to depend upon no one but herself. Men were not to be trusted. She was and would remain, in every way, her own woman.

Sadly, for all these good intentions, she didn't love him any the less. Archie's relationship with Dixie was cordial enough but Kitty often wondered how he would react if he learned the truth: that *he* was Dixie's father, not Frank. Perhaps it was partly hurt pride but she stubbornly clung to the hope that one day, against all odds, he might suffer a change of heart. Then she could confess and they would live happily ever after.

The next instant she would scold herself for nurturing such fanciful notions, for how dare she even consider her own happiness at the expense of poor Esme, who seemed destined to be a victim? She'd clearly been ill used by her father, lost her ability to act and struggled through a severe bout of depression from which she'd miraculously surfaced into some sort of contentment over recent months. Kitty put this all down to Reg's influence, and hoped and prayed they would one day find true happiness together.

As for her own, that must lie with the LTPs. The company was her life and, in the main, worked well. There were occasions, however, when all might seem happy and chummy during the performance on stage when in reality nerves would fray, tensions mount and tantrums become a frequent hazard in the wings.

This crisis ended, as they so often did, with Charlotte bursting into furious tears and claiming everyone disliked her, which was probably true, and that nobody understood her, which certainly wasn't true at all. Understanding Charlotte was remarkably simple; living with her day in and day out was the hard part. She considered herself to be the self-appointed focal point, the star in this firmament of jobbing actors. In Charlotte's own opinion, she was the sole reason for the success of the Lakeland Travelling Players.

She remained in a sulk at the technical run through prior to the full dress rehearsal. Her acting was wooden, her mouth in a perpetual pout, and she kept stopping every few minutes to complain about the lighting, the set, the script or the other actors. Anything and everything. She was, in short, the most miserably uncoordinated Cinderella Kitty had ever seen.

'Turn *into* the audience, Charlotte, not away from them. You should know that by now. And, for goodness' sake, *smile*! The children are more likely to go home weeping instead of happy after such a diabolical performance.'

Charlotte stormed to the front of the stage, hands on hips, to glare across the footlights at Kitty's unseen figure in the darkness. 'How can I smile, or turn in the right direction, when Felicity is under my feet the whole time? For pity's sake, can't anyone remember their damn' moves?'

Kitty sighed. There was really little point in a slanging match at this point in the proceedings. 'Let's all have a cuppa then go straight into the Dress, shall we?'

From then on the situation deteriorated rapidly and everything that could go wrong did. Tessa couldn't unlock the piano and had to run back to their digs where she'd left the sheet music. When she did finally get going with the song and dance routines, Charlotte complained she was in too high a key. Jacob, as Cinderella's father, missed his first entrance and was found wallowing in self-pity, whisky bottle in hand, slumped in the green room. He had to be thoroughly doused with cold water and black coffee to rouse him back into action. Rod and Sam, who were playing the Ugly Sisters, took far too long in make-up, and the costume Felicity had hoped to wear as principal boy didn't fit.

'I've put pounds on since last Christmas. Oh, fizz!' she mourned.

Too late to point out that it should have been tried on earlier, or even that a diet might have been a good idea, for within twenty-four hours they would hopefully be playing to a packed house.

The audience, however, on that first night, was decidedly thin. For once the weather seemed to have beaten them. Outside a veritable blizzard raged, snow building up in drifts against the stage door.

'We're done for. Nobody will come out in this,' Archie moaned gloomily.

'That's right, cheer us all up,' Kitty said, coming to stand beside him at the open door and gazing upon a scene of fairy-tale whiteness. 'So far we've an audience of fourteen, not counting the caretaker.'

'This'll finish us, Kitty. We've not been doing as well as we should lately and pantomimes are fiercely expensive to put on. If we don't get a good audience this week, we could end up with a serious loss.'

'Let's not think the unthinkable, shall we?' Determined to remain buoyant, she stepped out into the road to check if a queue was forming. It wasn't. She shivered, rubbed her hands up and down her arms to warm them then walked back inside, closing the door against a blast of icy wind. 'It's early yet. How's Charlotte?' she brightly enquired. 'Feeling more relaxed?'

Archie's face was expressionless as he assured Kitty that she seemed perfectly recovered. They both knew this to be untrue. Charlotte was becoming an increasing worry to them all, constantly flying into a rage for no apparent reason, or playing the primadonna and seeming to revel in making everyone's lives a misery. But the faintest hint of criticism about her irascibility and Archie would spring to her defence, citing first-night nerves or the difficulties of a childhood which still haunted her. As he was the only one who could get any work out of her, it was quite impossible to oppose such arguments.

Jacob appeared at that moment, loudly complaining of a poor House and begging Kitty to forgive him for his unspeakably unprofessional behaviour at the Dress. 'Gone on the wagon now. Won't fall off it. Honest injun.'

Laughing and shaking her head in despair and disbelief, she hugged him, a feat in itself in view of his increasing girth. 'I have every faith in you.'

Jacob's predilection for imbibing 'Dutch courage' in order to counteract his stage fright was beginning to be quite a problem, too. Archie merely smiled and said nothing, as usual. 'However small the audience is tonight, once they've seen Rod and Sam as the funniest Ugly Sisters ever, not to mention our delightful chorus of nymphs and shepherdesses, they'll spread the word around town and everyone will come in droves tomorrow and for the rest of the week. See if they don't.'

Jacob stuck his thumbs in the pockets of his yellow checked waistcoat and grumbled that the dancing was too *avant-garde* for his taste.

Usually Kitty valued his opinion because of the extent of his stage experience. She smilingly tolerated his puritanical views, his eccentricities, even his fondness for the bottle, because she loved him dearly and appreciated the fatherly concern he always showed her. And because he remained a gifted actor – when completely sober. On the subject of the chorus, however, they were completely at odds. 'You mean, *you* don't approve, you old fogey.'

'I'll admit half-dressed females aren't my forte. They make me rather hot about the collar.'

'Yet it's *art, dahling,*' Kitty giggled, realising the words reminded her of what Archie used to say to her in those early days in Ealing. She turned to share the joke with him but found he was no longer beside her, being in deep and earnest conversation with Charlotte in the wings.

Thankfully the seats did fill up considerably, in spite of the bad weather, but Charlotte took her revenge for losing the argument over the ballroom backcloth by delaying curtain-up by ten minutes. As if that wasn't bad enough, she changed several of her moves and omitted a number of essential cues which made it look as if Felicity, in her role as Prince Charming, or Rod and Sam, were the ones at fault as they desperately tried to guess what she might say next and where on earth she was in the script.

A row erupted, of course, the moment they stepped off stage, Archie valiantly defending Charlotte by saying that she was in dire need of a holiday. 'Tired out, poor love.'

'Aren't we all?' Kitty, performing as the Fairy Godmother as well as directing, since they never had quite enough people for all the parts, wished she could wave her magic wand and turn Charlotte into a calm, sweet-natured, quiet person like Esme. But then that would be too much to hope for. Charlotte was arrogant, demanding and completely selfish while Esme was – Esme. Even now she was apologising to Charlotte for not having given her a prompt.

Charlotte tartly pointed out that she'd also failed to produce the pyrotechnic flash on cue, which made poor Esme's cheeks grow pink for that certainly wasn't the case. Next she berated Kitty for not speaking loudly enough, Archie for being the worst Buttons in the history of the theatre, and Rod and Sam for being wooden and never in the right place at the right time.

In truth, as the Ugly Sisters, they'd been an absolute riot, keeping the audience hooting with laughter through-out, almost completely upstaging Cinderella, which was probably the cause for Charlotte's foul temper. It took all of Kitty's tact and diplomacy to placate everyone and get them back on stage for the second act.

Amazingly, despite all of this, the audience responded well, clearly loving every minute of the show judging by their laughter and applause, proving the pantomime to be a great success. The rest of the cast, ever responsive to an audience's mood, were buoyant as a result, sharp on cues, almost flirting with witty ripostes, till even Charlotte was driven to lift her performance if she was not to be outshone. Which she did, of course, magnificently.

Love her or hate her, the girl had talent.

Chapter Fourteen

The weather improved as the week progressed, much of the snow melting away in a massive thaw. The second night's audience had been equally thin but by the third night the auditorium was almost half full.

'That's more like it,' Reg happily remarked as the chorus, comprised largely of young girls and children provided by a local dance troupe, swarmed about making him look rather like a harassed Pied Piper. It took a considerable amount of shushing and hushing before they were all quiet and in position for the opening number.

Each evening as the actors prepared to go on nerves were stretched to breaking point and Kitty made it her duty to set about calming ruffled tempers, soothe battered egos and lift everyone's spirits. Some could be found huddled in a corner going over their script, while others would pace about the stage. Tessa Crump always required one of her 'little pink pills' and a frantic search for her sheet music. Felicity too often arrived only moments before curtain-up, frightening them all to bits by this habit she had of taking a spin on her bike when she should be in make-up. Nothing Kitty could say would persuade her to take the exercise earlier.

Then there was Suzy, practising her scales in the wings, within earshot of the audience, her response to criticism being always to turn Kitty's attention to some other worry, such as old Jacob's spirits being a touch too high, and urging her to take a much firmer stand with him.

'I thought you promised to stop this,' Kitty would gently scold the old actor, removing a bottle from the pocket of his ancient dressing gown.

'Gets harder. That pit-of-the-stomach feeling,' he'd mourn, looking thoroughly dejected and sorry for himself. 'Won't touch another drop, Kitty. Honest injun.'

It seemed to be a never-ending battle to make the company toe the line, and despite Kitty's carefully going over what the stage manager had already checked a dozen times, there were the usual small panics and mini-crises. Some essential item of costume would tear and Mrs Pips would be found sewing frantically. A No. 9 make-up stick would be 'borrowed' or Esme would be chasing an actor for a prop that hadn't been returned to her precious properties table after use the previous evening.

The two-minute call would be given and several of the youngsters would look green, as if about to be sick. Even the old hands would declare this was their very last show. Never again would they go through this nervous torture. And then the opening number would begin, hearts would slow their frantic beat, chins would lift, deep breaths would be taken and off they would go, bouncing on stage with a smile and a song, delighted to be there and loving every minute.

Much to everyone's surprise and relief, they played to packed Houses all that week. There was always some heckling of 'Pip, Pip!' and 'Ho there, yokels,' from the back row when the nymphs and shepherdesses appeared, but then an audience was expected to participate in the fun of a panto. By the last night, not only was every single seat taken but people were actually standing at the back. Esme, adjusting her glasses so she could peep through a crack in the curtains, grinned with delight.

'Standing room only. Lord, it's time to ring the two-minute bell. Quick, Reg, do the honours. That lot at the back look a bit rough. Do we put in the nymph dance or not?' she whispered to Kitty, as the moment for the harlequinade approached.

'Of course.' Wrinkling her nose mischievously at Jacob's dour expression, she added, 'Why on earth not?'

As the dancing girls in their flimsy, knee-length dresses of palest green gauze floated on to the stage, the gasp from the audience was audible. Kitty always loved this moment of surprise and met Esme's raised eyebrows with a smile. 'They love it.'

Perhaps they might have, given the time properly to appreciate the clever choreography, but a voice from the back row called out, 'They're naked under them frocks. *Shame on the hussies!*'

Within seconds pandemonium had broken out. People were standing up and shouting at each other, rotten fruit and rolled up programmes were flung on stage and for a while it seemed that one or two of the more exuberant members of the audience might charge up there too. The poor dancing girls fled in terror for their lives.

Grabbing Rod and Sam, Kitty thrust them into the wings. *'Do something! Quick!'* And like the professionals they were, the pair galloped on stage and, to a loud drum roll, started flinging custard pies at each other as fast as Esme and Reg could fill plates. Within minutes the audience had become diverted into laughing at the antics of the Ugly Sisters and the situation was saved.

Kitty drew in a long breath of heartfelt thanks when the curtain came down on the final scene. But the nasty incident left everyone dry mouthed and with fast beating hearts. 'That was a near thing. Lord, I wouldn't care to go through that again.'

When the week in Kendal finished, they again took to the road. The first stop was at a village hall in Gosforth, situated at the meeting of the ways from Eskdale and Wasdale. Then on to the head of Esthwaite Water and the higgledy-piggledy streets of Hawkshead where they performed in the tiny square to a lively crowd of interested villagers. After that they took in a string of villages from the White Hart Inn at Bouth to Meaburn Hall at Maulds Meaburn, from the Parish Rooms in Shap to entertaining the brick workers and miners in Seaton.

They performed a scaled-down version of the panto in a billiard hall where they had to compete with the clicking of the balls, and in a Salvation Army hostel with hymn practice going on in the next room. On one never-to-be-forgotten night, they performed in a school room close to Barrow docks, with the sound of ships' hooters intruding at every wrong moment. But none of this worried them in the slightest.

Their digs varied greatly. They stayed in one extremely grand, if draughty, mansion, which housed them all though it made their battered suitcases look extremely shabby. Even worse was the prospect of a chambermaid unpacking their even shabbier garments.

At the other extreme they were lodged in miners' cottages where tables were rarely cleared, where they often had to share beds with other members of the household and watch with horror as the poor overworked wife would dole out plate after plate of hot food to a constant stream of sons, daughters, husband and other family members, who all seemed to come in to eat at different times. The poverty of these people's existence, and yet the generosity they offered to the Players, was a shocking and moving contrast to their own relatively safe and sheltered lives. Esme, frequently moved to tears, spent hours longer than she could afford making toys for the children and helping the women to sew and cook.

As the pantomime season drew to a close, Kitty was already thinking ahead, making plans for *A Spring Revue*. Rehearsals began while they were still performing *Cinderella* and were soon well under way. There were a few moans and groans with the cast complaining they were all in dire need of a rest but when Kitty pointed out the size of the company's bank balance, they all knuckled down to work.

Charlotte, however, was another matter.

It was the final week of the season and Kitty was making her usual tour of the dressing rooms just before curtain-up. Charlotte was adding yet more lipstick to an already vivid mouth; next came a liberal dusting of powder to her rouged cheeks before she flicked off the excess with a rabbit's foot. She'd never looked less like a virginal Cinderella.

'A touch less colour, perhaps?' Kitty tentatively suggested, knowing her remarks would be ignored. 'Cinders doesn't transform into a beauty until the end of Act One, remember,' she gently reminded her.

Charlotte paused in the application of yet more carmine to her cupid's bow mouth and, ignoring Kitty's comment entirely, said, 'I've decided to take a couple of weeks off, so you'll have to line up an understudy for the start of the next tour. Got to go and see my dear old mother.'

A Spring Revue was already booked solid from the very next week, the first in March right through to the end of May, and, as always, young females were hard to come by. So even if they could find someone, there was no time left for extra rehearsals.

Kitty side-stepped Mrs Pips as she bustled past to pin up a torn hem on one of the dancing girls, thereby gaining herself a moment's grace before answering. 'Sorry, Charlotte, that's not on, I'm afraid. We're pretty stretched as it is. Everyone gets three days as a breather and that's all.' Then she lifted her voice to address the entire company. 'Chin up, everyone. Break a leg.' She offered the usual alternative to 'good luck', which theatricals believed brought anything but.

Clearly fuming at having her plans thwarted, Charlotte turned her back on Kitty and screamed at Mrs Pips. 'For God's sake get this rabble out of here. I really should have a dressing room to myself. Where's me bleedin' fan? I'm that hot, me make-up's running. And, Pips, make sure you dress my wig properly this time. It looked like a wrung out dish-mop last night.'

Ida Phillips opened her mouth to protest and then snapped it shut again.

'Beginners please,' Kitty called in her brightest voice, trying to avoid the mute appeal in the sideways glance Mrs Pips cast in her direction. The one-time housekeeper did attempt to waylay Kitty, just as she was making her escape, saying she really would like to have a word about Charlotte, if she'd a minute to spare.

'There's summat going on with that young madam. Summat we should get to the bottom of.' But Kitty didn't have a minute. She was far too busy to bother about Charlotte's tantrums.

There was a mildness now to the spring breezes, and the winter wildness of the garden was pierced by spears of new growth, of crocus and snowdrop, wild daffodils and violets. The barren fells still wore their cloth of Hodden Grey, like that once woven in Kendal town itself, and the rivers gushed and gurgled with the melted snows from the mountains. For the first time in months Kitty had time to think and draw breath, time to lie in her cosy bed with her delightful baby daughter crawling all over her, gurgling happy nonsense.

The exhausted cast was enjoying three glorious days of rest and recuperation at Repstone Manor before the start of *A Spring Revue*. Kitty meant to take full advantage of the break herself by staying in bed all morning, instead of bouncing up to do her usual million and one tasks. She might even snatch an hour or two from her endless planning and organising to take Dixie out on the fells this afternoon, and quietly reflect upon these last weeks and those ahead. Hopefully Archie would find time to do the accounts at some point during the weekend, if Charlotte permitted. Even as the thought came to her she heard the smash of crockery from the room down the hall. Dixie, busily engrossed in trying to push open her mother's eyelashes to bring her properly awake, gave a small start of shock and began to cry.

Charlotte made no secret of the fact that most nights she shared her bed with Archie. No doubt he'd brought her breakfast in bed and for some reason, it wasn't hard to guess what, she'd thrown it at him.

Kitty smoothed the soft down of her baby's hair. 'Don't fret, my darling. Only naughty Charlotte, having a bit of a tantrum.'

Three days was insufficient time, apparently, to allow her to visit her 'poor mother'. Rather unkindly, Kitty wondered if the mother in question might even be relieved. Somehow, Charlotte in the role of dutiful daughter didn't quite ring true.

Kitty put her head under a pillow, striving to blot out the sound of their noisy quarrel. Dixie, thinking this another new game, giggled all the more and was busily engaged trying to pull it off again when there came a knock on her door. Wearily, Kitty dragged on a dressing gown and went to answer it. It was Frank.

Perhaps it was a wish to escape the tension that was building up inside her, as well as inside the house, which led Kitty to abandon her plans for the day and agree to accompany him on a charabanc trip to Morecambe. Anything to get away. Besides, Dixie had never seen the sea, so how could she refuse?

Charlotte was indeed railing at the supposed injustice of Kitty's decision by storming back and forth before Archie's chair, fists clenched into fierce knots, the cerise silk tassels on her peignoir trembling ferociously. She couldn't remember ever feeling quite this angry in all her life. She was livid with fury, stamping mad, but then she'd always been able to 'play the drama-queen', or 'put on one of her paddys', as Archie teasingly termed her outbursts of temper. She could, in fact, quote directly from any script, play any role she'd ever done. Today, she was playing Kate from *The Taming of the Shrew*.

'I won't be dictated to. I need to be free.'

'Free to do what?'

'Anything. Take time off when I need it. To do as I please. I *hate* acting.' Which certainly was not the case. Acting was like a drug to her. Charlotte loved to perform. She adored having everyone's eyes upon her, admiring the way she moved or recited the lines, marvelling at her beauty and the wonderful gowns she wore. She also found it surprisingly satisfying to make people laugh or cry, or simply give them pleasure, something she'd never experienced before. The theatre was indeed wonderful, and Charlotte adored being the star of it, but it wasn't real life and she longed to shine even brighter in the wider world.

Her dream of ruling the roost at Repstone Manor would, of course, be far grander than anything Magnus could offer. Unfortunately it hadn't yet come about. Archie was a dear, sweet man and she adored him, but he could be vexingly stubborn as well as increasingly parsimonious for one so well placed.

She'd been berating him for a full ten minutes over her need to take some time off, perfectly convinced he hadn't taken in a single word she was saying. He just sat there in silence, reading his damned paper.

'Kitty doesn't *own* us for God's sake,' Charlotte stormed. It irked her that she must always seek Kitty's permission, and Archie's support was essential to achieve this. But how could she explain to him that her entire life was in danger of falling apart.

Despite their increased intimacy, she'd continued to make regular excursions home to visit her 'mother'. But these visits had grown less frequent in recent months due to the pressures of touring and Magnus was showing every sign of losing patience. His most recent letter, delivered via the Post Office box she held specifically for this purpose, had warned her that since she hadn't come home for Christmas, as instructed, he would sue for divorce if she didn't return at once. The very idea was intolerable. Terrifyingly so. She really couldn't risk losing access to all the lovely money which he so generously provided, in spite of her neglect of him. Not yet. Nor could she risk losing everything she'd gained thus far with Archie.

Archie shook out his newspaper, barely glancing in Charlotte's direction as he answered her pleas. 'We'll go on the next tour with the rest of the company, as usual.'

'*I* shall do as I please.' And now she did stamp her foot, making the crystal teardrops of the chandelier shake. Seeing the startled expression in his eyes, Charlotte wondered, momentarily, if perhaps she'd gone too far.

'Kitty needs you here.' Never had he taken such a firm stance against her, and it enraged her all the more. 'I really don't understand why you're making all this fuss.'

She snatched the newspaper from his hands and tore it in two. 'For pity's sake, listen to what I'm telling you and then you might.'

There was a long and terrible silence. Sometimes Archie found her tantrums amusing, even titillating, her passion always reigniting a spark in him that the traumas and disappointments of his life had very nearly destroyed. At other times he saw them as nothing short of trying and pettish. He quietly picked up the two sections of his newspaper and carefully folded them back together before taking both her hands and drawing the now weeping Charlotte down beside him on the sofa.

'Sweetheart, you're working yourself into a fine lather over nothing. Whatever's the matter, for goodness' sake? There's an article about Asquith rejecting a bill on compulsory military service which I'd like to read, if I may. So explain it all to me, calmly and quietly if you please, without tearing up any more of my newspaper.'

'Oh, Archie, you're so kind to me.' She was at once contrite, snuffling up her tears like a small child caught out in some misdemeanour. She hiccuped slightly, blew her nose on his white linen handkerchief and, snuggling against his shoulder, adopted a more wheedling tone. 'I feel you and I should have more time together. Alone. Why don't we take a long cruise down the Nile or spend a few months in Venice? Or even a lovely long weekend in town, just the two of us. So romantic! See some *real*

FREDA LIGHTFOOT

shows, dine out at *divine* little restaurants, patronise my favourite shops. Wouldn't that be much more fun than embarking on yet another dreary tour?'

'I'm sorry if you're tired, sweetheart, but we can't go away just now,' he patiently explained. 'We're both needed. You in particular, my precious.' But even flattery failed to calm her.

'And I say we *will*! I'm utterly exhausted and in need of a long rest.'

'Then I suggest you go back to bed and take one while you have the chance, my darling. We leave here first thing on Monday morning. So best make the most of the weekend.'

Whereupon Charlotte picked up a Chinese figurine and flung it into the fireplace. It smashed into a dozen pieces and Archie, infuriatingly enough, informed her from behind his newspaper that he'd never liked it anyway.

A soft spring breeze chased chip papers and old bus tickets into the gutter, propelling people along the promenade like steam trains. Kitty and Frank walked along the sea front together pushing the pram just as if, he commented, they were a proper family. They ate cod and chips for lunch in a café on the front where the waitresses wore white frilly caps and aprons and had notebooks dangling from strings on their waist-bands.

Throughout the long afternoon Kitty asked herself why on earth she'd come. Dixie would have been quite content with a short walk on the fells, then she could have taken the opportunity for a quiet session with the accounts or to put the finishing touches to her script. Instead, here she was seated on a wind-swept beach while Dixie poured sand into a bucket which Kitty would turn out into a pie so that her beloved child could smash it with her spade and shout with baby laughter.

Frank, of course, remained as brazen and chirpy as ever, still urging her to name the day, saying how much she needed him to look after her.

Kitty was feeling distinctly harassed.

'I simply don't love you and never could,' she said at last, driven to blunt honesty as every other excuse so far had failed to convince him.

'But don't we always have a good time together, duchess? And don't we owe it to Dixie to provide her with a proper ma and pa?'

Gritting her teeth, Kitty drew her scarf more tightly about her neck, trying to keep warm as the breeze turned chill in the late-afternoon. 'You and I both know that you're not Dixie's father, no matter what anyone else might think.'

Frank's smile was one of studied blandness, which did nothing to reassure her. 'Nevertheless, she can't go through life without a dad, nor you without a man. Besides, you wouldn't want Dixie's *real* father, whoever he might be, to learn the truth, now would you?'

She glanced up at him sharply. 'What are you saying? That sounded suspiciously like blackmail.'

'As if I would do such a thing. Dear me, whatever put such an idea into your head?' Then, reaching for Dixie, he purred softly to the child, 'Come to Pops, my darling. Come to Pops.' As Dixie happily reached out her chubby arms to him, gurgling prettily, Kitty snatched up the toddler to hold her close.

'Don't you *ever* use that name in front of her again. Look, it's starting to rain. Let's go home.' By the time she'd reached the promenade Kitty had calmed down somewhat. 'I'm grateful, Frank, for your not telling the truth about Dixie. But not *that* grateful. I won't marry you, nor will I have you assuming any rights over her or interfering in my life in any way whatsoever. Is that perfectly clear?'

He gazed at her for a long moment, an errant breeze lifting a strand of lank hair and slapping it against his shiny forehead. 'As crystal. Though perhaps one day you might think differently.' And again he smiled, only this time the chill that shivered all the way down her spine had nothing to do with the cool spring breezes.

Monday morning came and *A Spring Revue* was ready to take on the road. Kitty was determined that it should do well. The first night opened to a full House and got off to a cracking start with Suzy singing a lively number, 'The Call to Arms'. Although her voice possessed nowhere near the range it had once had, it was sounding good. The audience were joining in with the chorus in no time. Jacob did a stand-up routine poking fun at the old aristocracy and then made some jibes at the mining barons and cotton kings, so as not to show prejudice, which brought a storm of cheers from the working-class audience. Tessa, swathed in cardigans and complaining bitterly about the merciless draughts, searched frantically for the song sheet she wanted, her constant cry being,

'I know it was here a moment ago.' Then out of the maelstrom came her breath-stopping rendition of 'What Shall We Do With The Drunken Sailor?' which brought a standing ovation as always.

Kitty herself had written a parody on suburbia and had spent a good deal of time agonising over rhymes. 'What rhymes with afternoon teas? Sneeze. Sweet peas. And what about golf? Oh, dear, writing poetry isn't as easy as I thought.' But everyone had simply smiled, knowing that she always suffered a crisis of confidence when she was writing and that all would be well in the end.

And it was. In those first weeks there were the usual colds and sniffles. Poor Archie had a bad spell of 'flu which was very worrying as it kept him in bed for the better part of a week. It should have been twice as long but he stubbornly insisted that 'the show must go on'. Kitty would frown anxiously whenever she heard him sneeze or cough quietly into his handkerchief. It reminded her of those early days in Ealing when he'd seemed to be clinging so narrowly to life.

She felt at times as if she too were hanging on to life by a thread, always keenly aware of the pitiful state of their finances. And coping with a small baby in addition to the Players took a great deal out of her. Kitty knew she couldn't have managed at all without the help of Esme and Mrs Pips, who took turns to mind Dixie when she was busy. Not that she was a fussy child. She'd sit on anyone's knee so long as they gave her the undivided attention she demanded. And she'd been known to woo the heart of more than one cantankerous landlady.

But constant touring wasn't easy. Good lodgings were

sometimes hard to find. They often arrived late, were unpunctual for meals, slept at odd hours, none of which endeared them to landladies who expected guests to be out of their rooms from ten till six each day and sit down to dinner with everyone else. Wherever possible they procured invitations to stay in people's homes, though that too presented difficulties: over-familiar husbands, stage-struck daughters, and housekeepers who didn't approve of theatricals at all.

And then there were the freezing halls, the tuneless pianos, the stuffy rooms with windows nailed down, the smell of mildew and the fear that the stage might collapse at any moment under the weight of the scenery. Caretakers who spied on the female cast as they changed, audiences who made more noise than the players, or no sound at all which was worse.

Yet she wouldn't have missed any of it, not for the world. Wherever they'd performed, whether it be in a traditional theatre or a leaky shack, she'd loved every minute of it, and not even Charlotte's sulks could diminish Kitty's enthusiasm for the life.

Sometimes she would remark how lovely it would be to have a theatre of their own. She even once tentatively suggested they might convert the old barns at Repstone but Archie simply shook his head and laughed, saying it would be far too expensive even for his pocket.

And then all talk of theatres became lost in the rumours of a possible war in Europe.

'That'll be the end for us when it comes,' Suzy mourned, but Kitty pooh-poohed such a notion, saying they'd just have to change their tune and give audiences more fun to keep morale high.

By this time they'd acquired a van, somewhat beaten up and decrepit but which carried their equipment with greater ease than the trailer, although space was still limited. For this reason any number which could be performed without props or with the minimum use of scenery was welcomed with open arms. Mimes to music were popular for this reason, as was poetry, either epic or novelty being favourites so that the audience could join in.

Jacob proved his brilliance, stone cold sober, as Joseph Surface in a short extract from *The School for Scandal*, with Charlotte as Lady Teazle positively bubbling with energy throughout. Her quick movements and expressive gestures were a delight.

Afterwards she could usually be heard declaring how perfect she was for the part, chirruping with just the right degree of hauteur: 'Breeding isn't everything, you know. Some of us are born with class in our veins.'

She spent hours every day closeted with Mrs Pips, discussing, trying on, discarding and altering any number of costumes. And she had no conversation beyond whether she should wear a stole with her crinoline or if her wig bore sufficient curls and ringlets, even disagreeing heatedly with Kitty over the size of her fan. She had a preference for anything overlarge and heavily feathered.

Kitty never felt any jealousy over Charlotte's talent as an actress, because it was genuine. Over her relationship with Archie, however, it was quite another matter.

Chapter Fifteen

A Spring Revue was a hit and if Charlotte hadn't been a star before, she certainly was now. Young men would hover at the stage door begging for her autograph, or, more daringly, to take her to supper. She never accepted their invitations but loved to tell Archie about them in an attempt to rouse his jealousy.

Vexingly enough, the ploy never seemed to have any effect as he would simply smile and tell her that she was far too talented and beautiful to waste herself on stage-door johnnies. Archie seemed less biddable these days, which troubled her. Charlotte longed for an Italian count or a prince of the realm to appear one day, which would surely make him sit up and take notice. Though it was admittedly unlikely that the village halls and schoolrooms which normally comprised the Players' venues would feature on the itinerary of the theatregoing aristocracy. Yet another reason, in Charlotte's opinion, for herself and Archie to leave the stage and concentrate on developing a more stylish lifestyle.

She had of course a further, more pressing reason,

which she really must address before too long. Magnus's threat of divorce still hung over her, a dark and growing fear. Charlotte was perfectly certain that she could cajole him into relinquishing such scandalous nonsense if only she could secure sufficient time off to go and see him.

Life recently had been a bit of a juggling act. For all she had, in theory, won the battle for Archie's affections, keeping him was proving far more difficult than she had imagined. She could see his eyes constantly following Kitty; would notice him huddled in corners deep in conversation with Esme, which was even more infuriating. Charlotte's main task in life was to keep the three at odds with each other. Archie seemed perfectly content to amble on in this live-for-the-moment fashion. In one respect she adored this trait in him, since it made him so delightfully hedonistic, but at the same time Charlotte began to dream of a permanent future. She needed security. But how to achieve that seemingly impossible goal?

One evening after the performance, Frank approached her, begging Charlotte to help him in his own efforts to win Kitty. She promised to give it serious consideration. Who knew when an alliance with him might come in handy? So many balls to keep up in the air and under control.

One slip and she could lose everything.

In addition to performances every evening and twice-weekly matinées, Kitty insisted on continuing with rehearsals during the day, to keep everyone's performance up to scratch. This developed into a tiring regime and, ever mindful of her cast's state of health she would keep a vigilant watch that all was well. Archie's moods in particular proved to be a worry as she would often see anxiety and exhaustion etched into his pale face.

'Do say if I'm overworking you,' she told him one wet Monday when they'd gone through an entire extract twice over.

'Kitty dearest, I never mind working hard. My problems aren't with your work schedule. I'd move heaven and earth for you, you know I would.'

'Would you?'

He gave a little half-smile and then fell into a fit of coughing. When it was over, he drew out a cigarette from a silver case and lit it. 'Anything within my grasp,' he remarked vaguely, his gaze holding hers for a long moment. He didn't often smoke, but tension sometimes drove him to it.

'You really shouldn't smoke till that cough is better.'

'I know, dear heart. But a chap must have some hobbies.' The next moment he was confiding in her his increasing anxiety over Charlotte; how she seemed to be growing ever more irascible and neurotic, so much so that she'd once or twice driven him from her bed.

Kitty, not wishing to be privy to this information, concentrated on making notes on her director's script, then in a voice carefully devoid of interest, dryly remarked, 'As with any woman, Charlotte moans about one thing when it's quite another that's troubling her.'

'And how is a poor confused male to decode the signals correctly?'

Kitty glanced across at Dixie who was chuckling with delight at being dangled on the knee of the ever-adoring Frank. 'Ah, but we can't have you understanding us too

well. That would never do.' And she started to walk
away, her mind resolutely turning to the changes she
must make in the last scene, when Archie caught her
arm, drawing her close so that he could press his mouth
against her ear.

'I once thought I understood you. That something
special was growing between us. Yet I was evidently
wrong.'

Kitty seemed to stop breathing, perhaps her heart
even stopped beating as she became all too aware of
his fingers curled so warmly, so possessively, about the
soft upper flesh above her elbow. What could he possibly
mean? Though she might still feel a lingering love for
him, he was not and never could be hers. Or could
he? Esme was no longer a consideration as she seemed
to be more content with Reg's company these days.
Charlotte had been Archie's all-consuming passion for
some time, but now he seemed to be indicating that
this was waning, so why should she continue to hold
back?

She lifted her eyes to his. 'Archie Emerson wrong?
Never.'

'I'm glad to hear it.' And after an achingly long
moment, he let her go.

The company was heading north, progressing through
picturesque Westmorland villages with grey-stone cottages where sheep could be found grazing on wide greens.
Appleby and Kirkby Stephen, Penrith and Carlisle; some
of the loneliest roads of England. It seemed as if they were
on top of the world, often passing gypsy caravans making

their slow progress to the Appleby horse fair which took place every year in early summer.

Kitty announced that they would next be heading for Yorkshire as she handed round a list of venues which made Charlotte pale. Some of the towns Esme had booked were just a little too close to her old home near Leeds for comfort. In one respect being in Yorkshire would make it easier for her to get time off to see Magnus. In another it created a serious risk. For all she quite enjoyed living on the edge of danger, discovery was not part of Charlotte's plan.

But that was next week, or the week after that, for now she was revelling in her hour of fame. She went around using words such as 'chic' or 'smart', wearing hats with veils pulled almost, but not quite, over her face whenever she took tea in whatever town they were currently playing in. This was most afternoons during the run of the revue so that people would have the opportunity to recognise her for the star she undoubtedly was, for all she declared her intention to be quite otherwise.

'What fun to be incognito,' she would say to Archie as she sat scarlet-lipped, gazing around some crowded tea-room with delighted anticipation. 'I feel like a film star.' And with luck someone would be sure to have seen *A Spring Revue* and scurry over with a napkin for her to scrawl her signature upon it. Magnus, she decided, would have to wait.

Charlotte had never been the kind of actress to avoid eye contact with the audience. She always loved to see the adulation in their faces. And it was at a small theatre in Richmond that she thought she saw him, seated in an invalid carriage in the side aisle. Her heart very nearly stopped beating. Fortunately, the man turned out to be a stranger but having recently received yet another irate letter from her husband, the incident left her badly shaken. It was a moment which reminded her very sharply that the tinsel fame of a touring company, however delightfully flattering, would never provide her with the funds she needed to keep her in the style she enjoyed. The problem of Magnus must be addressed.

Charlotte made the decision that it was long past time the LTPs discovered just how much they needed her. They'd never properly appreciated her talent so perhaps they needed a jolt like this, just to remind them. It would teach them all a lesson. *A Spring Revue* could never survive without her, now that she was so famous. Besides, hadn't she begged to be allowed a proper rest? Kitty should have given her one weeks ago. Fortunately, she was close enough to home now to risk Kitty's displeasure.

When the curtain came down at the end of the first act, she quickly changed while everyone else was snatching a much-needed cup of tea before the start of the second. No one would miss her until it was too late.

As she slipped out through the stage door Charlotte was convinced that no one had seen her go. In this, however, she was quite wrong. Her hurried trip to the dressing room to gather together her things had been her undoing for, tucked behind the screen, enjoying a well-earned forty winks with Dixie on her lap, was Mrs Pips. She'd made no sound as she heard Charlotte furiously clattering about, snatching up bottles and jars from her dressing table and pulling on clothes in a tearing hurry. But as she crept out of the door, Mrs Pips followed.

She handed the still-sleeping child to Esme in the wings, saying she had some urgent business to attend to and snatching up her own coat and bag, hurried after the retreating figure.

As her taxi cab drew away from the kerb, Charlotte did not notice a silent figure quickly step into another, right behind.

Even as she agonised, Kitty could hear the audience growing restless, also a few whistles and catcalls. It wouldn't take more than a few minutes' delay to have yet another riot on their hands, and the memory of the last one was enough to make her blench. She found herself gazing imploringly into Archie's eyes, as if expecting him to spirit Charlotte out of thin air. The extract from *The School For Scandal* was due to start but, having confirmed that she was nowhere to be found, that every corner of the theatre had been searched twice over, he simply shook his head and reached desperately for his cigarette case.

'How could she do this to us?' That Charlotte could walk out halfway through a show was, to Kitty, beyond belief.

It was Reg who saved the day. He took Esme by the shoulders and gently urged her to act as understudy. 'You'll do it, lass, won't you? You must know the words by now, acting as prompt.'

'No, no . . . I couldn't . . . Really, I . . .'

'The show must go on. And thoo'll do it gradely weel. None better.'

Esme stood stunned for an achingly long moment, but the sounds of discontent from the audience were growing ever more alarming and finally she gave a small nod. 'All right. If I must.' Which galvanised Kitty into action.

'Three minutes to change while I send Rod and Sam on to entertain the audience. Mrs Pips? Where's Mrs Pips? Oh, God, don't say she's missing too.'

Suzy grabbed Esme and whisked her away to the dressing room, saying she was the speediest quick-change-artist in the business and they'd be ready in two minutes and not a second later.

Charlotte disported herself on the *chaise-longue* in the blue and gold parlour, a cup of Earl Grey tea beside her on the marquetry table. It felt almost as if she'd never been away. Mrs Pursey, appearing at the door like an avenging angel, had looked utterly taken aback to see her.

'By heck, you're the last person I expected to find standing on me doorstep at this hour of the night. Why didn't you send word? Your room isn't even aired. Had enough of globe-trotting, have you?'

The whole household, including Magnus, imagined that she spent half her life travelling. Rome, Venice, Paris, Geneva. She'd been compelled to read a good many Baedekers in order to be entirely convincing.

Charlotte had also been compelled to develop a system whereby she could dispatch letters from various parts of the country as well as from Europe, by the simple ruse of paying various landladies or actors she met on tour to post them for her. Whoever she could find with friends or relatives in suitable places from which to forward her mail. It was laborious and expensive, but thankfully worked. Money, she found, could generally buy such favours, and even discretion. No doubt they imagined them to be letters to a secret lover. But it was quite impossible to acquire a picture postcard in advance, so when Magnus complained of the lack of them, Charlotte insisted that a long letter was far superior; that only shop girls sent picture postcards. Despite his grumbles, however, the system seemed to work.

A surreptitious tour of the house while she'd waited for her tea to be brought, revealed to Charlotte that many changes had been brought about since her last visit eight months before. Doorways had been widened, and rails installed at various strategic points. She could hardly believe what her eyes were telling her. Further enquiries confirmed that the blue sitting room had been turned into a ground-floor bedroom for Magnus. 'Aye, that's right, so's he can enjoy having the French windows open out on to t'back garden,' Mrs Pursey tartly informed her as she'd set the tea tray down. Magnus had evidently come to terms with his condition and was making every effort to rejoin life and adapt. 'All thanks to good nursing. Luggage?'

'I beg your pardon?'

'Your luggage, madam. Where would that be?'

Charlotte was instantly annoyed to find herself again wrong-footed, as she bore the onslaught of that fierce-eyed glare which seemed to see right through her. She hadn't given a thought to luggage. In her haste to escape unseen, she'd only brought her make-up case, and could hardly have toured Europe out of that.

'I – I haven't brought any. I'm having it sent on later.'

'Of course,' remarked Mrs Pursey dryly. The click

of the woman's heels as she marched away seemed to emphasise her disapproval. 'I'll see to yer room then. Tha'd best not disturb the maister till t'morning.'

Now Charlotte sat sipping her tea, listening to the slow clunk of the pendulum in the grandfather clock that stood in the hall, worrying about what she would say to her husband in the morning. How would he react? She hardly expected a warm reception and cursed herself for leaving it so long. It would be extremely dangerous to risk losing Magnus until she was certain Archie would agree to provide her with the life she craved.

She'd no idea of the extent of Archie's wealth, though she assumed it to be considerable judging from the size of his estate. But she was also attracted by his impeccable style, all those little details such as his crystal cufflinks, silk shirts, and penchant for always wearing cravats. More importantly, he possessed the one essential which could not be bought: undisputed status in society. Married to Archie, one of the landed gentry, she could, and should, be rubbing shoulders with the titled rich. Charlotte smiled sadly and reached for her cup. If only it were possible.

Yet instead of enjoying the easy life, as he was surely entitled to do, he persisted on remaining with the Lakeland Travelling Players.

Charlotte admitted to herself that the attention she'd received as a result of *A Spring Revue* had been exciting and thrilling, but it couldn't satisfy her for long.

Were she to be 'discovered' by some professional producer and granted the opportunity to 'star' in a West End production, then that might be a different story. Charlotte would welcome such fame with open arms.

Otherwise, she'd no intention of spending her entire life living in squalid digs and touring the country with a second-rate theatrical company. Far more fulfilling and rewarding to devote her life to a man of stature and note. Charlotte rather enjoyed the sound of that, so she repeated it: 'devote her life'. Yes, that was good. To a man who could offer her not only money but the position and power she deserved.

It wasn't until after Mrs Pursey had led her to a hastily prepared bedroom, its drawn curtains gleaming rosily in the lamplight, that Charlotte thought to enquire who exactly had brought about this change in the home of her husband.

'Miss Mahon. His companion and nurse.' And who else could it be since you're never here? her tone seemed to imply as she closed the door.

'Good morning, Mrs Radcliffe.' Charlotte, finding her own name sounding strange after long disuse, sat up in bed to be confronted by a formidable young woman dressed in an ankle-length blue dress and starched pinafore. Her neat brown hair was almost entirely covered by a white cotton cap tied with ribbons under a firm chin. Her figure was tall and angular, as rigidly formal as the uniform, and the tone of voice uncompromising. Charlotte stared in stunned dismay as the woman ordered a young maid to set down a breakfast tray. Curtains were drawn briskly back, just as if the newcomer had a perfect right to allow the morning sun to pour into the room without even asking Charlotte's permission.

'I couldn't wait to meet you, madam, since I'd heard such tales about you.'

For all her lively tone of voice, there was something about the way she said 'madam' and 'tales' which stirred a chill of discomfiture in Charlotte even as she struggled to sit up and take in what was happening. Sybil Mahon was now ordering the maid to withdraw, instructing her to fetch hot water and towels as well as suitable attire from madam's wardrobe before presenting Charlotte with a face that had surely never known despair. Beneath that hideous cap was the image of an angel, even to a charming dimple just to the right of her smiling mouth.

'You'll want to be entirely presentable before visiting your husband, madam. Though when that will be, I cannot say. He rises late.'

'Have you informed him that I am here? I'm sure he'll be most anxious to see me.' Charlotte was filled with fury at being outmanoeuvred. Mistress of the house was surely her role.

'Mrs Pursey will attend to that shortly. Now, if you're quite ready, breakfast?' The interloper indicated the laden tray. An egg, lightly boiled no doubt. Hot buttered toast. The delicious aroma of freshly ground coffee. Charlotte stubbornly declined, despite the fact she was near faint from hunger since she rarely ate before a performance and had eaten nothing since. 'As you wish.' And without allowing a moment for Charlotte to change her mind, the girl swept up the tray and departed with it, saying madam would be informed when the master was ready to see her.

Charlotte was filled with a sensation far worse than

stage fright. If this was how Mrs Pursey and the nurse treated her, with barely disguised contempt, what kind of reception could she expect from her husband?

Esme was elated. She could hardly believe how well her performance had gone. She hadn't fluffed a single line, had remembered every move, performed with style and aplomb and been given a standing ovation at the end. She was beside herself with joy.

'I can't quite believe it.'

Kitty was hugging her, Archie was patting her on the back, everyone smiling and kissing her and telling her they'd known all along that she could still act. They all got rather drunk in the Star and Garter, not simply because they were pleased at Esme's return to the stage but also because it was their last night in Yorkshire, and the tour was going well. Tomorrow they would take *A Spring Revue* up to Northumberland for three weeks. By the end of that run, they'd need to have made a decision about what they were going to do next.

Esme, hiccuping gently as she sipped celebratory champagne, told Reg he was the one she had to thank for her success. 'If you hadn't bullied me into it, I might never have found the nerve.' He laughed and hugged her and for once Esme didn't pull away. 'You can't keep a good actor down. You're a star too now, love, just like Charlotte.'

Esme said that she'd be more than happy to go back to prompting and helping backstage on Charlotte's return, which met with howls of protest.

'Real talent should never be neglected,' Jacob remonstrated with her.

'Competition does no one any harm,' Suzy agreed.

'And will keep that little madam on her toes,' muttered Felicity, half under her breath.

'But where is dear old Pips?' Archie muttered as he refilled champagne glasses all round, a question no one could answer.

When the moment of their confrontation finally came, Magnus gazed upon his wife as if she were a stranger to him. For Charlotte that look was entirely disconcerting. She'd coped with Magnus's rages, his brutality, his dictatorial rules, even his perversions. Indifference was something totally unexpected and quite beyond her ken.

She'd taken great care with her toilette that morning, and in choosing what to wear, opting for a modestly plain gown from her old wardrobe that must be a good ten years out of date. Her face was almost bare of make-up, save for just a dab of rouge to give her lips colour.

Determined not to let him see her unease, she sauntered to the window to examine the familiar view. The smooth humps of distant hills; the grey rooftops of the neighbouring village, most of which Magnus owned; the rooks still flying from the small copse that made the front of the house so gloomy – it all seemed to draw her back in time. Yet the house seemed almost poky after Repstone Manor, and Charlotte wondered how she could ever have liked it.

'So, you've deigned to pay us a call? How very kind.'

She swung about and even to her own ears the normally musical tone of her laughter sounded false. 'Dear, dear, not still in a sulk, are we? You know the rich and famous never live with their own husband. Too banal for words, darling.'

'And are you living with someone else's?'

'Of course not. I need space in which to flourish, that's all. You wouldn't deny me that. It gets so terribly claustrophobic here. But I'm always happy to come home, Magnus, you know that. I miss you desperately when I'm away.' To emphasise this essential fact she went to kiss him on the cheek but he turned his face away at the last moment, avoiding her. To cover her startled embarrassment, Charlotte clapped her hands together, as if in delight. 'And you're looking so much better. What marvellous progress you've made these last months.'

'I am much better.'

'I'm pleased to hear it.'

'Well enough to know when my wife is making a fool of me.'

She felt her heart contract with fear. Surely he couldn't know where she'd been living, and with whom? Ever the consummate actress Charlotte held her nerve and, kneeling beside him, allowed tears to form in her eyes as she took his hand and pressed it to her lips. 'In what way, beloved, could I ever make a fool of a man as strong as you? If matters had not got into such a sorry state between us, nothing would have driven me from your side. You know how the memory of your dreadful accident still torments me.' A tear fell upon his hand.

'Then why has it taken you so long to return?' He was softening, she was almost sure of it. Almost.

She lifted two pale and slender hands and fluttered them in a typically feminine gesture. 'Oh, that was naughty, I admit. But I was having such *fun*. Met so many *lovely* people, you wouldn't *believe*. You won't scold me too much, will you, darling?' She pronounced it 'dahling', with no sign of an accent, knowing he would approve of her improved diction. And the ploy seemed to be working for his lips were curving very slightly into a smile, and he was tilting up her chin with one finger.

'You don't change, Lottie, I'll say that for you. Except to become even more beautiful. You are absolutely incorrigible.'

'And you are still the same handsome charmer who rushed me headlong into marriage.'

He hooked a hand about her neck and drew her towards him for a kiss, full and sensual, open-mouthed and demanding. One large square hand drew up her skirt as she knelt before him and slid between her legs, fingers moving, exploring. To her appalled disbelief, Charlotte found herself responding to his caresses and when he finally released her, gazed at him out of blue, startled eyes while he regarded her with triumph.

'That was simply to make it clear to you, Charlotte dear, that although I may not be a whole man, I am far more capable than you may imagine. What you choose to do now is of complete indifference to me. You can stay and be as good a wife to me as circumstances permit, or you can leave and suffer the consequences. I've changed my mind about a divorce. It would be too much to your advantage to allow you to be free, let alone make some other man's life a misery. No, since I am tied to this damned chair, why should you not be equally so. Love me or hate me, Charlotte, I'm your husband and will ever remain so, despite the consolations Nurse Mahon is most able and willing to offer. Unless, or until I choose otherwise, you understand. But that decision will be mine, not yours.'

For an instant she could barely take in what he was saying, but there was no mistaking his meaning. Magnus was back in control.

While Charlotte simpered and smiled, assuring him that she would stay for as long as he needed her, white hot fury hammered in her head and fear curdled her stomach. Despite all these months of careful planning, her situation seemed ever more precarious. She must continue to play the role of the adoring wife, at least until she had secured Archie's undying devotion, in order to keep her husband sweet. Otherwise, she might well lose everything she'd gained.

Chapter Sixteen

The advantages of Charlotte's prolonged absence became all too apparent as time went by. Instead of the usual carping, with someone eagerly taking offence at the least sign of criticism, the rest of the cast were readily putting forward suggestions as to how they could improve on their own performances, quite happy to put in the extra time needed to perfect the changes. Everyone seemed somehow far more relaxed; making jokes, laughing and teasing each other, and getting through so much more work with far fewer interruptions.

Charlotte can stay away as long as she likes, Kitty thought. She's not nearly so indispensable as she imagines.

As a rule, touring generally became easier during the summer months when the LTPs could often stay in one place for as much as a week, simply because more people were willing to come out on lighter nights. This summer, however, was like no other. Everyone felt as if they were existing on borrowed time.

While politicians talked long into the night, the Kaiser

continued to flex his military might, determined to challenge Britain's domination of the seas. A long period of prosperity seemed to be coming to an end in a show of aggression. Although Britain remained anxious to maintain the peace, she nonetheless observed with increasing concern the militarisation of Germany. In Manchester or Delhi, Winnipeg or London, Sydney or Wellington, patriotic fervour set young men joining up in their droves, all demanding to know how quickly they could get to the Front.

But life for the Players continued as normal. Kitty took to sticking 'Business as usual' over their posters and every night they'd be packed to the doors, just as if the British people wanted Fritz to know they weren't afraid. Witty parodies became popular, and mawkishly sentimental songs as well as the rousingly patriotic. The LTPs went from strength to strength with Esme gaining in confidence daily, not only because she'd finally lost her fear of the stage but because she now had Archie all to herself. His utter devotion, which he made no attempt to hide, surprised and delighted her.

Early-afternoon was devoted to rehearsals but by three o'clock Kitty would call a halt and he would take Esme out to tea or for a walk, bringing her back in good time to bathe and change for the evening's performance. On Sundays he'd take her on a lake steamer, for picnics on the shore or long walks over Loughrigg Fell, and they would lie in the sun, kiss, make love and talk of anything and nothing at all, as young lovers do.

They never spoke of the coming war or of how all their lives might be about to change. Nor did they ever speak of Charlotte.

'Let's have some fun,' Archie would say, and Esme would wholeheartedly agree, vowing not to ask for any more than he was prepared to give. She was not entitled even to that, she privately believed.

Nevertheless they became almost inseparable and Esme began to nurture a hope that he might at last love her as much as she did him. Everyone was remarking upon their closeness and Mrs Pips, who had been uncharacteristically quiet since joining up with the company again in Hexham, a whole week after her inexplicable absence, seemed to go out of her way to assist the pair, finding them maps and boots for their hikes, putting them up splendid hampers of food to take with them on their trips in the old Jowett. She said not a word about where she'd been, or what she'd been doing. Not even Esme could prise it out of her.

Kitty watched the love affair develop with mixed feelings. While she was delighted for her dear friend, still her own heart ached with longing and she wished it could be her blessed by such love. She had her lovely child, of course. Dixie was always with her, Kitty even carrying the baby on her hip during rehearsals. But how she longed to share this joy of parenthood with someone.

In addition, Kitty was forced ruefully to acknowledge that perhaps she'd driven her company too hard over these past weeks. She agreed to keep Sundays free. Surely they deserved a little relaxation during this blissfully hot summer when all too soon harsh reality might hit them. Yet for all their hard work and the fact everyone had clearly suffered from the punishing winter programme, there were few complaints and most of them were already looking forward to the next season.

'War or no war,' Felicity would say.

'It'll all be over by Christmas if it comes at all,' Suzy would insist, while Tessa would worry about her low blood pressure if the excitement of it all got too much.

'Best foot forward and march in step,' declared Jacob, who'd never seen military action once throughout a long and peaceful lifetime. Rod and Sam made no comment at all but their eagerness to be a part of the action was clear in their eyes, for everyone to see.

It was towards the end of July when Charlotte caught up with the Players again. She returned to Repstone and found them enjoying a weekend break. She looked remarkably refreshed and bright-eyed, more beautiful than ever; in startling contrast to the somewhat jaded appearance of the rest of the company.

'My word, you all look worn out,' was her opening remark as she regarded them in a suitably languid pose; exquisite in black and white silk, a tightly sculpted hat framing the perfect oval of her face. Nobody attempted to deny it.

'At least you're looking fully rested now, Charlotte,' Kitty said, kissing the air half an inch from her cheek and trying to sound genuinely welcoming. The scent of Attar of Roses was almost overpowering in the small parlour. 'Taking care of your sick mother wasn't too onerous then?' And if Charlotte gave her a somewhat sharp look, Kitty merely lifted her eyebrows in polite enquiry and smiled.

'I feel frightfully guilty for having let you all down,' she said, hooking her arm lovingly through Archie's and smiling graciously round at them all, eyes brimming with instantly manufactured tears. 'Have you missed me, darling? It can't have been easy for you to manage without me. Or for dear Esme, having to step into *my* shoes.' She turned her winning smile upon the hapless girl. 'Archie tells me that at least one audience started baying for me to appear and poor Kitty had to go on with excuses.'

Felicity gave a bark of laughter. 'Not a bit of it, old fruit! Esme stood in like the trouper she is and played a stormer every night. Developed into quite a little gem, has this gel.'

Charlotte's face tightened with instant temper while Esme, flushing furiously, quickly demurred. 'It was nothing, really. I'm just an old ham.'

She was far more concerned by the fact that Archie seemed to be abandoning her in favour of Charlotte. As he hovered indecisively between the two of them, Charlotte clicked her fingers and he hastened over to fetch her wrap. It was a significant moment and a wave of nausea hit Esme, a presentiment of what was to come.

'The audience doesn't seem to think so,' Jacob was smilingly reminding her. 'What about when you played Ophelia in *Hamlet*? That was a brilliant performance. You had them cheering in the aisles. A standing ovation no less.'

With some amusement, Kitty watched Charlotte swivel her startled gaze back and forth from Esme to the various members of the company who were all eager to chip in with evidence of her accomplishments. It was being made abundantly clear that not only had she valiantly held the fort in Charlotte's absence but become a shining light at each and every performance, a star in her own right.

Kitty silently prayed that Esme wouldn't have to pay too high a price for this show of solidarity. But Charlotte's next remarks proved how easily she could discard such troubling concepts as professional rivalry.

'You were evidently fortunate to play to audiences who were prepared to be generous, despite their disappointment at being palmed off with the understudy,' she caustically remarked, just the faintest hint of condescension in her tone. 'But then, with the threat of war, anything would amuse them, would it not? Now that I'm back, you are relieved of duty, Esme dear.'

'I don't think so, Charlotte,' Kitty hastily put in. 'Esme is already well into the part of Nora in *A Doll's House*, and has made it her own, so she might as well continue until the current season is over. Perhaps you could help backstage for a while until we start rehearsals for the autumn production. Then we'll see if there's a part in it for you.'

'Backstage?' Judging from the thunderous expression on Charlotte's face you would have thought Kitty had asked her to scrub floors in a workhouse. 'I *won't* be ignored, Kitty.'

'Indeed I'm sure that would not be possible.'

As Charlotte swept away, she resolutely had the last word. 'Of course, it may all turn out for the best. I have my dear mother to think of so it is *exceedingly* useful to have such a *willing* understudy. Even one who is no more than second rate.'

Her exit, as always, was superb and Kitty could only marvel at how this tiny Yorkshire girl could have transformed herself into such a consummate primadonna.

*　　　*　　　*

Charlotte was in a towering rage. Never in all her life had she felt quite so angry. Esme was proving to be far too competent. She'd clearly ingratiated herself not only with the company but with the audiences as well. Even Archie could all too often be found hovering around the girl, effusively praising her performance, checking that she'd taken sufficient rest or offering to fetch her a cup of tea. It had to stop.

And all because Charlotte had been forced to stay away far too long. It had proved well nigh impossible to break free from Magnus, for all his feigned indifference. She wouldn't have stayed a moment longer than necessary, were it not for that prissy little nurse worming her way into his good books. Charlotte had soon come to the conclusion that, despite his intention to keep her bound to him forever, Sybil Mahon had other ideas and would not be averse to becoming the next Mrs Radcliffe. As if that wasn't bad enough, it seemed that all those balls she'd been busily juggling were now flying all over the place. She had to get them back under her control.

Yet it was becoming increasingly clear to her that time was running out. She must achieve her objective. Either Archie must give up this nonsensical way of life and offer her the security and place in society she craved, or she'd be forced to write him off as a failed enterprise and return to Yorkshire and Magnus. An early resolution to the crisis was vital, particularly with rumblings of war in Europe growing ever louder. Kitty had begun to talk about entertaining the troops and Charlotte certainly couldn't see herself in a dugout, for God's sake, entertaining Tommy Atkins.

The first few days following her return continued to be difficult, and she overlooked no opportunity to reassert what she considered to be her superior position in the company.

Charlotte made it clear that she considered it quite beneath her to work backstage, confining herself to sitting elegantly in the prompt corner, taking enormous satisfaction in correcting mistakes. She naturally refused to don Esme's dungarees or risk in any way getting her hands dirty, which would quite spoil her nails. She declined absolutely to lift scenery, or hoist the backcloth into position. Repainted several times since it had been first used for the *Cinderella* ballroom scene, it now depicted a Victorian garden for the final scene in Kitty's latest home-grown offering, *Answering the Call to Arms*, yet another patriotic piece full of insipid sentimentality. Whenever Reg called upon Charlotte to check the stage for props before curtain-up, it was amazing how often she just happened to be occupied elsewhere.

And no matter how busy they were, she always insisted on a lie down in the afternoon.

It was during one such siesta that Mrs Pips came to see her. She walked boldly in, without even knocking or a by-your-leave, and closed the door behind her. If Charlotte was irritated by the intrusion, she quickly bit back any complaint for one glance at the old housekeeper's expression told her that the situation was even more dire than she'd appreciated.

Mrs Pips certainly wasted no time in coming to the point.

'I followed you that night, the one when you ran off

during the interval,' she bluntly informed Charlotte, folding thin arms across her narrow chest. 'I know where you went, and I know why. I know all about that invalid husband o' thine, too. It took no more'n a few questions round and about to find out the whole sorry story. And I'm telling you straight, little madam, if you don't leave my Archie alone and give him and Esme a proper chance to make a go of their relationship, I'll tell him, tell everyone in fact, what you're up to.'

Charlotte listened almost open-mouthed to these pronouncements. They came quite out of the blue, entirely unexpectedly, and shook her more than she could say. She hadn't even begun to shape any sort of reply before the old woman was walking out, her parting shot being that she'd give Charlotte twenty-four hours to think on it.

After she'd gone, Charlotte stormed back and forth in the green room of the small theatre, ranting and raving so that anyone hearing her changed their mind about coming in and scurried away. Except for Frank.

His opportune visit, just an hour after that of Mrs Pips, shed a completely new light on the entire problem. It was really most fortuitous that his anxiety to remind her of an earlier promise to help him persuade Kitty into matrimony, and the further information he now offered in his desperation to succeed, handed her the very ammunition she needed to bring about a solution to her own problems.

Charlotte was a model of diligence during that evening's performance. Reg never needed to call her twice for she would be there, smiling serenely at his elbow, whatever task he'd required of her dutifully completed. And if during the interval she spent longer than necessary on stage, checking furniture and props, testing the winding gear which hoisted and lowered the backcloth, no one remarked upon it. Nor did anyone notice her slip front of house or see coins being slid into back pockets among the riffraff standing at the back. So it came as a surprise to them all when the riot started.

It began as a groundswell from the back of the hall. A soft wave of complaint and grumbles that ebbed and flowed till they washed over the back stalls, peaking to a roar with individual voices calling out louder than the rest.

'Where's little Lottie? We want our Lottie!' The cry was taken up by several more.

'Take this boring play off,' they yelled.

'Bring back the dancing girls.'

'Aye, them in the flimsy frocks wi' nowt underneath.'

'Bring us our Lottie.'

And then it seemed as if the wave rose and broke right over the stage itself, for the cast were suddenly swamped by brutish young men clambering upon it, picking up furniture and breaking it to bits, smashing stage crockery, throwing props about and causing utter mayhem. Esme had her hands to her mouth, screaming with fear. Suzy stood frozen with shock while Felicity rushed on stage to join in the affray by battering the rabble-rousers over the head with her bicycle pump. Jacob and Archie ran front of house to try to stem the tide while Reg fled to call the police.

Mrs Pips was standing where she always stood, at the

back of the stage with Esme's change of costume in her hand, utterly transfixed by the scene before her. Somebody shouted to her to step back and, although she wasn't certain from where the voice came or whose it was, she obeyed instinctively and upon the instant, afraid of the crush that was swelling towards her. Ida Phillips didn't hear the winding handle creak and spin out of control, nor the rope snap as someone cut it, because of the noisy bedlam all around her. And she never even thought to look up as the backcloth, complete with its weighted chain and the heavy crossbeam that usually held it secure high up in the flies, came careering down upon her head.

Because Archie was so desperately upset by the death of his one-time housekeeper and companion, Charlotte left it until the week following the funeral to break her news to him. She allowed him to stumble across her seated on a dressing trunk behind the scenes, weeping softly into her hanky. She brushed the tears quickly away of course, feigning bravery, for this always appealed to the gentleman in him.

'What's wrong now, Charlotte, old love? No more sniffles allowed. We have to go on. Pips would expect it.'

He'd quite misunderstood and for a moment she was nonplussed but, actress that she was, didn't allow this to show, merely used it to her own benefit. 'Oh, Mrs Pips was such a *dear* friend, and I'm in sore need of one of those right now.'

'Won't I do?' He took away the soggy scrap of cotton and offered her his silk handkerchief in its place. Charlotte used it to dab at her crocodile tears.

'Oh, dear, I'm afraid you're going to hate me.'

'Never!'

'Promise?'

'Spit it out, Charlotte. You know how I hate prevarication.'

'Well – I'm afraid that our little moments of intimacy, our hi-jinks, have had an unexpected – no, not entirely unexpected, I suppose – an *unasked for* result.'

His eyes widened with shock. 'You don't mean . . .'

'I'm afraid so.'

'Lord, are you sure?'

Charlotte nodded. It wasn't true, of course, but only she was aware that pregnancy was impossible following her fall from the horse. A timely 'miscarriage' could be manufactured once she had achieved her objective. 'Why do you think I ran away? I'm so filled with shame. I know how you feel about responsibility, commitment, *encumbrances*, and I don't want to add to them,' she whimpered. 'But I couldn't cope with being an unmarried mother as Kitty does. I mean, I know how you felt when she was in the same boat, so why should I fare any better? Your first responsibility should be to her, shouldn't it? It's all so *awful*!'

'To Kitty?' He came to sit beside her on the trunk. 'Why would I have any responsibility towards her?'

Charlotte gazed at him in moist-eyed innocence. 'I mean, because of the baby. Of course I know she lied, pretending that Dixie was Frank's child. Everyone knows. I mean, you did too, didn't you, deep down? Though you *really* only thought of her as a sister, didn't you, despite the fact you must have – well – at least once, I suppose. Which I'm quite certain must have been at her instigation.

But if you were ever prepared to take on the responsibility of a child, it should be Dixie first, shouldn't it? By rights.' Charlotte ran out of steam, which was perhaps just as well, judging by his reaction.

For a moment she thought he was about to strike her. His face went bright scarlet, then bleached white, finishing up a sort of dull shade of purple. 'Are you trying to tell me that Dixie is *mine*, and not Frank's at all?'

'Well, yes. Oh, dear, I thought you *knew*! I've said the wrong thing.' Charlotte considered it judicious to begin weeping again. The cold fury in his expression was really quite alarming. 'Oh, Archie, you do see why I didn't dare tell you about *my* condition?'

Without a word he strode from the room and she was half afraid that he'd gone to confront Kitty with this new information. But she should have known better, of course. Archie hated confrontations, would do anything to avoid one. It was Frank he spoke to and, once having satisfied himself of the true facts, it took no time at all to bring her scheme to a satisfactory conclusion. None of this helped Frank's case, of course, not one little bit, but why should she care? She'd got what she wanted. At last.

It was Esme who came to Kitty with the news. She was weeping uncontrollably, her face pinched with distress, and although she'd done little else since the death of her dear friend, Kitty saw at once that something more had occurred.

'What? What's happened, Esme? Tell me.'

Esme handed her a note. It was from Charlotte and stated briefly that neither herself nor Archie would be available for the next tour. It said she was carrying his child and that they'd eloped to Gretna Green, following which they'd be heading for Italy on an extended honeymoon.

Kitty stared at the letter in stupefaction before screwing it up into a tight ball. Whatever she might have said, or felt, or thought about the situation, no one was ever to learn for Jacob too arrived a moment later with far more serious news.

It was the first week of August 1914 and a state of emergency had been declared. Mobilisation was under way. The war that was to change the course of history was about to begin.

ACT TWO

France and the Lakes

1915

Chapter One

Kitty had never expected war service to be easy. She'd embraced the idea of embarking for France to entertain the troops as a much needed antidote to self-pity, but never for a moment had she expected it to be like this. Already she longed to turn and run and forget the whole madcap scheme, yet it had barely begun.

They'd embarked on a glorious autumn day in 1915, the sun striking the chalk cliffs that normally gave shelter to the local fishing fleet and Channel steamers rather than transport ships full of soldiers and artillery, going off to war.

She'd spent most of the crossing hanging over the rail being stupendously sick while young boys masquerading as soldiers stood about in their life-jackets, smoking and joking as if they were off on a Sunday School outing. Feeling rather sorry for herself, Kitty had marvelled that they could be so light-hearted when they were about to face the bitter cold of mud trenches, the whine of bullets or the horror of poison gas.

'Give us a crack at Fritz,' was their only response

whenever they were asked their feelings on the matter.

Several of the older men were clearly returning to the front for even more punishment after recent hospitalisation, wearing their gold wound bars like a badge of honour.

Throughout the gruelling journey from Folkestone, her one thought had been for Dixie. The need for her child was a constant ache about her heart. How could she abandon her, for all she was safe with Archie, her own father? Kitty could only hope that some good would come out of this enforced separation, by giving father and daughter time to get to know each other better.

Since Archie's marriage, they'd learned to rub along for a while, for the sake of the company, but the closeness of their earlier friendship was quite gone. Archie had other loyalties now but it was fortunate that his relationship with Dixie remained good, and, since he'd been rejected for military service because of the poor state of his lungs, he'd actually volunteered to take care of her while Kitty was away.

Even Charlotte had agreed to be 'a loving mother' to the little girl. For weren't they all still friends, she'd said, smiling sweetly. So what was there to worry about? Dixie was safe.

Now, having to her great surprise survived the rough voyage, Kitty stood with the rest of the company on the harbour at Boulogne amongst a pile of boxes, bags, and even a small piano, while a sea of khaki flowed around them. A brighter sun was now reflected on the guns carried by men swarming down gang planks. Others loaded supplies on to trucks; motor cycles careered off in every direction with messages of great urgency; ambulances lined up, patiently waiting to place the wounded on board before the ship set sail back to Blighty – assuming it could ever manoeuvre its way out to sea again through a harbour mouth thickly congested with submarines, destroyers, ammunition carriers and craft of every description. Overhead was the constant drone of aircraft, adding to the general cacophony of noise which did nothing to ease her aching head or sense of disorientation.

'Are you feeling better?' Jacob's kindly face came into view, his faded eyes peering anxiously at her while his spectacles dangled uselessly, as always, from his waistcoat pocket. Scarlet checks today. Ever the dandy.

'I'm just about to organise a cup of tea for her,' Frank portentously informed him, as if such things could easily be procured in a French harbour in wartime, served in wafer thin china on a silver tray with *petits fours* no doubt. He jostled the old man to one side and shouted to no one in particular. 'Tea. Over here please. Someone unwell needs tea.' If anyone did in fact hear, they gave no sign as the confusion continued to swell and flow unabated about them. Frank's ridiculous pomposity did, however, serve to lighten her mood and Kitty actually smiled, despite her queasiness.

'I don't think we can expect waitress service, do you?'

'Perhaps it's the tweeny's day off,' Felicity said with a guffaw of her barking laughter.

'Miss Kitty Little? If you're the Travelling Players, follow me please,' a voice boomed in her ear above the din.

'That's us!' Kitty yelled back with relief. Moments later the small troupe was being led through the mêlée. 'Captain Dafydd Owen Williams will be in charge of you. He'll be along shortly. The Army's wheels are oiled by punctuality.'

Their boxes of props, costumes and other belongings were swiftly loaded on to the back of a small truck and they were brusquely ushered up afterwards, each of them being handed a tin hat as they climbed aboard with firm instructions to 'wear it at all times'.

'I believe we're to go to the new military theatre that has been built behind the lines. We're keen to get there today if we can. Is it anywhere near the Front?' Kitty enquired.

'Ask no questions. Just do as you're told,' she was bluntly informed and before she had time to thank their saviour, he had clicked his heels smartly together, saluted and vanished into the crowd.

'I suppose there's order somewhere in all of this,' Jacob grumbled, struggling to fasten his helmet and bringing forth a burst of giggles from Kitty when he finally succeeded, for it was several sizes too small. Her own was no more comfortable, coming halfway down her cheeks. Swapping them produced a slight improvement but it still felt so awkward and clumsy, she abandoned all thought of wearing it.

'Don't start developing Charlotte's airs and graces,' Suzy warned.

Felicity said, 'Perhaps she wants to look her best for Tommy Atkins.'

'To hell with Tommy Atkins. It just makes my head ache all the more, that's all. Anyway, if a bullet has your

number on it, a tin hat isn't going to save you, is it?'
She shrugged in a what-the-hell gesture, holding up a
warning finger when Frank looked as if he was about to
start on his usual fussing.

After almost an hour of sitting packed like sardines
in the vehicle with the mayhem continuing unabated
around them, they all got out again to stretch their legs.

'Oiled wheels of punctuality, my foot! Where is he,
this Captain Dafydd . . . whatever-he's-called? Can't we
set off without him and meet him on the road?'

'I have my orders to wait here,' said their young
driver, appalled at the very idea of taking such an initi-
ative.

Another hour or more went by and only Reg with
his more pragmatic approach to life seemed able to
withstand the pressure of the enforced delay. Felicity
was in a lather of impatience, Suzy had smoked a whole
packet of cigarettes, Jacob was mopping his brow every
five minutes and threatening to go in search of the nearest
pub. Tessa had vomited ferociously and was now laid out
among all their worldly goods and chattels, moaning that
she would take the next ship home if someone didn't get
her some fresh air soon. Kitty herself felt as if her head
would burst. Finally she'd had enough of kicking her
heels and doing nothing.

'Nearly three hours we've been stuck here. If we're to
arrive before dark we should get going.'

'He'd have my guts for garters for breaking an order.'

'He can have my guts if he likes, or even my garters,
but if you know where this dratted theatre is, let's go.
My head is splitting from all this noise. I need a bed, a
wash and some food.'

'Not necessarily in that order,' Felicity grumbled, and with one accord they all piled back into the truck.

The young corporal climbed reluctantly behind the wheel and with a jolt and a lurch they were away, rattling off at a cracking speed along the rutted road. At every crossroads, military police directing operations seemed to be fighting a losing battle against traffic rushing in on them from every direction. Despite the bursts of high speed at times, progress was frustratingly slow as the LTPs' truck frequently got held up behind ranks of new recruits marching to replace the depleted forces at the Front, or their passage would be blocked by the abandoned wreck of a vehicle or empty trucks returning to Boulogne as well as those loaded with guns, army boots and other flotsam and jetsam of war being sent home to be repaired and restored to full service. Often they would be forced to pull over to make room for a speeding ambulance or shrieking dispatch rider who always had right of way.

Kitty, together with Tessa, who was in an even worse state than herself, sat up front with the corporal and from their vantage point could clearly see the pitted ground where shells had landed. They passed through several villages and small towns which had been ruthlessly shelled, with many buildings reduced to rubble, signs everywhere warning of the dangers of falling masonry.

'What have we come to?' Kitty murmured, half under her breath as the truck rumbled on.

'Hell,' came Suzy's voice from behind, and as the cack-cack of gun fire sounded close by, the corporal casually suggested they might care to put on their helmets. A shell hit the ground no more than fifty feet away, sending a cloud of dust high into the air, and they did exactly that, all earlier resistance forgotten.

Kitty closed her eyes in the hope that forty winks might make her feel halfway human again and calm her stubbornly churning stomach. It came to her then that the Theatre of War was nothing like as much fun as the more traditional one. And the thought that perhaps Esme had been right to refuse to accompany them did cross her mind.

This last year, following Archie and Charlotte's return from honeymoon, everything had changed for the LTPs. Repstone Manor was no longer available as a base for the company to rehearse in or even for rest periods. Within days of settling into her new home, Charlotte had embarked upon a programme of refurbishment, as if to firmly establish herself as if she were Lady of the Manor. There was no room at Repstone now for a 'second-rate group of travelling players'. Charlotte's description. Nor for those who were once close to Archie, and perhaps still nurtured a lingering fondness for him.

It wasn't surprising in the circumstances that the whole troupe had been behind Kitty when she'd put it to them that instead of touring the north of England, they should entertain the soldiers in France. Taking the show on the road for another season had somehow lost its appeal and she longed for a new challenge, perhaps even personal danger which might drive the devils of self-pity from her soul.

A few enquiries at the War Office ascertained that this was feasible, so long as the Players confined themselves to base hospitals and rest billets, at least one of which had been equipped with a theatre of sorts. The whole company had readily volunteered to go with her, except for Sam and Rod who had joined a Pals regiment together, and of course Archie and Charlotte. And Esme.

Kitty had sat on the bed watching her friend pack, begging her to change her mind. 'Where are you going? Where can you go?'

'You think I can't survive without you? I did before. Why not now?'

'I thought we were friends. Friends should stick together.'

Esme had put her arms about Kitty then and wept silent anguished tears. 'This has nothing to do with our friendship. You know it hasn't. If Archie were coming too then it would be different. But while he remains here, so must I.'

'He's *married*, for God's sake.'

'It doesn't matter. It can't last. Not with Charlotte. How could it? And I must be here in case he should ever need me, at least as a friend.'

'When? How long are you going to wait for him?'

'I don't know.' And a faraway look had come into her eyes. 'But if I can't have Archie, I don't want anyone.'

Kitty clenched her fists in frustration, but no matter how much she sighed and argued, ranted, railed or reasoned, it did no good. Esme had made up her mind. Her decision was unshakeable. The most Kitty could get out of her was that as soon as she found another theatrical troupe to join, and got even half settled in some digs, she'd write.

'Every day.'

Esme hugged Kitty close, chuckling softly. 'How will I have time to write every day if the new director works me even half as hard as you did? I'll write regularly, though, I promise.'

'Where will you go?'

'Wherever there's work. Perhaps the pier at Blackpool or Morecambe. And Manchester's full of theatres. I don't know but I'll find one that'll take me up, don't worry.'

When Kitty woke the next morning, Esme had gone. There'd been only one letter before they embarked for France, postmarked Accrington. It gave a cheerful account of a week's work she'd found at the Hippodrome. After that, Esme said, she intended to take the bus to Preston where she'd heard of a new rep starting up. That was months ago and, worryingly, Kitty had heard nothing since.

She was jolted awake by her head banging against the metal door frame as the truck lurched into a pot hole. Loud curses from the corporal soon made it clear to them all that they'd suffered a puncture and almost with sighs of relief they all scrambled out, eager to ease their aches and bruises while the driver set about the gargantuan task of replacing the wheel and repairing it.

'Where's the jack and the chocks?' Reg said, rolling up his sleeves.

'At least he's happy,' Suzy dryly remarked. 'Otherwise I'd say war was no fun at all.'

It was then that Kitty heard the tramp of tired feet and around the corner of the dusty track that passed for a road came a company of soldiers, each weary man weighed down by his pack complete with entrenching tools and rifle.

'Here we are,' she said, brightening upon the instant. 'Our first audience, I do believe.'

*   *   *

Charlotte swept her critical gaze about the shabby sitting room, at the threadbare carpets and peeling wallpaper, creeping mould on the ceiling and woodwork that hadn't been repainted for a hundred years at least. Yet given proper care and attention, not to mention a raid on those funds Archie kept squirrelled away, it could all be so different. She picked sulkily at a tapestry cushion, threadbare and grubby.

'You can be vexingly mean, you know,' she complained. 'All I want is to do up this dreary room so we can entertain properly. What's so wrong with that?'

Given her head, she would refurbish the entire house in a more *avant-garde* style, as the smart set were doing in Belgravia. She longed for white sofas and deep-pile carpets, Chinese porcelain and drifts of ice-cool lilies in every room which she would brighten with marvellous pictures in sea-washed colours reflecting the new Futurist mode. And she would hold smart little dinner parties to which everyone would simply *ache* to be invited. Now that would be real stardom. Instead, she'd been confined to the redecoration of their own bedroom suite and one small parlour. It was really too bad of Archie to be so parsimonious.

It had come to be a familiar scene, Charlotte railing while her husband buried his head behind his newspaper. Sometimes he made no response at all. Today, his dry, quiet tones broke into her fantasies. 'What utter tosh!'

She pouted. 'I want us to take our proper place in society as your mother must have done, and no doubt her mother before her.'

'Ma? Lord, she didn't give a fig for society, only her own little clutch of friends. Cackling hens, Pater called them. Affectionately, of course, don't you know.' And he scowled suddenly, gazing across the room as if he could even now see her seated behind the huge silver teapot with whiskery Aunt Grace and scrawny Mrs Pilling, gossiping away twenty to the dozen as they consumed scones and fancies to their heart's content.

Charlotte stamped her foot and a cloud of dust burst forth from the faded Persian rug which raised her temper another notch. Even finding staff to keep the place up to her immaculate standards was proving vexingly difficult, since all the young men were joining up in a fever and young women taking over their jobs on the farms and in factories, scorning poorly paid domestic service. There were even days when she'd come close to regretting having disposed of the irritating Mrs Pips since the woman had had her uses. 'Well, I *do* care a fig, so don't compare me to your stupid, unfashionable mother!'

The look on his face then was dreadful to behold, warning Charlotte that she'd perhaps gone a step too far. She mellowed her tone upon the instant. 'Darling Archie,' she wheedled, kneeling beside him as was her wont. 'I didn't quite mean that as it sounded.' The nearest Charlotte could ever come to an apology was to deny what she had said. 'I know you do your best. It's just that you give so little credence to the importance of society because you've always had a secure place in it. You take it for granted. But don't you see what it would mean to me? I need to make my mark in this new world I have entered, as your wife.' She dabbed at a manufactured tear.

'You have already, judging by the bills for frocks and furbelows I've received,' he coolly reminded her.

'Drat you, Archie Emerson, you're being deliberately difficult. And who are you to talk? Aren't you always quite the man-about-town yourself?' It was in fact one of the things she admired most about him. He'd always insisted on the very finest worsted suits, even a matching cap for his knickerbockers when he went bicycling. She simply adored his crimson silk dressing gowns and velvet smoking jackets, his Moroccan leather travelling case which held his cut-throat razor, stick of shaving soap, toothbrush and tin of Calvert's Carbolic toothpowder. Archie was fastidious to the point of obsession, which fascinated and infuriated her all at the same time; particularly if she was waiting for him to come to bed and he was still fussing in his dressing room. 'You're ashamed of me, that's what it is,' she shouted, patience exhausted.

'Perhaps I'm sick of being used as a walking bank account.'

'How *dare* you!' Charlotte was on her feet, face scarlet with fury. Her own attire that morning was, as usual, equally fashionable, being a beige silk suit with an ankle-length narrow skirt over which she wore a modish overtunic that reached almost to her knees so that as she yelled and screamed, throwing herself into a fine paddy, she took great care not to crease it. And as she did so, her Yorkshire accent thickened, deliberately so. 'Tha thinks I'll let thee down. Well, 'appen I will.'

'Calm down, Charlotte. You'll hurt yourself. And you don't normally speak so broad, so why adopt that dreadful accent just to make a point which is completely fallacious?'

'Fallacious? Fallacious? What's that when it's at home?'

She put her hands on her hips and rocked back on her heels, laughing at him, loud and long, the raucous sound of her voice frighteningly close to hysteria. 'A girl from t'gutter wouldn't know the meaning of such fancy words. The kind of words that would've made your precious ma faint clean away. Words like "bugger" and "whore". That's what I am, tha knows. A bleedin' . . .'

'That's enough!' Archie leaped to his feet and flicked out one hand as a warning for her to stop. But he'd forgotten he was still holding the newspaper and the corner caught her cheek, grazing it and shocking her into a stunned silence.

'You struck me.'

'Charlotte, I didn't . . . I never meant to.' She slid to the floor in a paroxysm of tears, surreptitiously adjusting the overskirt so that it billowed beguilingly about her as she fell. Archie held her shuddering body close, giving her shoulder awkward little pats and murmuring pitiful apologies about how the fault was all his, recognising in himself a weakness he loathed.

There had been moments in recent months when he'd bitterly regretted this hasty marriage, particularly since Charlotte had lost the baby. He should never have allowed himself to be talked into it. And all because Kitty had lied about the father of her baby.

What was it they said? It takes only a weak man to do nothing for evil to flourish. No, no, it takes only a *good* man to do nothing. But he wasn't good, was he? Never had been. Else why would he treat people in the offhand way he did? He'd hurt Esme badly. Oh, yes, he recognised the flaws in himself only too well. If only he'd seen them in Charlotte before they tied the knot, but he'd been besotted, captivated by her sensual charms. Perhaps it was the lack of a child, or her disappointment in Repstone Manor and the life she'd taken on as his wife, but she was becoming increasingly difficult, selfish, vain and utterly profligate with money. But worse than that? Surely not.

'When I think of all I've done for you,' she wept, 'even agreeing to taking in your by-blow.' She was playing the poor wronged wife to perfection and Archie's sense of guilt soared for all he recognised the role. 'Yet have I once complained about the poor motherless infant?'

She was turning her body into his now, pushing her hand down to cup him, making him groan with guilty pleasure. Charlotte lifted her face and the moist pout of her lips, the suppleness of her lovely body and the touch of satin-smooth skin beneath his fingers, precluded any need for him to answer her. He simply couldn't get enough of her delectable body. Charlotte was utterly irresistible, and for all her histrionics and natural misgivings, had been kindness itself to Dixie. Much as he still held a fancy for Kitty and adored Esme's sweetness, Charlotte was infinitely more exciting, appealing to a part of him he didn't care to examine too deeply.

He pulled the flimsy tunic roughly aside to grasp one rosy nipple with his mouth and suckle her, making her gasp with pleasure. God, how he needed her.

Excitement was mounting in him. Now she was unbuttoning his trousers and he was frantically trying to free himself from their encumbrance; the erotic squeak of silk underwear urging him on as she too fought to free soft flesh for his delight, all consideration for her gown now quite abandoned. He entered her as she lay on the dusty Persian rug, though she was by no means submissive for Charlotte was never that, but an equal willing partner in their search for new delights. Sometimes she would straddle him, riding him like a horse to hounds; at others she would play the innocent maid succumbing to the wolfish demands of her lord and master while enticing him on. Or she would scold him as if she were his nanny and he a naughty schoolboy. Her facility for acting any part, even in their lovemaking, never ceased to amaze and enrapture him. Sensation swamped him. Nothing else mattered, all cares faded away, no other thoughts existed beyond his need for Charlotte.

Much later, as they lay together in the huge four-poster bed, he carefully explained that he was not half so rich as she seemed to imagine. Even so, Archie knew he would at least take her up to town on one of her gargantuan shopping sprees by way of recompense for her disappointment over the shabby house he'd saddled her with. Tight as his finances seemed to be these days, he'd find the wherewithal to stay a night or two in a small hotel he knew in Kensington where they could enjoy long breakfasts in bed together.

'Silly boy. You worry far too much.' Charlotte gave a little sigh of pleasure as she tenderly stroked his dark curls. At first she used to laugh when he expressed such concerns; now she took them more seriously. 'There are always ways and means of getting more money. If we really are so hard up, then I must put my little brain to coming up with a plan to ease this temporary difficulty. Don't I always find a solution?'

Before he knew it Archie had agreed not only to
the redecoration of the main salon, including the new
white sofas she coveted, but also to a grand dinner party
afterwards to show them off. How he would manage to
pay for it all he had not the faintest idea, but then didn't
Charlotte always get her way?

Chapter Two

They entertained the soldiers there and then on the road. Some of the men were injured and had to be set down with care by their comrades but the whole troop squatted or sat in enthralled silence throughout the performance apart from the huge swell of laughter which greeted a short parody of a sergeant-major on parade, and a rousing chorus of 'Tipperary' in which they all joined with gusto. Somewhere in the distance was the crump of shells falling but here, in the middle of the dusty French countryside, the voices of British soldiers drowned out the sounds of death for once.

'Let the Huns hear we're not beaten yet!' roared one young private, his ashen face a mask of pain as he nursed an arm strung up in a makeshift sling.

They were the merriest group Kitty had ever met, for all their sorry appearance, and she'd never enjoyed herself so much in all her life. Her headache was quite gone.

'What the *hell* do you think you're doing?'

She whirled about, stunned by this angry interruption from a voice that resounded above the din, drowning out even the soldiers' lusty singing. The men, she noticed, began desperately scrabbling to their feet as quickly as their injuries would allow.

Ignoring her completely, the newcomer sharply informed them that if they did not get on their way in double quick time he would personally extract their lily-livered hearts from their puny bodies and make them eat them for breakfast. Having issued this dire threat, which was instantly acted upon, the Captain, for such he undoutedly was, turned his ferocious glare upon Kitty.

'Don't you realise you could have got all these men killed if they'd been spotted by German scouting planes?'

The gall of the man was beyond belief. Afterwards, the mere recollection of his arrogance brought Kitty out in a lather of hot sweat. But at this precise moment, merely looking up into his face robbed her of breath, leaving her quite speechless. His tall, commanding presence emanated an aura that was both compelling and disturbing. Perhaps it was the rust-red hair which haloed his somewhat square head with unruly curls, or the deep set, greeny-grey eyes glittering in an undoubtedly handsome face that caused her to judge him so harshly. She caught the scent of his hair cream, all mixed up with the smell of dust, smoke and cordite. Rich. Woody. Intoxicatingly masculine. He really had no right to smell so *good* in the middle of war-torn France. She took a half step back and rallied her attack. 'Don't be ridiculous. They were walking along the road anyway. We've just improved their morale, that's all.'

'You shouldn't even be here.'

'*You* didn't show up. What kind of army discipline is that?'

'Army discipline is about doing what you're told, without question. In this case, waiting by the harbour for me to collect you and issue your next orders. *Even if it meant waiting all night!* And where, exactly, did you imagine you were heading?'

'To the military theatre behind the lines. The corporal said he knew where it was.'

'The corporal had his orders. Now he's in breach of discipline. And you are supposed to be in Boulogne tonight, at the military hospital, entertaining the wounded.'

Kitty's cheeks fired with embarrassment. 'Well, I didn't know that, did I?'

'If you'd waited, you would have found out.' She could hear the hint of caustic amusement in his tone, which infuriated her all the more.

'I've told you, we *did* wait. All dratted afternoon, to no avail. Where the hell were you? Oiled wheels of punctuality indeed.' The phrase, repeated because she rather liked it, was not received quite so placidly by this man as it had been by the young corporal.

Captain Williams leaned forward, thrusting his great square head close to hers while Kitty's fascinated gaze traced the line of his full upper lip. 'I happened to be delayed by a road blowing up in front of me. There is a war on in case you hadn't noticed.'

Now she felt guilt as well as shame, though not for the world would she let him know it. Kitty rolled her eyes heavenward as if she had never heard anything so extraordinary in all her life. 'So that's what all this banging and shooting is about? Well, fancy that! And there was me thinking it was some sort of Continental

Carnival.' Behind her, she heard Felicity give a loud snort of laughter.

The Captain was not so amused. 'In the truck. On the double.'

'You can't order us about in that manner. We're not in the Army.'

'You are now. Under my command. Get in.' It sounded very like a threat. 'And put that hat on.'

Kitty had, naturally, taken the helmet off during the performance. But the road was now empty, their audience having departed at double-quick speed, as instructed. A cold wind had sprung up over the darkening countryside, bringing with it the return of her headache and a sickness in her stomach which had nothing to do with the sea. Even so, as she climbed back into the truck, she was the only one of the Players who did not wear a tin hat.

The base hospital in Boulogne was situated in the Casino, the largest ward being in what had once been the Baccarat room. It seemed almost obscene to imagine such hedonistic pleasures had ever existed. Now the room seemed strangely bare though it was spotlessly clean, no doubt scrubbed out twice a day at least for the smell of disinfectant and lye soap was strong as the LTPs entered. Men lay in cots, bandaged from head to foot it seemed to Kitty; eyes watched them with burning interest and without exception every face was smiling; brave, cheerful, strong, for all there was evidence of pain in the drawn tightness of pale skin.

The ward sister had told them the boys were desperate for entertainment, anything to take their mind off their plight, which might be a future with a missing limb, poisoned lungs or little or no sight.

'We thought you weren't coming,' one called out.

'Had you forgotten us?' cried out another.

'Heavens, no. Sorry we're late. The taxi broke down,' Kitty quipped. 'You need to get the roads mended round here.' And they all roared with laughter.

The LTPs had changed their act from the scenes of Shakespeare and other worthy dramas they'd usually performed to lighter pieces. Music and laughter were the order of the day now, since they were what the soldiers most needed. Something to brighten their hearts and lift their morale. Since Esme and Charlotte were no longer with them, Suzy had spent hours giving Kitty singing lessons, training her voice to a standard that would hopefully pass muster. When Kitty had embarked on this plan, she'd thought her ability, or lack of it, didn't greatly matter. After all, the wounded would be glad of anything, wouldn't they? Now she looked into these young soldiers' eyes and knew they'd paid dearly to be among her audience tonight, and she wanted to give them the best she could offer.

Aware of the Captain standing close behind, who would no doubt be only too pleased if she fell flat on her face, she lifted her voice, determined that was one thing she would never do.

Kitty smiled as she sang, the lovely wide winning smile that had once won the heart of an unknown porter in a dusty London theatre. Now it won over the hearts and minds of a ward full of wounded soldiers who had moments ago been in despair.

They listened to her, entranced, and as she neared

the end of her song Kitty knew she had reached into their very souls, so absolute was their silence. When the piece was over there was a great tumult of sound, a roaring in her ears which she realised was the hammering of crutches on the floor and the rattling of bed pans. She laughed with delight and, half turning to Captain Dafydd Owen Williams, gave a small smile of triumph, one which faded slowly as she met the intensity of those enigmatic sea-green eyes. Kitty could not read his thoughts but nor could she tear her gaze from his. The tumultuous roar seemed to wash over them both as his silent stare held hers, then he turned on his heel and abruptly walked away, leaving her feeling oddly bereft. She turned back to her more appreciative audience, lifted her arms for silence and began to sing again.

The rest of the show went off every bit as well as that first number, proving that the Lakeland Travelling Players were indeed a success and Kitty Little herself a hit. Even the good Captain was forced to admit as much when pressed to do so by the ward sister. But on matters of military discipline, however, he was inflexible.

'In future you'll go *where* I tell you, *when* I tell you, and always do *what* I tell you. Without argument or dispute. Is that clear?'

'Perfectly.' Kitty paused then added, 'Except for that bit about *what*. I make the decisions about what my own troupe does or doesn't do. I'm as much responsible for their health and safety as you are. Is *that* clear?'

His eyes narrowed most alarmingly. 'You may decide what they perform. Which songs they sing or which recitation they give. What costume they wear. Every-thing else is under my jurisdiction. Military discipline prevails.'

Kitty was almost jumping with fury and thought she might explode if she heard that word 'discipline' one more time. But before she had a moment to think of a suitable response, he blithely continued: 'And you will also wear that damned helmet.'

She placed it on her head, tipping it to a rakish angle, and saluted him with a mocking smile. *'Yes, sir!'*

He looked at her long and hard, the grey-green eyes clear and probing which for some reason made her heart beat faster. Then he turned slowly on his heel and marched off. His silent reaction to her sarcasm left her with an odd feeling of embarrassment, so that she had to bury her head in the props basket to hide her burning cheeks.

Kitchener's Army was to be sorely tested during that long painful autumn. With severe communication problems, half-trained men and a serious shortage of ammunition, they faced the enemy with incredible bravery, resorting to hand-to-hand combat when they ran out of bullets. The Battle of Loos casualty list was to be numbered at over fifteen thousand dead and twice as many wounded. Yet it was not entirely in vain. For the first time the German line had been breached and morale remained high.

Each day as the LTPs woke in the green French countryside, with the sound of birdsong in their ears and the Somme meandering smoothly on its way, it seemed impossible to imagine the loss of all those young lives. It became all too clear to Kitty and her team as Christmas approached, however, the river mists rose and the rains came, that their own role in keeping hearts and spirits strong could not be underestimated. Not that Captain Williams agreed with her on this. The cost of bringing the LTPs to France was, in his opinion, a waste of taxpayers' money.

'Don't think this is some sort of picnic you've come on,' he would constantly say, as if they needed any reminding. 'Don't you know the good folk back home are suffering a forty per cent increase in taxes for you to parade around here in your fancy frocks?'

'No one is paying us anything, as a matter of fact, and we provide our own costumes. The boys like us to look good.' The Captain simply shrugged and walked away, leaving Kitty damning him to hell as usual.

Another time he commented, 'Dear me, it's bully beef for supper again tonight. How you must be missing smoked salmon and strawberry tarts.'

It was true that much of the time the Players were cold, dirty, hungry, tired to the point of exhaustion and frightened, but not even Tessa complained. They each of them acknowledged and then dismissed their fear, for weren't the soldiers even braver? What right did they have to object to a few discomforts, when they'd chosen to come here of their own free will? They learned to live with that tight feeling of anxiety deep in their stomach, keeping it under control with the patience and dogged determination they'd observed and admired in the young men around them facing possible death.

It was the soldier boys themselves who made all the suffering worth while. They always welcomed the

Players with great enthusiasm, joined in lustily with the singing, and laughed till they wept with joy at the jokes and parodies.

The day after their success in Boulogne they'd entertained a couple of hundred roaring, cheering men in a YMCA hut. Another night they performed at an *estaminet*, which was a sort of pub where the men went to relax. Then it was time to pack up the truck, or *camion* as it came to be called, and roll on to the next rest billet, and the one after that. And always the Captain would ride in his Army car some distance ahead.

'What use are you as an escort, so far in front?' Kitty once asked, in that tart no-nonsense manner she usually adopted when addressing him.

The Captain's response was bleak but honest. 'No point in us all being blown to smithereens if a crump lands, is there?'

Punctures continued to be a problem but Kitty always used the opportunity for impromptu rehearsals on the road, despite Captain Williams's disapproval. The old men and women working in the fields around would stop and listen, then creep over to watch, delighting in these wandering minstrels who had happened by. The French peasant farmers, all who were left to work the land now their young men had joined up, would laugh and clap though they understood not a word. And always, in the background, was the steady throbbing of guns, like the rumble of distant thunder.

At times as they drove along the air would seem to crack apart from an explosion; clouds of dirt would rise from a nearby field as shells struck, one after the other as if pursuing them on their route. On one such occasion the *camion* careered out of control and they all had to leap for their lives, flinging themselves into one of the many hollows that pitted the soft earth, to avoid being blown into extinction.

'What on earth possessed you to come to this hell-hole?' the Captain asked, as they lay face down in a ditch. Kitty could not only smell her own fear, she could taste it in the bitter bile in her mouth while from overhead came the constant drone and squawk of enemy aircraft, threatening further death and destruction.

'Always did love all that *Boy's Own* adventure stuff,' she quipped, when she had her breathing back under control.

He gave a grunt which, if she hadn't known how ill-humoured he was, Kitty might have thought to be laughter.

'Well, that makes a change from the usual one of thwarted love like so many newly recruited nurses on their noble mission.'

Kitty made no reply except to say that this was a pretty damning indictment of dedicated medical staff.

They were heading for yet another anonymous château in some unknown part of the French countryside. She never knew exactly where they were since there were few road signs to guide them and Captain Williams never properly enlightened anyone about anything.

'What do know about this rest billet?' she asked through gritted teeth, anxious to move the subject away from the sensitive topic of love.

'Only that some official is to speak to the men first about pensions and war loans, and then it's up to you to lift hearts and roof, as they say.'

There was the roar of a plane above, strafe fire studding the road, followed by another almighty explosion. Kitty buried her face in her hands on the basis that what she didn't see wouldn't hurt her. After a moment or two when silence had settled back upon them she heard a bird sing and lifted her face to the weak winter sun. 'As we always do,' she remarked with a smile. 'What more could they ask than for Kitty Little herself to entertain them? The Nightingale of Flanders no less.'

Right at this moment she felt more like a mole than a nightingale. As she sat up, picking lumps of dirt out of her nose and mouth, and brushing soil and seeds from the front of her blouse, she was surprised to see him actually grinning at her for once. Kitty even found herself grinning back. It was almost a declaration of friendship. Almost.

'I see that at least you've decided to wear that damn' hat,' was all he said.

'He might be showing the smallest trace of a sense of humour but must he always make his dislike of me quite so plain?'

They had arrived at their billet, unpacked, eaten, and were now waiting for the show to begin. But Kitty was still stinging from her caustic exchanges with the Captain. Thwarted love indeed. How dare he? It was almost as if he knew, but that was quite impossible unless he had a sixth sense.

Jacob patted her shoulder, a comforting gesture that had become almost a daily ritual between them. 'How would you feel, my dear, if you were a military man and had been detailed to nursemaid a troupe of travelling minstrels?'

Kitty gave a short laugh. 'I should thank my lucky stars for a cushy number!' But she was thoughtful for the rest of that evening.

The audience waiting in the main salon of the château seemed livelier than usual, having had an opportunity to rest and recuperate. After a battalion had been at the Front for their required period of duty, they were pulled out and sent to a rest billet. Here they would have the chance of a bath and to be disinfected from lice, fleas and other verminous sores brought about by the trenches, get clean clothes and have small wounds and irritations tended to, not least the dreaded trench foot. Once all of that was dealt with, there would be drilling routines to maintain army discipline, of course, but also good food, plenty of sleep and a glass of beer now and then.

They welcomed Kitty with a roar of approval. Just the sight of her tall slender figure walking on to the wooden stage that had been roughly knocked together brought an eruption of cheers and a great stamping of feet. The room seemed filled to bursting with men. If they couldn't find a chair, they sat on windowsills or every available inch of the floor. The rest were content to stand, packing the back of the hall with their boisterous presence. It was almost overwhelming.

And as always the show was a huge success with the men taking Kitty Little to their hearts.

Immediately it was over, she went straight off to bed. She was so exhausted she could hardly keep her eyes open, yet the moment her head hit the pillow she was instantly awake, her body stiff and aching, her mind a turmoil of emotion and stray thoughts.

As she lay waiting for a sleep that refused to come throughout that long night in yet another freezing cold camp bed, Kitty wept with longing for her child, worrying over whether Dixie was missing her. Then she grew anxious about Esme, wondering where she was and if Charlotte or Archie would think to forward any letters they received from her. Surely she would have found a new theatre company by now?

Her thoughts moved on to the pain of losing Archie. 'Thwarted love' as the Captain termed it. She couldn't help herself. It was like poking at a sore tooth. Dear Archie. How she had loved him. Would there ever come a time when she no longer looked back and wondered about what-might-have-been? He'd been a part of her life for so long, it was hard to wake up each morning and know that she wouldn't see him.

How far they had come since that first fateful night they had spent together. When she'd gone to him then, it was as a young girl seeking enlightenment and love. Later, Kitty had imagined he might truly come to love her and perhaps he had, in his way. That was Archie's problem. He'd always meant to commit himself to one or other of them, but had never quite managed it.

She turned over endlessly in her mind whether there was anything at all she could have done to win him yet knew, in her heart, that there wasn't. Charlotte had meant to have him from the moment she'd set eyes on him and Archie had been too weak to resist. She'd manipulated them all, exactly as she pleased. Kitty realised this now. Neither she nor Esme had ever stood a chance.

Kitty liked to think that she was getting over losing Archie though it still hurt that he'd been prepared to father Charlotte's baby but not her own. Her pride, if nothing else. But then, Charlotte had told him the truth while she herself had refused to give any indication of the identity of Dixie's father on the grounds that she'd no wish to trap him into marriage. Thinking about it now, though, Kitty wondered whether her determination to keep the baby's parentage secret hadn't also come from more selfish motives. She'd been so involved with her life as actor-manager of the Players, so thrilled to be starting out on this adventure, that hadn't a part of her resented the possibility of giving up that freedom, even to a man she supposedly adored?

As a result, Archie had never quite forgiven her for keeping him in ignorance.

What fools she and Esme had been. And what right did she have to criticise her friend for hanging on to the impossible dream of wanting to win Archie back, hoping against hope that Charlotte would grow bored with him in time or that he would 'come to his senses' and give up on his hasty marriage? Wasn't Kitty's own way of dealing with the pain even more radical? A drastic solution to her girlish folly.

Sadly, Captain Williams's taunt had come closer to the truth than he realised. For losing Archie had indeed been the main reason she'd come to France and not, to her shame, any altruistic purpose at all. He was right. Running away to war was hardly a sinecure or a *Boy's Own* adventure story. It was harsh, raw reality. A matter of life and death. And the truth was that she was nowhere near brave enough to cope with it. Kitty turned her tear-streaked face into the hard pillow to smother her sobs.

'Oh, Archie, what have I done? I needed you so much. Why wasn't I enough for you? I need someone now, someone by my side to love me.'

After a short burst of self-pity, Kitty sat up and sternly blew her nose, scolding herself for this childish indulgence. She wouldn't make that mistake again. After all, she was no longer a foolish girl but a woman, one even more determined to be independent, to have done with men and love and all the problems such weaknesses brought. So if the image of one arrogant Captain slid into her dreams when sleep finally came, it was only by way of warning what she must avoid: emotional entanglement of any sort.

Thank goodness Dixie at least was safe which, in the end, was all that really mattered. It was going to be a long, hard campaign and Kitty wondered what exactly she had let herself in for.

Chapter Three

Charlotte was wondering very much the same thing. This wasn't at all the life she had imagined when she'd plotted and schemed to get her hands on Archie's wealth. In fact she'd acquired little more than a cold damp house in dire need of repair, a restless husband who was proving to be extremely mean with his money, and her chief rival's snivelling child.

Now two and a half, Dixie was proving to be a vexing nuisance, not least because Archie was so besotted by her. He spent hours in the nursery every day despite the child's having a perfectly good nanny to take care of her every need. Admittedly she was fretting for her mother, but was that Charlotte's fault, for God's sake? The child was becoming a real little madam, spoiled beyond endurance, and all because of Archie's guilt.

If she refused to wear a certain pair of shoes then Dixie would be allowed to choose another pair, a pink rather than a blue ribbon in her hair, or play on the swing in the garden instead of taking a healthy walk in the park. If Dixie declared a dislike of cabbage or rice pudding, then Nanny was instructed not to give her any, despite its being good for her. And if she did not get her own way, she would fling her dinner across the room in one of her 'little paddies', as Archie termed them.

Evenings were the worst. At least a dozen of Charlotte's carefully planned dinner parties had been disturbed by Archie's abandoning their guests to go and attend to the screaming child. If she ever did sleep at night, no one would know it. Even now, at well past midnight, he was sitting with her, no doubt telling her stories and singing lullabies, which was surely the nanny's job.

It simply wouldn't do. He should be here, with her, in their grand four-poster bed. If there was one thing Charlotte could not abide, it was a rival for his affections. She hadn't taken all those risks, or abandoned Magnus, to be supplanted by a child.

Around two o'clock she was vaguely aware of Archie creeping into bed. She kept her back firmly turned towards him, her mind a seething mass of resentment. Something had to be done.

There were more pressing concerns the next day, however, when the draper failed to keep his appointment to measure up for new curtains in the drawing room. Instead he sent a formal little note informing her that he could not accommodate her at present until she had settled her outstanding account. 'Dear Lord, must I do everything myself?' she railed, storming through the house on a tide of fury, seeking Archie upon whom she could cast the blame for this oversight. She found him, as expected, on his knees in the nursery, playing at building bricks with Dixie.

'Drat you! Why haven't you paid this silly little man

for his paltry curtains?' She flung the letter at him then turned her temper upon the nanny. 'And *you* can take that dratted infant out of my sight. *This minute!*' Nanny hastily gathered up the now screaming Dixie with more haste than dignity, and fled.

'Charlotte, calm yourself. It is not the child's fault. My dear, if you continue spending in this vein, we shall be bankrupt within the year.'

She bunched her fists into tight balls of barely controlled fury. 'You only say that to annoy me. Why won't you even try to please me? I know why, because you don't truly love me. You never did.'

'Utter tosh, old thing. You know how I adore you.'

'No, you don't. You give all your time and attention to that child and no longer care a jot about me.' She swung about on her heel and sailed off along the landing, forcing him to follow her.

'That isn't true.'

His calmness inflamed her to such an extent that she snatched up a Japanese vase which had probably stood in that particular niche on the landing for the better part of a century and flung it with both hands down the sweeping staircase. Archie's appalled expression as it smashed into a hundred fragments gave her immense satisfaction.

'See what you have driven me to, with your meanness and neglect?' she screamed. 'I gave up everything for you and this is the bleedin' thanks I get!'

Archie frowned but responded with studied calm. 'What exactly did you give up, Charlotte? The stage? The LTPs? You said you were bored with all of that?'

He was looking at her now with that all-too-familiar coldness in his gaze which sent a shiver down her spine.

Charlotte had spoken without thinking for she'd given up Magnus, of course. At least, she'd failed to visit him in almost a year. But since Archie didn't know about this other part of her life, about the man who truly was her husband, and indeed must never know, how could he ever understand? Anxious to disguise her slip, Charlotte frantically searched her mind and impulsively decided to turn her blunder to her advantage.

'You must see that it's difficult for me, witnessing your joy over Kitty's child when I can have none of my own.' Having 'lost' the child she'd claimed to be carrying at the start of their 'marriage', Charlotte had finally owned up to a genuine truth by telling Archie that she was no longer able to bear one. At the time of this revelation it had proved to be an excellent way of cementing their relationship, of drawing him closer in his concern for her. Fortunately he showed no desire to rear a dynasty of his own, but he had developed a surprising fondness for Dixie.

Now Charlotte recognised that she'd struck exactly the right note as expressions of shock, concern and remorse flitted across his face.

He was taking her in his arms and apologising for his crass insensitivity. 'I never thought. How utterly selfish of me. Of course, it must tear you apart. My poor darling.'

The tears were very nearly genuine for Charlotte did indeed long for a dynasty. Nothing would have pleased her more than to give Archie a child, one who would inherit the house and land and oust this little interloper for good and all. Without a pregnancy, and there was little hope of one following Magnus's past treatment of her, how could she ever be secure? The only way was to rid herself of Kitty's little monster. Archie was kissing her cheek, stroking her hair, begging to know how he could make it up to her.

'I never meant to hurt you, my darling.'

Charlotte took both his hands in hers and kissed each in turn. 'I do agree that we should keep a careful eye on Dixie. She is, I accept, still your child for all the pain it causes me to admit as much, but to witness the evidence of this relationship, day in and day out . . .' She half turned away in her distress. 'It is too much. Couldn't we . . . No, you would never agree.'

'Agree to what?'

A sob broke from her and Charlotte put a hand to her mouth that trembled to just the right degree. 'To the child leaving this house. She could keep Nanny, of course, but be accommodated elsewhere.'

'I really can't afford to set up two homes. This one is costing me a small fortune.'

Drat the man! Always money, money, money. Charlotte smiled beguilingly up at him, blue eyes shimmering with tears. 'Oh, I never meant you to provide her with a whole house of her own. She is but a child after all. But there must be good homely accommodation to be found somewhere locally, perhaps in Windermere or Ambleside or nearby Carreckwater. And you could still visit her whenever you wished.' But not spend every waking moment with her, or half the damned night!

Archie gazed at Charlotte, his face thoughtful and sad. 'I promised Kitty I'd keep her safe.'

'She still would be safe. Just not in my sight all day, reminding me of my failure. Distressing me.' Again that sob, with increased anguish this time.

'Would you find that more bearable, my dear?'

'I would.'

After another long pause he said, 'Then how can I object? We must find little Dixie a new foster home. But it must be clean and homely, the people kind and good to her.'

'Dear Archie, of course. Perhaps she will thrive in it for she seems far from happy here, constantly fretting and screaming. I shall begin making enquiries first thing tomorrow.' And so it was agreed. Charlotte kissed him and then remembered the note from the draper and the more pressing concern of her new curtains. 'Oh, and do remember to pay the draper's bill, darling. Perhaps you will be less forgetful of such matters once you no longer have a demanding toddler on your hands.'

As she swung away down the stairs, Archie watched her go in fond though troubled silence. Then he picked up the letter and paled as he read the amount.

Once the draper had been pacified and duly put to work measuring and sewing cretonne and voile, Charlotte set about the task of finding a new home for Dixie with enthusiasm. In the end, levering the child out of Repstone had proved far easier than she had anticipated. Hopefully, this would have the added advantage that the child's mother would have no reason ever to come here again. Any lingering friendship Charlotte might once have felt for Kitty had long since disappeared. She was now seen as a bitter rival and must be banished from Archie's life completely.

When Kitty had first declared her intention to go to

France and take part in the war effort, Charlotte had imagined she would vanish as easily and completely as the blessed Esme who'd packed her bags and never been heard of again, give or take the odd letter. All such hopes had been lost when Archie had volunteered to care for Dixie. *His* child after all! It seemed that the presence of the very creature who had helped Charlotte to win him was now proving to be a far fiercer rival for his affections than either of the two previous ones.

After firing off numerous fruitless letters which brought no result, Charlotte put a small advertisement in the *Westmorland Gazette* and in this morning's post had come, at last, a response. The letter was from a Miss Frost who, together with her sister, owned a small 'home from home' boarding house idyllically situated on the shores of Carreckwater. The letter stated that they would consider it their Christian duty to provide a home for a child while its mother was away in France. Charlotte decided to pay the Misses Frost a visit without delay.

She drove herself to the tiny village of Carreckwater with its slate walled cottages and narrow winding streets. These radiated outwards and ever upwards to the surrounding fells and hills from St Margaret's church in the village centre. After parking the motor by the old boatyard she strolled along the path by the lake, pulling her warm coat about her in the February chill. The sun was shining, sparkling on the wave tips like diamonds, and all around the crags and hills seemed sharp and clear on this bright winter's day. Charlotte longed for her heart to lift at the sight of such beauty but she was shivering, and not simply because of the cold. A cormorant took off as she approached to fly low over the sheen of water, beating its wings till it was a mere speck disappearing in the distance. Sometimes she half wished she could vanish just as easily. Fly away to a new life, a new beginning. But she'd already done that once before, hadn't she? So what had gone wrong?

Despite all the effort and planning she'd put into this new life, Charlotte felt she'd still failed to attain the riches or status she deserved. Having recklessly married Archie to thwart Esme, despite not being free, she now lived in fear of his learning their union was a sham. It wasn't as though she expected, or asked for, great happiness – merely security and a degree of comfort and contentment. Yet now, deep in her heart, she craved it. Why couldn't she be happy like everyone else?

Laburnum House was a tall, grey stone property situated on the corner of the Parade overlooking the lake. In no time, it seemed, Charlotte was seated in a small parlour, heavily furnished in the Victorian style complete with aspidistra standing to attention in the bay window, drinking tea out of dull brown and white china and doing her best to appear interested in what her hostesses were saying.

The Misses Frost had apparently once been débutantes and exceedingly pretty, they assured her, in their day. All suitors had sadly fallen short of their exacting standards however and now, thirty years on, it was far too late even to consider matrimony.

'Though you can never be sure,' Miss Bebe said and giggled quite disarmingly.

Her elder sister cast her a somewhat reproving look before continuing with their life story. 'When Papa died, leaving us quite comfortably off, we chose to retire to the Lake District and open this boarding house.'

'Where we live somewhat vicariously by sharing the lives of our many guests,' Miss Bebe concluded, and now both sisters glanced at each other before bursting into paroxysms of laughter.

'I beg your pardon, Mrs Emerson, but we are often fascinated by the eccentricities of our lodgers. Those who keep goldfish in the bath. Others who won't eat meat except on Thursdays, or young men who dash off to their employment in odd-coloured socks. They are an endless source of entertainment. All quite harmless, you understand.' Miss Frost seemed a little ashamed of this show of levity while Miss Bebe was still gasping into her handkerchief.

Charlotte, having suffered more than most from boarding-house life during her days with the LTPs, understood perfectly. She guessed the Players had often provided similar amusement for any number of land-ladies. Nevertheless, she decided upon this evidence that the two sisters were both quite mad but also honest and well-meaning. There was a regal quality about them with their straight-backed posture, high-necked old-fashioned gowns and neatly coiffured white hair which entirely suited their name.

Miss Bebe's dress was in polka dots, navy and white today as it was a weekday she'd blithely informed Charlotte, though on high days and holidays she claimed to splash out on red or green. Miss Frost, as the elder, more serious sister, clearly thought it more fitting to wear a restrained beige, though she had rather spoiled the elegant effect of this on Charlotte's arrival by being weighed down with an armful of dirty linen. Even so, she'd managed to retain a considerable degree of dignity as well as her good looks over the years, despite being well past sixty.

It took no time at all for Charlotte to discover they'd taken such a keen interest in the LTPs that they'd never missed a show. They congratulated her on her recent marriage and understood perfectly that she would, of course, wish to abandon such a racketing, nomadic lifestyle for the more demanding one of lady of the Manor.

They were all getting along so famously that the moment Miss Frost bustled off to the nether regions of the house to refresh the tea pot, Charlotte edged forward in her seat and confessed there was one rather delicate matter she should mention – that of the child's status. 'I must be honest with you, for she is not . . . not quite . . .'

Miss Bebe interrupted. 'Healthy? Normal?'

'Oh, no, she's perfectly healthy *and* normal. A charming child. Only her mother isn't . . . She never . . . I mean . . .'

'Ah, you're trying to say that she's illegitimate, aren't you? Dear, dear. Well, we mustn't condemn the child for that, must we? It wasn't her fault after all. And there is a war on.' As if that excused the lack of morals. 'Perhaps we can help the poor mother to repent of her immoral ways and be saved.'

Charlotte put her hand to her mouth and dropped her gaze, as if she were shocked by such bluntness, though in truth she was striving to smother her laughter. The very idea of Kitty being 'saved' was an utter delight.

Miss Bebe's voice dropped to a confidential whisper.

'Don't tell Hetty, though. Not yet. She isn't quite so liberal-minded as myself, do you see? I shall break it to her gently, later.'

'Ah, yes. I do see,' Charlotte whispered back in the same tone, not seeing at all.

'She tends to be a woman of opinions, which is why she never quite caught a man, if you take my meaning. I, of course, had any number of proposals all of which I refused because of my responsibility to her. I couldn't leave her alone, now could I?'

'No, no. Of course not.'

'Though I could still find a husband tomorrow, had I the inclination.'

Charlotte agreed that she probably could and smiled for the first time quite genuinely, itching to say that husbands were really so very easy to find, one could even have two if one wished. She decided there and then that this was the place for Dixie. These two eccentric old dears appeared ideal for a wayward, wilful child. Good, clean-living folk who would provide proper bedtimes, simple, wholesome food and chapel every Sunday; otherwise Archie would be dragging her back home again in no time. 'Would you like to meet her? May I bring Dixie on a visit?' Miss Bebe clapped her hands together in delight and as her sister set down the refilled tea pot, Miss Frost declared she'd been about to suggest the very same thing.

'We are ever of one mind,' Miss Bebe said, on a note of placid satisfaction.

There then followed a short discussion on the practicalities of accommodation, costs incurred (which they assured her would be modest), and the nanny who would naturally be employed by Archie to take care of the child.

Charlotte was careful not to give any reason other than that of common humanity for him to be paying for all of this. The two sisters appeared overwhelmed by this evidence of his benevolent generosity to a fellow actor, and spoke movingly of their own Christian endeavours during these dark days of war.

'We have rolled goodness knows how many yards of bandages.'

'And no one can knit balaclavas and mittens as quickly as dear Hetty,' Miss Bebe informed Charlotte with pride. 'We are happy to do what we can for our boys in France.'

'There is just one small concern,' Miss Frost cautiously pointed out. 'We can't be doing with a lot of mess about the place. Because of our guests, naturally. Or noise for that matter. I mean, the fact that she's a girl is the only reason we're prepared to consider the idea. A boy would be quite inappropriate, you understand.'

'Yes, I do see that.' Charlotte privately thought that the money might come in rather handy too, judging by the age of the wallpaper and the shabby old furniture in the dark parlour, though she judiciously refrained from comment. Instead she thanked the sisters for their goodness and charity though even she was beginning to be concerned about the costs involved. The total would amount to a fair sum each month, of which Kitty would be contributing nothing. Money was becoming an increasing problem in these inflationary times. Perhaps she'd be forced to reconsider her position and pay 'Mother' another visit after all.

'She is a good, quiet child, isn't she?'

'You'll hardly know she's there,' Charlotte agreed.

*   *   *

There was absolutely no danger of the Misses Frost ever forgetting that Dixie was in residence at Laburnum House. Her tantrums and screams whenever Nanny tried to coax her into doing something she didn't care for seemed to vibrate through the tall house with alarming frequency throughout the day. She point blank refused to sleep in the cot they provided, choosing instead a mahogany Empire bed which had to be moved 'specially from another room.

They soon abandoned the notion of allowing her to eat with the other guests in the dining room, as Dixie would toss lettuce leaves, which she loathed, over the sides of her high chair, or tip the pudding dish upside down upon her head. This always caused great amusement to the other diners but was not, in Miss Frost's opinion, conducive to encouraging them to return.

She was once found seated quite comfortably in the coal house, crunching on lumps of coal. Her clean frock, impish face, even her little pink tongue and white teeth, were caked in black dust.

But there were rare moments when the child was a delight. She loved to help Miss Bebe make gingerbread men or jam tarts and then they would say how one day she might be a great help to them in the kitchen. Though even these apparently harmless pursuits could give way to another tantrum if she wasn't allowed to eat as many as she wished. And if she didn't get her way, Dixie would lie on the kitchen floor and drum her heels while the two sisters would wring their hands and wonder what on earth they were doing wrong.

Nanny, poor girl, seemed out of her depth, constantly apologising for her small charge but quite unable to control her. Miss Frost would insist that the child required more discipline, though even she could be melted by Dixie's charm at bath time when her angelic baby face would glow pink from the heat and moisture. She would sit contentedly pouring water from one bottle to another, humming little tunes to herself until the water had gone quite cold.

'Perhaps she will be a chemist when she grows up,' the sisters would speculate.

'Or a doctor.'

'No, no, she'll become a fine cook for some country gentleman.'

All speculation was brought to an end the day Miss Frost opened the lid of the piano to play her favourite ditties and Dixie pulled up a kitchen stool, climbed upon it and began to sing. From that moment on, they were her captives for Dixie had the sweetest, truest voice you could ever hope to hear.

Chapter Four

The LTPs travelled fifty miles or more every day, moving from one rest billet to the next. Kitty had attempted to persuade Captain Williams to allow them nearer to the Front, but he wouldn't hear of it. Passing through the ruins of Arras proved to be dangerous enough, surrounded as they were by coils of barbed wire through which they must negotiate a safe passage. So many of the French towns were little more than skeletal ruins with no hope of ever being rebuilt; smashed houses, hollow-eyed women, children crying, the stink of gas and the sweet sickly odour of decay. And often on the outskirts would be a row of simple wooden crosses – a testament to the bravery of lost youth.

The roads too were choc-a-bloc with ammunition trucks, supply carts and wagons laden with the detritus of war. Occasionally they would pass encampments seething with men and horses, and everywhere there were guns.

Nevertheless Kitty was determined to reach as many of the battalions as they could so pushed them ever onward, despite the group's increasing weariness, making their way parallel to the Front Line. She always found time to stop and talk to any company of men they met along the way, exchanging news, listening to their troubles, agreeing to see that letters were safely dispatched back home to their loved ones.

Captain Williams worried if the group on the road got too big, or dallied too long, and would urge them to move on before they were noticed by the scouting planes. Sometimes Kitty would heed his fears; at others she'd have Reg unstrap the small piano, for all they were generally short of time, and go straight into an impromptu concert there and then on the muddy road beneath the trees, or even once in a shell crater. The soldiers loved it and would always go on their way singing, their hearts lifted.

It was after one such performance, as they stood in the mud and rain helping to reload the *camion*, that Kitty ventured to ask the Captain the question which had been bothering her ever since Jacob had mentioned it.

'Might I ask why you were chosen for this job? It can't be much fun wet-nursing a troupe of actors.'

He answered without hesitation, 'Because I was the best man for the job.'

Kitty gave a shout of laughter as she tossed a blanket into the back of the truck. The arrogance of the man was beyond belief! 'And clearly the most modest,' she mocked, aware that he was prevaricating. As ever, he avoided answering a direct question.

'Maybe I have a fancy for the thespian life myself.'

'You'd be happy to grace any stage, any tin hut or shell-hole, in any part I cared to offer, is that the way of it?' She wiped the rain from her face and pushed back her hair, eyebrows raised in disbelief. 'So that you can fulfil your fantasies?' For a moment he made no reply, simply gazed solemnly down into her face. Kitty was tall, but this man topped her by inches. The collar of his greatcoat was turned up against the weather. Even so, his face appeared blue with cold, deep lines of weariness carved into his cheeks to either side of his mouth, and she had a sudden longing to put up her mittened hands to warm it. Then came a rare smile.

'I trust you would never offer me a small part, Miss Little.'

'Kitty Little, if you don't mind. *Miss* makes me sound rather like a Sunday School teacher.'

He laughed. 'I fear your troupe is tired and in need of some new blood. Who knows? Perhaps I could provide it.'

Kitty felt her cheeks start to burn as she heard murmurs of assent from the others who were standing around stamping their feet against the cold and blatantly eavesdropping on this conversation. The implication that they weren't up to the task in hand irritated her enormously and her response was tart. 'We certainly lack young men. What acting troupe doesn't these days?'

'Then why couldn't I do my bit?'

'You're a soldier, not an actor. You have no experience.'

Reg cleared his throat and politely intervened. 'Hmmph, Captain Owen does have some experience, as a matter of fact.'

Kitty glared at him. So it was Captain Owen now, was it, instead of the more formal Williams?

'Indeed,' he calmly agreed, his voice all affable charm and bonhomie. 'In civilian life I did tread the boards a little. Even directed my own small theatre company for a short time, though sadly it was closed down and turned into a cinema. Which probably answers your first question as to why I was the one chosen to wet-nurse you. Your choice of phrase, not mine.'

Feeling increasingly wrong-footed Kitty bluntly informed him that had she ever been fortunate enough to own a small theatre, she would never have allowed such a terrible thing to happen. Cinema, she informed him loftily, was a passing fad.

'If you say so.'

The next twenty minutes were taken up by them all putting their shoulders to lifting the piano back up into the back of the truck. 'Small it might be but it ain't light,' Reg complained as he did every time it was moved.

'Then don't get it out unless you have to. The roadside is not the place for a concert,' Captain Owen warned, though he too had said this so often, no one listened any more. They all climbed up alongside it, sitting with their backs to one side of the *camion* and their feet propped against the piano. Kitty closed her eyes, suddenly bone weary and desperate for sleep.

'Ah, but your motives for performing are so much finer than mine,' came that persistent soft voice in her ear, as irritating as a bluebottle. 'Taking art to the masses, isn't that what you used to do? Very worthy. Even being here, in this Godforsaken place, speaks volumes for your charity. So noble of you. Not a sign of a lost lover anywhere. Whereas I'm in this dratted war just because it's my duty.'

Kitty bestowed upon him a narrow-eyed glare, wondering if there could be any sincerity at all behind those words in spite of their ironic tone. She itched to hit back, to smack his arrogant, handsome face with the flat of her hand. Instead, she found herself leaning heavily against his shoulder, eyelids drooping, head nodding, while she sternly informed him that, tired though they might be, they were still perfectly capable of hard work. 'My cast may have their problems – who doesn't?' she mumbled, already half asleep. 'But bully-boy tactics would never work with them.'

'Bully-boy? Is that what you think I am?' he whispered against her hair. 'I was merely voicing an opinion that there are one or two members of your team in need of a boot up the backside.' He nudged her gently awake again and nodded in the direction of Tessa, who spent much of her time hunched in the cab, particularly when there was work to be done, and now seemed intent on stuffing half a dozen pink pills down her throat. Then over to Jacob, who had fallen instantly asleep, the neck of a whisky bottle protruding from his coat pocket which spoke volumes about why he was snoring so loudly.

Kitty groaned as she took in the significance of all this. The same old problems yet again. Should she send Tessa home? She was clearly far from well and had spent much of last night on the latrine. Was the poor old boy getting past it, too, this whole trip too much for him? Perhaps it was too much for them all.

Captain Owen said, 'How about an audition at least? I may well have much to offer your little company, not least my renowned skills as a director should you ever have need of one.'

She would do no such thing, Kitty sharply informed him, closing her eyes and struggling not to let her head droop. She was both actor-manager and director of the LTPs and would remain so, war or no war. Really, the barefaced cheek of the man left her gasping. Her head lolled and came to rest against the rough fabric of his greatcoat. It felt slightly damp but comfortingly solid. Pressed so close together in the crowded vehicle, how could she avoid it? Kitty could feel every muscle of his taut body and when he whispered in her ear that she should sleep, the fan of his breath on her cold cheek was deliciously warm. No scent of hair cream on this cold, wet day, but somehow still intoxicatingly masculine. She gritted her teeth, meaning to inform him coolly that the LTPs would carry on just as they were, thank you very much, but sleep overtook her before she could.

Dafydd Owen Williams did indeed join the Players and transformed all their lives. They'd been stationed at the military theatre for a couple of weeks and during this supposedly settled period, everything had changed.

He said he'd no intention of interfering in any way.

She insisted that for all his cleverness, his undoubted enthusiasm for the theatre and winning ways, he rarely agreed with a single decision *she* made.

He might consider himself a genius but *she* dubbed him simply perverse.

She addressed him frostily as Captain.

He told her to call him Owen, as all his friends did.

'Is that what I am? A friend?'

'You could be.'

As always when he made some remark that she couldn't cap, Kitty turned on her heel and walked away, head high, aware of his soft laughter following her.

They were planning a music hall extravaganza to entertain the troops. Something special which they could perform first here, in the relative security of the military theatre, and then with a few modifications take out on the road to the various rest billets. But they could agree about nothing.

If Kitty asked someone to come on from stage left, Owen would shake his head and say stage right would be better. If she put in a new song and dance routine, he would dismiss it as tawdry or inappropriate. When she choreographed the traditional walk-down for the finale, he insisted it was old-fashioned or the stage was too small and the cast should simply stand in line to take their bow and sing the final number. Most infuriating of all, whenever his suggestions were tried, they generally worked well. Confidence began to leak from her like a drain, affecting her ability to make sound decisions and causing her to become ever more reckless.

She'd received another letter from home, this time from Charlotte, which rambled on about Dixie's tantrums and how impossible she'd become. Kitty grew more anxious by the day over her child, wishing she could pack her bags and go home this minute. She felt suddenly isolated and vulnerable here in France, working with this difficult man whom she could barely tolerate while the rest of the cast seemed utterly captivated by him. Though even she had to admit he could be both charming and witty. When he took the time and trouble, that is. So why did he always manage to rub her up the wrong way? His complete self-assurance, of course. His arrogance. And for all he possessed considerable experience, Kitty remained stubbornly suspicious of his motives. He was still, in her humble opinion, a soldier, not an actor.

'I'm the director and if you don't do as I say, you won't be in the show,' she would sternly inform him.

'And if you don't start listening to other people's opinions *and* stop taking stupid risks over where you put on these damned performances, then you'll be back home in Blighty before you can say Tommy Atkins.'

Instead of the devil incarnate, she had Dafydd Owen Williams constantly peering over her shoulder, watching and commenting upon everything she did. It was both infuriating and disconcerting. Despite his claims of being content to take second place, he certainly expected to be given a starring role in the production.

'You promised you wouldn't give me a small part, Kitty Little.'

She *still* hated the way he used her name, almost as if it were false and simply a joke. Kitty had long since forgotten that that was exactly how she'd got it in the first place. 'I believe Shakespeare said there was no such thing as a small part.' But her rejoinder, however smart, hardly dented his arrogance one jot, nor wiped that devastating smile from his handsome face. He merely considered her solemnly, as if he could read every unsettling thought in her head.

'Why can't we work together properly? What are you afraid of? That I'll steal the show? Or perhaps that your company will follow my suggestions instead of yours?' His face cleared. 'That's it, isn't it?'

'Don't be ridiculous.'

'You're afraid of losing the LTPs?'

'Rubbish.' She turned away from him, desperate suddenly to get out into the fresh air, but he followed her, caught her arm and held her fast.

'I would never do that, Kitty. Even a blind, arrogant fool like me can see how important this troupe of travelling players is to you. Almost as if . . .'

'As if what?' She lifted her chin and met his gaze with blazing defiance. 'It were my whole life? My lover, husband and friend. That has been said so many times. Do try not to be trite.'

She saw compassion in his eyes now, and hated him for it. Then he gave her a little shake. 'Wake up, girl. Surely you don't intend to spend your entire life wandering the countryside like a medieval minstrel? Don't you have a dream, Kitty? Once this dratted war is over, what then? Back to your village halls and schools? Surely there must be more to life than that?'

'What we do is important.'

'I know. But it's only a beginning. You could do so much more.'

It was true, she did have a dream. Once it had been to create a troupe of travelling players, to take the best of live theatre into ordinary people's lives, to bring them entertainment and even some fun and laughter. Perhaps even at times to stretch their minds and make them think. Kitty thought she'd succeeded in that rather well. Once that had been achieved, she'd longed for a settled home for them all, a real theatre where they could grow and develop a secure future together. Archie had been a central part of that dream. She'd needed him to share it with her. Now that he was lost to her, it had all crumbled to dust.

'For an Army Captain, you show far too much interest in other people's lives. Let's stick to business, shall we? I really don't need you sticking your oar in every five minutes. Has that notion ever occurred to you?'

He had the cheek to smile. 'That much is obvious. But *why* is it so? Is your antipathy against Welshmen in general or myself in particular? Or are you just frozen up somewhere inside and it would be an act of charity if an Army Captain started a small thaw?'

Almost lifting her from the ground by the fierce grip he had upon her arms, he brought her so dangerously close to him that she could trace every fine hair above the curve of his upper lip, every pale freckle upon his brow, and feel the hard outline of his body pressing against her own. In that instant, Kitty was certain he was about to kiss her, and dizzily wondered how she would respond if he did. She found herself swaying and almost by instinct her eyelids drooped half closed. Then, quite abruptly, he let her go, his tone now matter-of-fact, almost brisk.

'However, the needs of the show should come before any personal animosity, do you not think?' And he strolled away, leaving her heart pounding, which put her in a snappy mood for the rest of the day.

The music hall show was a riotous success. Kitty brought the House down with 'Little Dolly Daydream'. If her voice lacked the range of Suzy's it certainly possessed greater strength, held humour and warmth and kept beautifully in tune; the kind of voice which actively encouraged the troops to join in and sing along. Later she had them all in tears with a heartrending version of 'Because'. Suzy, Jacob and Reg did a wonderful rendition of 'The Soldiers of the Queen', Tessa had them jazzing in the aisles with the 'Darktown Strutters' Ball' and Owen himself surprised them all by possessing a fine Welsh tenor voice which fairly lifted the roof when he sang 'Land of my Fathers'.

'You kept that under your damned tin helmet,' Kitty said afterwards. 'Why did we never hear you sing in rehearsals?'

'Perhaps I too relish my privacy. And we all have our secrets.' She considered him for a long silent moment, wondering what other secrets he might have and whether he would ever be willing to share them with her. For all she knew, he might well have a wife and six children back home in Wales. For some reason the thought depressed her.

After the show they enjoyed a noisy, jolly supper in which they all got rather squiffy, and then struggled to learn the foxtrot, the new dance which had become all the rage despite the war. It was the closest Kitty had come to happiness in months.

Not surprisingly their mood grew more maudlin as the wine took effect and the discussion more philosophical. Felicity wanted to know why they were fighting this damned war in the first place, and a lively discussion ensued as Owen and Reg struggled to explain, with the others chipping in their own opinions. Something to do with ruling the seas and the Germans being jealous of the British Navy. Kitty was unfortunately too sleepy to take it all in properly.

'When will it end, that's the point?' she asked in the midst of the debate.

'God knows. Ending a war is always a damn' sight more difficult than starting one. The Boche believed they could soon demolish our "contemptible little army",' Owen explained. 'But they were wrong. They took too seriously the troubles in Ireland early in 1914, thinking that would lead to civil war and distract us.'

'Or else that mutiny in India would put us off,' Reg put in.

Jacob, hiccuping loudly, muttered something about strikes and rebellion at home.

'That's right,' Owen agreed. 'But none of it came about. And when the war got going properly, the Hun thought we'd be all alone; that the colonies would let us sink rather than run the risk of losing lives. But that wasn't what happened. They all came in with us, Canada, New Zealand, India, the whole lot of 'em. And now, with the introduction of conscription, we'll beat them for sure.'

Kitty was leaning forward, her wine forgotten, taking in every word. 'You've been on the Front Line, haven't you, Owen?' It was the first time she'd used his Christian name and he blinked in surprise.

'I have, yes.'

'We're reasonably safe here, miles from the Front. Cold, wet, hungry, uncomfortable half the time, true, but privileged. If I wanted to go home tomorrow, I could do so. The boys in the trenches can't. I want to be with them. I want to see what it's really like, to feel a part of this battle in every sense.'

She expected him to ridicule her, to tell her not to be

stupid and childish, that only men could face the horrors of the Front. But although he sadly shook his head, he told her that he understood perfectly why she had that feeling. 'We all want to do more, to feel we're doing our bit.' He took a sip of wine, wiped his mouth. 'In the trenches there's usually three or four of you, in a group. One sleeps while one makes some effort to keep the trench clean, dry and habitable with a mug of tea and what might pass for food every now and then. And deals with the rats, of course.'

'Rats?'

'Catching them is proving to be quite a sport.'

Kitty felt sick.

'Where was I? Oh, yes, the others stand on the fire-step and keep guard. Woe betide any Tommy who falls asleep on duty. At night when you put your head above the parapet it can be like watching a giant firework display. Strafe fire, flares, shrapnel raining down all around – the whole sky can be illuminated. You can feel very exposed in spite of the battery of men firing steadily and methodically at the Hun. And then there are the firecrackers. Oh, you have to keep your wits about you for them, boyo. Watch out for each other at all times. And you have to listen out for Whistling Percys – that's a type of shell that heralds its arrival with a shriek – and the whizz-bangs do just what they say. But if one hits too close you'd never hear another. I lost my best mate that way.' He fell silent. Sipped at his wine some more.

Kitty had never heard him talk so much. She didn't interrupt. What was there to say? Platitudes seemed inappropriate and words of comfort impossible to find. She recognised the hard lines etched about his mouth now for what they were, raw pain which would no doubt always be there. Nor did any of the others speak but simply listened, appalled.

'Then there are sling bombs, hand grenades, trench mortar shells, anti-aircraft guns . . . Oh, it's a very modern war, being fought in a very old-fashioned way.' He turned back to Kitty, purposefully fixing a smile to his lips as if to conceal this brief glimpse of vulnerability. 'Your place is here, where you can lift the morale of war-weary souls seeking respite from death. You'll be relatively safe here.'

'I want to go, Owen. Just a fleeting visit will do. I want to *feel* the fear they suffer every day.'

But he was adamant. 'No entertainers are allowed anywhere near the Front Line, male or female. Though I believe Harry Lauder has been given special dispensation to do so. He's coming out sometime during the next few months.' Then he took her hands and held them, firm and warm, within his own. 'War is a game. A dreadful political game, played by men in shiny uniforms many miles from the mere sniff of a gun. But it's one that Tommy Atkins means to win.'

A silence fell upon them then as they thought of all the men, little more than boys mostly, who had already lost the game, despite a valiant show of bravery on their part. Kitty had learned a good deal about the views of these gallant young soldiers. They believed they fought for a righteous cause; that they moved on from this mortal life to another, more glorious one. If they fell in battle, that was not the end but a beginning. To talk to them, to see that belief in action, was a glimpse through the curtain of death into another dimension, one which was far greater than any they had known before. The thought put into perspective all Kitty's foolish earthly fears and concerns. What did the failure of a girlish love affair count for, set against such sacrifice?

'To victory,' she said now, raising her glass.

'To victory,' came an echo around the table, and as they drank, she smiled over the rim of her glass into Owen's eyes.

Chapter Five

Tommy Atkins was not winning. Not yet. The war on the Western Front continued unabated with neither side ahead. If it had been a game of football, Tommy Atkins said, it'd be considered a draw at this point, but he was hoping for better luck in the second half. The Germans had started their bombardment of Verdun in February but the French managed to hold on, minimising their losses by keeping the bulk of their troops out of the Front Line. But the future did not look promising, and men were losing hope.

It was March and the LTPs were weary too. They'd been in France now for almost six months, without any leave and with precious few letters, so it was with great excitement that Kitty heard of the arrival of a post bag. She set off at a run, hoping for news of Dixie, to be met by Frank.

'I thought you'd like these. Just delivered at great expense over land and sea.' He handed her two crumpled white envelopes with a sufficient air of disapproval to indicate, without her even looking, that one of them was from Clara. She recognised Archie's handwriting on the other and stuffed them both into her pocket, perversely quenching her anxiety. Not once had he written to her before, in all the years she had known him. Could something be wrong with Dixie?

'Thanks. I'll read them later. I'm rather occupied at present.' She certainly was not inclined to suffer another of Frank's lectures on her failure as a parent.

They were in the middle of rehearsal in an *estaminet* near Amiens which, within the next hour or two, would be filled with servicemen and no doubt thick with smoke. Tessa had played the overture twice through already. The room was freezing cold and Kitty was quite certain she was coming down with 'flu, so her tolerance level was low.

Frank remained where he was, obstinately blocking her path with his obtrusive presence. Resisting the urge to push past him, she drew in a slow, patient breath. 'I really don't have time for games this afternoon, Frank.' Still he made no attempt to move and she became filled with a sudden and infuriating sense of frustration. Why was he always *there*, under her feet, filling her with guilt?

'Clara has written to me, too. Are you going to write back? You should. You know she'd love to get a letter from you. I'll find someone heading home who can deliver it. You know I'd do anything for you, duchess.'

'Don't call me that.' Shooting him a fierce glare, Kitty jerked away from him as he put out a hand towards her, her skin crawling in that all too familiar way for she could barely tolerate his attentions.

'Did she send her love? She says in my letter that you don't rightly deserve it, neglecting her as you do.'

Kitty was at once awash with fresh guilt. Like it or not, there was an element of truth in the accusation. She had neglected her mother, not having visited her once in all these years. She dreaded to think how she'd feel if Dixie ever treated her in the same way. But then Kitty would never dream of trying to marry her off to a man she didn't love, in order to settle a few debts. Nor be discovered in her daughter's fiancé's bed. 'I'm surprised she notices I've even gone. You're more likely to be the one she misses, wouldn't you say? Though no doubt she's found some other young fool to warm her bed.' And Kitty walked briskly away before she could say anything she might later regret.

Following the rehearsal, the Players grabbed coffee and a bun before the start of the evening performance, though as usual Kitty was far too nervous to eat. Afterwards she would eat like a horse, of course, though it would probably be bully beef and mashed potato again.

She did find a moment's privacy to open the letter from Archie which informed her that things hadn't quite worked out as he'd hoped. Its tone was bitter: of his dissatisfaction with his marriage, how Charlotte was determined to bankrupt him, and how much he missed Kitty.

She gazed upon the words with awe. There was no mistake. He'd written it clear as clear, if in Archie's usual sort of blunt shorthand. '*Miss you Kitty, old thing. Still love you. Wonder sometimes if I married the right girl. What a rotter I was. Will you ever forgive me, I wonder?*' She felt herself start to tremble with shock.

He concluded with a postscript which informed her that Dixie was now staying with the Misses Frost, two delightful eccentrics who kept a boarding house in Carreckwater near Ambleside. Kitty scanned the rest of the page with dawning dismay, searching in vain for some reason, some explanation as to why he should be so heartless as to abandon his own child. It must be Charlotte's idea. How *could* she do that? Kitty took comfort from the fact that at least Dixie would still have Nanny, a plump, well-meaning girl who absolutely adored her young charge. But who were these Misses Frost? Would they give Dixie the love and care she needed? Kitty felt sick with fear. What on earth was she doing here in France when she should be caring for her own daughter back home in the Lakes?

Clara's letter remained in her pocket, unopened.

Moments later, while she hurriedly tidied her hair ready to go on, Frank turned up at her side again, just like a bad penny, Kitty commented. 'Sarcasm don't suit you, duchess. Beware of it,' he warned, breezily tying on the red bow tie he always wore as he showed the audience to their seats, even here for soldiers in war-torn France. She had to admire that in him, though it was probably more from vanity than respect for fighting men. He slicked down his hair and gave her one of his cocky little winks. 'Your ma says it's time you and me was naming the day.'

Kitty groaned. 'Not that old chestnut again?'

'Why d'you reckon I've hung around all these years? For the good of my health?'

'Because no one else will have you. Because you don't know how to keep your stupid mouth shut.' Kitty blamed him entirely for Archie's running off with Charlotte. Someone had told him the truth about Dixie, and it wasn't difficult to guess who. Perhaps that was why Charlotte had thrown Dixie out. Taking her grievances out on Kitty's child.

'You could do worse than take me on, duchess. Far worse. And, like I said, I don't mind waiting.' And with a cheery grin he strolled off to conduct his duties in his usual officious manner. 'Thank you, sir. That's five bob for two. Second row down the front in the orchestra stalls, so you can hide under the stage if we get bombed.' This was Frank's idea of a joke, for the 'theatre' was little more than a wooden hut with a tin roof, the performance was free and everyone grabbed a seat where they could. The two soldiers took it in good part, though, saying the show was cheap at twice the price to hear Kitty Little sing, and chose the two best seats in the front row.

'Five minutes to curtain up,' Reg called. 'Not that there is a curtain, but you know what I mean.'

Kitty was suddenly overwhelmed by emotion, by memories of past shows before the war, by her worries over Dixie, of missing dear Esme from whom there was still no word and of Archie who claimed still to love her. She dashed outside for a breath of cooling fresh air, flew round the back of the truck and ran full tilt into Suzy who was puffing on a cigarette stuck in her favourite tortoiseshell holder. Suzy put out a hand to steady her, chuckling softly until she saw the tears streaming down Kitty's cheeks. 'What is it? What's happened?'

'Nothing. Oh, it's Dixie.' And Kitty burst into tears.

'Oh, God, no. What's happened to her?' Suzy was hugging her, dabbing at her eyes, smoothing her hair. 'Tell me quickly. What is it?'

Kitty put her hand to her mouth and gulped back

the tears. Then she gave a shaky laugh. 'There's nothing at all the matter with Dixie really, only with her silly mother. Oh, Suzy, I miss her so much.' And then they were both laughing through their tears and Kitty began to tell her about the Misses Frost. Suzy quickly calmed her concern, saying the two sisters could well be a welcome improvement on Charlotte. After that it seemed perfectly natural for Kitty to pour out her frustration on the subject of Frank, and how he'd been working on her sense of guilt again. 'I'll swing for that man, I will really.'

Suzy's eyes were dancing with laughter, she being all too familiar with Kitty's fierce passions and her dislike of her one-time fiancé. 'What's he done now?'

Kitty brushed away her tears and began to smooth and tidy the trimmings and ribbons on the diva's lavender silk gown, one that was all too familiar. 'It's amazing how much wear we've had out of this frock.' She gave a harsh little laugh. 'Though it was intended to catch Frank.'

'Clearly it worked,' Suzy chuckled. 'He's hardly left your side since he first saw you in it, I shouldn't think. Perhaps it has magical powers. Would it catch me a fine young man too, do you think?'

'Frank isn't a fine young man. Frank is a *bore*! The dress doesn't work with the *right* man. At least it didn't with me.'

'Perhaps that's because you haven't met the right man yet. Or not recognised him as such, shall we say?'

'What? Of course I've met him. And lost him again. You *know* how I felt about Archie. How I *still* feel.' She did not dare mention what he had written in his letter about his own feelings.

'Sometimes it's best to let the past go. However . . .' Suzy gave a shrug and a wry smile and, tucking her arm into Kitty's, walked her back to the *estaminet*. 'Is Frank still going on about you two getting spliced?' And when Kitty groaned and nodded, she continued, 'I suppose it is rather daring of you, sweetie, to be quite so modern. I must say I admire you for not rushing headlong into matrimony but independence can be carried too far. Men can be utter darlings, or so I'm told. Don't you fancy being married to a lovely chap and having more little Dixies?'

'No, of course I don't. I'm not in the least interested in marriage or domestic bliss and all of that stuff. I have the LTPs, and that's enough for me.'

'Well, my dear, if that's the case and you truly aren't interested in either marriage or men, why are you crying?'

'I'm not crying.' Perversely, Kitty found tears were indeed still running down her cheeks and angrily slapped them away. Desperate to change the subject, she pulled out the other, still unopened letter, confessing to yet more feelings of self-pity for having neglected her mother.

Suzy dabbed at the tears with a large handkerchief and declared that everyone neglected their mother. 'That's the way of human nature, darling child. We take the poor souls for granted and never fully appreciate them until it's too late. You're tired. Take a break. Go home to Blighty and see her. It will do you good.'

'But it's *years* too late.'

'It's never too late to visit your mother. Go and make your peace. Take little Dixie to see her grandmother, why don't you?'

Kitty had a sudden longing to hold her child close

and breathe in the sweet scent of her. How could she have borne being away for so long? What was wrong with her, neglecting everyone she loved for the sake of a troupe of travelling players? How many times had Archie complained about her being far too independent? No wonder Charlotte was able to march off with him from right under her nose. Was it too late to win him back? The thought made her smile. Even so . . . 'When do I have time to take a trip to London?'

'Make time. We'll manage.'

'On the grounds that no one is indispensable?'

'You come very near it, my dear. Now perk up and dab some powder on your nose. We have a show to do and it's a brilliant one because you directed and star in it.' Which made Kitty cry all the more.

'I don't know how I'd manage without you and Jacob and all my friends. Everyone assumes I'm so strong.'

'While underneath you're as vulnerable and confused as the rest of us. I know, darling. Pardon me for saying so but you don't always give that impression.' Suzy kept her expression carefully bland as she stubbed out the remains of her cigarette. 'Perhaps you should let that vulnerability show once in a while.' Kissing Kitty on each cheek, she pushed her through the door. 'And don't worry about Frank. Why not persuade your ma to marry the little blighter herself?' Which set Kitty giggling so much, she went off happily to get changed.

Esme was starting the third show of the day, though the first of a new routine, and she was shaking with nerves.

From two o'clock onwards there hardly seemed a

minute to call her own. It was the tableaux only in the afternoon so not too taxing, followed by Egyptian dancing in the early-evening and later, when the lights were dimmed, came the lightly draped nymphs and goddesses. This routine often brought a smile to her lips as she recalled how far removed it was from the one of a similar title which Kitty had devised for the panto.

Live art, Terence called it. Those were the words he'd used when he'd first persuaded her to join his Theatre of Lovelies in Manchester and Esme still liked to think of it as such, for all that deep down she knew different. She only needed to catch a glimpse of the lascivious glint in the eyes of the watching men (the audience rarely featured women), and she understood completely the depths to which she had sunk. Yet without Archie, what did it matter?

Terence liked to think of himself as her Svengali. 'I always take care of my girls,' he'd say, and in a way this was true.

He'd find them good, clean accommodation close to the theatre, would cook them delicious meals if they were homesick. Terence's love of women was rivalled only by his passion for food, the evidence of which could be seen in his impressive size. And he was always ready to offer a strong shoulder to cry on should they suffer from the blues. He also paid excellent salaries and kept their wardrobes filled with the very latest fashions.

'Can't have my girls looking anything but classy,' he'd say. This wasn't strictly true since he might insist they be modestly and expensively dressed, right down to their silk panties, but the overriding image he sought from his

'Lovelies' was that they be sensual and salacious. He was fond of telling them how they were 'images to celebrate the beauty of womanhood; untouchable, unreachable, but infinitely desirable'.

In return for all this care and attention he expected them to work hard by doing three performances a day plus rehearsals, submit to whatever routines he planned for them and, should they choose to offer any extra 'services', he would naturally show his gratitude for that too.

From the start Esme had resolved not to fall into that particular trap. There was a limit, she decided, to how far she was prepared to sink. So long as she fell no further, she could survive.

At first Terence had pestered her daily, constantly coming to her dressing room, suggesting that he should pay her a call later, and on one occasion actually did so without asking her permission. She woke up one night to find him standing by her bed. Cold fear had shot through her and she'd yanked the bedclothes as high as she could. 'What the hell are you doing here?'

'Don't fret. Only calling in to check you were well, and to say goodnight. I thought you seemed a little off colour this evening.'

'I'm tired of your pestering, that's all. Leave me alone.'

'You have to be kind to me, Esme. It's part of the job.' He'd considered her in thoughtful silence for a long time, tugging at the whiskers on his chin before leaving, softly closing the door behind him.

The next night he came again, and the one after that, till she was jumpy from lack of sleep. 'Leave me alone,' she'd cried, desperate to make it clear that she was not on the menu.

'Can't I persuade you? I'd make it worth your while.'

'No.'

'Such a waste, Esme love.'

She was afraid. Panicking, she dispatched a hastily written letter to Charlotte, begging for her help. Employment had been hard to find of late. She had nowhere else to go since the kind of plays she'd usually excelled in were no longer being performed because of the war. She'd earned insufficient money so far from this new job to make her independent, and was concerned that unless she provide these extra 'services' he required, she might never actually do so.

She was not surprised when Charlotte did not reply. Why should she? Hadn't she been furiously jealous of Esme's success while she'd been away visiting her mother that time? Why should Charlotte be expected to come to her aid now? Filled with despair, Esme decided she had only one option. She must go back to the endless knocking on doors, the trek from town to town, and hope to survive.

Unfortunately, Terence found her hastily packing a suitcase. Esme guessed that one of the other girls had told him she was leaving. He came in, quietly closing the door.

'I wouldn't try to leave if I were you, love. You know that would hurt me very much and I'd only have to get one of my friends to fetch you back. You represent profit to me, girl. And a great deal of time and training.' He put his hand on her neck, caressing the skin while circling it almost entirely with his thick fingers. 'Just be a good little flower and do as you're told. The show must go on, eh?'

Bravely, Esme had looked him straight in the eye and demanded to know if these extra 'services' were obligatory, because if so, to hell with his 'profit', she was off right now. He'd calmly assured her this was not at all the case. 'This is a free country, flower. I may be a businessman with an eye to the main chance, as they say, but I hope I'm still a gentleman.'

Esme had simply lifted her eyebrows and said nothing.

'But a girl has to pay her way, one way or another.'

'I'm an actress, not a . . .'

He'd put a finger against her lip. 'Never use rude words, not in front of Terence. My mother always brought me up to be sensitive to a lady's needs. I understand women, believe me. You often say no when really you just need a little persuasion.'

'No amount of persuasion will make me change my mind. Ever.'

Something in her tone, and perhaps the fierce look in her eyes, finally made him believe her and although for a second the hold on her neck had tightened, he'd eventually removed it. 'Make yourself indispensable on stage and I might be persuaded to let you off any other duties. But don't even think of running. I won't be cheated out of my investment in you, Esme.'

She'd understood perfectly that although her boss might seem perfectly calm and reasonable on the surface, he possessed, without doubt, an underlying taste for violence. And he had friends with even fewer scruples. She saw enough of them in the audience, night after night.

It was then that Esme had made her decision. She

would take him up on his offer, since it seemed the lesser of two evils. If she was to be one of his 'Lovelies', she would be the best he'd ever had. She would do anything he asked of her – on stage. But nowhere else.

When Esme put this proposition to him she saw his eyes gleam with interest, watched with horrified fascination as he licked his lips, almost as if relishing the taste of her as a future dessert to titillate his palette.

He taught her to practise her art in front of mirrors. At least this helped to squeeze every last drop of embarrassment from her system. She couldn't do what he asked of her otherwise. Sometimes he would sit and watch her rehearse the routine from start to finish, over and over again, commenting and criticising, planning and adjusting her costumes, making suggestions, attending to each fine detail with scrupulous care.

And by the time the performance was over on this, its first public showing, Esme knew, with a terrible sinking of her heart, that she'd been wrong to think she could fall no further. She'd just taken another tumble.

It was a couple of months after she'd sent the letter to Charlotte that Esme spotted Archie in the audience. She could hardly believe her eyes. There he was on the front row, large as life and grinning at her from ear to ear, just as if his own heart was leaping as madly as her own.

That evening she found her performance more difficult than ever. Esme was awash with embarrassment to know Archie's eyes were upon her. Perhaps not judging her too unkindly, since he wasn't the moralistic sort, but he would surely be disappointed in her. This wasn't where she should be, or what she should be doing. They were both aware of that.

He came to her dressing room when the show was over and gave her a great hug but quickly silenced her hasty explanations. 'That was wonderful, old love. Never would've thought you had it in you.'

'I'm not sure that I have. Oh, Archie.' She let him hold her for a long time, revelling in the solid comfort his presence offered. Esme could sense freedom. She could smell it. Archie would take her away from this seedy existence she'd been forced to endure. He would sweep her up and take her back to Repstone, no matter what Charlotte might say. Hadn't she known, in her heart, that he would find her? He would carry her away like a knight of old on his gallant white charger, and she would be safe once more. Esme felt light-headed with relief, bubbling with delighted energy, laughing as she rained kisses all over his beloved face.

'You can't know how happy I am to see you.'

'My word, and I'm happy to see you too, my little ragamuffin. No, not a ragamuffin any longer, eh? You looked beautiful out there. By Gad, you had them eating out of your hands.'

It was these words which brought the first stirrings of disquiet.

He took her out to dine in a cosy Italian restaurant just off Deansgate where he filled her in on Charlotte's latest antics and histrionics, the removal of Dixie and how she was enchanting the Misses Frost. It was only when the waiter brought the bill that it occurred to Esme that he had never once asked about her.

'Don't you want to know what I'm doing here? How

I came to be part of that dreadful little theatre and one of Terence's Lovelies?'

'Why should I, sweetie? None of my business, eh? Besides, you were doing a splendid job so it's pretty obvious you've found your niche at last. Much better than being stage manager for the LTPs.'

'What?' She stared at him aghast. He didn't seem to understand. He thought she actually enjoyed degrading herself in front of all those men. And slowly her eyes began to fill with tears. 'Aren't you going to take me home with you, Archie? I hate it here. You must realise I wouldn't perform those – those lewd routines if I weren't forced to.'

He glanced up from counting out coins to look at her in surprise. 'Take you home? How could I do that, sweetie? Charlotte would never agree to having you at Repstone. Oh, but don't cry. I can't bear to see a woman cry. I'll come and visit you here. How would that be? We could become chums again, just as we used to be. Wouldn't that be grand?'

'Oh, Archie.' No knight in shining armour then. No white charger upon which to carry her away.

He stayed with her for much of that night, making love to her in her gloomy little room back at the lodging house, and left some time before dawn. At least she supposed he did since she never heard him go but, true to his word, he came to see her regularly after that, and they fell into a routine.

Archie would watch her act from the front row, then he'd take her to dinner at Romero's, followed by an hour or two of lovemaking in her room before he would dash off back to Charlotte, full of apologies and promising to stay longer next time. He never did, of course. And Esme soon realised that, despite her pleas, he never would mention her predicament to his wife. He had placed Esme in the role of mistress, which was no more than she deserved, and that was where she must stay.

So what choice did she have but to settle for what she could get? At least now she had Archie's occasional visits as consolation for allowing perfect strangers to ogle her naked body. It seemed to be the best she could hope for.

It was just before the interval on the last night of their stint at the military theatre and Kitty was singing 'Pack Up Your Troubles In Your Old Kit Bag', smiling at the audience, in particular at one young man on the front row who kept grinning or winking at her, nudging his mate in delight when she winked cheekily back. The pair had hardly missed a performance that week and Kitty liked to show her appreciation.

She was also keeping half an eye on Tessa at the piano, nodding her head in time to the beat, when there came an awesome, head-blasting explosion, a blinding white flare followed by utter pandemonium. One minute there were rows of smiling faces, the next there were flames everywhere, a terrible roaring and screaming in her ears. Thick, choking smoke. Sheets of corrugated iron from the roof slicing downwards into the mêlée, shards of metal and crossbeams falling as rain poured through, thankfully drenching the worst of the fire but creating its own mayhem as men blindly slid and fell over each other in their desperation to get out of the ruined building.

'Dear God, help us,' were the last words Kitty heard.

Chapter Six

Some time later, when she came round, she lay in her bed and listened with increasing horror as Felicity gently described the resulting devastation. 'About a dozen young soldiers were killed, several more wounded. Jacob and Reg were fortunately backstage. Suzy and I were in the kitchen, brewing tea and chatting.'

Kitty struggled to sit up, eyes dark hollows of pain. 'Owen? Where was Owen? Is he safe?' It suddenly seemed vitally important to hear that he was.

Felicity smiled. 'Perfectly safe. He was practising his scales, would you believe, in the dressing room at the back of the building. It was the front which took a direct hit.' She paused, stared down at her clenched hands, then back at Kitty. Even before she said the words, Kitty guessed what she was about to say.

'Oh, no. Tessa.'

'She didn't feel a thing. Death would have been instantaneous. Her hands were still on the keys.' Kitty read the pain and sympathy in Suzy's eyes, then put her face in her own hands and wept.

She later learned that it had been the young soldier who had winked at her from the front row who'd leaped up on to the small wooden platform to drag her to safety. But for his heroic act, she too would have lost her life that day. Kitty wasn't able to thank him personally, however, for he'd dashed straight back inside to find his mate and never returned. But she would always remember his courage with gratitude.

'I have to go home.' It was the following day and Kitty and Owen were sitting on a stone wall in the sun. A soft April breeze brought with it the scent of blossom from nearby apple orchards, just as if death and annihilation had never visited this French valley.

'I understand.'

'It's not because I'm afraid or because I really want to go. The others will be home too in four or five weeks, but I must go now and do what is right for Tessa. I must take her home to her family.'

He stared down at his hands, not looking at her as he spoke. 'What about you and your family?'

'I have a daughter,' Kitty told him, quite calmly. 'It's long past time I reminded her that I'm her mother. You spoke once of us both keeping secrets. Well, Dixie is mine. At least, she isn't meant to be a secret but I'd never mentioned her to you. Perhaps some of the others did. It wouldn't have mattered if they had.'

Owen smiled. 'Your company is clearly loyal for none did.' Again a short silence. 'You're married then?'

Kitty laughed wryly at this assumption. 'Oh, no. Perhaps I was prone to foolishness on the odd occasion but there's no need to make it a lifetime's pursuit, is there?'

He looked up and smiled at her, a mixture of interest and puzzlement in his eyes. 'Is that because he wasn't the right man after all, or do you have a natural antipathy to marriage as you do to Welshmen?'

Kitty pulled a face at him. 'Don't start all that again. I thought we'd called a truce.'

'We have. We have.' He laughingly held up his hands by way of apology. 'So tell me about this chap. What's he like? Is he the lost love you've also kept secret? Tell me what went wrong.'

Kitty jumped down from the wall and, before walking away, told him to mind his own business.

Owen naturally insisted on accompanying her safely to the ship, and it was not until they were bumping along in an old Army vehicle that the story began to unfold. Perhaps they both felt the need of something to occupy their minds, other than the coffin they carried in the back, but Kitty found herself pouring out all her troubles to this man she'd dubbed an arrogant Welshman. She related how she'd loved Archie for years, and how it had come about that he'd rejected that love and married Charlotte. 'Now he claims it was all a mistake, that he still loves me. It's almost more than I can bear.'

'Yet he betrayed you.'

'That wasn't entirely his fault.'

Owen gave a snort of disbelief. 'He was dragged kicking and screaming to her bed, was he?' Kitty flushed but said nothing and he continued in a quieter tone,

'There are many different kinds of love. Perhaps he loves you in a different way.'

'No, no. He says he loves me properly, not simply as a brother. Charlotte was wrong about that. It was her manipulations that drove him away from me in the first place. She was incredibly clever. You wouldn't believe the lies she told, how she poisoned his mind against us both. I can see it all now, looking back.'

'Both?'

'Well, there was Esme too. She's my friend. We both loved Archie but agreed that whichever he chose, the other would stand back.'

'And he chose Charlotte instead of either of you?'

Kitty looked out of the window at the countryside unravelling slowly like a bright green ribbon beyond the confines of the vehicle, wishing suddenly she'd never embarked on this discussion. It was so hard to explain to an outsider what it had been like. 'He loved us all in his way, do you see?'

Owen gave a shout of hollow laughter. 'So this man, who now claims he still loves you, also loved your friend and betrayed you both for Charlotte, to whom he is now married?'

'Something like that,' she agreed in a small voice.

'My God. How does he do it? How can you care for such a bastard?'

Kitty flushed with anger. 'Don't call him that! I knew you wouldn't understand. It was a waste of time trying to talk to you.'

'Sorry, sorry. Only you must see, Kitty, that he isn't worthy of you. If a man allows himself to be led by the nose by a manipulating woman, he must be either willing or a fool. Perhaps both. Do you want him to leave this Charlotte for you?' He negotiated a row of pitted holes in the road, lurching sideways as the truck bumped and bucked over the ridges.

Kitty grasped the door handle. Held on tight. 'No. Yes. Oh, I don't know.' Was that what she wanted? For Archie to abandon his marriage for her sake? It seemed such a shocking thing to do. He never would, of course. Too scandalous for words. 'Archie isn't a fool. Oh, I don't want to talk about it any more.' But he was weak, she thought. If she was honest with herself, she knew that. And he could at times seem quite cold and heartless, utterly devoid of emotion, while at others he could be entirely sweet and kind, generous to the point of carelessness with his money and possessions. But then, perhaps it was less generosity than a desire always to seek the easy route through life. Could it be that it was this very weakness which had allowed Charlotte's wickedness to flourish?

Tears were choking her as Kitty thought back over the pain Charlotte had caused; her utter lack of scruples in her efforts to win exactly what she wanted most: Archie. Or at least to get her hands on his wealth, which he didn't care about. Kitty knew that she really shouldn't allow this to bother her, not after all this time, that she should let him go. It was just that Archie had always been there for her, an essential part of her life ever since she was a young girl. Even more so since she'd lost Raymond, her beloved brother. Was that why she still clung to him, still defended him so tenaciously?

They drove on in brooding silence, neither speaking to the other. For much of the journey the Army truck had been slowed to a crawl by the usual congestion of military traffic. Now they were entirely alone on an empty road, skirting woodland that fringed green meadows where the occasional French farmer bent to his weary task. Some time during that long afternoon it began to rain, beating down on the truck, washing the windscreen so that visibility became increasingly difficult. They hit a stone or boulder on the rough road and the vehicle suddenly skewed crazily out of control and lurched to a halt. 'Damnation! We've got a puncture.'

Owen climbed out of the car and kicked the offending wheel in irritation. Even in the few seconds it took to examine the torn rubber, he was soaked to the skin.

Kitty stood beside him, equally wet. 'What now?'

As one they both glanced around them. It was past five o'clock. The surrounding landscape of woods and undulating fields already growing dark. 'We need to find shelter. Deal with this in the morning.'

'In the morning? Do you expect us to sit in this freezing vehicle all night?'

Owen again looked about him, his red hair now dark and slick with rain, and grinned as he pointed. 'I think we're in luck. That looks like an old farmhouse on the edge of that wood.' He snatched up the haversack containing some light provisions they'd brought with them and, ignoring Kitty's protests, grabbed her hand and started to make his way through the long wet grass, dragging her behind him.

'What about poor Tessa? We can't leave her alone.'

'She won't notice. And if we aren't to be joining her in that coffin, we need somewhere safe, dry and warm to lay our heads.' It made sense, harsh though it seemed, and Kitty made no further argument but ran with him through the rain.

It was little more than a cottage, the door swinging open as they walked through into the single room. It looked as if it had been ransacked or else someone had left in a hurry. Drawers had been pulled open, clothes strewn about, photographs of elderly parents left lying on the floor as if someone had rifled quickly through them, choosing what they needed and abandoning the rest.

'Let's hope they survived,' Owen quietly remarked.

They decided not to risk lighting the old wood-burning stove, in case the smoke alerted enemy interest. But it was cold in the farmhouse and Kitty shivered. Owen at once took off his jacket and draped it around her shoulders. It felt a strangely personal thing to do, to wrap her in a garment still warm from his body. 'Taking off my uniform jacket while still on duty. Another rule broken, but who is to know? Let's say I'm off duty now.'

As he broke the bread they'd brought with them into two pieces and handed one to Kitty, together with some cheese, she watched his fingers working, gazed upon the smattering of pale freckles on the backs of his hands. She hadn't realised until this moment how familiar those hands had become to her, and how much she would miss them.

They sat at the old kitchen table, munching gratefully on the food, thankful to put the horrors of war from their minds for a while; trying not to remember the devastating end to their last performance, or even think of poor Tessa outside in the truck, in the rain. Kitty felt she needed this respite, this time to clarify her thoughts before returning home and facing the more mundane problems of Archie and Charlotte. It felt so peaceful sitting here, so calming after the trauma of the last few days.

'I first went on stage at the age of six.'

Surprised that he should break the silence with this new, and unasked for, piece of information about his past, Kitty almost forgot to eat as he began to talk.

'When I was growing up, moving from place to place with my stage-struck parents, one month Paris, the next Rome, Switzerland or even far-distant India, do you know what I most longed for?'

Kitty smiled. 'A home of your own?' It seemed to be the logical desire for a boy who was constantly travelling, quite the opposite to her own dreams. He shook his head.

'For my parents to love me. The theatre has always been in my life. I loved acting; put my heart and soul into my work, gave every scrap of emotion I possessed to each part. Yet whatever I did, however hard I tried, it was never quite good enough for them.'

'For goodness' sake, why?' Kitty's eyes were alight with compassion.

'Because I wasn't my sister.'

'I beg your pardon?'

'She was called Francesca. Two years younger than me and not only exquisitely beautiful but an unusually gifted actress for all she was but a child. She died when I was fifteen. Drowned while out in a boat with a friend one warm spring afternoon. I knew from that day on that I could never compensate my parents for their loss. They'd much rather it had been me who'd died, you see, and not Francesca. She was their bright, shining star, their future. My poor mother, demented by grief, actually said as much once.'

'Oh, but that's terrible. Perhaps she didn't mean it. She was just upset.'

'Was she? I wonder. Perhaps it's only human nature to want what we cannot have. And they couldn't have Francesca, so they came to love her more.'

He gazed at her with those shrewd, assessing eyes of his, and Kitty found herself mesmerised by their grey-green depths. 'What are you trying to tell me?'

'Isn't it obvious? That maybe Archie only loves you because he can't have you. He married Charlotte, whether for the right reasons or not it's too late to say, and now finds he isn't particularly happy. What more natural than to yearn for the girl he might have married?'

Kitty flung back her chair and stormed to the other side of the room, putting up her hands as if wanting to stop the sound of his voice. 'That's the most callous, cynical remark I've ever heard in my life.'

'Hold on, don't be angry till you hear me out.' He came to stand before her and because there was nowhere for her to run to, her protests when he took her by the shoulders were faint. 'I'm not blaming either you or Archie. It's simply human nature, that's all I'm saying. I'm sure he does care for you, in his way, but he seems to have been easily led astray so perhaps you had a lucky escape.'

'That is complete tosh. Utter nonsense.' She was almost shouting at him now and saw how he winced, dropping his hands helplessly to his sides. 'If Archie says he loved me – *still loves me* – then he does. And I still love him.'

Owen actually laughed out loud, making the crimson in her cheeks flood right to the roots of her soft brown

FREDA LIGHTFOOT

hair. 'I wonder if you have enough experience of love to judge.'

'How dare you?' Kitty, thoroughly outraged, fought to restore her self-esteem. 'What the hell do you know about me? Are you implying I'm frigid or some sort of freak?'

He shrugged and a muscle tweaked the corner of his mouth into a wry smile. 'Are you saying that you *are* experienced? A woman of the world. Well, I suppose if you're unmarried and have a child, you may well be.' His hands were again gripping her shoulders, drawing her close, then sliding about her waist and pressing her against the hardness of his body. Kitty knew she should protest and push him away, but all resistance seemed to melt from her. His face was a mere breath away, close enough for a kiss; which is exactly what he did next. He kissed her. It was very soft, very light, quite casually done and with complete and utter tenderness. She almost felt like weeping. When it was over, Kitty had quite forgotten the thread of her argument.

He pushed a strand of hair away from her eyes, wide and brown and riveted upon his. 'Are you still cold?'

She nodded. 'A little.'

'We ought to get some sleep.'

'I suppose so.'

'I'll see what's upstairs.'

As he went to investigate, Kitty wrapped her arms protectively about herself, pulling his jacket closer. She didn't dare think what was going to happen next, or where, exactly, they were going to sleep. She didn't even know what she wanted any more. He was a good-looking man, and with more tenderness in him than had at first been apparent. Inside, she felt a strange ache, a longing for Owen to kiss her again. Yet she loved Archie, didn't she?

The sound of Owen's footsteps behind her on the wooden stairs brought her swinging about to smile calmly at him. Pleasant. Unemotional. Ready to discuss practicalities. 'There's a tiny bedroom,' he said. 'One bed. You can have it. I'll take the sofa.'

'Is there one?'

He shook his head. 'No.'

They lay side by side on the bed. Not touching. Not speaking. It seemed the sensible thing to do. They both needed rest. There was a war on. She couldn't expect him to sleep on the kitchen floor and there was nowhere else, except the truck and that was occupied by poor Tessa. How could she ask him to sleep with a coffin, out in the cold, dark, rainy night? All she had to do was let her eyes drift closed, and sleep. They remained obstinately wide awake, staring out of the curtainless window into the black night; the sound of the rain hammering on the glass now making her feel cosy and warm, protected.

'Goodnight, Kitty.'

'Goodnight.'

'Say my name.'

'What?'

'Say – goodnight, Owen. Only once that I can recall have you said my name. Say it for me now.'

She turned her head on the pillow and looked straight into his eyes. They gazed solemnly and steadily back at her. 'Goodnight, Owen.'

When he kissed her this time, it seemed the most natural thing in the world, the absolutely right thing to do. He unbuttoned her blouse slowly, kissing each newly revealed inch of flesh with tender care. He kept on kissing her as he slid off her skirt and petticoat. But it was Kitty who, as her desire mounted to match his, frantically helped him to untie the pink ribbons on her lacy combinations and rid herself of stockings and garters. Then she watched with undisguised interest as he divested himself of the rest of his uniform.

'Breaking more rules?' she softly enquired, and he smiled radiantly at her as he lowered himself beside her on to the bed. His body was lean and strong, lithe and tanned from the hours he spent bare to the waist on training exercises, and ready to love her.

Nothing that she'd ever experienced in her life before had prepared Kitty for how she felt at this moment. There was a burning need, deep in the heart of her, which somehow had to be quenched. They made love with equal passion and such intensity that she forgot all about her vow never to surrender herself to a man again. She had no wish in those intoxicating moments even to recall her need to be either independent or free. Kitty wished only to be a part of him, to meld her body with his and repay him with the same depth of delight that he was giving her.

Afterwards she lay with her head on his chest, listening to his breathing, feeling the strong beat of his heart. At last he spoke, soft words whispered into her hair, saying what was in both their minds. 'So what did all of that mean, Kitty Little? That you didn't love Archie quite so much as you thought?'

She didn't reply. How could she? Her mind was a turmoil of confused emotion and unanswered questions. Of one thing she was absolutely certain: she had never felt this way with Archie. Never. Lovemaking with him had seemed hasty and underhand, leaving her with a slight sense of embarrassment. But whether that proved it was Owen she loved, or that she simply desired him physically, was at this precise moment beyond her ken. She felt the pressure of his lips warm against her brow.

'What are your plans now? Have they changed? Will you still settle for being his mistress when you get home? Have him set you up in your own apartment as the kept women do in Paris? Or move in with the blessed Archie and Charlotte both, and begin a *ménage à trois*. On the other hand, you might just have come to your senses, I suppose.'

Kitty jerked up in bed to glare down at him. 'Is that why you made love to me – to spoil things for me with Archie? To prove that what I feel for him isn't love? Was that it? A little game to test me. You despicable, unfeeling, callous brute!' She was slapping at him, hitting his head, punching his nose, pulling his hair, and he was *laughing* even as he strove to hold her off, which somehow inflamed her rage all the more. 'Damn you to hell!' she cried, but he just kept on laughing, telling her he was in hell already.

Within moments her anger had subtly changed, the kicking and biting somehow reigniting their passion, and they made love again, this time with ferocious need. The third occasion, just before dawn, he took her more gently and with infinite care, slowly taking his time to love and caress her till Kitty felt she was drowning in sensation. She knew that she never wished to leave this bed; wanted to be held forever in his arms. Sated and exhausted, they slept entwined in peaceful abandonment but, despite her longings, inexorably and predictably, morning came.

When Kitty woke she was alone. Guessing that Owen was mending the puncture she dressed quickly, splashed her face in cold water, ran out to meet him. They stood in the cold light of early day, uncertain of each other, faintly embarrassed.

'You don't have to go home. We could make arrangements for the coffin to be collected.'

'I must. I owe it to Tessa. Besides, it will be good to have some time alone with Dixie.'

'Of course. I forgot. Your daughter. Yours and Archie's.'

'Yes.'

'And you'll see him.'

'Archie? Yes, I expect I shall.'

They drove the rest of the way to Boulogne in silence, not a word exchanged between them. When they reached the harbour Owen dealt with the loading of the coffin, saw Kitty safely aboard, stowed away her baggage in the cabin allotted to her then, as the ship's hooters sounded, he turned to go. Kitty stood rooted to the spot as he walked away from her without saying goodbye, without a kiss, without even a backward glance. He was halfway down the gangplank when she ran to the railing and called out his name.

'*Owen!*' As he half turned to glance up at her, Kitty grasped her skirt with one hand, held on to her hat with the other and ran pell-mell down the gangplank. Then she was in his arms, being held so tight it was as if he never meant to let her go. There were more unspoken feelings, more passion and desire in that single moment than Kitty could ever have dreamed possible. 'I'll be back. See that you're here waiting for me, safe and well.'

'I'll make damn' sure of it.'

Chapter Seven

The Misses Frosts' boarding house provided a haven of peace and tranquillity for Kitty after the dangers of France. Whatever fears she'd had when learning of Dixie's removal from her father's care had disappeared the moment she'd met the two sisters.

She'd been shown at once to Dixie's room where the child lay fast asleep, arms flung back over her head, rosy mouth pursed into a smile as if she were enjoying a happy dream. Choked with emotion, Kitty had laid her face against the warm soft curve of her daughter's cheek and breathed in that sweet scent which, in all the dreadful months in France, she had never forgotten. After a few emotional tears of relief, Miss Bebe had insisted she take a hot bath, made her a mug of cocoa and practically tucked her up in bed as if she were a child herself.

'Oh, my word, how this little one has changed our lives,' Miss Bebe had whispered as she'd folded the sheet back over the eiderdown beneath Kitty's chin. 'And for the better. Oh, dear me, yes.'

'She hasn't been a nuisance then?' And the old woman gave a chirrup of laughter.

'Of course she's been a nuisance! Aren't children meant to disrupt your lives? She is at a very demanding age, we realise that, and in the first few weeks after she came, the little madam drove us quite demented. Never stopped screaming for a moment, or stamping her little feet and generally throwing tantrums. Suffering from the "terrible two's", Nanny said. Of course, that was before she left us to train as a nurse. She's probably in France by now. You might even come across her. Charming girl.'

Kitty was appalled, and felt a sharpening of guilt. 'So you've had to cope all alone?'

'Oh, yes, but Hetty and I manage everything exceedingly well, don't you know. We like to be busy and are always in perfect accord.'

Even so, Kitty felt she really shouldn't have left Dixie with strangers. But then she hadn't, had she? Charlotte had done that. 'Perhaps she was missing me.'

'Whatever the reason she is perfectly cured now. We got Lad and she's been the sunniest natured child ever since.'

'Lad?'

'You'll meet him at breakfast. Now go straight to sleep and not another word.' And Kitty did just that, sinking blissfully into the duck down pillow.

Tessa's funeral took place on a bitterly cold April day at St Margaret's church in Carreckwater, with an even chillier reception from Charlotte and Archie, who barely exchanged more than a few words with Kitty. It was almost as if they blamed her for their friend's death. Charlotte planted a kiss some inches from her cheek and insisted she should call and take tea with them, just as soon as she was settled in. It was clear there would be no invitation to stay at Repstone and for once Kitty was glad.

It seemed blissful to have nothing more taxing to consider than Dixie's well-being. She would take her for walks in Fairfield Park or to feed the ducks on the lake, delighting in the fact that the child positively glowed with health.

Lad turned out to be a black and white border collie who had once belonged to an elderly widow, now deceased. He adored Dixie with complete and utter devotion. The two were inseparable, the child constantly chattering away to him while the dog sat listening, head to one side, tongue lolling. He'd lie at her feet while she ate or played, sleep at the foot of her bed, and trail behind her as she moved about the house. He came on all of their daily walks and demanded several extra on his own account for there was nothing he liked better than running about, chasing sticks, swimming in the lake and generally getting muddy. And when he wasn't being exercised in that way, he liked to have a ball thrown to him in the long back garden which he always managed to catch, no matter how far Kitty would try to throw it. Sometimes he would disgrace himself by chasing Dixie's favourite red squirrels up a tree, then sitting and barking at them long after they'd leaped away.

Kitty said this was the true meaning of 'barking up the wrong tree'.

In the evenings Miss Frost would play the pianoforte

so that Miss Bebe could sing 'Little Dolly Daydream' or 'If You Were The Only Girl In The World' in her thin, quavering voice. Miss Bebe was very fond of sentimental ballads, in particular 'Keep the Home Fires Burning' by Ivor Novello. Miss Frost preferred Chopin or Mozart. Lad would howl an accompaniment with them, though this never seemed to trouble the two sisters. Kitty would join in as best she could, though she was generally too weak with laughter.

On Saturday evenings Dixie would be allowed to stay up later so she could perform her party piece. The little girl would be stood up on a chair to sing in her high-pitched childish voice which nonetheless rang out clear as a bell. Or she would hold up her skirts and do a little dance routine for them all. Dixie lit up the gloomy parlour with the shining glow of innocent youth. Sometimes one of their other guests, very often a single gentleman or commercial traveller, would take the floor and do a recitation, or sing 'Drink to me Only With Thine Eyes'. Only after all of that, and when they'd played every one of Miss Bebe's favourites, was it judged time to stop and they'd all troop off to bed, tired but happy.

Kitty hadn't realised until now how very tired she was. The long winter of war had been exhausting and emotionally draining, and not without its quota of pain and suffering. She wondered if perhaps she should give up this foolishly dangerous life she was leading and devote herself to Dixie's care, as a good mother should; but then her dreams would be disturbed by memories of a certain

Captain, and she would itch to be back on that boat, heading for France.

Besides, hadn't she made a vow to do her bit? The boys sent to France couldn't choose to come home when they'd had enough, and neither should she. The rest of the Players were due home on leave in early-May, in just four short weeks, when this current tour of duty was over. The plan was that the company would take a month's leave to restore their flagging energy, then do some summer touring with the hope of returning to France some time in the early-autumn. Until they arrived, Kitty meant to consider this time with her precious daughter as a bonus, a special gift for them both.

Despite her resolve to be happy for Dixie's sake, she spent a lot of time worrying about her dear friends, wondering if they were safe and well, if they were managing without her. Dear God, she couldn't bear it if another of their number suffered the same fate as poor Tessa. They'd always found the little pianist's obsession with pills and potions faintly amusing; now her excessive caution didn't seem funny at all. Kitty realised that she'd never fully appreciated just how very brave Tessa had been to come to France with them and face such danger. The thought was humbling, almost shaming, and Kitty meant to honour her death by returning to her own self-appointed duties without complaint, just as soon as she was able.

But these well-meaning resolutions didn't stop her worrying about Owen. She'd felt her antipathy towards him gradually crumble. Now, following what had taken place during their journey back to the coast, Kitty found herself thinking about him more and more. She missed him. She wondered what would happen when the LTPs left? Would he then be sent back to the Front? A prospect which filled her with dread.

It confused her greatly that after two and a half weeks of cosseting by the Misses Frost, she still hadn't got around to paying that visit to Archie and Charlotte. Could she possibly be putting the moment off deliberately? Yet the protestations she'd made to Owen, claiming how much she still loved Archie, had seemed genuine enough at the time. But then she'd been so used to loving Archie, she was quite unable to imagine ever *not* loving him. Was that the way of it?

The visit, however, could be put off no longer.

Through the breakfast room window, puffs of white cloud danced over ranked tiers of mountains that shimmered blue with cold. After a sleepless night, Kitty's confidence was leaking rapidly away and she felt so nervous and filled with such unreasonable worry that she was quite unable to contemplate eating the excellent scrambled eggs set before her. Not a breath of wind stirred the crystal lake. It was a perfect, though cold, spring day, a day for walking over Loughrigg or taking Lad over Gummer's How. Instead she had to face what she guessed would be a gruelling session listening to Charlotte's imagined woes and tribulations, and Archie's disapproval of her going to France in the first place, which Tessa's death would seem to vindicate.

'Miss Bebe will be most upset, Mummy, if you don't eat up your eggs,' whispered Dixie in hushed tones. Kitty half smiled and glanced across at her daughter, happily tucking into her own breakfast with healthy gusto, under the close scrutiny of an ever-vigilant dog. 'I'm not hungry.'

Dixie puckered her little face into a cross frown. 'If we don't leave nice clean plates, Miss Frost will say we're wasting good food that the children in France would be glad to eat.'

This worthy ideal didn't stop Dixie from surreptitiously dropping a piece of her own toast, which was instantly snapped up by ever-open jaws. Though clearly not in the first flush of youth and with indifferent eyesight, the dog could still sniff out the smallest crumb at a hundred paces. When he was presented with the scrambled eggs, it took mere seconds for him to lick the plate clean and Kitty managed to retrieve it only just in the nick of time, before Miss Frost marched in with the toast rack. She glanced at the shining plate in surprise.

'My word, that didn't take long. You must have been hungry. Would you like a second helping, dear?'

Kitty shook her head with shame as she assured her generous landlady that she really couldn't manage another bite.

'Well, if you're sure. We can't have you fainting away from lack of sustenance, now can we?'

Dixie wanted to come with her of, course, trailing after Kitty as she put on her coat, collected her bag and hovered in the hall waiting for the promised taxi cab to collect her. Kitty had arranged with Miss Bebe for the sisters to take care of Dixie for the day. She would have taken the child to visit her father but decided Charlotte might prove difficult. Kitty also meant to tackle them about the success or otherwise of their promised search for Esme, so preferred her not to be present. Dixie, however, objected to this decision, not by howling, as some children might naturally think to do, but by complicated and persistent argument, punctuated by an endless supply of whys and buts so that Kitty laughed and told her she was far too precocious for someone not quite three and really should be on the stage.

Miss Bebe hastily came to the rescue. 'Why don't you come and help me in the kitchen while Mummy is away seeing her friends?' Kitty kissed her soft papery cheek in a rush of warm gratitude, whispering to her in a soft undertone so that the child couldn't hear, 'Thank you for letting her stay despite my lack of credentials. I can't tell you how much I appreciate your kindness.'

Miss Bebe did not entirely approve of Kitty's unmarried mother status but was cautious in her censure because she utterly adored Dixie and was half afraid Kitty might move the child elsewhere if she objected too strongly. Even Hetty had been persuaded not to attempt to 'save' Kitty, or preach to her on the possibly dire outcome of her immoral folly. Turning to Dixie, Miss Bebe offered her more toast soldiers.

'I expect Lad has taken most of yours, cherub, has he?'

'He asked very politely,' she explained.

'Well, that's all right then. And are you going to help me make custard tarts for tea?' Lured by this treat and finally admitting defeat, for the present at least, Dixie thanked her in the sweetly old-fashioned manner the two spinster ladies had taught her, and very solemnly informed Miss Bebe that she would also entertain her with a tap dance, if she liked.

'Well, how splendid. I should enjoy that enormously.'

*   *   *

Charlotte was all lightness and warmth, playing the diligent hostess to perfection. She sat, suitably draped in fur-trimmed silken wraps, pouring tea and serving tiny cucumber sandwiches and scones in the recently refurbished summer house. It had a new tiled floor, wicker chairs and even a fireplace where a small wood fire burned, presumably in an attempt to warm the cool atmosphere. She'd hardly stopped talking since Kitty had arrived, social chit-chat about tea-parties and luncheons with her new friends in which Archie made no attempt to join. He sat slumped in a chair, puffing on a cigarette in brooding silence.

It was some time before an opportunity presented itself and Kitty was able to intervene and stop the flow. Only as Charlotte sipped delicately at her Earl Grey tea in its bone china cup did she manage to ask the question which was beginning to haunt her. 'Where is Esme? Have you heard from her?'

Charlotte's lips tightened, as if in disapproval, while there was the first spark of interest in Archie's eyes. Nevertheless, the two glanced briefly across at each other before shaking their heads in unison. Neither had heard a thing, said Charlotte, not since that first letter telling them she'd gone to Preston. Kitty spoke of the many letters she'd sent from the Front, with no reply to any of them, and Charlotte responded by complaining of the way Esme had simply vanished, without a goodbye or even a word of thanks for the free accommodation Archie had provided her with over the years. 'She owes him a great deal, you know.'

It was perhaps this which finally broke his silence. 'Utter tosh,' he said. 'Doesn't owe me a damn' thing.'

And stubbed out his cigarette with fierce stabbing motions.

Charlotte set down her cup and wafted the smoke away, as if it displeased her. 'Where would she have been without you? I'll tell you where: skivying for a demanding mistress, or as companion to some old dear, no doubt. Esme's problem was that she was quite unable to accept her limitations, or to put the past behind her.'

Kitty very nearly responded that this had clearly never been a problem for Charlotte herself, but managed to bite the words back. She still wondered from time to time about Charlotte's background, and how much truth there was in the story of the tragic fiancé or her tales of an orphanage upbringing. It sounded far too much like something out of a penny melodrama. For now Kitty contented herself with the usual platitudes about how they were all struggling to do just that and returned to her chief concern.

'She must be involved with a theatrical group somewhere. She can't simply disappear. Have you made any enquiries at all?'

Archie shook his head. 'If Esme does not write and has no wish to be found, what are we expected to do?' A reasonable enough remark, Kitty conceded, which nonetheless did little to dispel the feelings of unease she had over her dear friend.

After tea they strolled in the gardens, admiring Charlotte's new rose bower, listening to her plans for restoring the remainder of the neglected acres, of rebuilding the glass houses and reclaiming the old irrigation system, though she complained that the war prevented her from finding a decent gardener, since all the young men had joined up.

Kitty half glanced at Archie, wondering what his reaction might be to these ambitious plans, and whether he could afford them. Generous to a fault he might be, but although he had always appeared to be comfortably placed financially, even Archie's bank account must surely have its limits. His face appeared pale and drawn, muscles taut, preoccupied with other matters, as if he wasn't listening to them at all. His next words seemed to prove this as he suddenly suggested they visit the theatre together in Kendal, the very next evening.

'For old time's sake. It's *A Midsummer Night's Dream*, would you believe? The nearest we'll get to art in these grim times. A welcome change from all the light music and sentimental drivel they've served up since war began.'

'Archie, what a snob you are.'

Charlotte gave a quick frown but smilingly agreed that such a trip might be quite pleasant. 'Of course it means I must cancel a long-standing engagement with Phyllis, my dearest friend, but . . .'

'Splendid,' Archie said. 'That's all settled then.'

While Charlotte went off to telephone and change her plans, Kitty and Archie strolled on down to the lake, as they had so often in the past. The daffodils were in full bloom, lining the banks, the hedgerows thick with blossom. Somewhere, high above, a skylark was singing.

'I shall always remember the first day we arrived here. I was so amazed that you even owned such a wonderful place. Pity we never did get around to converting the old barns into a proper theatre. But what a lot has happened since. Has it all been worth it, Archie? Have you been happy?' Kitty hadn't meant to sound quite so bitter but the words were out now; they couldn't be taken back.

'Do you mean with my marriage?'

'Yes, I mean with your marriage. With Charlotte.'

Archie looked into her eyes for the longest thirty seconds Kitty had ever known, sharpening the pain of regret that still lingered within. 'She isn't *you*, old thing. That's the trouble. And you know how I've always felt about you.'

Kitty felt a wave of panic. What on earth was he trying to say? She could hardly bear to hear this, to witness his distress, or read the deep unhappiness in those deep blue eyes.

Sighing deeply he put back his head to gaze across at the blue-misted hills, mouth a tight line, jaw rigid. 'Let's say marriage with Charlotte has been an interesting experience. I sought perfection in an imperfect world. Thought I'd found that in Charlotte. She was – *is* – so gloriously beautiful.'

'And have you found perfection?'

'Doesn't exist, old thing. Should've known that. We rumble along, one or two problems I have to admit, but nothing I wish to air in public. I made my bed, as they say, and must lie in it.'

Kitty was grateful for his reticence. She really had no wish to hear Archie's marital problems. She needed to believe that he was happy, that losing him to Charlotte had been worth the sacrifice. Eager to change the subject she returned to her concern over Esme and asked, quite bluntly, if it had been Charlotte's idea that no enquiries be made.

Looking uncomfortable, he made no reply to this but merely flickered his eyebrows in that way he had when he'd no real wish to state the obvious. Kitty felt a surge of annoyance, irritated that he couldn't better control his wife, and experienced a sudden insight into all the other times he'd infuriated her by not standing up to Charlotte's machinations. She would have pressed the matter further only she heard the sound of a car engine and saw that her taxi cab had returned, on the dot of five as instructed. 'I really must go. Dixie will wonder where I've got to. I'll see you both tomorrow evening then.'

Archie walked with her to the car and when she reached it, his hand gently cupped her elbow while his voice dropped to barely above a whisper. 'I meant it, you know.'

Kitty took a step back, out of his reach. 'Meant what?'

Archie pushed his hands into his pockets and stared grimly down into a flower bed, as if it were of vital importance that he should memorise all the flowers in it. 'All that stuff about the feelings I once had for you – still have. It's all true. I always did love you best, Kitty. Cared for all three of you gels but you were special, even though I married Charlotte.' He lifted his gaze from a clump of pansies, to smile regretfully at her.

Kitty was suddenly so filled with anger, shaking with such furious emotion, that she felt sure her knees would give way. 'For God's sake, what the hell are you trying to do to me?'

'Just wanted to set the record straight.'

A scrunch of gravel and, glancing back over her

shoulder, Kitty saw that Charlotte was hurrying towards them, calling out her name. As she reached them, Archie's tone subtly changed, though his smile remained in place.

'So I'd like to call in tomorrow afternoon to see Dixie, if I may? Is that all right?' He was looking at Charlotte now, as if anxious to gain his wife's permission. When she appeared to raise no objection, he continued, 'We can have a longer chat then.'

Owen had been entirely wrong. Archie did still love her. He'd always loved her. Yesterday, today and for always. Kitty felt jubilant, confused and terrified all at the same time. It was far too late for him to say such things. Loving her wasn't enough. He was married to another woman.

Owen had also asked what she wanted Archie to do about it, even if he did still care for her. Was divorce the answer, shocking as it may seem? Somehow Kitty doubted he would ever bring himself to divorce Charlotte, despite his evident regrets over marrying her. They weren't happy, that much was clear, both from the hints he'd dropped and from what she herself had observed. Even Archie could no longer deny that his most attractive feature, so far as his wife was concerned, seemed to be the depth of his pocket. But he had always been bad at making decisions, ever content to sit on the proverbial fence; ready with advice on what others should do while not being prepared even to choose between the three of them.

If only they'd not taken Charlotte up in the first place; if only she hadn't seen the advertisement in *The Times*; if Archie hadn't felt such pity over her tales of orphanages and being in service and losing her fiancé. If Kitty hadn't picked a quarrel with him over his being late and slightly tipsy for their first performance. Or if only Esme hadn't loved him too. Oh, so many 'if onlys'.

And if only *she* didn't still love *him*, Kitty thought, even now smiling through her tears. 'Ah, there's the rub.'

But did she? What of her feelings for Owen? What did they amount to? Had their brief affair simply been a celebration of life, in the midst of the terrifying and claustrophobic fear of death which had seemed to be closing in upon them in France. Or was there more to it than that?

And how could she ever trust a man enough to be sure?

Chapter Eight

So here they both were, in the Misses Frosts' overcrowded front parlour; a fitful ray of sunlight capturing the dust motes in the air and glinting on two bent heads as fingers rifled idly through programmes, tickets, play books and other clutter from their once nomadic life, wallowing in nostalgia while their eyes carefully avoided direct contact. It was the first time they'd been alone since Archie's marriage and it seemed odd, even uncomfortable. He smoothed down the lapels of his flannel blazer, immaculate as ever, always a perfect judge of the correct attire, even when visiting an old friend.

Kitty suddenly longed for others to be present; even Lad, the old dog, would have been a distraction, something to help ward off this sensation of stepping back in time, except that sturdy Miss Frost was, at this precise moment, striding over Loughrigg with him. Then again, she half expected Ma to pop in with a mug of beef tea or a list of chores for her to do, or for Archie to get out the old toasting fork and for them to indulge in a heart to heart over charred, over-buttered crumpets.

It was cold in the gloomy parlour and Kitty had lit a small fire, which burned fitfully in the iron grate. Now they both sat in contemplative silence, watching a thin spiral of smoke drift up the chimney.

She concentrated hard on keeping her breathing even as she watched him push his slender fingers through his dark curls in that old familiar way she'd once known and loved so well. Another image instantly intruded – one with red hair; another hand, liberally splattered with pale freckles. It served only to magnify the sense of chaos and confusion in her head. She blinked it away.

The silence stretched endlessly between them and then, as they both started to talk at once, he gave a half laugh. Kitty was saying how pale and tired he looked. Archie said how much he admired her dress. 'You look absolutely stunning, old thing. Blue suits you.'

It was a simple, linen, pleated day dress, quite fashionable before the war, now looking slightly dated and with a darn on the sleeve, showing the signs of wear exhibited on so many of Kitty's clothes. She gave an amused chuckle. 'I seem to remember you telling me blue was my colour once before, because I'm so tall and have such long, manly legs.'

He looked confused for a moment and then his face cleared and he laughed again, more naturally this time. 'Oh, I remember. *As You Like It*, wasn't it? I didn't mean it quite as it sounded at the time. Knew I'd blundered, but didn't know how to put it right.'

No, Kitty thought, you never did.

He leaned closer as he reached for a copy of the first poster they'd made to advertise the event and she could smell the scent of his shaving soap. 'Never ever meant that you actually did resemble a boy. I mean, you're a fine-looking woman, Kitty. That doublet and hose made your lovely legs look the absolute tops. Very shapely.'

She considered thanking him for the compliment but somehow it all seemed too long ago, insignificant now. 'I'm sure the outfit suited me a good deal better than a lavender gown,' she joked.

'Did that dress ever miss a play?'

'Not that I noticed. Do you remember Mrs Pips endlessly baking biscuits to sell in the interval?'

'Dear old Pips.'

'Remember the time you had a puncture in the Jowett.'

'Heavens, yes, and you giving me a pasting for getting squiffy on that home-made wine someone gave us. And Felicity insisting that a bicycle was much more reliable.'

'Old Jacob in those dreadful yellow waistcoats, telling us, "Never listen to your own voice or you'll lose touch with your character and forget your lines." He was right, though. It's true.'

'Lord, I remember. Is he still sneaking nips from that whisky flask?'

'Of course. I think his liver must be thoroughly pickled.' And they were both laughing now, chortling with glee while recollecting treasured moments.

'We had some good times with the LTPs.'

'Yes, we did.'

'I miss you all, don't you know.'

'You could have come with us to France. You were invited.'

'Charlotte wouldn't have enjoyed it.'

'No. Of course not.'

Perhaps it was the recollection of Charlotte, and what might-have-been, which caused them both to fall silent again. With remarkably steady hands, considering the tumult of emotion she felt within, Kitty pulled out a folder. Programmes and newspaper cuttings about the LTPs scattered haphazardly over the table but she could see nothing for a blur of tears suddenly blocking her vision. So many memories, so much pain. Surreptitiously, she brushed them away and began to rub her hands up and down her arms as if warding off a chill of despair. Or perhaps because she was afraid they would reach out for him.

Did she want Archie still? Or was she in fact cured yet still nostalgically trapped by their shared experiences, still striving to see the best in him when really he didn't deserve it?

His voice broke into her thoughts. 'You asked me if I was happy, Kitty. I shall ask you the same thing. Are you?'

'You mean, as a single woman, an unmarried mother, a woman of loose morals – isn't that how everyone sees me? Perhaps I'll end up like the Misses Frost, or like Ma, running a boarding house for theatricals.' Kitty spoke with pseudo-brightness, struggling to find a way out of the quagmire of self-pity she'd landed herself in, but somehow unable to.

'Marriage was never high on your agenda though, was it? Not your thing nor mine.'

Not quite knowing how to respond to this, Kitty reminded him that she'd had no example of married bliss, not with Clara as a mother. 'I'm glad you at least found it – married bliss, I mean – with Charlotte.' Since they both knew this not to be the case awkwardness descended again and they sat for a long while watching the glowing remnants of coal turn to ash in the grate.

'What about Frank? Is he still around?' Archie asked at last.

'Oh yes.' She tried to make a joke of it. 'The ever present burr in my side.'

'Why didn't you marry him? At least he was prepared to do the decent thing.'

Kitty stared at him in utter disbelief as seconds ticked by, then the question simply popped out, of its own volition. 'Would you have *done the decent thing*, if you'd known Dixie was yours?'

'But I didn't know, did I? I mean, I didn't think any the less of you for getting into such a pickle. I've thought since, of course, that no decent gel would come to a chap as you did to me that night, if she were untouched. A virgin. Shows a slackness of morals, don't you know. So it made sense for the child to be Frank's.'

Kitty's cheeks grew hot, though whether from shame or anger, she couldn't rightly have said, not just then. 'You mean it mollified your sense of guilt. Yet it was all right for me to have been with Frank in that way?'

'Well, you were engaged old thing. Bit different eh? As your fiancé, he was entitled to a few more – favours, as it were. Naturally you were piqued when he behaved like a cad with your ma. Still, he did regret the slip afterwards and tried to put the matter right. Though if you'd been honest about Dixie, told me what was what in the first place, that she was mine and all that, I dare say I would've married you, not Charlotte. Everything would have been different then. Funny old world, eh?'

Somehow, his casual nonchalance at the way life had turned out jarred Kitty's stretched nerves almost to bursting point. He'd been a willing enough participant in those pleasurable moments which had resulted in their child, yet ever since had been anxious to deny all responsibility, now daring to accuse Kitty of 'slack morals'.

It came to her in a moment of rare clarity that all Archie really cared about was himself. While experiencing this new insight into his character, she also realised that for all his declared intention of coming to see Dixie, he hadn't even enquired how she was, let alone that she be allowed to join them in the parlour. 'Perhaps I thought that expecting you to *do the decent thing* wasn't a particularly good reason for matrimony.'

'You should have settled for Frank then,' he continued, quite matter-of-factly, as if it were of no real moment. 'He'd've made young Dixie a better pa than I ever would.'

Kitty bridled. 'You think that's all I was looking for, a father for Dixie? Anyway, it isn't true. Frank would have made a dreadful father.'

'So would I, old sport. So would I. Still a child myself, don't you know.'

Oh, how true that is, she thought. Suddenly weary of this dissection of her past life, Kitty went to rest her forehead against the mantelpiece, momentarily closing her eyes as the remnants of her depleted energy drained from her. Would everything have been different if she'd told him the truth immediately? Could they have been happy or would Archie indeed have felt trapped, as she'd always feared? It was so ironic. She'd left him free for

Esme, only to have Charlotte snap him up. Desperately striving to keep her voice light, she turned back to him with a smile. 'Why go over all of that now? I did what I thought was right at the time. So did you. I didn't expect to – lose you – in quite that way.'

'You haven't lost me, Kitty, old sport. You still have my . . .' He stopped, put out a hand to touch her. Startled, she looked into his eyes and he into hers and there was no sound but the ticking of the mantle clock, echoing the loud beat of her heart.

Finally Kitty found her voice, barely above a whisper. 'What? What do I still have?'

'My friendship. Forever, my friendship.' He seemed to have moved imperceptibly closer, letting out a deep sigh, and the echo of his sadness pierced her to the heart. 'I've grieved for the loss of that special relationship we once enjoyed,' he whispered.

'Have you? Me too.' Deeply touched by this admission, she felt drawn almost to tell him about Owen, to discuss the confusion of her emotions, but he was still talking, marvelling aloud at what a lucky chap he was for Charlotte to put up with him when he'd made such a muddle of things. 'That's what she calls me. A dear old muddle-head.' Despite his words, his voice sounded hollow, even bleak, not at all that of a man celebrating his good fortune. 'You look tired, Kitty. You're the one in need of rest.' He pushed back a wayward strand of her hair and she jerked away, startled by the unexpected intimacy of his touch.

'Don't – don't do that.' What was it that she wanted? If only she knew.

'Why not? I've been wanting to touch you for so long.

There was a time when you'd hang on to my arm, kiss my cheek, even tuck scarves round my neck. You never do any of those things now.'

'That was a long time ago. And you're married.'

'We're still friends though, aren't we? I still want you, Kitty. I could offer more than friendship, should you ever have need of it.'

She felt herself start to shake. What did he mean? In what way did he want her? As a friend? Surely he meant as a friend? She didn't dare ask, couldn't even bring herself to lift her head and look into his eyes. She only knew that if he touched her again, she might fling herself into his arms and completely shock him, or else burst into undignified tears. Then suddenly his lips were on hers and she wasn't pushing him away.

He felt so good, so dearly familiar. At least at first he did, but then the sensation subtly changed and the lines of his hard body against hers began to feel odd, entirely wrong, even strangely repulsive. Kitty found that she wasn't responding to his caresses as she would have expected; in fact she desperately wanted him to stop. She felt herself stiffen, her hands coming up to his chest in an effort to push him away. Her mind seemed to be clearing, as if finally managing to assess what was going on in her head, and yet a part of it was still listening to what he was saying – something about Charlotte not finding out.

He was mumbling into her neck as he pressed kisses upon it. 'We don't have to tell her about this, do we, old thing? A chap deserves the comforts of his old friends, eh?'

The scent of his hair cream seemed suddenly over-powering, making her long for another more woody scent, for the French countryside and the feel of another man's arms about her. It came to her then, if not as a blinding flash then with a sure and certain knowledge that it was not Archie she wanted at all. It was Owen. It was Owen she loved; Owen whom she longed for, to hold her in his arms and speak of love. Yet Archie was growing more daring, pushing open her lips to probe the delights of her mouth with his tongue. She felt his hand at her skirt, pulling it up, his fingers sliding between her legs. And then she was thrusting him away, yelling at him to stop.

'For God's sake, Archie. What the hell do you think you're doing? You're married. Is this all you ever think about? *Your* comforts? *Your* needs. What about *mine*?'

Drawing in a shaky breath, Kitty brusquely handed him his coat and hat. She could bear no more. How dare he make such a proposition to her, as if she'd come back just to see him, as if she had no other life, no feelings at all? For the first time, she came near to hating him but then he was mumbling apologies, begging her forgiveness, telling her he never meant to offend and just as quickly as it had come, her temper had drained away and she was scolding herself for overreacting.

Archie was like a child, a creature of simple pleasures. He often acted without thinking but he meant no harm by it. She must remember that.

As Kitty led him down the lobby and firmly out into the street, she spoke with calculated crispness. 'We can't turn back the clock. This wallowing in nostalgia won't do at all. Charlotte is right. Best to let the past go.'

Archie looked startled and a shadow, almost of accusation, seemed to darken his blue eyes, as if she'd rejected him in some way. 'Never forget that I always loved you best old sport, right from when we were in Ealing. I mean, I knew you didn't care a fig for me but . . .'

'*Archie!* How can you say that? I *adored* you! You must *never* say such things to me now, nor touch me ever again. You really mustn't.' And without waiting for him to respond, she whirled on her heel and went back inside, slamming the door of Laburnum House far harder than it had ever been slammed before.

The trip to the theatre was an inspiration to them all. Kitty knew she loved it still, even after all these years. Merely to enter its plush interior was like stepping into a magical world, a world where anything could happen; where hearts could be lifted, or broken at the will of an emotionally adept actor. The smell of the greasepaint, the sound of the pianist playing the opening bars, brought a spurt of excitement akin to fear to the pit of her stomach, whether she herself were going on stage or not. Kitty's love for the theatre ran through her veins like blood. But she wasn't the only one affected on this particular evening.

Archie sat enraptured throughout, drinking it all in like a thirsty man finally given a drink. He hadn't realised how utterly bored he had become, living in the country with Charlotte.

As for Charlotte herself, she was utterly captivated. Not so much by the performance, though it did bring back fond memories, but by the fact that during the interval a young man approached her. Diffident, shy, he nonetheless asked if she was *the* Charlotte Gilpin.

'Why, yes.' Charlotte was enchanted if not particularly surprised to discover that she had been recognised.

'I saw you play here on a number of occasions. *Much Ado About Nothing* was my favourite. You were brilliant as Beatrice. You were indeed the "incarnation of mirth and merry malice".'

'Oh, my dear.' Charlotte was overwhelmed and happily signed his programme, making it seem as if she had starred in this excellent production as well.

It was then that the idea came to her. Charlotte too was bored. Living at Repstone had its charms, naturally. She was highly regarded and greatly sought after as a guest for ladies' luncheons and bridge afternoons. But these were becoming something of a yawn. To date, she had not yet achieved what she had set out to achieve. She had not reached the upper echelons of society. Why weren't she and Archie receiving deckle-edged invitations from the Lowthers or the Somervells?

And watching this performance of *Midsummer Night's Dream*, not to mention the delightful young man who had recognised her, had reminded her of the adulation she had once enjoyed and so taken for granted.

Eyes bright, revealing that she too was not unaffected by the atmosphere, Charlotte was effusive as she sipped her sherry and complimented the show. 'It's almost like old times, isn't it? Not that we couldn't do much better, of course, than this amateur set-up. I do wonder, sometimes, if it wouldn't be absolute *fun* to make a comeback.'

'Comeback?' Kitty regarded her with mild amusement for Charlotte always spoke as if she were the only one among the Lakeland Travelling Players with any talent; as if the rest of them were all dead and gone now that she had left. 'We're still operational, Charlotte.'

'Oh, I know you're doing your bit, darling, and I admire you enormously for struggling on. However, it can't be easy without me, the focal point of the show as it were. Now do be honest.' She smiled condescendingly at Kitty who simply looked bemused. 'I've been thinking that perhaps I should put on a Benefit.'

Even Archie sat up and began to take notice of this surprising suggestion. 'What d'you mean, old love. A Benefit?'

'Don't call me "old love",' Charlotte snapped but quickly restored her angelic smile in case any more of her adoring fans were present and should recognise her. 'We could put on a show for the benefit of the soldiers – the wounded who are convalescing in the Lakes. And whatever money we make can go to the War Fund, for ammunition or whatever it is they need.' She finished this surprisingly well thought out plan to be met by stunned silence.

At last Kitty said: 'That's not half a bad idea.'

'Where could we stage it?' Archie asked, becoming interested despite his misgivings. There was always the fear that Charlotte might suddenly grow bored and the whole thing would turn into another nightmare of squabbling and histrionics.

But she had thought of this too. 'In the old barn at Repstone. Kitty always said she wanted a theatre. Well, why not turn that into one? Intimate, of course, but it has potential, don't you think?'

For the first time in years, Kitty felt a flood of warmth towards Charlotte. Wasn't this what she had always dreamed of? A theatre of their own. Somewhere to put on their shows without the constant travelling. She reached forward and planted a kiss on her cheek. 'Charlotte, I adore you.'

'So do I, old thing,' Archie said, crushing her to him in an all-embracing hug, so that she re-emerged looking flustered and dishevelled.

Oh, dear God, Charlotte thought later, as the effects of the sherry and the young man's flattery wore off. What have I let myself in for?

Chapter Nine

It was indeed like old times, the launch of the Lakeland Players all over again. Kitty felt she was in seventh heaven. Using Miss Frost's trusty bicycle, with Dixie seated in a carrier on the back and Lad running alongside, she would pedal madly along the country lanes each morning from Carrackwater out to Repstone; the sun glinting off the blue-hazed Langdales to her right, the glittering lake to her left, with the promise of spring in the air. It was more than three miles of winding, undulating track but worth every bit of effort to have the opportunity to fulfil a dream.

But what did it all mean? What would be required to get this Benefit production off the ground?

Long before Kitty could make any decisions about what actually to put into the show, it meant many late nights drawing up plans for the new theatre. It meant the procuring of a dramatic licence; the purchase and installation of rows of theatre seats, (since Charlotte insisted they have only the best and Kitty did not disagree.) It involved the construction of a decent-sized stage, complete with trapdoor, moveable set and wings, not forgetting a proscenium arch and curtains which pulled together smoothly without snagging. The barn had a high cruck roof so could therefore provide decent flies in which to store raised scenery, but its long narrow shape, with only an old dairy tacked on the end, meant a shortage of dressing rooms. Never mind, they could always use the house for now. And then there was the vexed question of lighting. Since there was neither gas nor the new electricity system installed in the barn, they would have to resort to their old-fashioned method of acetylene lamps.

'Anything but candles,' Kitty insisted. 'They are a positive hazard.'

But Charlotte would have none of that. 'I've been complaining to Archie for months now that we should have electricity installed in the house. Heavens, simply everyone has rid themselves of smelly old gas mantles these days.' So electricians were hired, cables laid, and in no time at all the newly built stage was fully equipped with footlights and spotlights, the very latest in lighting equipment, purchased from a specialised company in London at heaven knows what cost.

'Can you afford all of this?' Kitty asked, for whatever she suggested, Charlotte ordered and Archie paid for. It was really quite alarming.

'Don't ask me. Charlotte seems able to make my funds stretch twice as far as I can.'

Not that Kitty objected too strongly because of course she was privately thinking beyond the Benefit. She hoped this would not be a temporary project at all. It seemed such a waste to take all this time and trouble to turn an old barn into a theatre simply for a one-night war effort, however worthy, when a little stretching of resources could achieve much more than that. Kitty wanted a long-term future for the Barn Theatre, as it came to be called, and a long-term future for the Lakeland Players.

And she meant to be the one to manage it, if the dream came true.

The Great War had caused a boom in theatregoing but had almost killed off good British drama. Archie was right when he said that anything vaguely intelligent had been pushed aside by this craze for entertaining the fighting men with the light-hearted and the spectacular. Politicians, newspapers, even the church, insisted that everyone needed to be cheered and amused, and not be encouraged to use their brains as this was far too taxing.

Kitty went along with this to a degree, naturally. Hadn't she personally seen the benefits of raising a young soldier's morale while he was on a well-earned rest from the Front? But here, back home in Lakeland, she longed to rectify this imbalance. She wanted to bring back *art* to the theatre. She longed to put on new plays, to discover new talent. Some of these could be comedies, of course they could, but in no way vulgar, and she would retain some of the old favourites. Shakespeare, Ibsen, Shaw. Perhaps even *Hindle Wakes*, the new and, some would say, outrageous Lancashire drama by Harold Brighouse. Kitty could rather empathise with Fanny Hawthorn off on her weekend 'lark' with her young man.

When she put this notion to Archie and Charlotte neither of them raised any objections, though Charlotte did sink into thoughtful contemplation for quite a long while before asking: 'Are you saying that we should make the theatre permanent? You want to put more shows on after the Benefit?'

'Yes.'

'I'm not sure that I would have the time or the energy,' Charlotte complained, and Kitty tactfully commented that there were other actresses she could hire when Charlotte was too busy. 'And she'd have to pay us rent, wouldn't she, Archie? We couldn't allow you to use the barn for nothing, Kitty.'

She smiled. 'Of course not. I wouldn't expect you to. I'm sure we could agree a reasonable rent.'

'But would people be prepared to come out here, to Repstone, just to see your little plays? What sort of productions could you put on?

'New ones whenever possible,' Kitty said, her enthusiasm bubbling over. She would read dozens of plays every week in order to choose only the best, and not be influenced in the slightest by prejudice or critical reviews. She saw herself as becoming almost as famous as Miss Horniman of The Gaiety Theatre in Manchester.

For the Benefit, however, Kitty told them, the tried and true would hold good. They must have the audience laughing and singing and having a lovely, jolly time. There would be lively songs for the men to sing along with, plenty of rousing patriotism, and perhaps one or two amusing sketches. 'Charlotte, would you care to dress up as a soldier and do "Soldiers of the Queen"?'

She coolly declined, saying that she wouldn't sink so low. 'I prefer a splendid little drama to better show off my talent, naturally. I am the one they are coming to see, don't forget.'

'Quite right. I hadn't forgotten,' Kitty kindly agreed, hiding a smile and deciding she could always do the soldier act herself. Why not? She was itching to get her feet back on stage.

But no matter how many hours she spent each day working in the theatre, no matter how exhausted Kitty was when she arrived back at Laburnum House, she always found time to write to Owen. Perhaps it was only to add a page to a letter she would complete and send in a day or two, but never for a moment did she forget him.

Deep in her heart Kitty felt cleansed. She was finally free of all the nostalgia which had held her back in the past, had kept her clinging to Archie long after she should have let him go.

Would that he would adopt the same attitude, she thought.

He could hardly keep his hands off her, always seeking some excuse to slip his arm about her waist, peck a kiss upon her cheek, tweak her nose or tidy her hair, just as if he had the right so to do. Kitty found herself studiously avoiding being left alone with him. It was all most trying.

On two separate occasions while working late in the evening at the new theatre he'd suggested that she stay and not bother to return each day to Laburnum House. Kitty's response was always that the Misses Frost looked after them exceptionally well and that Charlotte wouldn't approve. 'She deserves some privacy. I'm intruding upon her life too much as it is.'

And yet again today he'd taken hold of her cycle handlebars as she was about to ride off up the lane, holding them fast while he informed Kitty that he and his wife occupied separate rooms; a fact she really had no wish to learn. 'It would give you and me ample opportunity to become – reacquainted,' Archie announced with a smile, and since there was no mistaking his meaning Kitty had laughed, unable to disguise her embarrassment.

'I shall pretend you never said that, or that I have mistaken your meaning entirely.'

'I'd rather you did neither.'

'Archie, we aren't foolish young things any more. You're a married man and I . . .' Kitty knew, with a certainty born of true love, one fed and nurtured by the weekly and sometimes daily letters she received back from Owen, that he was the man for her. Captain Dafydd Owen Williams, that obnoxious, cantankerous, unpunctual, arrogant, exciting and amazingly sensitive tyrant, was the face which haunted her dreams. He it was who filled her heart with longing and with the pain of worry over his well-being. Archie was her past, Owen her future. Kitty was sure of that fact, more than anything else. 'Prefer to turn the page and go forward,' was all she said now, then calling Dixie and Lad to her like a pair of recalcitrant puppies, got on her bicycle and set off back to the Misses Frosts' with relief.

As the day approached for the LTPs to arrive home on leave, Kitty's excitement and anticipation mounted. In his last letter to her, Owen had calmly announced that he would be returning with them. He was due some leave, he said, and had decided to take it with her, in Lakeland.

She could hardly wait. Kitty marked the days off on her calendar each morning, said a little prayer for his safety every night. Once, fleetingly, it crossed her mind that she still had to break it to the Players, and to Owen, that much of their proposed leave was to be spent rehearsing and performing the Benefit. Then she would quickly push these concerns away for she had every confidence that the LTPs would wholeheartedly co-operate with the project.

They arrived, as expected, during the first week in May. They were tired and travel weary, thankful to be safely back in England, yet despite their exhaustion and quite without exception they were excited to hear about the coming Benefit. But Owen was not with them. His leave had been cancelled. Kitty was bitterly disappointed.

'Something is afoot,' Jacob kindly explained, patting her shoulder in his kindly, fatherly way as she struggled to hold back her tears. 'We can't begin to guess what it might be, but he was ordered to return to base and assigned to other duties a few days before we left.'

'He's been sent to the Front, hasn't he?' she whispered.

Jacob shook his head sadly, wiped a tear from her cheek. 'I fear that may be the case, Kitty love. We can only pray that he will be safe.'

Kitty drew comfort from the fact that at least she had her friends about her again. Suzy and Felicity were always good-humoured and threw themselves into rehearsal for the new show with their usual enthusiasm. Jacob admitted to the need for a little rest, in view of his advanced age, which he was graciously granted while Reg and Frank set about bringing all the LTPs' equipment and fitup out of storage. Reg in particular was like a dog with two tails, so thrilled was he with the new Barn Theatre.

Kitty, in addition to all her other responsibilities, spent a good deal of time auditioning prospective actors, as the company was in dire need of some new blood.

On this particular morning, she was down by the lake taking a welcome break from rehearsals to throw a stick for Lad. The dog would plunge into the water, paddle madly out to retrieve the stick and then swim happily back, carrying it aloft. You could almost see the grin of triumph on his black and white face.

'It's when he hits the shore you have to watch out,' Kitty warned Archie, as he came to join them. The dog would run around in circles for a while before finally dropping his precious trophy and, as predicted, shake himself so vigorously he'd shower them with water, soaking them all through.

'Let me throw it this time, Mummy. I want to do it.'

'Well, don't throw yourself in, darling.'

Kitty and Archie stood together, watching the child toss the stick. Dixie put enormous energy into it, pirouetting like a little dancer on the shingle though the stick rarely went further than a few yards. Every now and then, simply to please Lad, Kitty would pick it up and toss it far out into the lake. In between, while dog and child were happily engrossed, she talked to Archie, saying how well she thought it was all going, and what a pity it was that Esme couldn't be a part of it.

'I think so too, but what can we do? God knows where she is by now.'

'Have you never tried to find her?'

Kitty sensed his hesitation, even as he remarked that he didn't think looking for her was such a good idea. 'I mean, if she'd wanted to be found . . .'

'Don't start that again.' Kitty turned her attention away from the lake to gaze more keenly at him, noting the way his eyes avoided hers, and a thought struck her. 'You know where she is, don't you?'

A telling pause. 'Whatever makes you think so?' He looked very like a small boy who had been caught out in some misdemeanour.

'Archie, look at me. You do know, don't you?'

A longer silence this time and then, 'As a matter of fact, I do. I found a letter once, that she'd written to Charlotte.'

Kitty struggled to hold on to her fast-disappearing patience. 'For God's sake, where is she?'

'At a theatre in Manchester, I believe. But I really don't think . . .'

'We must go. At once.'

His face was registering utter panic. 'I'm not sure Charlotte would approve.'

'To hell with Charlotte. I insist. Esme is so stubborn that if she were in any sort of trouble, and I'm not saying that she is, she'd never ask for help. Besides, we're her friends. We must at least check that she's well and happy.'

He gave a heavy sigh of resignation. 'Very well. If you insist.'

Relief that she'd finally made some progress in her search for Esme drained all the tension from Kitty. Smiling with pleasure, she was actually reaching out to thank him more profusely when Charlotte unexpectedly emerged on to the path from behind a clump of trees.

'You both look very secretive. What's all this hush-hush conversation about?'

'Not in the least hush-hush. Archie thinks he may know where Esme is after all.'

'Where she *might* be,' he corrected.

'We're going to go and look for her.'

'Well, well!' The polite smile froze upon Charlotte's face and, as Kitty had seen her do so many times in the past, she turned to address Archie in peremptory tones, ordering him to fetch her coat as the breeze was really quite cool. Without protest he obediently set out on his mission, almost as if it were a relief to escape.

Charlotte tucked her arm companionably under Kitty's and led her a little way along the shore line. 'My dear, perhaps we should have a teensy-weensy word about this fancy of yours to find Esme.' She glanced back along the path but Archie was out of sight, probably in the house by this time searching for her coat, or perhaps deliberately staying away.

Kitty stifled a sigh, determined not to make things easy for Charlotte. If she'd something to say about Esme, let her struggle to say it.

'The thing is, you see, I've really no wish to find her.'

Kitty was shocked. 'Why ever not?'

'Of course, it's delightful for all of us to be together again after – everything – well, you understand, for a little while at least. But we can't continue to accommodate you indefinitely at Repstone. We are not made of money.'

'I realise that, but I didn't think you were accommodating us. Every one of the Players is staying with the

Misses Frost at Laburnum House and, as I said, should
we use the Barn Theatre after the Benefit Night, which I
hope we do, we will of course pay Archie a reasonable
rent for it. We could have a lease drawn up. Always
best to keep things on a proper businesslike footing. But
what has all of this to do with Esme?' Kitty presented a
carefully bland face of polite enquiry to Charlotte.

'There were difficulties, if you recall.'

'Difficulties?'

'For heaven's sake, my back was turned for five minutes and she did her damnedest to steal him from me.'

Kitty almost snorted with laughter since both she
and Esme would have done anything at one time to
win Archie from Charlotte. She quickly disguised it as
a clearing of her throat as she recognised the seriousness
of Charlotte's expression. 'You shouldn't have spent so
much time away in Yorkshire then, or wherever it is your
poor mother lives. However, that was all a long time ago,
so what exactly are you saying?'

'That Esme's privacy, which she has been at pains to
guard, should be respected. I will freely admit that my
marriage with Archie hasn't been all sunshine and roses,
as I dare say he has mentioned, but I certainly don't
want him taking up with old girlfriends or being used
by them.'

'Friendship was always important to Archie.'

'Was it? I wonder. You really should appreciate that
he's only being kind when he says he wishes to see Dixie.
He feels it's his duty to take an interest in the child. He is
stricken with guilt at times, as if he let you down in some
way, which is all perfectly ridiculous since you have no
proof that she even is his.'

'Frank is prepared to admit I never slept with him.'

'Then it's your own fault if you lost Archie. You shouldn't have lied to him.'

'I never lied. I simply didn't tell him. I didn't think having a child was a good enough reason to stampede someone into marriage.'

'Quite so, darling. If they have no *wish* to be stampeded, that is. And it is *so* sweet of you not to hold it against me that *I* was his choice and not you, despite the – er – um – circumstances.' And Charlotte smiled triumphantly at Kitty, as if she had proved her point.

Kitty bit down hard on her lip, determined not to fall into the trap of arguing that Charlotte had done exactly the same thing, stampeding Archie into 'doing the decent thing'. Far too degrading. Besides, she had lost her child so it wouldn't be fair; assuming of course she had ever been genuinely pregnant. And was Charlotte happy now that she'd got what she wanted? It didn't seem so. In many ways, the pair of them deserved each other.

But where was the point in going over all of this when it was Owen she loved, Owen she longed for? Charlotte just had the knack of rubbing her up the wrong way. Gritting her teeth, Kitty said, 'I still think we should find her.'

'I'll be perfectly frank with you, Kitty. Finding Esme may well ruin my last chance to make our marriage work.'

'Oh, I think you underestimate your powers, Charlotte. I'm sure you have a much tighter hold on him than that. We'll go first thing in the morning.' And Kitty walked briskly away to collect Dixie and take her home.

*   *   *

Charlotte was furious. She sat writing posters and tickets with hands that shook with rage. How dare Kitty defy her? How dare Archie override her wishes in this way? Surely he wasn't still pining for that dratted girl? She'd grown sick and tired over these last months of being unfavourably compared to angelic Esme. And it was all so annoying that it had blown up now. Trust Kitty to spoil things.

Initially, she'd almost regretted her impetuosity at suggesting this Benefit. Then she'd realised that it might well turn out to her advantage after all, in more ways than one. She'd been secretly looking forward to re-establishing herself as a star, though only for the sake of the war effort, of course. Charlotte had come to look upon the money she was lavishing upon the theatre as an investment. Not in Kitty, for heaven's sake, or the LTPs, but in her own future. She certainly had no intention of giving up her ambitions in order to play in petty little dramas in the Barn Theatre week after week. Far too much like hard work. But being its Lady President might well prove beneficial. Evidence of involvement with some worthy charity, particularly one of an artistic nature, would do her no harm at all amongst Lakeland society. It might actually prove to be the key to the success she craved.

But Charlotte had believed herself to be fully in control. She'd milked Magnus of a small fortune over the years which she'd carefully hoarded and was now enjoying spending. Archie often teased her about making his money go twice as far as he could, not realising he was absolutely correct in this because she did indeed have twice as much as he imagined. But Charlotte was perfectly aware that was delicate. This affluence couldn't last forever. Ever since she had examined the state of her bank balance the previous week, she'd felt a nudge of disquiet. Yet for once, she hadn't an idea in her head how to put the matter right.

Charlotte hadn't visited Magnus in over a year, which she recognised now as a mistake. No doubt Little Nurse Perfect would well and truly have got her feet under the table by this time. But while it would be an advantage to be free, the scandal of a divorce could lose her Archie and ruin everything, leaving her virtually penniless.

It really was a pity that Magnus had survived that accident. It would have made her life so much less complicated if he'd simply died. If he died even now.

Charlotte nibbled on her pen and began to think. If he were to die, that would make her a rich widow – in theory. In practice, of course, she would remain 'married' to Archie. Only she knew that it wasn't truly legal. But then she could always persuade dear old Archie to go through with a ceremony again, to retake their vows as it were. They did only elope after all, with a hasty wedding in a blacksmith's shop. A proper church ceremony would be lovely and perfectly fitting in the circumstances. This notion brought a smile of amusement to her pretty face. Perhaps it was time to pay Magnus another visit after all, though she was rather tied up at the moment with the Benefit. The moment that was over and done with, she would go and see him – tie up a few loose ends. Her own cleverness never failed to amaze Charlotte: she always managed to get exactly what she wanted, in the end.

Smiling, she continued to address envelopes while

her mind weighed risks, played out various scenarios. It couldn't be too difficult, could it? He was a cripple, for heaven's sake. All she had to do was hold on to her nerve, and when had Charlotte ever failed to do that?

They drove to Manchester without a single hitch, not even a puncture. Arriving early in the morning, they spent the entire day wandering from theatre to theatre since Archie claimed to have forgotten the name of Esme's after all. Kitty, remembering her early efforts at searching for an agent in the streets of London, once again used her charm on theatre porters and acquired a list of all known theatres in the city, a surprising number if you included the new cinemas which, in their desperation, they did. One by one they crossed them off with no success. Not only was Esme not working in any of them, no one had even heard of her. It was most discouraging.

Now they stood helplessly outside the Manchester Palace, which was right back where they'd started, Archie complaining that it was all a waste of time and that Esme had probably left long since; Charlotte protesting as only Charlotte could that she was freezing cold and wished to go home. Both of them had been saying much the same all day. Kitty ignored them.

Again she studied her list. There were only a few names left unchecked. The Blossom Theatre Club, out towards Salford, with only two cinemas left after that. She hadn't the first idea where any of them were or even if they were worth the effort yet felt bound to try since they were on the list. 'We could ask someone,' she said, refusing to climb back into the motor as Archie seemed to be insisting she do. Spotting an omnibus driver making his way home after a shift, Kitty ran across to ask him.

Charlotte uttered a quiet oath under her breath and got back into the car where she sat tapping her polished nails in silent fury. She saw the man point, obviously giving directions, while Kitty nodded and thanked him. This wasn't at all the way things should have turned out. The last thing Charlotte wanted was to find Esme Bield. Drat the woman. Drat both of them.

They discovered the Blossom Theatre Club situated deep in the side streets and alleys of Salford. A gas light flickered indifferently over a scuffed door that looked in dire need of a fresh coat of paint. Stuck on the walls in the seedy-looking foyer were several tatty posters with the strangest play titles Kitty had ever seen. *A Night With Lil* was one. *Out on the Town with Our Bessie* was another. All most puzzling and not in the least prepossessing.

There seemed to be no one around to ask about Esme so they bought three tickets from the girl in the booth and made their way into the smoky atmosphere of a dimly lit room. It wasn't particularly large, what could be classed as an intimate little theatre. The stage was the usual proscenium arch with brown velvet curtains that had seen better days drawn across it. Unusually, from the centre of this came an extra platform which protruded out into the audience. Rows of plush seats were ranked to either side, beyond which were set a number of tables. It was at one of these that they sat. Archie ordered a bottle of champagne, saying they might as well at least enjoy the evening, and again Kitty marvelled at his seemingly bottomless funds. Would real life ever catch up with Archie? she wondered.

More people came in and the room gradually filled up, with about half the rows occupied and most of the tables. The bar was certainly doing good business and, if anything, the atmosphere grew ever more thick with smoke from the many cigars being lit up by customers. Two or three musicians wandered in and began to set out their music and various instruments, tune up and generally shuffle themselves into position.

Kitty's heart felt like lead. First impressions were not reassuring. Esme surely deserved better than this. It was surprising really that, despite evidence of a good deal of money changing hands, more wasn't spent on tidying the place up.

Lights dimmed and went out, footlights flickered on, uncoordinated notes were heard and a lively overture struck up. As the curtains opened there was a ripple of lukewarm applause.

Kitty gazed upon the scene in stunned amazement. Never, in all her life, had she seen anything like it. Six girls stood as still as statues, which was presumably what they were meant to be. Their arms were raised as if in supplication, heads thrown back or tilted artistically to one side. They looked exactly like Grecian goddesses except that they wore no clothes. They were completely naked, their pale nude bodies glimmering like silver in the footlights.

Charlotte muttered something about knowing all along it would be a mistake to come and Archie coolly remarked that as long as the girls didn't move, this was considered to be a new form of art.

Kitty cast him a look of quelling disbelief.

Only one girl was dressed. Wearing a flowing gold

cape over a silver satin gown she knelt centre-stage, head bent, long fair hair falling forward so that it swept the bare boards.

As the music gradually slowed and changed its beat, she rose from her crouched position, lifted one arm and flung back her hair to reveal eyes like bruises in a painted face; scarlet lips that smiled bewitchingly at her audience. She moved forward on to the projecting rostrum and began to dance. Stunningly graceful, bewitchingly rhythmic, the dance was utterly and erotically sensual. And as she moved, the girl unclipped and discarded the cape. Next, she began to slip the gown from her shoulders. Ribbons were untied, hooks unpinned, silken layers peeled away one by one, a garter tossed into the cheering audience, followed by a sheer silk stocking. Kitty found, to her complete shock and horror, that she was watching a young girl disrobe in public before her very eyes. Worse, she'd finally discovered the answer to the question which had haunted her for so long. She now knew exactly what had become of her dear friend.

Chapter Ten

'How can you do this? How can you sink so low?' Kitty's instincts were to gather Esme in her arms. But the woman seated before the fly-specked mirror bore no resemblance to her dearest friend. This woman's face was hard-edged and brittle with no sign of emotion or vulnerability. This woman was a stranger.

She reached for another costume, bright orange, liberally trimmed with feathers and even more tawdry close to than the one she had so beguilingly taken off moments before on stage. Esme slipped it on and began to fasten up hooks and dozens of tiny glass buttons. No one came to assist her so Kitty got up to help, only to be brusquely informed that wasn't needed, thank you very much.

The stale smell of fish and chips and sweat dominated that of grease paint and Kitty began to feel slightly nauseous, feeling a sudden longing to be out in the clean soft May evening. 'You can surely do better than this, Esme? You certainly have the talent.'

'Some of us just have to settle for what we can get, deal with life as best we can. We can't all make it big, you know. We can't all become the glorious Charlotte or be the indomitable Kitty Little, Nightingale of Flanders. Oh, yes, I've heard about your success overseas. Bully for you.'

'But this?' Kitty waved her hand to indicate the stiflingly small dressing room, filled at this moment with what seemed like dozens of girls in various stages of undress, then let them fall to her sides again in despair. Kitty turned to Charlotte. 'For goodness' sake, you say something. Talk some sense into her.'

It was the interval and Archie had remained in the wings backstage, no doubt on his third cigarette by this time, while the two girls attempted to talk some sense into their friend. They weren't making much headway. But then most of the effort had come from Kitty. Charlotte sat with a handkerchief soaked in Eau de Cologne pressed to her nose, as if she had never in her entire life endured such conditions. Now she remarked that really Esme had only herself to blame. 'You always suffered from low self-esteem, my dear, which is pretty stupid. If you don't respect yourself, who else will? That's what I say.'

Kitty could not fault the argument, but the smug manner in which Charlotte delivered these words somehow left a nasty taste in her mouth.

'And where were you with your damned advice when I asked for it?' Esme said, not attempting to disguise the bitterness in her tone.

Kitty picked up on this instantly. 'When did you ask for advice? Was it of Charlotte?'

'Yes, it was of Charlotte. She preferred to ignore me. Too busy playing Lady Bountiful.'

Kitty felt weak with exasperation. 'Drat the pair of

you! You, Esme, for never answering *my* letters, of which I wrote dozens, and you, Charlotte, for not telling me that you'd had another letter from Esme.'

She shrugged elegantly. 'What could you have done? You were in France, for heaven's sake. And if she stays in this rat hole, it must be because she enjoys the work.' She spoke as if Esme wasn't even present, then she turned to her and asked, 'Do you offer other services? More lucrative ones, shall we say?'

Esme's face became ashen while Kitty leaped to her feet in a fury. 'For God's sake, Charlotte, that's enough. If you can't say anything useful . . .'

'. . . I should take my leave. I'm most happy to do so. It is really no concern of mine how Esme chooses to disport herself. And it is only sex, after all, in which apparently she is an expert.' Charlotte rose gracefully to her feet, aware that as she pushed her way through the crowded room several pairs of envious eyes swivelled to watch her go. At the door she paused, smiling back at them all in the happy knowledge that she could pamper herself with pure silk and genuine furs, not crêpe de chine and rabbit. 'As a vicar's daughter, you should try wearing a dog collar or cassock. That would really excite the customers.' Then she swept out. As usual, her exit was superb.

Esme actually laughed. 'Good old Charlotte. She doesn't change, does she?'

'Esme, please come home with me. You can stay at Laburnum House. Everyone's there and would love to welcome you back. We're working on a Benefit Night at the moment, for the wounded soldiers. We'll give that a short run this summer, have a bit of a rest,

FREDA LIGHTFOOT

then head back to France come September. You could join us.'

'And get myself blown to smithereens? No, thanks.'

'But why stay here? I don't understand.'

'I've told you, Archie is the only good thing that has ever happened to me. Without him, I have nothing. So what does it matter where I work or what I do now?'

'What about our friendship? Does that count for nothing?'

For a second the old Esme was visible behind the tears that welled in her pale grey eyes. But before she was able to respond a booming voice came out of nowhere, making everyone jump and the room fall silent.

'*Esme! Why the hell aren't you on stage?* One minute to your number. Fifty seconds for the rest of you.' The man was massive with a shiny bald head and hairy chin, about as wide as he was tall, seeming to fill the tiny room. Like a huge block of granite half blocking the doorway, he clearly had no intention of moving as the girls squeezed past him one by one to get to their place on stage. And, as each struggled through the impossibly small gap between his stomach and the door jamb, his hands would slide over their thighs, squeeze their rump or pat their breasts. Kitty found herself holding her breath along with them, and sharing their relief whenever they wriggled free of his odious proximity.

'Lord, so that's who you work for. Is that how it is?'

Esme snatched up a powder puff, flicked it over her nose then tossed it aside. 'You don't know a damn' thing about how it is. Go home, Kitty. Don't you preach

440

to me. Just leave me alone.' And as she swept out, the huge man surprisingly stepped politely out of her way.

Kitty couldn't bear to watch the rest of Esme's performance but nor could she bring herself to agree they should leave and go home, despite both Charlotte and Archie urging her to do so. They returned reluctantly to their table to order more champagne while Kitty hid her distress and embarrassment by hovering in the foyer, peeping through a crack in the door from time to time to see if the show was over. When it finally was she urged Archie to try his luck.

'Persuade her to come home with us. Perhaps she'll listen to you. You were always the one with influence over her and she still adores you. Please, please try.' She was desperate for him to get Esme on her own while the fat man was still occupied front of house. Archie's response was that there was little point in trying and Charlotte declined to get involved. Yet, because Kitty was so insistent, he finally gave in.

'All right, old thing. I'll give it a shot. But you stay here with Charlotte. Let me try on my own.'

'I want to come with you.'

'No. You must trust me to deal with Esme. I'll try my best, I promise.'

'Yes, all right. Only do it now. Please.' Kitty would have agreed to anything.

After he'd gone, she and Charlotte sat silently for several long moments. Having had time to give more thought to the situation, Kitty finally asked, 'Why didn't you answer that letter she mentioned, when she apparently asked for your advice? Why didn't you respond to her cry for help? Or tell *me* at least, so that I could've done something?'

Charlotte gave a brittle little laugh. 'And you would have come rushing home from France, would you?'

Kitty knew she couldn't have done any such thing. Nevertheless it pained her that Esme had written asking for help and clearly received none. Again she asked Charlotte why she had done nothing.

'Because I owe her nothing. I did explain why I had no wish to do this.' Charlotte topped up her glass with the last dregs of champagne, her every movement declaring she was bored sick with the whole business. 'Esme Bield can do as she pleases so far as I'm concerned. She makes her own choices, as do we all. She doesn't have to stay in this flea pit. She could leave. *Now* if she wished. She's her own woman with a mind of her own and I'm not her nursemaid.'

There was such a painful truth behind these harsh words that Kitty couldn't bear to sit and listen to them any longer. She got up and fled backstage, relieved to discover that most of the chorus girls were making their way home. Perhaps Archie would have more success than she. If only the fat man would stay away for a while longer. She put her ear to the door and began to listen.

It was Archie's voice she could hear. 'I thought we might be happy but now even she doesn't care a jot for me. Old Archie, the weak-kneed bore. Isn't that what you all think of me?' Kitty heard him chuckle, as if trying to make light of it.

Esme's voice now, coming out in a strangled little croak. 'Archie, all I ever wanted was for you to be happy. I didn't care who with. No, that's not true. Of course I cared. I desperately wanted you to choose me. But when you clearly preferred Charlotte, I respected your choice. I wanted you to be happy with her. I remember your telling me that was partly the reason why you ran off with her, because you were so good together. And why would you not be? I know she's highly strung, but Charlotte's a lovely woman and extremely talented.'

There came the sound of weeping, and Kitty could imagine him gazing at Esme from out of dark, soulful eyes as he mopped up her tears. 'It's all too much for me,' he moaned. 'Charlotte's never satisfied. She's utterly grasping, I've learned that much. Never stops complaining or haranguing me, and rarely lets me touch her nowadays. Not unless I'm prepared to fund her excesses in this social whirlpool she's concocted. Almost as if she's playing a role in a dratted play, an act I have to pay admission to. I spend my life desperately searching for fresh funds as you know, my sweet. It's a nightmare.'

'It might not be an act Perhaps she truly does care for you, in her way. She stays with you, doesn't she? Oh, and I do wish she wouldn't.'

'Ah, yes, but what can I do, sweetie? I married her. "For better, for worse. For richer, for poorer".' His voice was sharp with irony.

'Preferably for richer if Charlotte has any say in the matter.' And they both laughed, though there was little

443

mirth in the sound. 'Oh, Archie. What are we going to do?' Silence followed this pitiful cry during which, to her shame, Kitty pressed harder against the panels of the door in a desperate attempt to identify the muffled sounds within. She could make little sense of this conversation except that Esme was still potty about him and Archie was moaning as usual. When was he going to ask her to leave, to come away with them now, tonight?

Eventually, when she had almost given up hope, Esme's voice again, low and breathy. 'I love you so much, Archie. I'd have nothing without you. I don't *care* if you feel you must stay with Charlotte so long as you don't stop coming to see me. You won't, will you? You know how much I need you. You make my life bearable. I mark your visits in my diary. They're my red letter days.'

Visits? Red letter days! What was she saying? Kitty could hardly believe her own ears. Had Archie *known* where Esme was all along?

He murmured, 'Always did love you best, Esme my sweet. Cared for all three of you gels but you were special, even though I married Charlotte.'

Behind the door Kitty felt as if someone had kicked all the air out of her lungs. Those self-same words had been used by Archie to herself just the other week when he'd called to see her at Laburnum House; when he'd actually had the nerve to proposition her. Lord, what the hell was going on? Did all this mean what she thought it meant? Well, they always said eavesdroppers never heard any good, either of themselves or others. She took a step back from the door but then, unable to resist, put her ear back to the door panel. Archie was still talking.

'. . . so that is why, my own sweet darling, my visits here make life bearable for me too. We'll always be friends, forever and eternity. More than friends. You know how I've always loved you best. But I must go soon, my angel. We can't risk the odious Terence finding me here.'

'Oh, not yet. Not yet. Please . . .'

Again there followed a prolonged silence but this time the origin of the muffled sounds was only too evident to Kitty. They were making love. She could hear Esme's little gasps of pleasure, Archie's grunts of intense satisfaction. Kitty did back away now, staring at the door as if she could actually see the pair through its solid surface. Then she turned and ran.

When Archie returned to their table some twenty minutes later, as coolly immaculate as ever, Kitty had composed herself and was calmly discussing with Charlotte the relative merits of blue and gold against red and cream for the new curtains and decorations they planned for the Barn Theatre, just as if she had never left her seat. She was saying this place too looked to be in dire need of a lick of paint.

'Though it's got character in its own way. If only . . .'

'. . . it were in a more salubrious neighbourhood. Quite. I doubt Shakespeare would bring the crowds flocking in here, do you?' Charlotte finished with a wry smile, and even Kitty had to chuckle.

She glanced up as Archie approached with a frown of anxious enquiry. 'Well, did you get anywhere? Is she coming?'

He sadly shook his head. 'Won't budge. Think she's afraid of the fat man. Mr Terence, they call him.'

'And she likes the money, no doubt,' Charlotte said, draining her glass and getting to her feet. 'Now will you take me home this instant? I am quite worn out.'

Kitty said, 'I'm not coming.'

'What?'

She was adamant that she would stay on in Manchester for one more day in order to make further attempts to speak to Esme. Archie surprised her by arguing forcibly against the notion.

'Why won't you leave her alone?'

'Because she's my friend. We struck a bargain years ago that we'd look after each other. That we'd never give up on our friendship, no matter what. I trust she'd do the same for me if the situation were reversed. Please warn the Misses Frost for me, won't you? I'd hate them to worry.'

But he wouldn't let go of the argument. Never had she seen Archie so angry. He ranted and raved at Kitty, accusing her of being stubborn and interfering, obstinate and bossy, insisting that she was wasting her time. Charlotte continued to complain that Esme had the right to mess up her life, if that was what she wished to do. Kitty, however, remained resolute.

'I can at least try.'

Archie suddenly changed tactics. 'In that case, I shall stay with you.'

This was the last thing Kitty wanted. She felt the need of some time alone in private with Esme. And time to think. Only when Charlotte finally lost her temper with him did Archie storm out of the theatre, jump in behind the wheel of the Jowett and drive away, leaving Kitty standing alone and vulnerable on a dark, wet city street.

If she had expected to spend a sleepless night in the small hotel she booked herself into, she was surprised to discover that after writing her usual loving letter to Owen, which she meant to post first thing in the morning, she must have fallen instantly asleep for in no time at all she was opening her eyes upon a new day.

She should have been rushing back to put the finishing touches to the Benefit Night as well as to spend some precious time with Dixie. Instead she was consumed by the terrible anger building slowly within her. *Archie had lied about forgetting the name of the theatre. He'd actually visited Esme there!* Yet he had not admitted this either to herself or, presumably, Charlotte. Why was that? The reason had to be only too evident from the sounds she had heard behind the closed door. He and Esme were having an affair.

In itself that was not so surprising, Kitty supposed, but the realisation brought with it two unanswered questions. If he'd decided that marriage to Charlotte was a mistake (and who could blame him for that?) and he really loved Esme, then why had he propositioned Kitty? Not simply once, but on numerous occasions since her return.

Secondly, why hadn't he persuaded Esme to leave that dreadful theatre? What kind of man would be prepared to have the woman he loved take off her clothes for other men? There was something seriously wrong here. Kitty began to wonder, for the first time, if she knew Archie at all. He suddenly seemed like a complete stranger to her. And for all she and Esme had both once loved him, never for a minute had they been prepared to share him.

Chapter Eleven

Theatricals usually stayed in the same boarding house, within walking distance of the theatre, so it didn't prove too difficult to discover where Esme lodged. She looked more her normal self this morning, young and fresh-faced if a little tired and not in the least surprised to find Kitty on her doorstep.

'I thought you'd come,' she said, as she led her inside.

Dressed in an old tartan dressing gown, she was taking a late breakfast in the tiny bed-sitting room she occupied. It was a gloomy place, containing little more than a bed and a chest of drawers with a few hooks on the wall which held Esme's few clothes covered by a curtain. In one corner stood an old sink and cupboard, single gas jet, table and two chairs. It was here that she was preparing porridge. Kitty declined any for herself but accepted a cup of tea. The two girls sat at the table in the window, sipping their tea with little more than polite comments about the weather and perfunctory remarks about the war as they gazed out on to grimy mill chimneys and roof tops beyond. It was reminiscent of Kitty's old attic room at Hope View in Ealing and she shivered, almost as if she had come full circle, for wasn't she still suffering at the hands of those who obtained their pleasure at the cost of others?

The effort at small talk was finally exhausted and Esme said, 'I know why you've come.'

Kitty looked up at her in surprise. 'Do you?'

'You've found out, haven't you? About me and Archie.'

A short pause, a sip of the scalding tea. 'Not until I heard you both last night at the theatre, as a matter of fact. I'm sorry, I dare say it was rude of me to listen but I couldn't help myself. I came backstage again to add my weight to Archie's efforts at persuasion and found – well – you know what I found. But don't worry, I shan't tell Charlotte.' She was speaking quite quickly, still staring at the chimneys, reluctant to meet Esme's enquiring gaze. 'None of my business. Though how long you think you can go on without her finding out, I can't imagine. Charlotte isn't going to take kindly to being betrayed. All hell will be let loose then.'

'She isn't the only one who's been betrayed. He left me for her, remember, the moment she came back from Yorkshire that last time.'

'I know, love.' Kitty hesitated, wanting to reach out to her friend but not quite knowing how. Should she tell Esme about how he'd tried to seduce her too? Or had she been mistaken? Kitty was so used to making excuses for Archie, she found herself doing so yet again but then remembered that if she hadn't stopped him, he would have been perfectly prepared to enjoy a little romp there and then, in the Misses Frosts' front parlour. It all suddenly seemed rather tawdry, and all the time he had *known* where Esme was, being no doubt a regular visitor to this seedy little room. Suddenly the anger boiled up in her again and Kitty set down her cup with a clatter.

'Can't you see how he's using you? How he's used us both? He's every bit as manipulative as Charlotte in his own selfish way. Archie doesn't love any of us. He only loves himself. He loves being the centre of attention, not having to make any effort or decisions about anything. He'll always take rather than give, whatever brings him the most pleasure. It could easily have been me making love to him last night.'

Esme's face flushed bright pink. 'That's a lie.'

Kitty told her then, quite bluntly, about how Archie had made it clear he still wanted her. 'He's even told me their sleeping arrangements, which apparently leave him free for nightly trysts whenever he chooses, though how true this is I don't care to know. But he's made it abundantly clear that he's more than willing to take up where we left off. He can't keep his hands off me; doesn't give a damn about any of us. He's as fickle and as utterly self-centred as . . . as . . .'

'I don't believe you.' All colour had drained from Esme's face, the pain in her grey eyes terrible to behold.

Kitty softened her tone. 'Oh, Esme, *if* he's so wonderful, why hasn't he insisted that you leave this dreadful place? Why does he allow you to demean yourself in this manner? Why do you stay?'

A deep sigh, which seemed to be drawn up from the bottom of a deep dark well. 'I-I've got myself into a mess, I admit it, allowing myself to be taken in by the likes of Terence Lee. I met him in Preston and he seemed genuine enough at first, assured me it was all quite respectable. I just had to sit there and look beautiful for men to admire. No movement or anything. Nobody ever had admired me before and it seemed safe enough. But then – he started asking for more. So we reached a compromise.'

Esme seemed to run out of words but then continued in a voice so low Kitty could hardly make them out. 'Charlotte was right in one respect. I did think too little of myself. Always have, I suppose. Hiding from memories of what my father did to me, I came to expect bad things to happen. It seemed normal. But that other accusation she made isn't true. I only dance. Nothing else. I have the respect of the audience, even of Mr Terence. It's called Live Art.'

Kitty slammed her fist down on the table, knocking over the abandoned cup so that tea spilled over on to the linoleum floor. 'Utter rubbish. It's *sleaze*! You're titillating men's fantasies. And for heaven's sake, Esme, you deserve better than that.'

'I've told you, I need the money. And it won't be forever. Just till I've got myself . . .'

'What do you need money for?' Kitty interrupted, barely having the patience to listen to any more excuses. 'The lack of it has never bothered you before. Why now? Besides, you could get a job in any normal theatre, music hall, variety. Even the pierrots would be better than this.'

'None of that pays anything like as well, even if the work were available.'

'So where's the evidence of all this money then?' She

moved about the room, indicating the shabbiness of their surroundings. 'What do you do with it? What do you spend it on?'

'I'm not spending it. That's the point. It's for *our* future, Archie's and mine. He's saving it for me. He does mean to tell Charlotte about us. Quite soon. But he can't leave her just yet. Not till she's perfectly well again. She lost the baby, you know. She's been quite low since.'

Kitty stared at her dear friend in pained disbelief. 'I don't believe she ever *was* pregnant. I think it was all a ruse, to force Archie to marry her.' Poor Esme. She was really far too naive for her own good. Kitty went over and gathered the cold hands between her own. She could feel them shaking. Very gently, she asked, 'How do you know that he'll ever leave her? Whatever it is that Archie feels for Charlotte appears to be unshakeable. Whether he loves you or not, he's still completely besotted by her. Besides, it would demand action on his part to leave her, for him to make a decision, and you know how Archie prefers to avoid difficulties and anything the least bit unpleasant.'

'But he loves *me*. He's told me so over and over again.'

Kitty bit her lip in frustration and tried again. 'Then why try to seduce *me*?'

'You may have been mistaken.'

'Esme, I wasn't. Archie prefers his relationships to be purely physical because he isn't capable of truly loving anyone. And what proof have you that he is saving this money? Have you seen the work that's being done at Repstone, even before the Barn Theatre? Someone is funding Charlotte's dreams for this new role of hers. Have you considered it might well be you?'

'That's a despicable thing to say! Archie wouldn't allow such a thing to happen. And he has plenty of money.'

'I'm beginning to wonder. He complains all the time about the likelihood of being bankrupt within the year. Look, you've been a fool. We both have. I believed in him just as much as you did. But I was *wrong*! He'll sleep with either one us and be unfaithful to all three without a thought for the effect this might have upon us. He'll follow anyone who leads him down the path of dalliance. And he hasn't an ounce of true feeling and emotion in him, it's all superficial gloss.'

Kitty stopped speaking because she could think of nothing more to say to prove her case.

And now the silence was so complete, even the dust motes whirling in a streak of stray sunlight seemed like a noisy intrusion. Esme sat and wept silent, heartbreaking tears while Kitty put her arms about her friend and held her close until they were all spent.

'I thought he truly loved me.'

'I know.' Kitty made more tea and they drank it in silence.

'I wish Mrs Pips was here,' Esme said finally. 'I didn't realise how much I depended upon her advice until after – after her death. It was all so sad, so cruel that the winding gear should break just when she was standing underneath it. I mean, we'd never had any trouble with it before, had we?'

Kitty was staring at Esme, a thoughtful frown puckering her brow. 'A tragic coincidence, that's for sure. Made me jittery about props and set ever since, I can tell you. Nor did we ever find out where she went just before she died.'

'Charlotte was away too at about that time though, wasn't she? And then when Mrs Pips came back, I suppose we were busy and forgot to ask, and then it was too late.'

Their gazes locked, as if with the same thought. Kitty said, 'Did she never speak of her trip to you?'

'Only to say that she'd felt a desperate need for a short holiday, and stayed at a charming inn called The King's Head in a small village near Leeds.'

'Leeds? Isn't that where Charlotte goes to visit her mother?'

'You mean the one who has never come to see her daughter perform in all the time . . .' Esme stopped, and focused on the look of startled concern in Kitty's eyes. Her voice shook slightly as she continued, 'She may, of course, not be fit enough to travel. She does seem to fall ill a good deal.'

'True, she may not. But Charlotte rarely speaks of her mother except when she's wanting to pay her a visit.'

'Almost as if there wasn't really a mother at all.'

'Then who does she go to see?'

'Lord, are you suggesting that Pips followed Charlotte in order to find out?'

'What happened to her things?' Kitty asked.

Esme got up and drew from a cupboard a cardboard shoe box. 'Everything's here. Not that she had much. Sad really. A housekeeper all her life with very little in the way of family beyond her beloved Archie. There are lots of photos of him as a boy of course, all stiffly posed in sailor suits. A purse with a few coins, programmes of shows we did, and a diary. But I've already looked through that. Nothing of any note.'

They looked through everything again but Esme was right. There was nothing of any interest at all. Both of them now fell silent for neither dared voice the growing fear that perhaps dear Mrs Pips had indeed discovered an answer to where Charlotte went on her frequent trips away, one which Charlotte objected to her knowing and had therefore put an end to the old housekeeper's curiosity for good.

Kitty said, 'We could always pay a visit to Leeds ourselves. Explore some of these villages. There can't be too many with inns of that name, can there? We could just make time before the Benefit Night, if we hurried.'

Esme looked at her for one long stunned moment, then reached for her coat.

The Benefit proved to be an enormous success. The Barn Theatre was packed to the doors, standing room only. Each song and sketch met with a joyous response from the audience. They even took kindly to Charlotte's extract from *She Stoops to Conquer* with its humorous tangle of mistaken identities, though not perhaps with quite the enthusiasm she had hoped for, nor the standing ovation she believed she deserved.

Kitty, dressed as a soldier, was now waiting in the wings for her own entrance. Mouth dry, nerves strung high, beads of sweat trickling between her breasts, this was the moment she loved and dreaded more than any other, as all actors do. The fear she felt in this instant was so all-consuming, so utterly numbing, that she longed to turn and run; then the curtains parted, the music played and she was striding out on stage and the rush of pleasure she experienced as she started to sing, was utterly intoxicating. An addiction no less. The roar of greeting from the audience when they saw her was almost overwhelming, drowning out even Kitty's powerful voice for several seconds. Some actually stood up and called out her name, others whistled, but they were soon hushed into silence by their comrades and a complete stillness fell upon the audience as she sang. She marched and sashayed, swung her stick, saluted and flirted outrageously with them, and when the song was done almost the entire audience erupted from their seats as one, cheering and roaring and yelling for more, while others stamped their feet, clapped and whistled.

Kitty Little, as always, was a triumph.

In the wings Esme, Felicity, Suzy, Reg and the rest, even Frank, were laughing and applauding and cheering just as madly – glad for her – believing she deserved this success after all her hard work. Archie was looking on with a stunned expression on his face and Charlotte was purple with rage.

She absolutely refused to take part in the final curtain and, loudly complaining that the audience must be illiterate peasants, flounced off to her dressing room where she glared in the mirror as if defying it to find any flaw in her own image. Pinching her cheeks, trailing a finger to test the firmness of her chin, Charlotte came close to asking herself if she could possibly be past her best. This was dismissed almost instantly as quite impossible and the blame for a less than adoring response from her usually devoted fans laid entirely upon Suzy who had dressed her hair. Snatching up a pair of scissors, she began to snip and tidy silken strands but when they only made the image worse, she flung them back into her hair pin tray. Perhaps she should have gone to a proper hairdresser, tried one of the newer, more daring styles. Perhaps she'd worn the wrong dress, crimson or pink suited her far better than this dull maroon. Charlotte began to rip it off, tearing the fabric in her fury.

'Kitty overheard us that night in my dressing room at the Blossom Club.' Esme spoke these words with creditable coolness and Archie appeared nonplussed, caught out, like a naughty boy again; an expression quickly masked as the lines of his face hardened and tightened.

'I see.'

Kitty smiled. 'Don't worry, I've promised to say nothing to Charlotte. She's *your* problem. But I would recommend that *you* tell her. I may be a touch over-sensitive on the matter, having had more than my fair share of betrayal myself, but I happen to think it's a pretty lousy thing to do, however awkward and difficult your wife happens to be. Particularly when it's with a mutual friend. It's not as if you didn't have the chance to choose Esme instead before you married Charlotte, is it?

'You *were* going to tell her about us, though, weren't you Archie?' Esme said, eyes bright and trusting. 'Ask for a divorce and marry me, as you promised.'

'Of course.'

Kitty said, 'Why don't you explain to Esme about your being quite prepared to betray her as well as Charlotte?

Oh, yes, I've told her about your recent efforts to seduce me. You've hardly stopped trying since I came home.' She flung the accusation at him like a lance, brown eyes blazing.

'You aren't going to believe this nonsense, are you, Esme?' Archie smiled disarmingly at her before turning his narrowed, icy glare full upon Kitty. 'It was unfortunate you should find out about my affair with Esme in quite that way. In normal circumstances betrayal, as you so beguilingly term it, might well be considered a pretty rotten trick. But these aren't normal circumstances.' He began to cough and mop his brow.

'Why aren't they? Because there's a war on? I'm talking about before the war. Admit it, Archie. You shamelessly use your charm to *exploit* people.'

'I knew I shouldn't have agreed to our all getting together again. I thought it would lead to trouble. But I never deliberately exploited either of you. We're old friends after all. Therefore I can take whatever you're willing to give.'

'But what do *you* give in return, Archie? Nothing. You *use* us for your own selfish purposes. You even help yourself to Esme's earnings. That is utterly despicable.'

He looked suddenly like a stranded fish caught on the end of a line, gasping for air. Esme ran to grasp his arm. 'I told her it wasn't true, Archie. You'd never do such a thing, not now you've declared your love for me.'

Something inside him seemed to snap then, as if he wanted an end to all pretence and prevarication. He shook her impatiently away, reaching for his cigarette case. 'Love. Love. Love. That's all I ever hear from the pair of you. What good is love? I ask you. I've seen what love can do, it can destroy a man. I saw what it did to my father and I vowed never to allow such a thing to happen to me. He adored my mother and do you know why she didn't come to the concert with us that night? Well, let me tell you. Because she had an assignation with her lover. She died in the hotel fire in another man's arms, and yet it was my father who was driven mad over losing her. Love? I do assure you, I've been happier without it. Causes far too much pain. My one aim in life has been to protect myself; to live a life of ease and comfort without commitment or responsibility of any sort, and so long as one or other of you was prepared to provide me with those comforts, why not? What are friends for? That's the long and short of it.'

'Dear heaven,' Kitty said. 'You're the one who's mad. Unfeeling, insensitive, calculating – entirely cruel and self-serving. Amoral.'

'Nonsense! Our *affaire* was most enjoyable, quite titillating in its way. And seeing Esme cavort in front of all those leering men, knowing I was the only one she allowed anywhere near her, was really most entertaining.'

'But you'd never any intention of giving Charlotte up, had you? Because you suit each other admirably. You're two of a kind.'

Archie simply smiled. 'Of course. Charlotte may be demanding in material ways – money, *objets d'art*, nonsense of that sort – but she makes no demands on me emotionally, do you see?' He drew on the cigarette and blew smoke down his nostrils, considering them both through narrowed eyes. 'I loathe emotion.'

Esme was quietly weeping now. 'But what about our

plans for you to leave her? For you to divorce her and marry me?'

'Never actually said that. Never told you any *real* porkies, sweetie. You heard what you wanted to hear. I always think it's best not to disagree with people and let them believe what they like, don't you?'

Kitty was beside herself with fury. 'We can clearly see the extent of your cruelty – your unfeeling heartlessness. We should have recognised it for what it was years ago. You've made fools of us, Archie, by your determination to think only of yourself. You and Charlotte both. But perhaps you've been hoist by your petard, as it were.'

'I beg your pardon?' He was laughing at her now, which enraged Kitty all the more.

'Perhaps it's time to put an end to secrets.' So saying, she swivelled on her heel and made for the dressing room. Archie's shout was ignored as, closely followed by Esme, she thrust open the door and stormed into the room. 'Well, are you going to tell her, Archie, or shall I?'

'Tell me what?' Charlotte, seated at the dressing table in her silk dressing gown, set down a pot of cold cream, picked up a wad of cotton wool and began calmly to wipe her face as she considered their reflection through the mirror.

Archie went to bend over his wife and plant a kiss upon one greasy cheek. 'That you were superb in the show, my darling, no matter if the audience didn't fully appreciate the chosen extract.'

Kitty said, 'Go on. Tell her, or admit to Esme you'd never any intention to do so. I think you owe her that much. It's long past time there was an end to all this subterfuge.'

Charlotte glanced from one to the other of them and then snorted her derision. 'What subterfuge? What is it Kitty wants you to tell me?'

Esme edged forward, chin high, a glassy look in her clear grey eyes. 'About our affair. Archie has been visiting me at the theatre for months. We're just as much lovers now as we ever were.'

Charlotte's smile remained fixed upon her lovely face and for a moment Kitty thought the revelation might pass off in a quite civilised fashion, and then she suddenly launched herself from her seat and lunged at Esme, polished nails extended like claws, grasping her hair, shrieking like a harridan.

'You little *whore*! You *tart*!' Whatever other epithets she might have found to use were lost as the two girls fell grappling to the floor. It was the most appalling, undignified tussle Kitty had ever witnessed and throughout it all Archie did nothing. He stood by watching with an expression almost of amusement upon his handsome face and Kitty knew that this was true arrogance. He was completely detached and cared nothing for any of them.

It was Kitty herself who fought to drag the two screaming girls apart, a battle she was clearly losing as nails scored deep and teeth bit through torn flesh. But it was good old Reg, bursting in through the door, who saved the day. He dragged Esme clear and held her safe in his arms where she burst into a loud paroxysm of cathartic sobs.

'There, there. Let it all come out. That's right, love. Never fear. No one will hurt you ever again. Not if I've aught to do with it.' And when the sobs finally abated, allowing him to wipe her eyes, Esme offered up a watery smile.

It made Kitty wonder if Reg's patience might be rewarded after all.

Archie helped Charlotte back to her seat, smoothed her hair and poured her a glass of restorative champagne. 'Sorry, Esme old sweet, but Charlotte was much more to my taste. I'd never leave her for either of you. When she brought it all out into the open about Dixie, thought I'd best settle for marriage after all and make the best of it, even though I guessed that her own supposed pregnancy was a figment of her imagination. Far too damned convenient, and she'd been away for some time. But we do suit each other rather well, don't you know. No strings. And I didn't want Kitty to start staking claims on me.'

Charlotte smiled triumphantly at them all. 'He only has to keep signing those lovely banker's drafts and I'm his forever.'

Archie actually laughed out loud at this, as if it were all a jolly joke. 'Think yourself lucky, the pair of you. I make a dreadful husband. At least Charlotte doesn't expect anything from me that I can't afford to give.'

'And which I don't return tenfold between the sheets at night,' she finished for him. And they smiled at each other, in perfect accord.

Kitty said, 'So all that separate beds tale was rubbish too?'

' 'Fraid so.'

'You disgust me.'

'I disgust myself at times, but there we are. Such is the

harsh reality of life and – would you believe it? – here I am, married after all.' He laughed.

'I wouldn't be so certain about that.' During the preceding conversation, no one but Kitty had been aware of the door opening. Now it swung wide so that an invalid carriage could be pushed fully into the room by a young and pretty nurse. 'Allow me to introduce myself. Magnus Radcliffe, at your service.'

A strange silence fell as all eyes focused on the stranger.

'Mrs Emerson, what a delight to see you again after this long while. Or should that be Charlotte Gilpin, or even Charlotte Radcliffe? I am correct in saying that we never did get that divorce, aren't I, my dear? You are still *my* wife, or certainly were the last time I looked at our marriage lines which admittedly was some days ago. Who knows what might have happened in the interim.'

Charlotte had turned a deathly white, staring at Magnus as if she were seeing a ghost. 'What the hell . . . ?'

'. . . am I doing here? I do assure you that I've come by invitation to your Benefit Night. I received a mysterious, complimentary ticket in the post yesterday morning. What a coincidence, I thought, seeing the name upon it. I mean, how many Charlotte Gilpins can there be? Perhaps it was unwise of you to use your maiden name. You should have put your new married name on the programme instead, foolish girl. But there I go, getting it wrong again. How can you have a new married name when you haven't yet rid yourself of the old one. Mrs Radcliffe.'

Archie took a step forward, opened his mouth to

address Magnus, then swung about to face Charlotte. 'What the hell is he saying?'

'That you aren't her husband at all. *I* am. Can you still go to jail for bigamy, I wonder?'

Archie looked aghast. 'You mean, I've suffered this damned marriage for nothing?'

'Drat you!' Snatching up the scissors, Charlotte flew at Magnus like a screeching banshee. Everyone stood frozen in horror with only Archie making any attempt to stop her. They heard him call out her name, heard Charlotte's furious scream that she'd damned well make sure she killed him this time. Then she'd be free. At last.

'Get out of my way Archie!' It was then that Charlotte lunged. But in the seconds it took for the scissors to plunge into soft flesh, Archie had again stepped forward, desperately begging her to be calm. Only when he fell to the ground with her name still upon his lips and her husband in his wheelchair unscathed, did Charlotte realise what she had done.

October 1918

Chapter Twelve

Kitty's eyes struggled to adjust to the darkness. A bat touched her cheek. Out in the mass of the unseen audience she could hear muted laughter, the pulse of anticipation. This was to be their last performance; their finale. She could sense, even before they began this farewell concert, that the men were happy, more relaxed than they'd been in years.

Germany was desperately seeking peace despite its bragging that it could fight again if it must. The soldiers who comprised Kitty's audience tonight knew the truth. The enemy was in retreat. They had them on the run.

During the last two years the LTPs had done three tours of duty in France. They had seen the wounded and the dying being brought back from Ypres and the Somme. They'd experienced the gunfire, dodged the shells, watched in horrified disbelief as battle planes chased each other to destruction across the skies; heard the orders ring out for the Allied guns to engage fire. Only once or twice had they faced the kind of bowel-weakening fear the soldiers faced every day in the trenches, but it was enough. They understood.

Today, weary soldiers had spent the day bathing and sunning themselves and, as darkness fell, had grown increasingly eager to get on with the show, knowing that deliverance from hell was within their grasp.

But even though the end was in sight and peace within their grasp, Kitty knew that tonight was important to them. She'd learned how some of the young men were secretly fearful of going home. They worried whether they would have trouble adjusting to civilian life again. Would their wives still be waiting for them? And how would they ever get over losing so many of their comrades, and perhaps their own health? Kitty had no answers to these questions, had fears enough of her own.

All she could do was bury herself in her work.

The war was almost over and still she went on singing and entertaining the troops, almost as if she were two people. One part of her was Kitty Little the performer, the much loved Nightingale of Flanders. The other was still Katherine Terry, the girl from Ealing who had had a dream.

Kitty had finally visited her mother, introduced Clara to her grandchild, and a peace of sorts had been declared between them. Ma was older now, and tired, but still running Hope View in exactly the same way as before, though her guests were more sailors than theatricals these days. The two of them would never be close, but at least they could be friends. Kitty was glad of that.

Following Archie's death Charlotte had been taken

away by the local police, still cursing and screaming hell-fire and damnation upon them all. Magnus had returned to Yorkshire with his devoted nurse, and the friendship between Esme and Reg was coming along nicely. Dixie was a healthy five-year-old now, well cared for by the Misses Frost, and showing every sign of having inherited her mother's talent as well as Repstone Manor and the Barn Theatre from her father.

In every respect but one, Kitty's life was fine.

But one fear overwhelmed her: would Owen come home safe? It was so long since she'd last seen him and so much had happened since, she hardly dared to hope. She didn't even have an idea where he was, not having received a letter from him in weeks. Kitty told herself that they'd probably been held up by the war and would all arrive together, in a bunch, but underneath she feared the worst. Their correspondence had always got through before. If there was silence now, then there must be good reason. She believed he must have been taken prisoner or killed.

She'd arrived late tonight, as usual, sparing precious minutes calling at the depot to check on the mail, always pushing too much into her days; and now she watched in humble amazement as lights flickered on, one by one, candles illuminating the darkness, almost as a defiant warning to the Boche to stay away.

Kitty realised with a jolt that the men seated patiently before her were numbered in their hundreds, perhaps as many as two thousand. The sound of their voices, their expectations of her that night, very nearly overwhelmed her.

She felt choked with emotion, turned helplessly to

Jacob. 'I don't think I can do this. There are so many of them. It's too much.'

He beamed at her. ''Course you can. The show must go on.'

'They all love you. Because you're Kitty Little,' Felicity added, while Suzy quickly tidied the heavy chignon and pushed her out into the arena.

And of course this was what she was meant to do. Kitty must cheer them on their way, lift their hearts and give these boys the courage to face what might be an uncertain future. This was what she loved to do. To give of herself. This was where she felt most alive.

A hush fell as she lifted her face to the night sky and began to sing. *'How can I bear to leave you? A parting kiss I'll give you.'* A gigantic roar of approval met the song.

'Come home with me, Kitty!'

'Give me a kiss too!'

Song after song she gave them, sometimes joined by the rest of her troupe, often entertaining them with silly parodies and bawdy humour, bringing gales of laughter from her devoted audience. But grown men wept that night as she touched their hearts as never before. *'Morning will come. Each day the sun will shine,'* she sang. *'Greet it with joy.'*

The show was over and, as always, had been a great success for Kitty Little and her troupe. It had been more than a concert, it had been a triumph of survival over adversity, a celebration of victory. When it was done, she turned to the others with a joyous smile. 'Thanks everyone. Thanks for everything. Suzy, Felicity, Reg, Frank, and Jacob of course. Esme.' There were tears in her eyes as she gathered them one by one into her arms. 'The tour is over. The war is won. I think we can go home now.'

But they said nothing, merely dabbed at the tears in their own eyes, faces expressionless, and Kitty's heart lurched with fear. 'What is it? Tell me. Has something happened to Owen?'

'Only that he wants a kiss from Kitty Little too.' And suddenly there he was, standing before her; a dusty, crumpled mess with one arm in a sling but alive and well and all in one piece. She walked towards him like one in a trance, touched his face in wonder.

'It is you.'

'Yes, it's me.'

'It's going to be all right, isn't it?'

'Yes, Kitty. Everything's going to be just fine. All we have to do is go home together and fetch little Dixie.'

Then she flung her arms about his neck and he winced as she jerked the injured arm but held her as tightly as he could with the good one. The roar of approval this time came from all her dear friends who crowded around to share again in the hugs and kisses, this moment of joy for their beloved Kitty, for weren't they a team? And now they had gained a new member, a new theatre, and a new beginning for the Lakeland Players.